Bella Novela

CHARLOTTE HARRISON-KING

FOUR PARROTS PUBLISHING®

For Ada and Maz

This novel may contain triggers for people struggling with an eating disorder.

The Girl

Tall, curvaceous and long-limbed, Catherine Lish walked briskly along a picture-perfect beach one afternoon in Riviera Maya, Mexico. She had been there for around a week already and thought it was paradise on Earth, despite the fast-approaching storm clouds out at sea, which she was hurrying to avoid. It wasn't long, however, before the shadowland of a pre-storm swallowed up the colourful landscape and a strong wind began to ruffle the bright white umbrellas that dotted the area.

As the light drained away, Catherine grimaced and increased her pace, while around her, sunbathers packed up quickly and ran soggy with saltwater back towards the hotel, staff speedily tidied furniture away, and birds swooped erratically through the darkening sky. The storm was a surprise to everyone, it seemed, but eternally uneasy Catherine still cursed herself for not having checked multiple sources for the day's weather predictions before walking so far up the beach; it was a rookie error, especially when travelling during hurricane season.

She was a traditional English rose but for her dark purple nail polish, pierced nose, and the trail of tattoos across her ribs which were covered by a floaty dress that kept whipping up in the quick breeze. The offending wind was also aiding her always-wavy, strawberry blonde hair in its attempt to strangle her. Adding further to her discomfort, her sunglasses were still in her room, meaning grains of sand flew unimpeded into her half-closed, blue eyes, and as she walked barefoot along the blustery beach, her feet sank deeper with every step.

This blinding spacewalk was made even worse by the large bag flung gratingly over one sunburnt shoulder, and the fact that she was having to juggle gritty sandals and an unruly wet towel. Most annoyingly though, her swimwear was damp and cold against her skin. Paradise or not, she couldn't wait to get off the damn beach.

Then, just as she began to feel thoroughly enraged – a throwing her sandals into the sea level of angry – she looked up and saw something that stopped her in her tracks. Catherine had seen the small, neglected girl a few times and it always pained her to just walk by and do nothing. Any animosity she was feeling therefore towards her inaccurate weather app, the sand in her oesophagus, or seashell cuts to her toes, instantly melted away.

The child was sitting next to the wall between the hotel and the public beach. She was unkempt and scrawny, with light-brown skin and jet-black hair and, as Catherine got closer, her heart broke at the familiar sight of bruises along one of her thin arms, and small blisters on the soles of her feet.

Catherine stood in front of the girl, holding up a hand to block the barrage of beach that the wind was hurling at her. Absorbing the heavy dose of perspective offered by the clear mistreatment of the child, she took a deep breath and then said, 'Where's your mummy, sweetheart?' Catherine spoke in Spanish, which she could manage well as long as she wasn't drunk or hungover.

2

'She's at home,' said the little girl without looking up.

'Maybe you should go home now? She will be missing you, and it's going to rain.'

'Mama won't miss me.'

Catherine frowned, and once again glanced at the girl's bony ankles and bruises. 'What's your name?'

'Gloria,' said the child, finally raising her sad eyes from the floor.

'I'm Catherine.' She flashed a smile that she hoped appeared comforting. 'You can call me Kitty; it's what we sometimes call a cat in England. So, you're just going to sit right there all night, are you?'

'Yes, but if it rains, I will go and hide somewhere safe.'

As she stood there looking at the girl, Catherine's feet sank even deeper into the soft sand, right down to the coolest layer and, like her feet, she felt stuck. She couldn't bear to leave the child alone in such a state, but there was also the nagging sense that the situation wasn't for her to resolve, and that she should just keep her nose out of it and go back to her room.

Catherine thought back to all of the times she had been warned about the child street urchin while travelling, tragic waifs supposedly sent by Fagin-esque parents to con tourists out of loose change for drug money. She had heard this warning from Cambodia to Poland to right there in Mexico, and usually she just walked on, leaving the neglected kids to go and dance around someone else for cash. But this felt different.

'Gloria, how old are you?'

'I'm six.'

'When you're six, you should be inside, safe, during a storm.'

Gloria shrugged.

'I have an idea,' began Catherine, crouching down to be at Gloria's eye level, and wobbling as her new sand-boots refused to budge. 'I'm staying in this hotel. My room is big and there is a spare bed in the corner of it.' She paused. Was she really going to offer this? 'Do you want to come with me tonight? You can have a nice bath, and eat lots of food and watch cartoons if you want to?'

Gloria was looking at her, her dark, almond-shaped eyes taking in every word that Catherine was saying.

'Now, you shouldn't go with strangers. Ever. Some strangers can be very bad, but I promise I'm not bad. I can't leave you here on the beach when there's a storm coming.' Catherine looked over her shoulder at the choppy sea and at the sky, which was turning gunmetal grey. 'You can sleep in the spare bed, or if you want to leave after dinner you can do?'

Gloria just carried on looking at her, blinking, seemingly scanning Catherine for signs of being a bad guy.

Scan complete, the girl rose and held out her hand to Catherine, who wriggled her sandy feet free, stood up and took a step forward. She shoved her shoes into her beach bag, cringing at the thought of all the sand contaminating the bag's innards, and took Gloria's tiny hand in hers.

'So, what do you want to eat? Do you like burgers? Fries? Quesadillas? Chocolate cake?' she asked as Gloria bobbed along beside her, but then Catherine started to wonder what it would actually be sensible to feed the little girl. Images of liberated concentration camps kept filling her brain, as did her history teacher's sad revelation that the kindness of strangers had caused many prisoners of war to die from overfeeding. She looked at the thin girl beside her, and thought she probably wasn't as malnourished as a prisoner of war and that a small portion of chocolate cake should be OK.

They didn't talk much on the way to Villa 61, and thankfully they didn't come across any hotel workers or other guests, who might have found them quite a strange pair. The hotel was not like those in Europe where everything was in one building.

Instead, the lobby, restaurants, bars and spas were all in separate structures dotted around the complex, and instead of corridors connecting them there were winding paths lined with trees.

The hotel rooms weren't in rows stacked on top of each other high into the sky either; they were separated into three-storey, salmon-pink 'villas', each with an outdoor staircase and balcony, and housing around eight rooms.

Catherine introduced Gloria to her room, giving her a short tour of the second-storey space, which consisted of a small entrance hall lined with a large wardrobe and drawers, a big bathroom, a king-sized bed, sofa bed, desk, and bistro dining table.

Once they had settled in, the little girl had a nice bath with lots of bubbles. Catherine stood outside the bathroom, wanting to give Gloria her privacy but also fearful that she could drown. Catherine didn't have much experience with children, and she wasn't sure what they were capable of at which ages. 'Are you OK in there, Gloria?' she asked repeatedly, listening intently for the gurgling sounds of a drowning child.

'Can you help me, Kitty?' said her little voice after a while.

'What can I help you with, sweetheart?' said Catherine as she stepped into the bathroom and saw that the bathwater had turned brown with dirt.

'Will you wash my hair?'

Catherine hesitated, wondering how she would explain washing the hair of a random child that she had essentially kidnapped, to the police. 'Of course I will, but first let's get rid of this dirty water and replace it with some more bubbles, shall we?'

Gloria nodded, and chuckled quietly as the bathwater drained noisily from the tub. Once the bath had refilled, and in the manner of a sommelier offering a sample of wine before pouring, Catherine held the bottle of shampoo beneath Gloria's tiny nose for her approval.

'That's nice,' said the little girl.

Catherine smiled, knowing she would give the same response herself, even if the Cabernet tasted like petrol. 'When I was little, my mum used to wash my hair for me and she would always get the shampoo in my eyes. I'm sorry in advance if I do that too.'

'My mum washed my hair too when I was small.'

'You're still small now,' said Catherine, more to herself, before squirting a vast amount of creamy coconut shampoo onto the child's thick black hair and gently rubbing it in.

Catherine offered a large white fluffy dressing gown to her tiny guest, who was considerably cleaner than an hour earlier, but as the gown was about three times the size of her it had to be tied tightly to stay in place. Gloria settled on to the room's big blue sofa while Catherine turned on the TV. Soon, American cartoons filled the screen, hypnotising the girl just like any other child, although Catherine was fairly sure she didn't understand English.

Catherine handed her guest some snacks from the minibar, and went back into the bathroom to start washing her small clothes with the bottle of travel wash that she always packed, a habit from her backpacking days. Just as in the bath, the sink water soon turned the colour of sludge, and it took several rinses before the water ran clear. Using the hairdryer, Catherine dried the small items of clothing with care and finally gave them back to Gloria, folded and in a neat pile.

'They are just like new!' said Gloria, unfolding them with Cheeto-dust fingers.

Catherine's heart broke as she eyed the remaining stains and the rips on the little yellow T-shirt and denim shorts, but she supposed that to Gloria, they did look new again without the layers of dirt and sand.

'We'll go to the shop tomorrow and see if they sell any children's shoes, if you like?' she said.

Gloria nodded and smiled slightly.

Once Catherine was showered and dressing-gowned too, they ordered a feast from room service, laughed at cartoons and got ready to go to sleep. Gloria used a spare toothbrush and cleaned her teeth, something she didn't seem familiar with at all, and Catherine brushed the child's wild hair, which thankfully seemed to be lice-free. At around nine o'clock the little girl fell asleep, her tummy full of chicken quesadillas, fries, crisps and chocolate cake.

When Catherine woke up the next day, she rolled over and saw Gloria dressed and ready to go. She was sitting at the edge of the sofa bed waiting patiently for her host to wake up, her little legs dangling far from the ground.

'Buenos días cariño, cómo estás?' said Catherine. She ran a hand across her face and tried to muster the energy to get out of bed.

Gloria didn't speak; her eyes simply widened a fraction.

'What do you want to do today? Do you want me to take you home?' said Catherine in Spanish.

The little girl shook her head and fixed her gaze on the floor.

'Shall we go to the shop and find you some shoes first?'

Gloria looked up and nodded eagerly.

'OK. Have you brushed your teeth?' Catherine thought this seemed like a grown-up thing to ask. It was like they were performing in a play and she had to pretend to know the lines while Gloria improvised alongside her. *Is this what parents do?* she wondered, and as Gloria responded by running into the bathroom to brush her teeth, Catherine was left impressed by her own commanding performance as a fully-fledged adult.

They held hands as they walked along the paved maze through the hotel grounds, past well-manicured lawns and beneath palm trees, spotting big lizards as they went. Catherine didn't exactly like these spiky, cat-sized creatures that were so different from anything that roamed wild in England. During her first few days in Mexico, she would scream every time she came across one lying on a path sunning itself. She was getting used to them, but was still startled whenever she spotted one and this amused Gloria greatly. The little girl started pointing them out to see Catherine's reaction, and Catherine was happy to play along and exaggerate her shock and horror at the mini-dragons to put a smile on Gloria's face.

When they reached the row of hotel souvenir shops next to the lobby, Catherine immediately spotted some pink sandals hanging on hooks next to one of the front doors. Gloria's face lit up as her eyes alighted on them too, and she grabbed for a pair at least four sizes too big for her.

'Let's see what size you need, shall we? Sit down for a second.' Catherine took a couple of pairs from their hooks and held them against the soles of Gloria's feet. The sizes were American, which always confused Catherine, just like a change in currency always perplexed her.

The shopkeeper, a stout, middle-aged woman with chestnut-brown hair, soon came over to see if she could help, and looked between Gloria and Catherine with a slight frown.

'Is this the girl from the beach?' she asked in English with the hint of an American accent.

'Yes, it is,' whispered Catherine, turning her back to Gloria. 'She was in a really bad way yesterday, so I took her in and gave her some food and now I just want to buy her some shoes before I send her home.' Catherine spoke quickly, keen to avoid any misunderstanding.

The shopkeeper put her hand on Catherine's arm. 'That was a kind thing to do. This one has been running around here for a long time, her parents are not good people,' she said, indicating the bruises on Gloria's arm with a flick of her eyes.

Gloria, who had wandered off to look at some of the toys in the shop, appeared oblivious as the shopkeeper continued to describe her parents as 'drug-addled scum that should be locked up'.

'Why has no one done anything for her before?' asked Catherine, kind of annoyed that everyone seemed to know that this was happening and hadn't done anything.

'Guests and staff give her food when she will let them, but she usually runs off if anyone tries to help. The authorities here don't have the time to chase street kids out of the goodness of their hearts. She must have trusted you, or maybe she's hit rock bottom?'

'Probably rock bottom. I'm no mother, I fed her so much chocolate cake last night, she was almost sick!' Catherine sighed, and rubbed her eyes hard with her fingers, feeling a stress headache coming on.

The older woman smiled. 'She looks happy enough to me,' she said as she glanced over at Gloria.

'So, you know who her parents are, then?' asked Catherine.

'I do. She looks just like her dad, only much prettier. They live in a big apartment block about half a mile inland. Her dad has always lived around here. My good-for-nothing ex worked with him at a wholesale company, they're friends. I last saw Jorge a couple of years ago when they delivered some stock here and he didn't seem so bad back then, but things went downhill, I guess. I heard him and his wife have a baby boy now too.'

'That's sad.' Catherine felt sick at the thought of a baby being neglected as Gloria had. 'Do you know of any other family members? Would your ex-boyfriend know more?'

'I'm sorry, that's all I know. And no one has seen or heard from my ex in a long time, which is for the best.' The shop-keeper turned to Gloria. 'So, you want some sandals?' She spoke in Spanish, getting her attention.

She measured Gloria's feet and selected the perfect pair, and as she strapped them on securely, she saw the blisters and gave the little girl a look of sympathy. Then, clicking back in to sales mode, the stout woman showed them her selection of children's T-shirts, shorts and underwear. Catherine purchased two of each.

'What are you going to do?' asked the shopkeeper, whose name, it turned out, was also Gloria.

'What makes you think I'm going to do something?' said Catherine.

'I just get the feeling that you might.' She smirked, and handed over a translucent carrier bag that was stuffed full with the clothes. She patted Catherine on the arm, then unhooked a blonde doll from the display next to the till and placed it in little Gloria's delighted hand as a gift.

With Gloria at her side, Catherine walked a few steps away from the shop and then came to a standstill. The sun was beaming down on them, the previous day's storm having been swiftly replaced by bright light and humidity. Even at ten o'clock in the morning the sun was a hazy, blurring glow, too bright to look at, and Catherine could feel it sizzling her fair skin as she stood there. Gloria stayed close, playing with her new doll's frizzy mop of hair, and wriggling her own toes, seem-ingly trying to get used to wearing shoes again.

Catherine looked up at the cloudless blue sky as if waiting for a sign, not that she believed in such things but she was all out of ideas and didn't know what to do next. After a few minutes, she beckoned Gloria to follow her inside the hotel lobby, which was long and wide with a cavernous wooden ceiling. The windows were left flung open at all times and the floor was marble, shiny and slippery, with swirls of black and white, and speckles of purple. At one end of the rectangular room was the reception desk, flanked by a concierge, timeshare and excursion sales reps. The rest of the huge space was taken up by tables and chairs, enormous plants and a long bar.

'I need you to get me a family lawyer and a police officer, right now,' said Catherine in Spanish, sliding a $100 bill across a large glass desk towards the flabbergasted concierge. 'Please,' she added as an afterthought, her manners having temporarily evaporated in that moment of impulse and insanity.

'A family lawyer and a police officer, madam?' he said, his face creased with concern as he peered over the desk to see Gloria.

Catherine slid another $100 bill at him and affirmed that it was urgent. 'Tell them it will be worth their while, I can pay. But they need to get here as soon as possible.'

The concierge offered a nervous smile, and agreed to try his best to find what she had asked for.

'We will wait over there so please don't just try, please get them here as soon as possible.'

Catherine and Gloria took seats at a table in the lobby bar and sipped lemonades as they waited. Catherine glanced sporadically at the concierge, and each time she did he looked more and more flustered. His big eyebrows were set in a deep frown and his hands flapped around as he made repeated telephone calls.

Eventually, he came dancing over to them, the frown replaced by wide eyes and a smile as he informed Catherine that he had managed to arrange for both a lawyer and a police

11

officer to arrive in the next couple of hours. Catherine thanked him, and apologised for being so bossy. Around three hours later, a brown-suited man in a hat arrived, holding a briefcase, and the concierge immediately pointed him in their direction.

Catherine wasted no time explaining the situation to the kind man whose glasses kept sliding down his nose as he listened. They spoke quietly as Gloria played with her doll nearby, and just as their conversation was concluding, two grumpy-faced policemen sauntered towards them. She repeated her explanation of what she knew of Gloria's home situation, and they looked thoroughly uninterested until she brandished a wad of $50 bills.

Thankfully, Mr Hernandez, the kindly lawyer, offered to accompany the police officers to the apartment building to see what could be done to help Gloria and her baby brother. If it was as bad as Catherine was envisioning, the lawyer might be needed to arrange for someone else to care for the children – an aunt or uncle, perhaps – and if that were the case, there would be paperwork involved that she didn't want leaving to chance. It was agreed that Gloria could remain in Catherine's care until after their visit, which was just as well as at the mention of her going home, Gloria held tightly to Catherine's hand, not letting go until the policemen had disappeared from view.

Catherine thanked the concierge again, who now seemed most intrigued by the situation. She guessed that he was probably about ten years older than her; he wore a dark suit and his black hair was styled perfectly, as was his beard. He gave them a complimentary one-day guest wristband for Gloria, and emphatically wished them well, clearly enthused by the change of pace that their presence had injected into his day. Catherine and Gloria went to the huge buffet restaurant for lunch before heading back to the hotel room for a siesta.

Later that day, while Gloria was still sleeping, there was a light knock on the door and Catherine was surprised to see Mr Hernandez. After some whispered pleasantries and an explanation that Gloria was asleep, the two of them crept out onto the large balcony, which had views of the jungle.

'Please sit down, Mr Hernandez. Do you want something to drink?' said Catherine.

'Just some water would be nice.'

She moved quietly back into the room and pulled out some bottles from the minibar.

'I am sorry to come to your room like this,' Mr Hernandez said, accepting the water from Catherine and watching as she closed the sliding balcony door softly. 'The thing is, I have some sensitive information and I didn't want to explain the details in public.' He removed his suit-jacket and hat, looking quite flustered.

'Are you all right?' asked Catherine as she took a seat next to him.

He glanced at the closed balcony door, as if to make sure that Gloria could not hear what he was about to say.

'We went to the apartment building that you described to us. The policemen spoke to a few neighbours to get an idea of what has been going on, but none of them have seen the family for over a week. Gloria lived with her mum, dad and little brother. He was about a year old.'

'He ... *was?*' Catherine repeated, her stomach swirling.

'When we got to the apartment, we knocked but there was no answer, but the door was unlocked so the policemen went in. I'm sorry to say that there was a woman, Gloria's mother, deceased on the hallway floor. Her father and brother were also found dead.' All the colour had drained from the lawyer's face as he recalled what must have been a horrific sight.

'Oh God,' said Catherine, feeling sick. 'Was it drugs? I was told they may have been drug users?'

'I'm not sure. As soon as the police realised what they were dealing with they got me out of there. I only saw the woman, Gloria's mum. They are treating their deaths as suspicious.' He took a sip of his water, his hand shaking slightly.

'I'm so sorry that I put you in that situation,' said Catherine.

'No, dear, don't ever apologise. Better that we old men found them in that state than the girl. It's just not what I'm used to. The police weren't shocked by it, they acted as though they see that kind of thing every day, but not me ... I won't forget today in a hurry.'

They sat in silence for a few minutes. Catherine tried to imagine the terrible scene, and wondered if Gloria had witnessed what had happened. She shook her head. 'What will happen to Gloria now?'

'Their neighbours didn't seem to know of any other family members living nearby. And according to the police, there was nothing obvious in the apartment to indicate anyone close, no photos or address book, and the only mobile phone in the home was smashed. The authorities will continue to look but, in the meantime, Gloria will need to be cared for.'

'We could ask Gloria. She's a bright kid, she would know if she had family living nearby, surely?'

'We could try that, but as she is so bright, it makes it even less likely. If she knew of local family members, would she not have gone to them instead of living on the beach?'

'You're right. Oh God, how will we tell her what's happened?' said Catherine, tears spilling down her cheeks.

The lawyer shifted uncomfortably in his chair.

'Are the police going to come and take her?' Catherine asked, trying to pull herself together.

'Well, that's why I'm here, actually.'

'To take her?' said Catherine, wiping her face.

'No. I was wondering if you might be happy to keep her with you?'

Catherine blinked. 'For how long?'

'Indefinitely. Until a family member can be found.' Mr Hernandez gave a careful smile.

'Wow, OK. That is a big commitment. I was just trying to help, I don't want a kid,' said Catherine, feeling lightheaded.

'If you don't take her, she will go to an orphanage.'

'Oh no.' Catherine put her head between her knees. This was all like some kind of strange nightmare. She pinched her leg, and when she didn't wake up, she stood up and bent her head over the balcony railing, thinking that the air beyond it might not be as thin as it currently felt on the balcony itself.

'Wouldn't Gloria be better off with someone local, who will understand her culture and everything? Wouldn't it confuse her to live with me in a hotel surrounded by white English people on holiday?'

'She trusts you. From what the neighbours said, whenever they tried to approach her in the past, she would run away. For some reason she let you help her so, personally, I think it would be best for her to remain with you.'

'What are the orphanages like here?' said Catherine.

'Orphanages all over the world try their best, don't they? But it's hard to care for one child, let alone dozens, so they can be a little ... bleak. Would you want a child to go into an orphanage in the UK?'

Catherine walked to the balcony door and looked in at Gloria sleeping. 'No, I wouldn't.'

'It's a sad fact that we have many children living on the streets here, and we just don't have the infrastructure to care for them all. If their communities or families can't help, and the orphanages are full, they can fall through the cracks.'

'OK, I'll do it.' Anxiety punched Catherine hard in the stomach. 'I'll foster her.'

'You are a good person, Mrs Lish.'

Catherine squinted at the lawyer; such an unassuming man in appearance but a wizard of persuasion. She felt like Frodo, conned by Gandalf into taking the ring to Mordor. 'What happens if they don't find any family?'

'The authorities will only look for her family for around a month. If they can't find anyone, then she will be put up for adoption, and while she waits to be adopted, she will be placed in an orphanage. Although, I should state the obvious here: not many kids her age get adopted, unfortunately.'

'Oh, God.'

'I have all the papers here to enable you to become her temporary guardian, all you need to do is sign them. I will take a scan of your passport and I'll get you the necessary visa so you can stay here more long term. I have a friend who works at the embassy, are you happy for me to ask for her help?'

'I'll take all the help I can get. I have a scan of my passport that I can email to you?'

'That would be helpful.'

'Don't you need to check that I'm not a child-molesting, serial killer before you let me take care of her?'

'A social worker will visit you either tomorrow or the day after, and part of your visa application will involve them checking your criminal history. You don't have any convictions, do you?'

'No. But I can't stay here forever. I have a life in England, a business. Let's hope they find someone who can take her.'

'Yes, let's hope so.' He handed her a pen to sign the documents. When they were completed, he said, 'Here is my card. I will send you an invoice for my time today along with your new visa and copies of this paperwork.'

The lawyer placed all of the papers back into his briefcase, and they moved silently back through the room towards the front door.

'Thank you for your help, Mr Hernandez.'

'The police may want to question Gloria about what she saw. Don't be alarmed if they contact you, but call me straight away if they do, OK?'

'I will,' said Catherine, holding his business card in the air, feeling uneasy.

'This isn't England, Mrs Lish, remember that. I promise I will do all I can to help you and Gloria. I wish you all the best.' He smiled at her, put his hat and jacket back on and walked towards the stairs.

Once the door was closed, Catherine put her body against the wall and slid down it until she was sitting on the cold floor, wondering what the hell she had got herself into.

Catherine was twenty-six years old and, other than her little brother, she had gone through her whole life never really having dealt with children before. She was six years older than Robert, and had mainly just wrestled, argued and joked around with him for the first twelve years of his life, leaving all the caring to their parents. She had taken on responsibility for Gloria, but had absolutely no idea what she was doing.

After Mr Hernandez left, the first thing Catherine did was to call her brother, her best friend in the world; she told him everything. He was shocked, he was supportive, they laughed that only she could get herself into this kind of predicament on an all-inclusive trip, and he promised to sort things out back home so that she could stay on for an extra month.

The next thing she did was to take out a notebook.

17

Catherine loved notebooks, and she wrote bullet points on how best to keep Gloria happy and, more importantly, alive.

She started by writing a reminder to add Gloria officially on the register as a guest in her hotel room. She would go and speak to the helpful concierge first thing the next morning and arrange this.

She then listed breakfast, lunch and dinner as being important not to miss. Catherine had a tendency to skip meals but she couldn't do that now. Regular mealtimes would help to establish a routine, and Gloria needed fattening up – something that should be easy to achieve in an all-inclusive resort.

Next, she penned ideas for Gloria to attend the hotel kids' club, and for a shopping trip to Playa del Carmen for more clothes and anything else a child would need, although she wasn't sure what else a six-year-old might need, so she also made a note to research this later on.

She had watched a lot of *Supernanny* back in the day, and was grateful that she knew all about naughty steps and time-outs should she have to discipline the little girl at all. As she looked over at Gloria however, still sleeping, she couldn't imagine the timid little thing ever needing a time-out.

Finally, she wrote down and underlined several times that the kid needed patience and love after everything she'd been through, and Catherine reminded herself not to be selfish.

Notes complete, Catherine quietly tidied the room and emailed Mr Hernandez a copy of her passport. She always had a copy on her phone in case she was mugged or arrested Bridget-Jones style and thrown into a foreign prison, a fear she had carried throughout fifty countries without a single incident.

'Kitty?'

'You're awake!' Catherine smiled. She walked over and sat at the edge of the bed. 'Shall we go and get some dinner?'

Gloria nodded sleepily.

'I have to tell you something,' said Catherine once Gloria was looking more alert. 'Your mummy and daddy have gone away and they're not coming back.' She paused. This could end up being traumatic for them both, she really should have googled how to break this sort of news to a child. She took a deep breath, and made sure Gloria was listening. 'Before they left, they asked me to look after you for a while. Is that OK?'

'They have gone away?' mumbled Gloria while playing with a crease in the bed sheets.

'Yes, sweetheart, I'm afraid so. But they loved you very much, I'm sure they did. I'm going to look after you for a while and we are going to have a lot of fun, aren't we?'

'OK,' said the little girl, giving Catherine a weak smile, as if sensing that she needed some reassurance. 'Where is my doll?'

Catherine looked around and spotted its legs sticking out from beneath one of the bed's many pillows. 'There she is, look,' she said, pointing.

'Oh, here she is.' Gloria smiled, holding the doll upside down. 'She looks like you, you both have yellow hair. I'm going to call her Kitty after you.'

'That's nice. We will have to get her a friend that looks like you, with dark hair?'

'Yes please!'

'OK. Let's go and get some dinner, then?' said Catherine, standing up.

Gloria climbed out of bed and sat on the hard floor to put on her new shoes. 'Can I have chocolate cake for dinner again, Kitty?' she asked the doll, and a mischievous grin lit up her little face.

Maybe she isn't so timid after all, thought Catherine with a smile.

The Boy

With Catherine's two-week holiday officially having been extended, and with two of them living in the hotel room, they needed to stock up on some essentials like shampoo and shower gel. Catherine was sick of using the tiny ones provided by the hotel, and whenever they were at the beach she kept picturing the plastic lids choking a sea turtle.

There were areas all along the seafront cordoned off to protect turtle eggs, and each time she walked past one of these roped-off zones, she felt guilty about her make-up wipes and water bottles too. She had even had a dream one night in which all the baby turtles had crawled out of the sand like zombies and flapped all over her, and frisbeed bottle caps at her in revenge.

So, in an effort to prevent death-by-sea-turtle vengeance, Catherine and Gloria got a taxi to a big supermarket not far from the hotel. Catherine had considered renting a car a few times, but the thought of driving on the wrong side of the road scared her, as did the size and chaos of the roads there, so she had shelved that idea for the time being.

She was happy with her decision to taxi rather than drive herself on that day especially, as the roads were a nightmare of honking horns and swerving cars; the taxi smelt of watermelon and the friendly driver offered to wait for them outside the shop.

Stepping into the supermarket felt like arriving on a spaceship after a walk on Mars; outside was so hot and dusty, but inside was ice-cold from the blasting air con, artificially lit and spotlessly clean.

They got a trolley, and Catherine handed Gloria the shopping list that they had written together earlier in both Spanish and English. Catherine, still not knowing at what ages children should be doing things, was panicked that Gloria didn't yet know how to read or write, or even understand basic numbers, so she was trying her best to teach her.

'What's first on the list then little lady?' said Catherine, pushing the trolley along.

'Shampoo.'

'Did you read that or did you just remember it?'

'I just remembered it.'

'Well having a good memory is a great skill too, which word says shampoo?'

Gloria examined the list, holding it close to her face.

'That's it!' said Catherine as Gloria pointed to the right one, probably just a guess but still, a correct guess.

They found the aisle with the toiletries and continued through the list, finding toothpaste, tampons, sun cream and dental floss. Catherine bent down to look at the different types of moisturiser they had, and when she looked up, Gloria was gone.

Catherine turned frantically to look in both directions down the aisle before abandoning their trolley and running towards the tills. She ran along the row, looking down every aisle, and as she really started to panic she began shouting Gloria's name. She couldn't find her anywhere, and when Catherine started to cry, the store's security guard meandered over to see what all the fuss was about. At that minute, however, the little girl emerged from behind a display, holding some snacks and a comic.

'Gloria, where did you go!' shouted Catherine, sprinting towards her. She fell to her knees and tried to hug her little runaway, but Gloria flinched. 'Sweetheart, you don't need to be scared of me. I'm sorry for shouting, you just scared me,' she said, putting a hand to her chest and taking some deep breaths.

'I scared you?' asked Gloria, looking at Catherine sheepishly.

Catherine gently took the items out of the girl's arms and put them on the floor. 'Feel my heart,' she said, taking the girl's hand and putting it on her chest. 'It's beating a mile a minute! I didn't know where you were, so I got scared and I ran around looking for you.'

Gloria bit her lip.

'Everyone thinks I've gone mad,' Catherine whispered, giving the confused security guard a sideways glance and smile. 'Please don't scare me like that again, OK? My heart can't take it.'

'I won't,' said Gloria, still looking scared.

'Gloria, no matter what you do, I will never ever hurt you, do you understand? Even if you make me really mad, I won't ever hit you or anything, I would never do that. I won't hurt you and I will do my best to make sure that no one else ever does either. I'll try not to shout, but I can't promise I won't ever shout again, OK?'

Gloria seemed to believe her, as she relaxed her shoulders and threw her arms around Catherine's neck, almost knocking her off balance. 'Sorry, Kitty, I won't do that again.'

Catherine hugged her tight and then picked up Gloria's shopping from the floor. 'Are these on the list?' she asked, holding up a big bag of sweets and raising her eyebrows.

'Yes, look,' said Gloria pointing at the word 'tampons' on the piece of paper.

Catherine laughed and they went to find their abandoned trolley.

That afternoon, with Gloria safe at the hotel kids' club, Catherine sat on the beach and had a quiet mental breakdown. Watching the waves, she took some deep breaths and tried to relax as her mind ran away with itself, as it so often did. She felt like shouting at it to shut up. She was questioning her ability to look after a child, chastising herself for being so inept at parenting that even a simple trip to the supermarket was difficult, and feeling guilty and anxious about shouting at poor Gloria. She couldn't stop thinking about her scared little face.

'Hey, I'm Stefano,' said a man suddenly as he sat down next to her on the sand with a thud. 'What are you looking at?'

Catherine jumped. 'Umm, the sea?' she said, pointing. She shot him a sarcastic look and flicked sand off her knee.

'You're just looking at the sea? I thought it must be a boat or something, you've been staring for so long.'

'Who are you?' she said, the annoyance at his interruption showing on her face.

'I'm Stefano.'

'Yes, I know that. I mean why have you been watching me watch the sea?'

'I work at the bar, I made you that drink?' he nodded at the cosmo in her hand. He had an accent she couldn't place.

'Oh, right, well thanks for that.' She raised the cup slightly and rolled her eyes.

'You seemed sad, so I thought I would check you weren't planning to throw yourself in the sea or anything, but maybe I mistook sad for rude. I'll leave you alone.' He went to stand up but Catherine took his hand.

'I'm sorry,' she said, her shoulders sagging.

'It's OK.' He shrugged and smiled.

His eyes were pale blue and his short hair was dark blonde and slightly curly; he had a golden tan, a thick beard and tattoos along his biceps. He was wearing the white polo-neck T-shirt and long, tailored shorts that Catherine recognised as the hotel staff uniform.

Some people can be described as having resting bitch face, but not Stefano. He was the opposite – he had the kind of face that looked happy all the time. Now that she'd made the connection with the hotel, Catherine remembered seeing him around. When he didn't agree with something, Stefano's mouth would turn downwards ever so briefly and he would shrug his broad shoulders and arch his eyebrows, but then his gleaming smile would spring back into position and any conflict simply dissolved. He was a people-pleaser, easy-going and funny, which made him popular with guests at the hotel, and from what she could recall, he had plenty of friends too. So, when Catherine turned to see him smiling at her again, she couldn't help but smile back.

'A smile! Mio Dio, I made her smile!' he shouted to the empty beach.

'Oh, you're Italian?' she said, nodding in recognition of the words, and now his accent too.

'Si, I am. How did you get that?'

'Mio Dio, my God, capisco benissimo,' she said, pointing at herself.

'I guessed that you were English, but that's odd, the English don't usually speak other languages,' he said, elbowing her playfully.

She nodded. 'We don't, we're a bit shit for that actually. I blame the government – now that's something we're good at doing!'

'Why do you speak Italian?' he asked, his voice gravelly, like that of a much older man.

'All the best boys are Italian, Stefano,' she said, and raised a shy smile.

'So why are you so sad?'

'I'm not really sad, just a bit overwhelmed with life right now. Why are you so happy?'

'I don't know, I just always am.'

'That must be nice.'

'Yeah, I guess it is,' he said, beaming at her once again with his infectious smile. 'So, what's overwhelming you? Life's not so bad, is it? You have a cocktail in your hand, sand beneath your feet ...'

'Nothing is bad. It's just complicated.' She frowned at the sand between her toes.

'You English people love to feel stressed!'

Catherine laughed. 'Stop generalising English behaviour! I know stressed people all over the world.'

'Are they all English people living in other countries?' he said, arching his eyebrows.

'Hmm. Some of them, I guess.' She gave a rueful grin.

He reached across and took hold of her wrist.

'What are you doing?' she said, trying to pull her hand away.

'I'm taking your pulse, checking for signs of stress,' he said, smiling again. After squeezing her wrist for no more than three seconds, he offered a diagnosis of severe stress.

'I feel like I should be stressed right now! Two weeks ago, I basically became a mum to a six-year-old!'

'Whoa. How did that happen? Remind me to never use that contraception!'

Catherine laughed out loud. 'I found her on the beach.'

'I don't think finders keepers applies to children, bella,' he said, patting her on the arm in mock condescension.

'I know that, you idiot!' She laughed, rolling her eyes, beginning to warm to this lovable stranger.

'I heard about this story,' he said, his smile faltering. 'You're looking after that little girl, the one that was always on the beach. Her mum died, right?'

'Yeah.' Catherine looked at the dimming sky and stretched out her long legs, her toes running through the sand. 'It's just a lot to get used to.'

'You have every right to feel stressed,' he said, more seriously.

'You heard about Gloria on the grapevine?' asked Catherine after a moment of quiet.

'The concierge was talking about it. He thinks you're great. Keeps telling anyone that will listen that he helped you to call the police. He's a friend of mine, so I've heard the story a few times now.' He smiled. 'It's a good thing that you're doing.'

'Thanks.'

'Do they know how her parents died?'

'The police won't tell me anything, it's an active investigation so I suppose they can't? But it's odd, two adults and a baby dying at the same time, and when I found Gloria, she had bruises on her arm,' said Catherine quietly, as though she thought the culprit might be hiding behind a folded sunlounger, listening to their conversation.

'Have you asked her about it?'

'No, I don't want to upset her, she's just starting to seem more settled.'

'Maybe she will tell you at some point.'

'Yeah, hopefully,' said Catherine.

'So where is she now?' Stefano asked, jokingly looking around for her. 'You didn't lose her already, did you?'

'Don't. I actually did lose her today, in the supermarket! It scared me half to death. She's in the kids' club right now.'

'See, you're acting like a mum already. You've ditched your kid and you're drinking cocktails!'

Catherine laughed, she tried not to but she couldn't help it.

'You can do this,' he said.

'She's a great kid. I just don't like change, I never have. I was just here for a holiday and now all of a sudden I'm responsible for a child.'

'But if you could go back in time, would you change anything?'

'Of course not. She needed help and I wouldn't change what I did.'

'Look, I work here almost every day. I usually work in the daytime, so I finish at six. You can meet me whenever you like and tell me about your day and drink cocktails, and I will help you to get used to it. What do you say?'

'Why are you being so nice to me?' she asked, narrowing her eyes at him.

'I have happiness to spare.' He grinned.

'No, really.'

'I'm extremely shallow and you're extremely beautiful?'

'You don't seem shallow.'

'You are beautiful though,' he said softly, looking into her sad, blue eyes.

'I'm Catherine by the way, but people call me Lish, it's my last name.'

'Lish ...' He pronounced slowly. 'I like it. You're also Eng-lish so it will be easy to remember. Come on, let's go and get you another cocktail before your kid comes looking for you.' He stood up quickly and offered her his hand.

He was much taller than her and she could smell his after-shave mixed with tobacco smoke as they walked, side by side, back to the bar.

The Rain

As the days went on, Catherine and Gloria developed a routine. They went for breakfast, they swam in the sea and in the pools, they had lunch, and then Catherine would try her best to impart some wisdom about basic maths and the alphabet. Then they would have a nap, for Catherine's sake as much as Gloria's, followed by dinner. After eating, Gloria would go to the hotel kids' club and Catherine would meet Stefano on the beach.

He was kind to her; he made her laugh, and each time she saw him he seemed to become more attractive. Best of all, he didn't demand anything from her, so while it didn't take long for them to realise they wanted to be more than just friends, neither of them applied any pressure. He said simply that they were 'seeing each other', which she liked the sound of, but for that reason there was no plan for him to meet Gloria. Catherine didn't want this free and uncertain relationship to confuse the little girl. She had gone through so much already.

Two weeks of their evening meetings had passed by quickly, and once again Catherine stood excitedly waiting for Stefano on the beach. However, just as she spotted him rounding the corner, a warm, fat rain droplet splattered off her cheek, and soon the sand around her was bouncing beneath a sudden, heavy downpour.

Soaked in seconds, laughing uncontrollably and without thinking too much about it, they ran as fast as they could towards her hotel room.

Their hair and clothes were drenched from the rain, and they stood dripping and giggling for a few seconds in her room's entrance hall, a pool of water collecting on the shiny floor at their feet.

'This is the first time we've been alone in private,' she said, touching his beard lightly and smiling as water trickled down his neck like it was spilling from a sponge.

He stroked the wet skin of her cheek and closed his eyes. His fingers drifted southwards to her cleavage and then as quickly as his eyes snapped open, he was kissing her.

The water from both of their faces and the dizzying surprise that it was happening made the kiss feel aquatic, like they were kissing under water, swirling in circles as they drifted to the ocean floor. They stopped and looked at each other for a minute after coming up for air, as though they were double-checking telepathically that this was a good idea.

Stefano looked at the curve of her breasts beneath her soaking wet dress and took off his T-shirt. 'I should let it dry,' he explained in a whisper, placing it on the back of a chair.

Catherine looked at his body, at his toned stomach and the hair on his chest, and after they kicked off their shoes, she helped to slip his shorts from his hips. She turned her back to him and he kissed her shoulders while slowly unzipping her dress, letting it fall to the floor.

'Oh my god,' he whispered, 'you are so beautiful.' He pressed himself against her, moving his hands along her waist before cupping her naked breasts from behind.

She arched her neck as he kissed it and felt him harden against the small of her back.

'Is this OK?' he asked, moving his hand down her body and slipping his fingers into her underwear. Still standing behind her, Stefano pushed her gently against the wall, and she began to moan softly in response, enjoying the sensation of her breasts being caressed by the smooth, cool wall as she moved against it.

When she turned to face him she saw that his usual smile was gone, replaced by a brooding look of concentration that made her knees tremble and goosebumps spring to life on her arms.

With more urgency, he ran his hands over her curves and then lifted her, his fingers digging into the supple skin of her thighs as he quickly carried her to the bed.

She wrapped herself around him, pulling him close to her, and as the storm raged noisily outside, they made love.

'Wow,' he said breathlessly as they lay entangled on the bed, his smile firmly back in place.

'Yeah.' She giggled, her head on his chest, her fingers running along the thick hairs on his arm.

'You have tattoos on your ribs, that's so hot,' he said sleepily in Italian, shifting onto his front and kissing the inked skin just below her breasts.

She stroked his damp hair and stared at the swirling ceiling fan for a long time before they snapped out of their drowsy trance, got dressed and splashed through the wet hallway, laughing as they took care not to slip on the tiles.

She kissed him goodbye and watched him skip out the door. 'Ciao,' she yelled after him.

He turned to smile at her from the top of the stairs, and then he was gone.

Before going out to collect Gloria, Catherine threw a heap

of towels down on the floor to soak up the water and then she made the bed. It felt like a crime scene, and Catherine wasn't sure it was appropriate to bring Gloria back into the room after what had just happened in it. She couldn't explain why, but leaving the window open a crack made her feel better, like the ghosts of her and Stefano's lust would blow away, and the room would be cleansed of their erotic encounter.

That night, while Gloria slept soundly, starfishing on the sofa bed with not a care in the world, Catherine went out and sat on their balcony. She didn't do this very often for fear of a giant lizard being out there, but she was starting to fear them less and less, and with the rain now having slowed down it was nice to be outside listening to the water splashing on the trees.

Just above the treeline she could see a sky full of stars, and she started to think about her husband.

The rain always reminded her of him. They had both preferred cold weather, always wishing for dark and dull days over sunshine, much to the disdain of everyone they knew. They scoffed at family members who would walk into their house and start opening blinds; they would pretend to burn up like vampires, and complain about the excessive heat if the temperature climbed above fifteen degrees. They loved the rain, especially on weekends when they could stay cosy at home, just them in a bubble. However, it had been raining on the day he died too, so now Catherine had a more complicated relationship with precipitation.

She felt bad about having slept with Stefano. He was not the first since Thomas had died but still, she always felt a twist of guilt, as though she was being disloyal to him.

An anxious cloud had filled her chest ever since Stefano had skipped out into the rain earlier that evening. She could feel Thomas's betrayed eyes stinging the back of her head, and tears began to creep down her cheeks. Catherine sat hunched on a chair, her knees pulled up under her, remembering her husband and worrying that one day she might forget something small about him, like the way he looked at her when he was annoyed or how it felt when he put his hands on her. She had forgotten so much already.

At just after midnight Catherine went to bed, exhausted and emotional, but despite her guilt and anxiety, she was excited about the idea of seeing Stefano again.

When his colleagues started to ask questions about them, she joked that they were passionately not in love. A couple of times he took her out into the local town dancing or for dinner, while the hotel provided a safe babysitting service by the hour for Gloria. The little girl was enjoying life at the hotel; she was looking healthier, happier and had more clothes and toys than could fit in the room's wardrobe.

They got to know people all over the hotel, from the bellboys to the waitresses in the restaurant, the gardeners and the children's entertainers. They would fuss over Gloria as they watched her grow in confidence, and would chat to Catherine and share their parenting stories and advice with her. Seeing them every day, the staff started to feel more like friends, and Catherine began to relax into her new life.

The Friend

ᦅᦆ᭙

'You will love them all, I promise,' Stefano said as he pulled hard on the handbrake of his rusty old car. 'I haven't told them that you speak Italian yet. They will be like, *Whaaaaaat?*' He mimicked the shocked expression anticipated from his friends, then got out of the car and ran into the bar, leaving Catherine to trail nervously behind.

Burgundy earrings swayed from her earlobes, complementing the crimson polish on her nails. Catherine loved floaty dresses with bold patterns; some days she looked like a wacky secondary school art teacher, and others she looked like she was going to a 1960s summer music festival. But she always tried to coordinate certain accessories, so even though she might clash with her surroundings like a tiger in the fabric aisle of a haberdashery, her toe polish always matched her bikinis and her finger polish colour had to be similar to that of her earrings. Without such rules, she felt firmly out of sync.

It was a week before Christmas, and Stefano had taken her to a bar to meet some of his closest friends. They had been dating for a couple of months, and he had finally met Gloria a few days earlier; it had gone well. He was basically a twenty-four-year-old big kid, so it was unsurprising that they had hit it off, and as Gloria had grown in confidence, Catherine was no longer worried about her getting close to someone new.

The bar was open-fronted on to a busy road, with just a handful of parked cars on the kerb separating it from the swooshing sounds and lights of the night-time traffic. Rock music pumped from old-fashioned speakers, tables and chairs were grouped everywhere in messy clumps, two big pool tables were positioned next to the back wall and a long bar ran down the left side of the large room. One barmaid sat behind the bar's taps and, as Catherine navigated her way through the maze of furniture towards the back of the room, she smiled in Catherine's direction as though she could read her anxious mind.

Stefano and his friends were clustered around one of the pool tables, swigging beers and talking in Italian. Catherine's insides swirled like she was on her way to a job interview. Her mouth felt funny, as if she were losing the feeling in her tongue. *Can you ever really feel your tongue?* she pondered while trying to remember how to walk in a straight line.

'Guys, guys!' shouted Stefano. 'This is Catherine. Lish, these are my friends.' He put a strong and comforting arm around her as each member of the group introduced themselves.

'Ciao, piacere di conoscervi tutti,' she said, the greeting uttered with moderate confidence. She was pleased to find that her tongue had woken up.

'Oh my God, are you another Italian? I thought you were English!' said a short man with a beard, big eyebrows and expressive hands, whom she recognised as the concierge from her hotel.

'No, I am ...' She stopped, looking at the tall man who had just joined their group and stood right next to her. He had lightly tanned, almost pale, skin, messy dark brown hair and big brown eyes. 'Wait, are you English too?' she asked, squinting at him as if to clarify his Englishness.

'How on earth did you guess that?' he asked in a northern English accent.

'I don't know, I just had a feeling. That's so weird!'

Stefano laughed. 'You can probably smell the stress on him, bella. This is my friend Benedetto. He's half-English, half-Italian. Beni, this is Catherine.'

'So, you're the mystery girlfriend? I was starting to think he'd made you up.'

Catherine smiled. 'Where in England are you from?'

'Manchester, what about you?'

'I have a house in the Peak District, near Cromford? Not that far from Manchester, actually.'

'Oh yeah, I think I know it. It's nice there, proper old-England with cottages and green hills?'

'That's it. It's a nice place to live.'

'So, you're *not* Italian?' The interruption came from a pretty girl who was standing on the other side of Stefano, her brown hair cut in a pixie style. She smirked. 'What, did you practise saying hello in Italian for us? How cute.'

Catherine's nerves dissolved into annoyance. 'Perché dovrei esercitarmi? I'm fluent,' she said. Her assertion was triumphant and, she hoped, casual, as if she proved that she was bilingual at least fifteen times a day and it was no big deal.

The unfriendly girl gave Catherine a dead stare.

'That's Valentina,' Beni said softly.

Valentina was shorter than Catherine by about a foot, slender and delicate, with Cupid's bow lips and big wide eyes. She was wearing a skater dress, black boots and had piercings all up her ears.

Catherine shifted her gaze away from her. 'Can I get a round in?' she asked the group with a jolt, hoping to defuse the tension.

'Yeah, sure!' they all chorused.

'Beers for everyone,' Stefano said. 'You're doing great,' he whispered into Catherine's ear, and then darted off to set up the pool table.

Catherine walked up to the bar and the friendly barmaid smiled again as she lined up four cold beers and a glass of wine. Speaking in Spanish, they chatted briefly before Catherine headed back over to the group, clutching the beers and wine with the help of the bushy-browed concierge, who had introduced himself as Anton. As they walked, he cooed about what a small world it was and asked after Gloria. Following a couple of games of pool – which she was terrible at – and lots of awkward laughter, Catherine escaped to the sanctuary of the bar and Maria, the barmaid, who it turned out had a little girl around Gloria's age. Maria was medium height, with long glossy black hair, beautiful tanned skin and a voluptuous figure. Catherine would come to realise that whatever the occasion, Maria would always be wearing jeans and a low-cut T-shirt, with beaded thread-and-bangle bracelets stretching up each arm, as though it were her uniform.

As the bar became busier, Catherine went to sit outside, the 'outside' of the open-to-the-elements bar being defined as the area no longer under the roof and as far away from the pool tables as possible, which suited her fine. She took deep breaths, her legs tucked beneath her on the wooden bench. She looked at the stars, sipped her wine and lamented how awkward she was in these kinds of social situations. Three glasses of wine still hadn't made her feel any better around these new people, and with Valentina's harsh gaze drilling into her she felt more uncomfortable than ever. Stefano – lovable, easy-going Stef – had no idea how she was feeling, he was too busy laughing with his friends, one arm slung casually over a smirking Val's shoulders.

'Are you OK?' The voice came from behind her, and Catherine turned to see Beni standing on the bar's front step.

He was wearing jeans, boots, and a checked shirt with the sleeves rolled up, unbuttoned over the top of a black T-shirt. Catherine couldn't help but notice how square his shoulders looked against the bright backdrop of the bar as he stood with one hand in his pocket, the other holding a freshly lit cigarette.

'Oh, I'm fine, thanks for asking. I'm just getting some air.'

'Yeah, there's not much air in this bar, with its missing wall.'

Catherine gave a wry grin and unfurled her arms and legs from the upright foetal position she had been in, suddenly conscious of how shell-shocked she must look.

'Can I join you? I need some air too,' he said, holding up his cigarette slightly.

'Sure, come and share the air.' Catherine scooted a millimetre to her left to indicate that there was room for him on her bench.

'It's overwhelming meeting this many people at once.'

'Is it obvious that I'm rubbish at this?'

'You just seem a bit nervous.'

Catherine nodded and studied the wine in her glass.

'Stef lives in his own world, doesn't he?' said Beni, pushing a hand through his hair, which was short at the sides and back but longer on top, wavy, seemingly with a life of its own as strands pointed in every direction.

'He really does.' Catherine smiled.

'He's a good guy though, he wouldn't hurt a fly. You met him at your hotel, right?'

'Yep, he's the fantasy holiday bartender I'll be telling all my friends about when I get home.' She laughed.

'You've been dating for months now though, not exactly a fleeting holiday romance, is it? And tell me to mind my own business, but how can you afford to live in a hotel for so long?'

'Well, it's a long story. I was only meant to be here for two weeks but then I met Gloria.'

'Oh yeah,' he said, 'you're sponsoring a local kid or something. Is that her? Gloria?'

'I'm fostering her. I'm just looking after her until we can find someone in her family to take her in. The police couldn't find anyone, so I've hired a private detective to help find a nice aunt or long-lost cousin or something. Fingers crossed. I gave him eleven months to find someone. I'll have been here a year by then.'

'Don't you want to keep her, if you've had her for a couple of months already?'

'I love her. But I don't want to be one of those white devils that come along and take the cute kid off the beach and rip her away from her culture and her home and her family. If there's a family member out there willing to love her, then that would be the best thing for her, regardless of how much it would break my heart to say goodbye to her. And it's a huge commitment. Am I really ready for a kid? I'm not sure. I've kept her alive so far, I guess.'

'You're an interesting person, Catherine.'

'Call me Lish.'

'Lish? Why Lish?'

'Everyone calls me Lish, it's my last name. Gloria calls me Kitty but only she's allowed.'

'So, what's your story, how did you come to be in Mexico ... Lish?'

'Well, in the literal sense, I got here on the flight from hell.' Catherine smiled at the memory.

'Why was it so bad?'

'I don't know where to start! I got to the airport nice and early, I always try to be a punctual three hours early for long-haul, as they suggest. I checked in my bag and was handed a piece of paper that told me the plane had been changed. I thought, never mind, it won't be too different, surely?'

'I love the suspense you're building here.'

'I sat myself down in the airport café and thought, it's all right, just a short two and half hour wait now until take-off. But no. No sooner had I sat down than the first catastrophe of the day hit. A text pinged through on my phone to tell me of a delay.'

'Those bastards.'

'Then, when we finally got herded onto the plane four hours later, it was like travelling back in time. It was like a plane you would hop on to fly from Birmingham to Belfast, not one you'd want to be on for eleven bloody hours! There was no entertainment, the staff were all stressed out and the only food on offer was sandwiches, sandwiches and more sandwiches.'

'So, the disaster was that you couldn't watch free films and eat microwaved salmon?'

'Without the films, Beni, the vast majority resorted to drinking, and by the time we were halfway over the Atlantic we had a full-on riot on our hands.'

'Oh no, did you have to turn back?'

'We had to turn back,' Catherine said, pretending to look furious. 'They had to strap the worst troublemakers into their seats. I mean, it provided the entertainment we were lacking, but still. It was another six hours back to the UK, and then we all had to get off the plane while they found us a new crew and

pilots because they can't work that long of a shift. The slackers.'
She laughed.

Beni shook his head and tutted. 'It's so selfish when people refuse to work a twenty-four-hour shift so that other people can go on their holidays.'

'I know, right?' Catherine smiled. 'Anyway, after another few hours, which I mostly spent lying on the cold floor of the airport, I was starting to feel like Tom Hanks in *The Terminal*. I was about to give up and accept that I would just have to live there forever, when we got given a plane by another airline.'

'OK, that does sound like an ordeal. How long did it take to get here in total?'

'About a day and a half!'

'Wow, that's rough. Why were you travelling here on your own in the first place?' he asked, glancing at the ring on her left hand.

'That's another long story.'

'I have all night.' He shrugged.

'My husband died, it's not a very fun one,' she said, looking at the floor.

The smile fell from Beni's eyes in an instant. 'I'm so sorry. When did he die?'

'It's been about three years.'

'Want to tell me about it?' he said, putting out his cigarette under his boot and stretching his long body into a comfortable listening position.

'OK,' said Catherine, unsure where to start, or even how to tell this story that she had never really told anyone. She wasn't sure why she was going to tell Beni, but his expression was so endearing that she couldn't say no.

'My dad died when I was young; there was a knock on the door and my mum's life changed forever. It was always in the back of my head that the same thing could happen to me, so I planned for it.' She stopped, Beni's eyes were big and brown and distracting so she looked at the floor.

'I knew I wasn't as strong as my mum. I thought I wouldn't be able to live without my husband so I wanted to prepare myself, to have a plan in case I ever had to. I imagined that if it happened to me, if he ever died, I would go to Norway, to this big beautiful cliff that people dangle their legs over for amazing selfies, and I would throw myself off and be done with the pain in an instant. Having this wacky plan comforted me somehow.' A smile spread across her lips at how ridiculous it sounded, and she continued gazing at the floor.

'So, when it happened,' – she paused, smile gone, embarrassed that her eyes were glazing with tears that she was determined not to cry – 'when I got the knock on the door to tell me that he'd died, I cried of course. I cried for days and I planned the funeral, and I lay in a dark room for a long time and then finally I went online and booked my flight to Norway. I got myself to the airport, I got myself to the National Park. I hiked up to the big rock and then I just sat there with my legs crossed far away from the edge. I looked out at the amazing view and I realised that I was capable of doing crazy shit without him and that my life wasn't over. I thought, if I can get myself to the edge of a cliff in Norway, what else am I capable of?'

She finally looked Beni in the eye, scared of what his reaction might be to this harrowing tale, but he was smiling, kind of. His thin lips naturally arched downwards and his chin was square, matching his broad shoulders. His smile wasn't like Stefano's; when Stef smiled, he did so with his whole face, but when Beni smiled it was mainly just with his eyes. Without this slight hint of smile he looked kind of angry. Making a happy person smile was one thing, but making Beni smile felt like a real achievement, so it was just as infectious.

'Pulpit Rock? Your suicide plan was to throw yourself off of Pulpit Rock?' he said, arching his eyebrows in surprise.

Catherine smiled, impressed that he knew exactly where in the world she was talking about.

'That's very dramatic,' he said. 'My plan included a bottle of vodka and some pills. I feel like I lack imagination now.' His smile faltered as he let his admission linger between them.

'Well, then I'm glad you lack imagination,' she said as they held each other's gaze for a couple of seconds.

'How did he die? Your husband?'

'Car crash, just like my dad,' she said, looking at her wine glass again.

'Shit.'

'Yep. So anyway, I got back from my jaunt to Norway and I realised I had a shit-ton of money from Thomas's life insurance and there were pension schemes and all sorts on top of that, so I quit my job in an office and I bought a couple of run-down terraced houses and I did them up. I sold them for a profit and I did it again and again. It was hard work, but soon I was rolling in it.' Catherine let out a burst of laughter, half pride and half surprise at what she had achieved, like it had only just hit her. 'My brother works with me now. I set up a lettings company. He's dealing with everything at the moment while I'm out here, bless him. I think he's glad I'm not there bossing him about any more.'

'So, why Mexico?' asked Beni.

'Just a holiday. Don't worry, I didn't come here to throw myself off the Coba temple.'

Beni smiled almost imperceptibly and nodded.

'What about you, how did you end up in Mexico?' asked Catherine.

'Oh, you know, it just kind of happened,' he said, not looking at her.

'Come on, I told you my story, now you tell me yours. Fair's fair.'

'It's a long story.'

'Well, it looks like Stef has forgotten I'm even here, so go ahead.' It was a joke, but she was glad he had forgotten her, so that she could carry on hiding outside.

'It's not a happy story,' he said quietly, his turn to stare at the floor.

'The best friends are the ones who drink cheap drinks with you and listen to your sad stories, and so far you're my best friend in Mexico. Now let me be yours?' she said, leaning in to give him a gentle nudge with her shoulder. *Ahh yes,* she thought, *the wine is working its magic now.* She was feeling much more sociable, and clearly comfortable enough to spout shit to strangers.

'Well, my mum died.'

'I'm sorry.' Catherine reached out instinctively and gave his hand a squeeze.

'I was twenty when she died. My dad had done one years earlier so when she passed that was it, I was on my own. We had no money, the council took the house back, and I ended up living on my mate's floor for a few weeks. Then I got a job repping in Spain.' He shifted on the bench. 'That was great. I had somewhere to live and the job was good, I had a few different jobs out there actually, so I was always busy. I was starting to feel OK, but then I got offered a job working the party circuit and things kind of got out of control. I was drinking every single night to stay social and to fit in. I was drinking so much and was shagging about and doing everything else you associate with the club scene. Anyway, one night my room-mate popped some pills and went flying off our balcony.'

'Oh my God, Beni, that's awful, I'm so sorry,' said Catherine, squeezing his hand again, but this time she didn't let go.

'I didn't even realise until the police arrived. They shook me awake and asked me what had happened, I had no idea. I felt so guilty. If I'd been sober maybe I could've stopped it. He must have been high as a kite, thought he could fly. It's a tale as old as time, or at least as old as drugs and high-rise buildings.'

Catherine watched as his stubbled jaw tensed, he was clearly upset.

'It could so easily have been me,' He pulled his hand from Catherine's grip and leaned forward, resting his elbows on his knees and his head in his hands.

They sat in silence for a couple of minutes and Catherine watched cars drive past and listened to the laughter coming from the back of the bar while she thought of something to say.

'Anyway, it shocked me into quitting the drugs, and I didn't drink for a long time. I got a job in another hotel, calling bingo numbers for pensioners and teaching aqua aerobics. It was good, but I needed to leave Spain and I didn't fancy being back in England at that point, so I went to the airport and booked the first flight I could afford to somewhere they spoke Spanish. That was six years ago, I've been here ever since.'

He looked at Catherine. Her eyes seemed to be searching his face for something, she was frowning slightly, she looked sad.

'That's a really sad story, Beni, I'm sorry that happened.'

'It was a long time ago now. Sorry, I've depressed you, you look so sad,' he said, looking into her worried eyes, wanting to make her smile again but not knowing how.

'I'm fine. Are you OK?'

'I haven't told anyone else here about all that. Don't tell Stef, will you? Definitely don't tell Anton, he can't keep anything to himself.'

'Of course not, I haven't told anyone about Thomas either,'

she said, blushing as she realised that she'd told this stranger more than she'd told her boyfriend.

'I won't tell anyone,' Beni said.

'So, you met Stef and everyone here?' Catherine asked. 'I thought you knew them from back home. Did you meet them at an "Italians in Mexico" help group or something?'

'No! Although we could probably start one,' he said. 'I met Stef while working in the hotel.'

'You work at the hotel too? What do you do? You don't look like a bartender.'

'What do I look like?'

'Kind of like a construction worker?' She laughed.

'I'll take that! I work in the hotel next door to yours. I'm a bar manager, but sometimes they pull me across if they're short-staffed.'

'So, is it your dad that's Italian then?'

'Yeah, mum was a northerner, and I was born and raised in the north too, but my dad and my dad's mum, my nonna, taught me to speak Italian and to cook.'

'When were you last in England?' Catherine said, picturing him making pasta with his grandma in a Manchester suburb.

'Umm, my mum died about eight years ago, so yeah, eight years. God, that's a long time, isn't it?'

'And you speak Spanish?'

'I do, not perfectly, but people seem to understand me. You speak it too, I heard you chatting to Maria. And how on earth do you know Italian, by the way?'

'A boy, of course.' She laughed, and finished her wine with one last gulp. 'So, you drink now? You're not completely teetotal?' Catherine said. 'You took one of the beers earlier,' she added, in response to his quizzical look.

He nodded. 'Ah. Yes, I drink, I can handle it. I've just had a couple today which is why I can offer you a lift back to your hotel if you like?'

'Are you sure?'

'Of course. I don't think Stef is in any fit state to drive you. It's eleven thirty – do you want to go now if you have a babysitter?'

'Yes please, let me just say bye to Stef.'

Beni watched as she crossed the room to her boyfriend, locking her arms around his neck and pulling him in for a deep kiss. He was surprised at the small knot of jealousy that formed in his stomach. He watched as she waved goodbye to everyone, even running over to Maria behind the bar and pulling her in for a quick hug.

In the quiet and closeness of his car Beni could smell her perfume, as well as coconut which he guessed was from the shampoo she used. He took off his checked shirt and threw it on the back seat, then started the engine and turned up the air conditioning.

Catherine glanced at him sideways, at his frowning face as he pulled the seat belt across his chest and at the black sleeves of his T-shirt that hugged his strong arms.

'I'm glad that's over!' she said, relaxing into the passenger seat. 'I hate meeting boyfriend's friends. I'm definitely someone you have to give time to warm up to!' Her laugh was self-conscious and she knew it, but somehow it didn't matter.

'You seem to have become friends with Maria and me already, and my friends really aren't a fussy bunch. Well, not all of them,' he said, pulling the car onto the busy road.

'That's all right then. Valentina though, she seems a little bit of a, umm ...'

'Ice queen?' said Beni.

'Sure, let's go with that.' *It certainly seems to suit the frosty reception she gave me.*

'She's been Stefano's best friend since they were back in Italy.'

'I wonder if she loves him?'

'Maybe. Would that bother you?'

'No,' she said without hesitation.

'You wouldn't be jealous of her loving your boyfriend? You know they live in the same building, right? Not together, but just a few doors away.'

'Well, I'm not planning on loving him, so someone should.'

'I didn't realise love could be planned.'

'I don't plan on loving anyone again; with Gloria as the exception. I don't think I could even if I wanted to, it's too painful.' Catherine pulled at a loose thread on the car seat. After a moment, she glanced at Beni. 'Don't tell him I said that to you. God, was there truth serum in that wine?'

'I won't tell him.'

'What about you, have you ever been in love?' she asked.

'No, I haven't ever really had a proper girlfriend. I kind of did in college, and there were a few girls in Spain that I dated.'

'You said "Shagged" earlier.' She softened the reminder with raised eyebrows and a smirk.

Beni grimaced. 'I'll have to watch you, you're like a tape recorder!'

'I don't believe that no one has loved you.'

'I don't really give anyone the chance.'

'What about here, in Mexico? Any sexy señoritas?'

'No. Well, me and Val kind of danced about the idea for a bit.'

'Wait. So, you and the Ice Queen – who may be in love with Stefano – did the titillation tango?'

Beni snort-laughed. 'What? What is that?'

Catherine was now giggling uncontrollably. 'I'm sorry' – she flapped a hand, regained a little, but not much, composure – 'wine makes me laugh a lot, and use random alliteration.'

'Alliteration? That's it, I'm not telling you my last name. You would die laughing.'

'Now you have to tell me!'

'No! You can either have more info about me and Val, or my last name. Which will it be?'

'What happened with Val?' Catherine asked, still giggling.

'We went on a date, but nothing ever happened beyond that.'

'Why not?'

'Neither of us were really interested in the end.' He shrugged.

'I see.' Catherine bit her lip, trying to stop inappropriate questions from bursting out of her mouth. It rarely worked, especially after this much wine and with cool air suddenly hitting her bloodstream. 'So, when did you last have sex?'

'That last swig of wine has really loosened your inhibitions hasn't it?' Beni said, checking his mirrors and then turning down a side road.

'I'm sorry!' She laughed, watching his arm muscles tense as he changed gears.

'About a month ago. Holiday romance, a girl from Southampton here with a group of friends.'

'Oh, Beni,' she said in mock disappointment.

'I know. *I'm* the fantasy holiday bartender!'

She stared out the window at the passing trees and Beni looked at her sideways, at her bare legs and her wavy blonde hair.

'Do you remember her name?' Catherine said after a while.

'Whose name?'

'The girl from Southampton.'

'Amy?' he said. 'Maybe.'

'Was she beautiful?' asked Catherine dreamily, closing her eyes and leaning her head against the vibrating window. Wine also put her to sleep. 'Were you sad when she had to go home?'

'Not really.'

Catherine sat up and looked at him for a while, her eyes narrowed.

He frowned. 'What?' he asked eventually.

'Did you tell her you were from Italy? Did you put on an accent?'

'What? Of course not!'

'Come on, you can tell me, did you pretend to be Italian?'

'I am Italian.'

'You know what I mean. Did you tone down Beni the Northerner, and emphasise Benedetto the bravissimo pasta prince?' she said theatrically, in a bad Italian accent.

'Pasta prince?' He raised his eyebrows.

'Shut up.'

'You were being alliterative again!'

'I know, it's a curse.' She thrust her palm to her face and laughed.

'I've actually never told anyone about my nonna teaching me to cook before.'

'You haven't? Why did you tell me?'

'You're like a talk-show host. You've extracted more information from me tonight than anyone ever has.'

Catherine smiled. 'Are you really telling me that you don't assume a mysterious Italian stallion persona to help you woo women?'

'When you look like this, you don't need any of that fake shit,' he said, posing behind the steering wheel, the smile in his eyes.

'I'm sorry, I thought you said it had been a month since Amy, stud?'

53

'Just because the goods are this tasty doesn't mean I'm giving them away for free!'

She cringed. 'Please! Never call yourself tasty again!' Lost in another fit of giggles, she grasped the car door handle with one hand and held up the other to hide his face.

'I don't think I've ever met anyone who laughs as much as you.'

'Not even Stef? It's all the wine, I'm usually much more stoic.'

'That's a shame, I like your laugh.'

'Tell me your last name then.' She grinned.

'Nope. I'm saving it for a rainy day,' he said, looking at her so he could see her smile again.

'So, is Stef a Lothario like you?'

'A Lothario?'

'Does he seduce many lonely hotel guests?'

'No, you're the first I think.'

'Yeah, right! You can tell me the truth you know; I can handle it.'

'I'm serious, I've never seen him with any girl apart from Val.'

'How can that be? He's so ...'

'Impossibly handsome?'

Catherine shrugged. 'Yeah.'

'I know, I try not to stand next to him if I can help it. He's all blonde and tanned and smiley.'

'You have the strong silent thing going on though. Like a hitman.'

'First, I'm a construction worker, now you think I look like a hitman?'

She nodded. 'You're like one of those men that chase Jason Bourne around Europe.'

'So, not Jason Bourne, but one of the anonymous henchmen sent to kill him?'

'That's you.' She laughed. 'Before you came to speak to me outside tonight, you hadn't said a word to anyone. Hitmen are rarely chatty.'

'What do girls prefer, the stoner or the hitman?'

'It depends on the girl, I suppose? Stef didn't mention Valentina to me, you know. Maybe he does like her?'

'You sure you don't mind that?'

'Would it matter if I did? What will be will be. Oh, I love this song!' She turned up the volume on the radio and began to sing along.

'You have a nice voice,' Beni said after a couple of minutes of listening to her, of watching her dance in her seat.

'I'm sorry, your poor ears. You must be regretting driving me home at this point.' She laughed, looking embarrassed.

'I promise, I'm not. Have you ever done any singing professionally?'

'Oh God, don't flatter me!'

'Come on, have you?'

'A bit, just for fun. I was sometimes the girl sitting on a stool in the corner of the restaurant, singing her heart out while no one listened. It made me so nervous every single time but I loved it.'

'Why don't you sing here?'

'I haven't done it in years, I'm not good enough for the big stages they have in the hotels here.'

'Sing something for me?' he said, switching off the radio. 'Go on, don't be nervous, I'll tell you if you're good enough.'

'OK.' She took a deep breath and sang a few verses of an Aerosmith song.

'Oh wow, you're breaking my heart,' he said with a sigh.

'Why?' she asked, covering her face. 'That bad?'

'No, that good. You should sing for more people. I'll talk to Anton in the new year, he'll get you a gig, even if you just start in the lobby bar.'

'I feel nervous already.'

'Don't be nervous,' he said, frowning at the road.

Catherine turned her attention outside the car too. 'We're here, it's just up there, The Shell.'

Beni turned to look at her. She seemed to have already forgotten that he worked in the hotel next door.

'Oh right, you knew that. Damn the wine! Thank you for giving me a lift.'

He nodded and swung his car in next to the white marble steps up to the lobby, where the bellboys all stood to attention.

'It was nice meeting you, Beni, hopefully I'll see you again soon?'

'Yeah.'

'Have a nice Christmas,' she said, hugging him briefly before sliding out of the car and fist-bumping a waiting bellboy.

'Lish!' bellowed the khaki-suited man in further greeting.

'Buenas noches, Javier,' said Catherine, and then she turned to give her chauffer one more wave and a smile.

Beni watched her walk through the lobby, her golden hair bouncing behind her, and his stomach somersaulted.

The Audition

The pool at which Catherine and Gloria chose to spend most of their time was the quietest in the resort. Catherine liked this, especially as she often tried to teach Gloria poolside; she could do without the distraction of too many other kids, or boisterous teenagers hormoning all around them.

She also liked it because you could hear the lapping waves but didn't get sand blown all over you thanks to a well-placed towel hut, and because there was only one predictable lizard that rarely moved an inch all day whom they had decided to call Walter. On the rare occasions that he wasn't there, both she and Gloria would worry, for very different reasons, about where he might have gone.

It was a warm but cloudy day and Gloria was sitting cross-legged on a sunlounger in the shade. She was practising writing letters of the alphabet, and Catherine gave her encouragement in between spells of people watching and applying copious amounts of sun cream to them both.

'Hi, Anton, what are you doing here?' said Catherine, concerned there might be a problem with their room.

'Everything's fine,' he said, sitting down on a lounger next to theirs with a flourish. 'A little bird told me that you can sing and that you want to do a set here at the hotel?'

'I didn't think he would actually talk to you about that.'

'Beni said your voice is beautiful but you're not very confident.'

'Did he now? He's quite the chatterbox that bird, isn't he!'

Anton smiled kindly. 'He said you used to sing back home?'

'I did, but like I told him, it was just in bars and restaurants. And it was a long time ago.'

'What did you used to sing?' Anton asked. His Italian accent seemed somehow stronger in the brightness of daylight.

Catherine stopped herself from fidgeting. 'All sorts really, but my favourite was singing obscure Eurovision songs.'

Anton grinned. 'That might be fun. After all, we get people from all over the world visiting us, and with all-inclusive drinks you can pretty much sing anything and people will be happy. I'll talk to our entertainment manager, but first I want to hear you sing.'

'When shall I sing for you?'

'Well, I'm not busy now?' he said, leaning back, clearly enjoying the warm light on his face as a gap in the clouds revealed the sun.

'I'm not going to sing right here; people will think I've lost my mind. Oh, by the way, Gloria, this is my friend Anton.'

'Come on, Gloria, do you think Catherine should sing us a song?' he asked in Spanish.

The little girl looked up from her notepad and nodded. 'Kitty, please sing a song.'

'Oh nice, using the child's cuteness against me? Oh God, I feel sick. OK, what the hell, what shall I sing?'

'Give me some of your best Eurovision?'

So she did. She sat up straight and sang 'Calm After the

Storm' with all her heart, and when she was done, the few people around the pool clapped with cheerful, slightly confused expressions on their faces.

'I'll go and talk to Jose. I like this Eurovision thing, I will suggest that too,' said Anton, beaming at her.

Once Anton had left and Gloria had finished her writing practise, Catherine was glad to jump into the swimming pool with the little girl to cool down. Catherine was like an eel in the water with her long legs kicking quietly beneath the surface, moving her along at speed. Gloria on the other hand was far less elegant, she looked like a bird trapped in the pool trying to flap its way out. Despite that, she was still a strong swimmer, so water was the one place that Catherine didn't have to worry too much about her little ward.

As Gloria splashed about, Catherine would float on her back, eyes watching the clouds drift and the pelicans soar, the water in her ears tuning out the world. Gloria would often copy her. They would float together, spinning gently this way and that with the breeze, holding hands, like otters, so they wouldn't drift away from each other.

Sometimes when they played this floating game Catherine would secretly stand up, then take Gloria's ankle and pull her along in the water. The little girl would laugh her head off as Catherine made a siren noise and told Gloria she was being taken to the police station. When Gloria had laughed so much that she couldn't float any more and water was coming out of her nose, they would tread water together and talk about all sorts of things, like why the sky is blue or where they thought Walter lived when he wasn't guarding the path.

On that day, however, Gloria asked a question that Catherine wasn't expecting, although she should have been.

'Are my mum and dad really not coming back?'

'They can't, sweetheart, they want to but they can't,' Catherine said.

'But why not?'

'They passed away, they died. Do you know what that is?'

The little girl shook her head and her chin rippled the water beneath it. Her face was now much fuller and, if possible, she was even cuter with her slightly chubby cheeks. Catherine had never been good with hair; at best her own was brushed, running down her back or tied in a messy ponytail. But she was getting better with it, and now, more often than not, Gloria's thick black hair was plaited into pigtails.

'Dying ... is when someone we love goes away and they can't come back no matter how much they want to, or how much we want them to.'

Gloria blinked, her eyelashes wet; she stayed quiet.

'My dad died when I was little,' Catherine said.

'He did?'

'Yes, and I miss him a lot. But when I miss him, I talk to him, sometimes out loud or sometimes just in my head.'

'And does he speak back?'

'Not in a way I can hear with my ears, but every time something good has happened to me I think maybe he's helped with it.'

'Where do they go when they go away?' Gloria asked.

'Everyone has their own ideas about that, but I like to think they just hang out nearby making sure we're OK.'

'I hope my dad is not nearby.'

'If you don't want him around then you can tell him to go away.'

'Shall I tell him now?'

'Yes. Go on, tell him to go away.'

'Despaparecer papá!' Gloria's shout was so sudden and loud that some of the pensioners around the pool clasped their chests in shock.

Catherine grimaced and raised a hand in apology, hoping that all of the singing and shouting wouldn't get them banned from the quiet pool. 'There you go, he's gone.' she said, turning to Gloria, 'Do you want your mum around?'

Gloria nodded.

'Then she will be with you all the time. You can talk to her whenever you want, and she can keep my dad company. Let's float some more?'

While staring at the sky, Catherine thought she should read up on the traditions of the Day of The Dead, but from the little she knew about it, you needed a photo of the deceased relative and they didn't have one of Gloria's mum, so until they did, she wouldn't mention it to Gloria in case it upset her.

Beni walked through the grounds of the hotel. He wasn't entirely sure where he was going, it wasn't as familiar to him as the hotel next door where he usually worked. Lost at the outskirts of the complex, he passed a pool with just a handful of people sitting quietly around it and was surprised to spot Catherine, floating in the water.

He walked over and stood at the edge of the pool, but she and Gloria were floating quite far away, their ears were submerged and their eyes were closed, so his attempts at a greeting were ignored, by them at least. Other guests started to look up from their books at the man who was disrupting their peace and quiet, and he began to feel very awkward.

Catherine opened her eyes to watch the clouds but instead

saw Beni standing by the pool. Surprised, she forced her feet down quickly and stood up. 'Oh my God, you scared me!' She laughed, and then choked on a tiny bit of water that had gone down the wrong way.

Recovering, she swam to the pool's edge, her long legs kicking gracefully behind her, Gloria splashing along at her side.

'I'm sorry. I saw you and thought I'd say hi, but you couldn't hear me and now everyone's giving me strange looks,' he said, crouching down to talk to her.

'We like to float, don't we, Gloria?'

'Hi, Gloria, I'm Beni.'

'Hola, Beni,' said the little girl shyly. She glanced at Catherine, and then kicked off the side and carried on swimming.

'What are you doing here? You look smart,' said Catherine, eyeing his white shirt, a far cry from the T-shirt and messy hair of their first meeting.

'This is my uniform; I work in the fancy bit of my hotel.'

'Ooh la la!' She smiled. 'What are you doing slumming it over here then?'

'They need help with a big stocktake in the new restaurant,' he said.

'Anton came to see me earlier. He's going to talk to the entertainment guy about me singing, thanks.'

'You're welcome.'

'Kitty, Walter has gone missing again,' said Gloria, doggy-paddling over to them, splashing water all over the place.

'Who's Walter?' Beni said in Spanish.

Catherine filled him in. 'He is one of those terrifying ungodly tiny dinosaurs that roam about the place. Walter stands over there all day long and gives me a heart attack every time I need to go to the loo.'

'Kitty is so scared of lizards.' Gloria laughed, her little hands clinging on to Catherine's arm, her toes stabbing into her thigh.

'Walter tends to wander off every now and then and we wonder where he pops off to. Any ideas, Beni?'

'Everyone has to take a break. He can't guard the path all day, can he?' He stood up and looked around, his hands in his pockets.

'But where does he go?' asked Gloria.

'Well, you didn't hear this from me,' he whispered, leaning down slightly, 'but in those bushes, there is a secret door that only iguanas can use, and it takes them to a tunnel, and from that tunnel they can get to anywhere in the hotel. So, when you see a lizard somewhere else around here, that could be Walter. Who knows? It's busy work protecting the hotel and he probably has a few paths he has to keep an eye on.'

'Kitty, is that true?' Gloria asked, looking sceptical.

'It's true. Look how smartly Beni is dressed. He works here at the hotel so he knows all about the secret iguana tunnels.'

Beni nodded, his expression solemn. 'I'll keep an eye out for him but I think he'll be back soon. He probably just had to go and check out another path for a while.'

Catherine laughed as the girl tried to clamber up her. 'Gloria, I'm not a climbing frame!'

'Then why can I climb on you?' said Gloria, and offered a mischievous grin that now rarely left her face.

'You can climb on rocks; are rocks a climbing frame?'

'Well, no. How about a nice hug then?' said the little girl. She wrapped her arms around Catherine's neck and dangled limply from it into the water.

'Are you trying to drown me? Beni, are you seeing this? You can be my witness!'

'No!' Gloria giggled. 'You're a cliff and I'm dangling off you.'

'I've got to stop her watching late night Stallone movies after I've fallen asleep,' Catherine said, prying Gloria's arms from her neck. 'Get off me, Sylvester!' She kissed Gloria on the nose and let her slip into the water.

'Yes, probably not great parenting that, Lish,' Beni said, crouching down again.

Catherine looked affectionately at Gloria. 'I have to hide the TV remote, don't I?'

'Kitty hides it but I always find it,' said Gloria, clinging to the side of the pool.

'Go and swim, crazy lady. Show Beni how far you can go.'

'OK!' Gloria swam away, limbs thrashing.

'When I was at uni, we got a kitten. I watched loads of Japanese horror films around that time and I'm convinced it's what turned it psycho.'

'What did it do?' said Beni.

'We had to use oven gloves to pet it, and it climbed the curtains like that baby climbed the walls in *Trainspotting*.'

'Stallone is usually the good guy to be fair. The worst that could happen is Gloria develops a cigar habit and a penchant for wearing bandanas. And why were you watching Japanese horrors with your cat?'

'Just a standard Friday-night thing to do?' she said with exaggerated blasé.

'You really don't seem like a Japanese-horror kind of girl, Lish. You're too blonde and cute, and you're terrified of Walter the friendly path guardian.'

'Don't judge a book by its cover, Beni, I could be a total psycho for all you know. But OK, you got me. I studied film at uni and I had a module on horror. I hated it. I can never unsee that man's ankle being sawn off with wire.' She grimaced, her eyes glazing slightly at the memory.

'You studied film?' he asked, raising his eyebrows.

'In thirty years, studying film will be like studying fine art.'

She feigned annoyance and flicked a little water onto his polished shoes.

'I didn't criticise,' he said, holding his hands in the air, smiling slightly. 'So, you think that one day Stallone films will be played on a loop in the National Gallery, in the room next to the Renoirs and Picassos?'

'No, because the best thing about film is that it's accessible. You don't need to see the original like you do with a painting. I don't know about you, but I've never pressed play on a DVD and thought, "God, I wish I had the original Super 8 of this that I could hook up to a projector!" I guess maybe some people think that, but most don't, because film is art for the era of mass production.'

'I don't know. Is film really art? It depends, doesn't it? On how it looks and everything.'

'With a painting, you need the original to see the brush-strokes; with film, they are always there, not just in the image but in the sound and movement too.'

'Wow, you really love films, don't you,' he said, watching her eyes sparkle and her nose ring glisten as the sunlight bounced off the water onto her face.

'That's why I studied it.' She smiled.

'Where will you hide the remote tonight?' he whispered.

'Maybe I'll tell her Walter has it in his lizard tunnel.' She grinned up at him.

'Or you could put it in your safe?'

'I tried that once. The little madam tried so many different passcodes it locked me out and I had to get hotel security to come to the room. I need to be firm with her but it's hard to be too cross, knowing what she's been through.'

'Her watching TV isn't so bad is it? Maybe she just can't sleep?'

'Maybe. I think I'll start reading to her before bed and see if that helps.'

'Beni, look how far I've gone!' shouted Gloria from the other side of the pool.

'Good swimming!' he shouted back.

Catherine smiled. 'She's a strong swimmer but she can only do doggy paddle. I think she taught herself. I've tried showing her some other ... moves, types, what do you call them? ... Strokes! That's it. I've tried to teach her some other strokes but I'm not a good coach. I can barely teach her the alphabet.'

'I taught swimming for a while in Spain?' Beni shrugged.

'You did? Would you help us?'

'Sure. I'm off on Monday afternoon, shall we do it then?'

'That's great! I'll pay you for your time, obviously.'

'No way. I'll help because we're friends. We are friends, right?'

'Of course.'

'Hey, what are you doing here?' Stefano said as he walked over to them in his much-less-formal work uniform.

'Hey, man,' said Beni, standing up and slapping hands with his friend. 'I'm here to help with the stocktake. Oh, shit, I should get going, I'm late,' he said. 'Bye, Gloria!' he shouted.

'Adios!' she shouted back.

'Will you both be at the bar on Saturday?' Beni said as he began to walk away.

'Maybe,' said Stefano.

'Have fun stocktaking,' said Catherine.

'Thanks, have fun floating.'

'Hey, Gloria!' Stef shouted the greeting, waving at the little girl as she splashed around. 'You and Beni seem to be getting on well?' he said to Catherine. He lay down with his stomach flat on the floor, and stretched over the edge of the pool to kiss her.

She laughed, and touched his face with her wet, pruning hands. 'He's great; I like all of your friends.'

The Song

❧

A
nton managed to persuade Jose, the hotel's entertainment manager, to let Catherine sing, and after a couple of weeks she was paired with a local guitarist called Miguel. He was a short man with a thick moustache and Catherine assumed that he was middle-aged but she wasn't sure and she didn't like to ask. He had a wife and two daughters of whom he spoke fondly at every opportunity, and had been playing guitar at the hotel for many years. He could have been annoyed at being paired with a novice, a foreigner whose friend had got her the job, but if he was, he never showed it and he was always friendly and patient with her.

For around a week and a half, every day while Gloria was in the morning kids' club, they practised tirelessly in one of the conference rooms. Catherine was nervous and wanted everything to be perfect, and as Miguel had never before heard any of the songs they were going to be singing, every minute of their three-hour rehearsals was utilised. On the third day, something clicked and they found their sound. Miguel performed with several other acts so had plenty of experience and he helped Catherine to feel more confident. They were a dream

67

team and the nerves she was feeling soon began to mix with excitement.

Before she knew it, she found herself standing in the corner of the lobby bar about to sing. The huge space felt daunting; it was a far cry from the tiny restaurants back in England, but similar in the fact that no one was paying them the blindest bit of attention. The guests were all far too busy talking and drinking or checking in at the reception desk and dragging their suitcases. It was a lot to contend with, but she took a deep breath, tapped the microphone three times and greeted the crowd.

She was wearing a long green dress with a cut-out back, and Miguel was sporting a light-yellow cotton shirt and mustard tie. As he began to strum his guitar something strange happened: everyone stopped talking and looked at them. Catherine wasn't used to this. She expected to sing to the sides of their chattering faces, not looking into their wide pupiled eyes as they sipped their cocktails as attentive mutes. She shot Miguel a look of panic but he seemed as calm as ever and gave her an encouraging smile. Heart beating fast, she clasped her fingers around the microphone and began to sing.

Her raspy voice curved its way around several Eurovision songs and a handful of well-known hits, all performed acoustically in a folk style, just like they had practised. She spoke to a couple of people in the crowd, asking where they were from and if they were enjoying their holiday, and Miguel danced on the spot as he played, harmonising a few lines here and there. A few exuberant couples even got up and danced, which was a pleasant surprise. Catherine bowed her head at the end and thanked Miguel, and a ripple of applause followed them out of the room.

Once outside, Beni, Stefano and Anton all appeared and congratulated them boisterously, as if they had just scored a winning goal.

Catherine laughed as they all hugged her roughly and patted Miguel on the back. 'Where were you three hiding?'

'Behind that big plant! We didn't want to distract you,' Anton said.

'Thanks for coming to see us on our first night.' She beamed, and hugged each of her friends again in turn.

'You were amazing!' said Stefano, with one of his trademark smiles. He kissed the side of her head as he pulled her in to a one-armed squeeze.

'Have you got a babysitter with Gloria right now?' Anton asked.

'Of course.'

'Then let's go and get a few drinks!' he said.

'I need to head over to the main stage, Catherine, for another set later tonight,' Miguel said. 'You did great.'

'Thank you so much for doing this with me, you're amazing. I'll see you on Sunday.'

Miguel smiled at her and then swaggered slowly away, holding his guitar.

'That was so good!' said Stefano as they walked through the dimly lit hotel grounds towards the beach bar. 'I had no idea you could sing like that.'

'It was fun. Beni and Anton, thanks for conspiring to arrange this for me.'

'It was all me,' said Anton, flashing a cheeky grin at Beni as he linked arms with her.

'Yeah, if I'd known you were going to use your talent for evil and sing Eurovision songs, I would never have got involved,' said Beni.

'You can make fun, but I bet at least one of those songs will burrow into your brain and you'll be singing it for the next month.'

Beni groaned. 'I think that's a bet I can safely make.'

'I don't know why people hate Eurovision so much. It's not like it used to be, some of the songs on there are so good!'

'Don't start her off! She'll be talking about set design in a minute,' Anton said.

'I'm making it my mission in life to spread the good word of Eurovision,' Catherine said. 'In the spirit of which, I need to up my costume game; I need a light-up dress before my next gig!'

'I don't know why you're looking at me like I might have one hanging in my wardrobe,' Anton said, deadpan.

Catherine laughed out loud and clasped his arm. 'I feel like Dorothy in *The Wizard of Oz* walking along this winding path through the trees, linking arms with you boys.' she said, and then she and Anton, attempted the skippy walk from the film.

'But who's who?' Anton said, trying to catch his breath and laugh at the same time.

'I don't know! You all have a heart, you all have a brain and none of you are cowards. If anything, I should be the lion because I'm terrified of lizards. Like that one!' she said, squirming. A shiver shot down her spine as she pointed to the iguana's head sticking out from a drain.

'I'll be Dorothy then!' said Anton, flicking imaginary long hair over each shoulder, 'Stefano is dumb and lovable so he can be the scarecrow.'

'He isn't dumb!' said Catherine, standing on her tiptoes to kiss Stef on the cheek. 'But his hair is a bit like straw, so OK.'

'Hey! It's the humidity,' said Stefano in a mock hurt voice, tickling Catherine in revenge.

'That means you're the tin man,' said Anton, scurrying over and knocking on Beni's chest, clicking his tongue to imitate a hollow sound. 'No heart in there! We need to find him someone to love, stat!'

Beni smiled faintly. 'Shut up, Dorothy!' he said, pushing Anton away.

Anton just laughed, and linked arms with Beni, forcing him to have a go at the skippy yellow-brick-road walk.

As they carried on over to the bar, Catherine looked at the three men and wondered how many drinks they had had while watching her sing, and whether or not to be offended.

The beach bar was busy; many of the tables were filled with couples, families and groups of friends all wearing their finest holiday clothes – the women in off-the-shoulder dresses, the men in their best short-sleeved shirts. The area was lit with fairy lights and, along with the faint music that was playing, the waves somewhere in the darkness provided a backing track. Drinks in hand, Catherine and her friends sat at a table near to the bar and the boys started to smoke.

'Blow it away, my hair will smell funny,' said Catherine, wafting her hands around, trying to stop the smoke from clinging to her skin and clothes too.

'Lighten up, Lish, there are bigger problems in life than smelly hair,' said Anton.

'This coming from the man I had to talk down off a ledge because Meryl isn't going to be the main character in the second *Mamma Mia* film?' said Catherine, her eyebrows arched.

'Good point,' said Anton, blowing his smoke in the opposite direction.

'This will freak you out,' Stefano said quietly. 'I overheard one of the reps say they found a tarantula in the staff bathroom in one of the hotels near here.'

'What?' Beni said, a look of horror on his face.

Catherine hummed to herself, spinning her wine glass slowly.

'Is that a Pendulum song?' Beni said, frowning at her in surprise.

'I can't hear the word tarantula without thinking of that track,' she said.

'I'm like that with the name Maria,' said Anton.

'I'm surprised you know a Pendulum song,' Beni said.

'Lish is a rocker at heart,' said Stef. 'This scar on her ear is from a mosh pit earring-ripping.'

'It's true.' She laughed, rubbing the scar with her fingers.

'I thought you liked poppy Eurovision-type stuff?' Anton said. 'Is our friendship a lie?'

'Can't I like different things? One more glass of wine and I'll be up there dancing to salsa music too.'

'I'm going to get you that glass of wine then!' Anton said, finishing his cigarette and walking over to the bar.

'Who were you seeing when your earring was ripped out?' said Beni.

'It was System of a Down, I think? It was at a festival. I hadn't showered in days, I thought I was going to lose the ear.' She laughed.

Beni turned his beer bottle over in his hands, and as it warmed, droplets of water ran onto his fingers. He shook his head. *That's it,* he thought, *the one thing that was stopping her being absolutely perfect, and it turns out she likes good music after all.*

'It was a long time ago now; my moshing days are over,' she said, pulling an embarrassed face.

'Remember when I pierced your ear, Beni?' Stefano said with a grin.

'How could I forget that trauma?'

'What happened?' Catherine asked, smiling at them both

but distracted by Stefano's fingers, which were running along the skin of her inner thigh.

'Stef decided I should have an earring. He thought it would make up for my lack of a beard.'

Stefano guffawed. 'I poured vodka on his head and then shoved one of Val's earrings through his ear.'

'And exactly how off your faces were you when this took place?' Catherine said.

'Extremely. It didn't get infected though. I bet I could still wear an earring,' said Beni, touching the tiny hole in his earlobe.

'Are we talking Boy George feather-dangler or a stud earring?' Catherine said, smirking.

'I wanted to stretch it, but I didn't dare mention that in case Stef tried to shove a pen in it!'

Stefano laughed and kissed Catherine's ear. 'I would have! So, what's the best band you've seen perform live? Foo Fighters are mine.'

'Rammstein for me,' Beni said, and took a swig of his beer.

'Did you see them in Manchester?' Catherine asked, tilting her head to one side.

'Yeah, it was in Manchester I think, why?'

'I can't remember what year it was, but I saw them there too. About nine years ago?'

'Me too, I think,' he said with a look of surprise.

'You were in the same arena all those years ago? How weird is that,' Stefano said.

'That *is* weird,' said Beni slowly.

'What's weird?' Anton asked as he sat down at the table again and handed out drinks.

'Lish and me were at the same gig years ago in Manchester.'

'But so were about 20,000 other people,' Catherine said.

'What gig?' Anton said.

'Rammstein. They're a German metal band,' said Beni.

'Maybe that's why you knew he was English when you first met him, Lish. Beni loves to have sex in public with strangers. Maybe you two had met before in a toilet cubicle?'

'Oh my God, I do not!' Beni said, throwing a coaster at Anton, who was laughing hysterically.

Catherine feigned incredulity. 'What makes you think I'm the kind of girl that would have sex with someone in the toilet of an arena ... and then forget what they looked like?'

'You're right, you couldn't forget a face like our Benedetto's,' said Anton, pinching his friend's cheek.

'Stop making out that I'm a sex maniac!' Beni said.

Anton smirked. 'Well, if the shoe fits ...'

'What's the best band you've ever seen live, Anton?' Stefano said, a tiny frown forming.

He gave this some thought. 'Backstreet Boys.' The other two boys winced, but Catherine was jealous.

'The Foo Fighters played in my home town once. It was a big deal for us,' said Catherine to Stefano. 'Why is it that we call it "home town" even if we live in a city or a village. We don't say home city, do we? Or do we?'

'Oh no, Lish is getting philosophical. She'll start talking about the dinosaurs soon,' said Stefano, his frown evaporating as he laughed and kissed her cheek.

Catherine smiled and nudged him with her elbow. 'I just can't believe there were once these massive scary monsters walking around on the exact same ground that we walk on now. It's amazing.'

'Technically, it's not this ground,' said Beni. 'We keep building on top of it and the ground level ebbs and flows naturally too, so the earth they walked on is either under layers and layers of dirt and tarmac or it was washed into the sea long ago. Look at all the fossils and bones that've been found. You have to dig for them, and it's not because they were buried on purpose is it?'

'That makes sense. There must be some places in the world where evidence is closer to the surface though. Haven't they found big footprints before?'

'Yeah, I think some have actually been found in England?'

'It's so interesting.'

'If you say so, Lish,' said Anton, rolling his eyes.

As the boys talked about video games, Catherine people-watched. She observed the band setting up and children running around; bored teenagers playing on their phones and slightly older teenagers doing shots, far from being bored. Parents looked content and older people sat quietly taking it all in. Everyone had the relaxed glow of having spent the day by the pool doing nothing and worrying about nothing, the aftersun cream on their burnt faces giving them a slight shine. Catherine listened to the waves and sipped her wine until the band had finished setting up and instrumental Latin music began to play.

As guests started to gather in pairs, Anton grabbed her by the hand. 'Balliamo,' he said, striding onto the dance floor with gusto.

Beni watched them, no longer focusing on what Stefano was saying. They were surprisingly good, he thought, stepping forwards and backwards in time with each other, side to side, wiggling their hips, clasping each other's hands and holding on to each other at the waist.

'Your turn, Stef, come dance with me?' Catherine called, as Anton skipped off to the bar looking pink-faced and worn out after the last lively song.

Stef didn't budge, he stayed slumped in his chair looking exhausted. 'I can't dance to this! Beni, you do it,' he said, waving his hands around like he was being attacked by mosquitoes.

'I can't dance either,' Beni said quickly, holding up his hands in surrender. But he edged forward in his seat.

'Come on, Benedetto!' Catherine said, dragging him to his feet. She bopped her way back over to the dance floor, leaving him to finish his drink in one big gulp.

'Val's finishing her shift soon, I'm going to go over and meet her,' whispered Stef.

Beni didn't say anything, he just glared at the back of Stefano's head as he watched his friend sneak away.

'Don't look so worried, I'll show you what to do,' Catherine said once Beni was standing in front of her. She got into position. 'You put your hand on my waist here, and hold my hand up like this.' She showed him the steps and they began to dance, badly.

'I'm no good at this.'

Catherine looked up at Beni's face, he was frowning more than ever as he concentrated on dancing, 'I can't believe we were at the same Rammstein gig, I love their songs, I know every word by heart.'

'You don't speak German too, do you?' he asked.

'No, I just memorised the lyrics, I don't know what any of it means.' She was lying and it made her cheeks burn briefly.

'Your hair doesn't smell of smoke, by the way.' He could feel the soft skin of her back through the gaps in her dress, her hand felt like a delicate bird in his and, as always, she smelled of coconut.

'That's good. Where's Stef gone?' she asked, looking over her shoulder.

'I'm not sure.'

'Has he gone to meet Val?'

'Maybe.' Beni shrugged.

'Don't look so serious, Beni. He's not betrothed to me, he can do as he pleases.'

'It's none of my business. And this is just my face, you know; I always look serious.'

'Oh, I know you do, but every now and again you look a bit less serious, and I take that to mean you're smiling at me,' she said.

'I never smile really, I'm not like Stef,' he said, not looking at her.

'I know you're not. One of your non-frowns is worth ten of that happiness-whore's smiles.'

'Alliteration,' he whispered, leaning in towards her. Now they weren't even trying to salsa, they were just swaying on the spot and talking, holding on to each other.

'The rest of the time you look somewhere between disgusted and not giving a shit.' She smiled.

'Finally, someone that gets me.'

Catherine laughed, and Beni looked away, doing his best not to seem too obviously happy to have his hands on her.

'See,' she said, poking the site of the frown line that had momentarily disappeared. 'You're un-frowning. Maybe all along you just needed dance therapy.'

Dancing with you would have made Emperor Nero a nicer guy, he thought, pulling her a fraction closer.

'How did you learn Spanish? When you were in Spain?' she said.

'I did it at school and it improved after living in Spain.'

'Is that what you studied at college too?' she asked in Spanish.

He shook his head. 'I did science A Levels. I wanted to go to uni to study geology or geography. I was saving up to do it when my mum died.'

'It's not too late, why don't you do it now? Get a loan? I had a whopping great loan from my time studying. It's not a big deal, you just pay it back slowly?' She shrugged.

'It's too late now, I'm twenty-eight.'

'Exactly. You're twenty-eight, not eighty-eight. What did you want to do with the degree?'

'Probably become a teacher?'

'Oh, wow.' She giggled.

'What?'

'If I'd had a teacher that looked like you when I was in school, I'd be much better at geography than I am now,' she said, then felt her cheeks flush.

'Well, if I'd had a teacher that looked like you, who was as passionate about film as you are, maybe I'd be in Hollywood now, serving drinks there instead of here,' he said, the hint of a smile pulling at one side of his mouth.

As Catherine laughed, her arms automatically pulled him towards her. The muscles in his shoulder flexed beneath her hand, and she became aware of the scent of his aftershave.

'What about you?' he said, drawing her attention back. 'I know you learnt Italian for a boy, was it the same with Spanish?'

'Do you think I have a man in every port, Beni?' She laughed again. 'I did it at school too, and I got really into watching Spanish TV shows. I'm lucky, I just kind of take to languages. Plus, I can be a bit obsessive with things. If I want to do something, I won't stop until I've perfected it – not that my Spanish is perfect!'

'You were amazing, you know; you sang so well earlier, better than I'd imagined.'

'Thanks for speaking to Anton about it. I never would have.'

'I should get commission as your talent agent.'

'You're getting a free dance lesson, what more do you want?' She smiled.

He slid his hand down her waist an inch and held her close. He had never wanted anything more than he wanted to kiss her in that moment, but he didn't. Instead, they began to really dance again, stepping this way and that. She laughed the whole time.

'Am I really drunk, or am I actually not too bad at this?' he said, dancing around with more confidence.

'You're doing great.' She smiled.

'Stefano is an idiot,' he said quietly, staring into her blue eyes, which were twinkling, reflecting the thousand fairy lights above their heads.

Catherine took a deep, contented breath and exhaled slowly. 'I don't care, it's fine. Anton is sitting alone let's go keep him company.'

Catherine continued to sing on Thursday and Sunday nights, her confidence growing with each set that she did. She and Miguel became popular, with some guests even planning their evenings around their little show, mostly thanks to Anton recommending it to guests as they made their restaurant bookings with him. Some guests came back on multiple nights of their holiday and Catherine would get to know them a little. Over time, she and Miguel made sure to learn a song from each competing Eurovision country so that they could take requests from the audience and wouldn't have to turn anyone down. Miguel, who had never even seen a single Eurovision in his life, let Catherine show him endless YouTube videos. He listened patiently to her non-stop prattle about production values and creativity and why it really was the most underrated thing on Earth, and he started to become a fan himself.

Catherine, who had stopped singing not long after she married Thomas, couldn't believe she had let something go that made her so happy.

The Scar

An hour up the main road from Catherine's hotel was a huge water park filled with wave pools, slides, lazy rivers, beaches, lagoons and waterfalls. Catherine had been eyeing the leaflet for a while and with Gloria loving swimming as she did, it seemed like the perfect place to take her.

She had mentioned this idea to Stefano who, thinking it sounded like fun, decided he wanted to come along too and invited his friends. Catherine was delighted with this as it meant more eyes to make sure that Gloria didn't go missing or drown; she was still uneasy when leaving the sanctuary of the hotel with her, especially after what had happened in the supermarket. So, one sunny day, Beni came to collect her, Anton and Gloria from the hotel lobby in his big white car.

'You have a booster seat?' said Catherine when she opened the door for Gloria.

'I looked it up. Gloria needs one at her age so I bought one.'

'That's so nice! I didn't even think about it,' she said, climbing onto the back seat and strapping Gloria in.

'Thanks for coming to get us, Beni!' said Anton, settling into the front passenger seat.

'Have you been at work all night? Aren't you knackered?'

'I'll be fine. We're so short-staffed I had no choice, but I'm off tomorrow, I can sleep all day. Did Lish tell you my car died?' said Anton, running a hand over his bloodshot eyes.

'She told me you wrote it off,' said Beni. 'Not exactly natural causes, was it?'

'Lish! You told on me? It wasn't my fault. Some idiot cut me up and I saw him too late.'

'Are you going to get another car?' asked Beni as they drove away from the lobby.

'I can't afford to at the moment but I will do in time. Thankfully, I can get a lift to work most days with Raquel, one of the waitresses – she lives near me – so I'm managing.'

'I can give you lifts too, just let me know what days you're working,' Beni said.

Anton glanced at him. 'Thanks,' he said, then did a double take. He seemed surprised at the offer.

'Say hello to Beni, Gloria,' Catherine said.

'Hola!' they said in unison.

'Is everyone ready for a day of Valentina being moody, then?' Anton said, drumming his fingers on the window ledge to the rhythm of the rock song playing on the radio.

'Shh, Valentina is lovely,' Catherine said through gritted teeth. 'Little ears, Anton, big mouth,' she whispered in Italian, poking the back of his arm.

'Ahh yes. Valentina is the best. Never in a bad mood, life and soul of every event,' Anton said in Spanish, sounding like a Latino robot.

Catherine smiled at Gloria, hoping she was buying what they were selling. 'Oh!' she said suddenly, glad of the distraction. 'I stole some pastries from the breakfast buffet.' She pulled out three sugar-dusted croissants wrapped in tissue paper from her bag, handed one to Anton and carefully gave Gloria hers on her knee.

'Beni, I didn't think this through, there's going to be a big mess back here!'

'It's OK. Where's mine?'

'Here.' She was sitting behind him, so leaned forward, put one hand on his shoulder and held the pastry to his mouth. He took a big bite, slightly licking her finger as he did.

'Eww, it's like feeding an alpaca, Gloria!' Catherine laughed, which made the little girl giggle, and flakes of pastry fell all over her like snow.

'Anton, why don't you ever bring me pastries?' said Beni, licking the sugar off his lips. Catherine watched him in the rearview mirror, and grimaced at the mess Gloria was making. Before Beni could turn to see it for himself, she quickly shoved the rest of the croissant into his mouth.

'Thanks,' he mumbled.

They met Valentina and Stef at the entrance and the chaos of the park was immediately apparent, with screaming coming from all directions as children and adults alike delighted in sliding, splashing and sunbathing. Catherine had instant sensory overload, flinching slightly at every laugh and scream a child made, like she was in Vietnam and bombs were going off.

After getting changed and putting their belongings into lockers, they all stood in a semi-circle around the park map in their swimwear. Catherine was uncomfortable being around Val who, in just her emerald bikini, looked far more petite and had so much tanned skin on show that Catherine felt like a lumpy albino rhinoceros in comparison.

'Wow, we look like the cast of *Baywatch*,' Anton said, peering over his sunglasses at everyone.

'Catherine, it's actually a nice rest for my eyes not seeing you wear so many clashing patterns,' said Val.

Well, it's not nice to see you looking so tanned and perfect, thought Catherine, but she couldn't actually verbalise a decent comeback; instead, she looked gormlessly at her feet and took comfort from the fact that her nail varnish matched her bikini.

'Duck off, Val,' Beni said, giving Gloria a small smile, proud of himself for remembering not to swear in front of her for once.

Catherine held one hand over her stomach and twisted away; with her other hand she held tightly on to Gloria. She had been firm with the little girl that morning that she was not to run away, that she shouldn't go anywhere with a stranger and – like Catherine used to tell her little brother – that if someone came near her, to scream bloody murder until all eyes were on her. They had all practised this screaming in the car on the way there, which Gloria had found very amusing.

'Where shall we go first then?' asked Stefano, cutting through the friction. He was just as tanned as Val, and was bouncing around like an excited Labrador about to be taken for a walk.

'I want to try that big slide,' Val said, looking thoroughly disinterested in the whole exercise.

'OK, let's do that then,' Stef said, leaning in to look at the map more closely to see how they would get there.

'I think we'll give that one a miss,' Catherine said. It was a bit too scary for a six-year-old and, secretly, too scary for her too.

'Me too,' said Anton. 'Gloria, do you want to try this wave pool out to start with? It looks fun. I need to start small. We'll meet back here later, shall we?'

Gloria happily took Anton's hand and they wandered over to the wave pool without looking back.

'I might go and try the lazy river then, since Gloria's taken care of,' said Catherine.

'I'll come with you,' said Beni.

Like Catherine, he was strangely pale for someone living in Mexico, but was still more tanned than her. He had long, dark-blue swimming shorts on and his hair had grown slightly since the last time she had seen him, giving him a small fringe as it flopped forwards. It was strange seeing her friends half-naked. When Beni was teaching Gloria to swim, Catherine sat near the pool fully-dressed as she watched them, not wanting to be half-dressed while spending time with her boyfriend's friend. Beni normally stood at the side of the pool and didn't get in either, so this was the first time she had seen him with his shirt off. As she'd suspected, his body was athletic, not skinny, but so toned that sometimes when he moved you could see a hint of his ribs. He had a messy line of hair on his chest and above his trunks. He was broad, and Catherine couldn't help but watch the contours of his strong back and shoulders as they set off on their walk over to the lazy river.

She smiled, content, as they walked along through the busy park, their flip-flops slapping along, sometimes squelching through puddles of water. 'When I flew over here on my own I never thought that I'd be going on a group outing to a water park with friends,' she said.

Her long hair was in a ponytail that kept swinging and tickling her back. Liking how it felt, she began swinging her head a bit more than usual, aware that it probably made her appear a bit erratic, especially as she was walking with her arms crossed and her shoulders slumped, still trying to disguise the fact she was just in a bikini.

'I'm glad we're here too,' said Beni, his eyes screwed up, his hand held in salute as a visor against the blinding sun. 'Your show's going well, I caught some of it last week.'

'How did you catch it?'

'Well, I say "caught it", but actually I came over especially to see you.'

'You did? Why didn't you say hi after?'

'I couldn't stop for the whole thing; I just nipped over in my break.'

'Beni, are you becoming a secret Eurovision fan?' She grinned up at him.

'I wouldn't go that far, but I like the thing you're doing where you sing guests songs from their home countries.'

She smiled. 'The only problem with that is, so many people in that hotel are English that I'm getting sick to death of singing Katrina and the Waves and Gina G.'

'Which country do you wish someone would say, so that you could sing it? I could come and act as a stooge if you like. I could don a moustache and stand in the crowd and act all shocked when you ask me where I'm from.'

Catherine laughed. 'Actually, no one ever says Italy!'

'It's a deal. I'll come over and shout Italy at some point.'

'OK.' She smiled, looking over at him briefly.

He was one of those cool people that only ever make slow deliberate movements. Nothing like her, a bouncing ball of anxious Flubber, or Stef, who bounded around laughing all day long like one of those inflatable waving-arm men you see outside car dealerships.

Confronted with his toned body, all she could think about was her thighs rubbing together and how wobbly everything must look in the skimpy bikini she was wearing. *Women are supposed to be wobblier,* she attempted to reassure herself, unsuccessfully, as she moved even more carefully and tried to tense her stomach.

'I heard you talking German to some of the guests. Why did you tell me you didn't understand it?' Beni asked.

'You're like a tape recorder, you remember everything I say,' she said with a smile, then shrugged. 'I just didn't want to seem like a know-it-all.'

'I think it's amazing. Don't ever feel that you have to hide knowing stuff from me, OK? Have you got stomach ache?' he asked as they stepped into some shade and, temporarily no longer blinded by the sun, he could see her holding her arms firmly crossed and walking like an uncomfortable ostrich.

'No.' She laughed, and raised a hand to her face. 'I just wish I was wearing more clothes; I feel all self-conscious.' She blushed and swayed her ponytail even more, half in an attempt to calm down and half to distract him from looking too closely at the rest of her.

'Everyone is wearing swimwear,' he said, looking around.

'I know, I've just never been that confident. Up until a couple of years ago I wouldn't even swim because I didn't want to wear a bikini in front of people. I considered buying one of those swim burkas and telling everyone that I was allergic to the sun.' This wasn't entirely a joke.

'So, what changed?'

'I don't know, I just stopped caring as much.' She shrugged. 'But it's one thing being OK walking from your sunlounger to the pool; it's another entirely walking through a park like this.'

'I'm surprised; I didn't think you'd be like that.'

'A self-obsessed idiot? Guilty!'

'No, I don't think you're self-obsessed at all. I just never imagined that someone who looks like you would feel self-conscious.'

'That looks like me? How do I look?' She tightened her arms around her stomach, feeling more conscious than ever of the shimmering stretchmarks at the tops of her legs.

Beni didn't say anything, just smiled slightly, nervously. He hadn't taken his eyes off her since she had walked out of the changing room. He kept glancing at the tattoos along her ribs, at the curve of her hourglass waist and at her perfect legs; he just wanted to reach out and touch her. He felt terrible about it, but it was like he was hypnotised; he just hoped no one else had noticed him staring, especially her.

'Here it is,' said Catherine. 'Are you going to remember the way back, because I won't!'

'Meet me here afterwards?' he suggested.

There wasn't a queue, so they were each given a rubber ring straight away as well as some rushed instructions and off they went, floating just a few feet apart from each other along the slow, winding river.

Catherine pondered what he could have meant by 'looks like you' while jungle noises played from speakers and a gentle breeze washed over them as they glided through the calm water. It felt a million miles from the chaos of the rest of the park and she wished she could stay in that rubber ring all day.

She was first to finish the ride and was standing at their meeting point beside a bin and a lot of foliage when she felt something grab her. She spun in a panic, wondering what creature had reached out of the leaves and pinched her skin, but instead, she saw two boys walking away, laughing.

'Did you actually just do that?' she shouted after them.

They stopped walking and turned around casually. 'Whatever, don't pretend you didn't like it,' one of them said in an American accent, as the other boy laughed even louder.

'It's sad that you have to go around grabbing women without their consent to make your friend laugh. What's wrong, boys, can't get a girl the old-fashioned way?'

'Ah, shut your mouth,' he said, rolling his eyes.

'Oh, no, this *is* the old-fashioned way isn't it,' Catherine said. 'You take what you want regardless of what the woman might want?'

'Fucking hell. Trust me to squeeze the feminist's ass. Most girls are just glad of the attention.'

'What's going on?' asked Beni, arriving at Catherine's side.

She didn't acknowledge him, she had tunnel vision for the boys. 'You know what? I didn't think I was a feminist, but if not wanting to be felt-up by some letchy teenager without my say-so makes me one, then I guess I am!' She flung her arms wide.

'We're not teenagers. Fucking hell, mate, your girlfriend is an uptight bitch!'

'What did you just fucking say?' said Beni, stepping forward and balling his fists.

Catherine put her hand against his hard chest, pushing him back a little. 'You're not teenagers? I'm sorry, I just assumed you were. You both look like you're taking puberty like a spanner to the face right now, and new hormones might have somewhat explained your disgusting behaviour!'

'Let it go, I only felt your ass.'

'He touched you?' said Beni, and strode towards them at speed.

Catherine ran ahead and stood between him and her young molester, her back leaning against Beni's body as she stopped him from getting any closer to them.

'Girls don't like being groped by strangers, OK? It's like stealing; you steal a tiny piece of a girl when you do that. And yes, most girls will laugh it off, but don't for one minute think she won't be reliving it for a long time after. She's not "glad of the attention", believe me!'

'Whatever,' said the ringleader.

'Sorry,' said his friend as they walked away.

Catherine grudgingly turned to face Beni, feeling guilty for wanting to spend a few seconds longer leaning her wet body against his. As she looked up at him in the bright light, she noticed a small scar protruding from his lower lip. She had the strongest urge to reach out and touch it but she didn't. From then on though, it was all she could do not to stare at it whenever he spoke or when the hint of a smile hit his lips.

'You should have let me beat them up,' he said, his muscles flexing.

'They're not worth it, but thanks for wanting to,' she said, taking his hand and leading him back towards the wave pool.

Catherine was grinning, feeling more confident. Not because of what that little perv had done but because of how she had reacted. She felt like Wonder Woman; if anyone else had a problem with her body, she would tell them off too! She relaxed her shoulders and uncrossed her arms, thinking she should set a better example for Gloria.

'What did you mean before, when you said "someone that looks like you"?' she asked, her new confidence bubbling inside of her.

'I feel bad,' he said, his insides bubbling too.

'About what?'

'Because I meant that you're crazy to be self-conscious because you look great, and I shouldn't say that. I don't want you thinking I'm being all predatory like those two losers.'

'You think I look great?' she asked, taken aback.

He nodded, and a tiny smile pulled at his lips as he watched her blush. He loved making her blush.

'It's not predatory to pay a girl a compliment. Thanks.' She knew she was as red as a fire engine and no amount of flicking her ponytail could distract from that.

'I wonder if Anton is bored with the wave pool yet?' Beni said, changing the subject.

When they got back to the park map, only Gloria and Anton were there, eating ice creams at a nearby café and looking thoroughly content, their hair still wet from the pool.

'Hi guys!' said Catherine as she and Beni sat down at the table.

'I love it here, we should get a season pass,' said Anton. 'We have had so much fun, haven't we, Gloria?'

Gloria nodded, smiling from ear to ear, clearly too interested in her ice cream to speak.

'How was the lazy river? Relaxing?' Anton said.

Catherine and Beni exchanged a look and smiled.

Val and Stef soon returned from the big slide, and this time they all went to the wave pool with Gloria. For the rest of the day, they darted around the park from slide to slide, pool to pool. They ate junk food for lunch, they reapplied sun cream a dozen times, had numerous bathroom breaks and laughed so hard at times that their abs hurt. After a while, even Valentina looked like she was having fun, though she and Stefano spent most of the day together, and even when with the group they would be off doing their own thing.

As their time at the park neared its end, Catherine, Anton and Val were sitting at the edge of a pool, their legs dangling into the cool water, the sun beaming down on them, while Beni and Stefano took Gloria for one last paddle. Catherine watched them, feeling lucky to have this group of friends. Val caught her eye and smiled at her, and it seemed as though she was feeling the same. It was a brief but nice moment, and they carried on watching as the boys splashed in the water with a giggling Gloria.

'I'm going to go to the bathroom,' said Valentina suddenly, her smile dissolving into her usual look of disgust as she glanced at Catherine again.

After she'd gone, a confused Catherine felt Anton's eyes on her and turned to look at him. 'What?' she asked.

'Nothing,' he said, but continued to look at her.

Now that she had seen him with his shirt off, Catherine could confirm that Anton was by far the most hirsute of her friends. Dark hair covered his chest and arms, his neck and face; the hair only really took a break for his eyes, but even they sat beneath extensive eyebrows and a neat but heavy coiffure.

'You're great with Gloria, I'm so glad we're friends,' she said, squeezing his hairy hand.

'Me too. Gloria's great. I like kids, it's a shame I probably won't get to have any of my own,' said Anton, pensively looking at his legs in the water.

'Why not? Being gay doesn't mean you can't have kids.'

'I know that, but I'm single, I'm nearly forty and my wages only just about take care of me. There is all of that to consider before even thinking about the small problem of having half the ingredients missing.'

'I don't know if they're any good or not, but you can always take some of my eggs when the time's right?'

'You would do that for me?'

'Sure, why not. I'm not doing anything with them. Or you could adopt? For now though, you can hang out with me and Gloria for practise.' She gave him a kind smile.

'Before you came along our group was drifting apart, but now look at us.'

'You were drifting? Why?'

'Too busy with work, the flimsy Italian connection bonding us ... I mean, a lot of people are Italian, aren't they. It doesn't mean they're all friends.'

'That's true.' She kicked her legs gently in the water.

'We hadn't seen Beni in about a month before that Christmas get-together, and now we see him all the time.'

'Maybe he's just not as busy as he was?'

'Lish, if I'd asked him to come to the water park with me a few months ago he would have told me to fuck off, seriously. And him offering me a lift into work – I nearly fainted when he said that.' He smiled. 'It's like a cloud is lifting.'

'He does seem quite detached sometimes. He never smiles, but that's just him. His eyes smile though, you should watch his eyes next time you say something funny, I bet you'll notice it.'

'You've only known him a couple of months and you know him better than all of us.'

'He's my friend and he's been good to me, you all have. He's a good person.'

'Oh, I've always known that. No matter how dark he gets, he is undoubtably good. I met him for the first time at Maria's bar, not long after he got here. A group of thugs took a dislike to me and my "lifestyle". Beni overheard and defended me, that's how we became friends. I love Mexico but Mexico doesn't always love me.' He flicked at a fly that had landed on his arm.

Catherine could see the sadness behind his smile. She stayed quiet, not sure what to say.

'It was sweet that he got a car seat for Gloria. It's nice to see him become something close to a humanoid with feelings again.'

'Talking of being devoid of feeling, where's Val got to?' Catherine said.

'She's over there. With Stef.' Anton pointed, and rolled his eyes.

They were sitting on the steps into the pool, half-submerged, laughing about something.

'Where's Gloria?' said Catherine, forgetting her jealousy, suddenly panicked.

'It's OK, Beni has her over there. Oh, and for her he smiles, look!'

Catherine watched as Beni and Gloria splashed around in the water. 'He's been teaching her to swim properly. He really is great with her,' she said, feeling a hundred butterflies flutter around inside her chest.

~

Anton travelled with Stefano and Val on the car ride home, leaving Beni to drive Gloria and Catherine back to the hotel. Gloria was asleep within the first few minutes of the journey and Catherine didn't speak for a long time, she just stared out of the window.

Beni glanced at her a few times; her hair was in a bun on her head, matted and messy. She was wearing a loose halterneck dress over her bikini and he could see part of her tattoo peeking out.

'You're quiet,' he said eventually.

'Sorry, I'm just tired from all the sun, and the chlorine I swallowed today,' she said, turning to smile at him. 'Did you have fun?'

'Yeah, I did. I didn't think hanging out with a kid all day would be fun, to be honest, but I was wrong.'

'She's a good kid, so happy all the time and chilled out. She's like the anti-Catherine.'

'I was kind of nervous about today.'

'You're great with her, Beni, she loves you.'

He chewed his bottom lip. 'Maybe I was nervous to hang out with you and Stef?'

'Why?'

'I don't know.' He shrugged. 'It was a surprisingly good day, and as a bonus I saw the lovely Lish get angry for the first time. I didn't realise you were so fiery.'

'Now you know not to mess with me,' she said, wagging a finger at him, not lifting her head from the headrest.

'You have a patch of sunburn you know, a tiny triangle just here,' he said, pointing to a part of her shoulder that she couldn't see.

'Must have missed it with the sun cream.' She shrugged.

'You have more freckles than you had this morning too.'

'Are you the UV police? We can't all have Italian blood and get a tan from a light bulb!' Catherine frowned in annoyance as she thought of Val's perfect olive skin. Her temples ached, her mascara was heavy and itchy on her tired eyes, and her almost empty stomach was somehow bloated. The for-no-reason stress was like poison; the irritation made her skin fizz and she couldn't shake it. She longed to be one of those women who always seemed confident and comfortable. She was seldom either.

'Your freckles are cute and you'll have a small pyramid tan.'

'By midnight me and my damn Viking skin will be lobster red all over. I didn't put nearly enough sun cream on.'

'I saw you reapply about ten times.'

She shook her head. 'I should just start wearing a beekeeper suit.'

'Next time we go somewhere for the day I'm going to write a word on your arm in sun cream to see what happens.'

'You will see that nothing happens. I will burn and then go back to looking like Casper the Friendly Ghost,' she said, turning to look out of the window again.

'You and Stef didn't seem to talk much today?'

'I noticed that too.'

'Did you have a fight?'

'No, I just can't exactly compete with Val in a bikini, can I?' She sighed.

'Don't be soft.'

Catherine smiled, amused at his use of a very English phrase. 'He was with her most of the day and didn't really speak to me. How else do you explain it?'

'I thought you said it didn't bother you how close they are?'

'I usually don't care, but I just felt so exposed today and it's just messed with my head. I'm being stupid, I know I am.'

After a while, Beni reached over and held her hand. She was trying to hide it, but it was clear that she was crying and he had absolutely no idea what to do. He knew she hadn't eaten anything all day, and as he stared at the road, he wondered how she could be so blind to how beautiful she was.

'Shall I turn the air con off? You feel cold,' he said after a while, drawing his thumb left and right across her skin to warm and console her.

Catherine turned to look at him; he was watching the road, one arm stretched to the wheel, his face set in its usual frown but somehow softer now. 'I'm fine,' she said, letting go of his hand and wiping her wet face. 'What word will you write on my arm?'

'I'll surprise you.'

'Nothing rude. I have a six-year-old that I'm trying to keep on the straight and narrow.'

'Prisons are filled with people that saw sunburn swear words as children,' he said, looking her way briefly so he could watch her smile.

Catherine grabbed a pen from the dashboard and took his hand again.

'What are you doing?' he asked, keeping his eyes on the road.

'I'm drawing on you. Just focus on driving.' She laughed, her nose and eyes still watery from being upset. 'It's pre-revenge for whatever Italian swear word you're going to write on my arm.' She held a couple of his fingers and rested his palm on her thigh.

He could feel the pen sliding along his skin but he couldn't work out what she was drawing. All he could think about was the millimetre of cotton separating his hand from the skin at the top of her thigh and had to focus really hard on not crashing the car.

'It's not hurting is it?' she asked as she moved the pen across his knuckles.

'No, it's quite nice.'

'Nice? Does it tickle?'

'Yeah.'

'Tickle.' Catherine laughed. 'It's such a funny word.'

'"Cosquillas" in Spanish.'

'When did you learn that word?' she asked, raising her eyebrows at him.

'My brain is filled with useless information.'

'I sometimes think I could be a brain surgeon if I knew less about films and lyrics to Eurovision songs.'

'I don't think those things take up *that* much space, Lish,' he said, giving her a tiny smile.

'Tell me something I don't know about you,' she asked while drawing.

Beni thought for a second, still frowning at the road. 'I hate champagne, it's horrible. Why do people pay so much for it? Now you.'

'I keep having a dream that sea turtles flap me to death because of my excessive use of plastic.' She laughed.

'They will soon take their revenge on us all.'

She finished drawing just before they pulled off the main road. She had penned circles, squares, swirls, diamonds and flowers all pressed together to form an elaborate pattern all over his right hand, which now looked like it belonged to an Indian bride.

He held it up, doing a Beyoncé-style hand twist as they drove slowly through the grounds of the hotel.

'I like it,' he said, pulling the car up to the lobby.

'Thanks for everything today. Thanks for driving us and for listening to my emotional vomit. I'm sorry I got upset, I'm just tired.' Catherine undid her seatbelt and hugged him close, blushing as she felt his arms slide slowly around her waist.

For once, she didn't smell of coconut. Instead, a blend of sun cream and chlorine flooded Beni's senses as he stroked his newly tattooed hand along the bare skin of her back. His lips were close to her neck, to a row of freckles he had discovered earlier that day and, as they remained pressed together, her cool skin and wet hair chilled the side of his face. Yet despite his increasingly icy earlobe, he felt warmer than ever.

'Thanks for never being boring, and thanks for my tattoo; I'll never wash this hand again,' he said quietly, still holding her, not wanting to let go.

'Please wash it,' she said eventually with a smile, tapping his arm twice and getting out of the car.

He watched her walk through the lobby with a still sleepy Gloria in her arms and a big bag slung over one shoulder, a smudge of ink obvious on her back.

The Television

Beni had invited Catherine, Stefano, Val and Anton over to watch a rugby match one evening at his third-floor apartment in Playa del Carmen. Catherine had spent the day shopping, and people-watching from an uncomfortable metal bar chair while drinking sweet yellow cocktails, relaxed in the knowledge that Gloria was being looked after. In the late afternoon, holding many shopping bags, she walked to Beni's apartment block and began the climb up the stairs to his apartment an hour earlier than planned. However, as she breathlessly reached the third floor, her phone dinged with a message from him to cancel.

She was just a few steps from his apartment by the time she stopped to read the message, and was worn out from her fast-paced hike from the high street in the hot weather, so she carried on and knocked on his door anyway.

Catherine could hear a commotion inside, with loud thuds coming closer and closer towards her. She quickly looked around, double-checking that she had the right address, and was relieved when Beni finally opened the door, just a fraction. His hair was sticking out in every direction, his usually smooth face was covered in dark stubble and his white T-shirt was stained.

'Hi, I'm sorry that I'm so early, it didn't take me as long to walk here from town as I thought. I only just got your message to cancel. What's up?' she asked.

'I just had to cancel, Lish, I'm sorry you've come all this way for no reason.'

'Are you not even going to invite me in for a quick cup of tea?' she said, while subtly trying to sneak a peek at his apartment. Then her eyes widened in realisation. 'Oh God, have you got a girl here?' She giggled. 'I'm so sorry, I'll go,' she whispered, turning to leave.

'No, there's no girl.' Beni sighed, and his jaw tensed as he let the door swing open to reveal his leg, bent oddly at the knee like a broken wing.

'Oh no! How did that happen?' she said, only then noticing his firm grip on the door frame as he used it to hold himself up.

'I haven't been able to tidy up or anything and I haven't got any drinks in or food. I was waiting for the last minute hoping it would get better, but I still can't put any weight on it.'

'Come on, you should go and sit down,' said Catherine, stepping towards him.

'It's a mess in here, I don't want you to see,' he said, attempting to pull the door closed again and wobbling on his good leg like a tipsy flamingo.

'Don't be silly!' she said, pushing him gently back into the apartment and watching him hop with heavy thuds to a black two-seater sofa.

The blinds were closed, so the room was dark but for a few lines of sneaky sunlight projecting along the back wall. There was a kitchen at one end of the room, a dining table in the middle and a sofa and television at the other end. Opposite the front door was a doorway that Catherine assumed must lead to the bathroom and bedroom. The place was a total mess; Beni hadn't been exaggerating. His bin was overflowing, the kitchen counters were piled high with plates and food wrappers, the small table and chairs were draped in dirty clothes and laden with books and magazines, and the living room floor was littered with even more books, cables, paperwork, and glasses containing half-finished drinks.

She sat on the arm of the sofa for a second and, as was so often the case with her, she didn't know what to say. He looked so embarrassed and she felt guilty for invading his space. She thought about leaving but he looked so helpless and dishevelled.

'When did you hurt your leg?' she asked, looking around.

'Are you trying to work out how long it's taken to get this messy?' he said. 'A few days ago, on Friday; I haven't been able to get out since.'

'It happened after the meal with everyone? Why didn't you say anything? I would have bought you some food and helped you.'

'I didn't want anyone to find out,' he said, looking at the ground.

Catherine couldn't stand to see him like that. 'You sit right here,' she said, dragging over one of the dining chairs and gently hoisting his leg onto it to keep it elevated. 'I'm going to clean up and then we'll eat.'

'No, you're not cleaning!' he protested, trying to stand up.

'Why? Have you got something you don't want me to find?' she said, standing with her hands on her hips. She was wearing a grey dress that hugged her curves and was short enough to show her long legs in their entirety, maroon pumps and, as always, her hair hung in waves down her back.

'What, like a human-skin lampshade and a box of teeth?

101

They're well hidden,' he said, his eyes running down her legs before he could stop himself.

'I want to help. I'm glad my husband isn't here to hear me say this, but I like cleaning and you don't get to do it when you live in a hotel.' She smiled.

'No! You can't,' he said, using his hands to lift his leg from the chair.

'Just sit here, watch the rugby, and take these.' She handed him some paracetamol from her handbag and made sure his leg was comfortably perched on the makeshift footstool again. 'Please just try to relax, but don't think I didn't notice you avoided answering my question about how this happened. Cleaning your apartment buys me that info, deal?'

He nodded and swallowed the pills.

'I'm guessing ice-skating championship went awry, or you had a go at Russian dancing?' she said with her eyebrows arched.

'I'll tell you later, I promise.'

'You weren't doing cartwheels on the beach were you? That's how Stef broke his toe.' She laughed, rolling her eyes.

'Later.'

'Oh, here,' she said, rummaging in one of her bags and pulling out a CD.

'A CD? What year is this?'

'Shut up, it has all your favourite songs on. One of the bellboys made it,' she said.

'One of the bellboys made you a mixed tape and you're giving it to me?'

'He's so sweet and actually really good-looking, but he's probably not even twenty-one. He asked me for a list, so I told him all of your favourite songs so you can listen to them in your car. It has a CD player, right?'

'Yeah.'

'I let him make me one for Stef as well, and now I'm going to try and set him up with a nice waitress who's about twenty-one too. I'm working on a whole plan to get them together.'

'I don't recognise this one,' said Beni, pointing at one of the handwritten squiggles on the back of the CD.

'It's Måns Zelmerlöw. He's the Hugh Jackman of Eurovision – he can sing, he can dance, he can act. I'm going to turn you into a fan if it kills me.' She smiled.

'Some of these are your favourite songs, Lish. Can I see Stef's CD?'

'Yes,' said Catherine, fetching it from the same bag and handing it to him.

'These are all actually his favourite songs, none of yours are on there.'

'I'm never in his car,' she said, chewing her lip.

'So, he has no Weezer or Billy Talent?'

'Nope.'

'No Eurovision?'

'None.' She laughed.

'Lucky him, can we swap?'

'No! So then, where's your cleaning stuff?' she asked, clapping her hands together.

She cleaned the kitchen surfaces and balled the dirty clothes hanging on the table and chairs into bags ready to be cleaned; she swept and mopped the floor and collected pots and glasses from all over the apartment and washed them up. It wasn't a completely selfless act; she looked at Beni, slumped on the sofa still in pain, and it made her feel good to help him.

Beni couldn't focus on the rugby, he kept thinking about her moving around behind him, touching his dirty clothes and cleaning his stained kitchen counter, and cringed at the idea that she might see him differently afterwards. Then, when she knelt on the floor in front of him and started tidying away his paperwork and books, it took all of his willpower not to stare too long at the hint of her underwear; it was torture.

'I'm done!' she said eventually, flopping onto a cushion on the floor and watching the rugby disinterestedly for a few minutes. 'Shall I go to the shop and get us something to eat?'

'No, you can't go out there on your own,' he said, clasping her wrist.

'I am a warrior woman; I can do anything I set my mind to!' she said in her best macho movie-narrator voice. 'I have my rape alarm, don't worry. Wouldn't it be nice if men would just stop raping though?'

She took the many rubbish bags with her to throw into the giant outside bins on her way to the supermarket and ignored Beni's protests for her not to go. She felt safe enough, his apartment was just a few streets away from the bustling tourist zone and there was still a little daylight left. From the supermarket, she bought as much as she could carry to keep him stocked up for the next few days, as well as a frozen pizza and some beers for them to have when she got back.

As she walked into his apartment, the smell of aftershave hit her and she could see that he had changed his T-shirt. Maybe, like the apartment, he had had a little spruce up too.

'What's that?' asked Beni, turning to look at her as she walked in laden down with shopping.

'It's a walking stick!' she said, beaming as she handed it to him.

'You can buy those from the supermarket?' he asked, examining its polished brass handle, which was engraved with a pattern.

'No, I spotted one of your neighbours on my way back in and he had one.'

'So, you stole an old man's walking stick?'

'No.' She laughed as she began to put the food away in the cupboards.

'I told him that you'd hurt your leg and I asked him if he had any spare walking sticks. Turned out he had quite a few. This is one of his favourites, bless him, he was so sweet to lend it to you. I'll have to send him a present.'

'He probably just fancied you.'

'Beni, he was about eighty!'

'Don't be so ageist. Eighty-year-olds can still find women sexy.' *Especially you,* he thought, watching her put things away in the kitchen, her dress riding up as she stretched to reach the highest cupboards.

'Well, anyway, he said you can keep it as long as you need to. His name is Francis, he's in number four.'

'How much do I owe you for all this shopping?' he asked.

'Nothing. You drive me places all the time and you never let me give you petrol money.'

Catherine finished putting away the shopping, cooked the pizza and finally sat next to him on the sofa feeling tired out.

'You didn't have to go to so much trouble,' he said, then bit into a slice of pizza.

'It's no trouble. I haven't used an oven in months, it's nice to know that I haven't forgotten how. Are you going to try and go back to work soon? I imagine you don't get sick pay here?'

'Hopefully I'll be able to walk by Friday, especially with my new stick.'

'If you still aren't able to get out, let me know and me and Gloria will bring you some more shopping, OK? I don't want to find you starved to death clutching an empty can of aftershave.' She smirked.

He cringed slightly. 'You caught me off guard showing up like that. I'd been wearing that T-shirt for two days, I didn't want to be the dirtiest thing left in the apartment!'

'You smell nice, it's mixing well with the gallon of bleach I just used in here. Actually, where's the spray? I think I need some too, I feel like I've run a marathon.' She laughed.

'Somehow, you still smell nice.'

'Shall I message the others and see if they want to come over now that the place is clean and you have beer in the fridge?'

'No, there's no point, the rugby is over.' He shrugged.

'OK. Are you still in pain?'

'Yes,' he said reluctantly.

'So, what happened, Beni?'

'Oh, it's embarrassing.' He groaned, pulling a hand over his face.

'It's just me; I won't laugh, even if you injured it skate-boarding like a big man-child.'

'I was mugged,' he said, not looking at her.

'That's not embarrassing! God, I'm sorry I've been joking around about it. What did they steal?'

'Nothing. I refused to hand over my wallet. They punched me a few times and I punched them back.' He held up his top to show bright purple bruising on his ribs, and Catherine noticed that the knuckles on his left hand were bruised and cracked in places too. 'But then they pulled a knife and I ran away like a little bitch. It was dark and I tripped on a step and that's how I hurt my leg.'

Catherine didn't say anything, she just stared at his worried face and finally put her hand on his. 'Running away doesn't make you a coward. It's fight or flight, it's a natural instinct.'

'And the tripping over part?'

'I want the CCTV of that bit.' Catherine smiled. 'Did you go to hospital? Are you sure it's not broken? Do your ribs hurt?'

'I'm 95% sure I've just pulled or torn a ligament. I did it a few times when I used to play rugby and it generally felt like this.'

'You used to play?'

'Yeah, just for fun,' he said.

'Can I tell you something?'

'You don't like rugby.'

'How did you guess that?'

'When you looked like you were having more fun emptying the bins than watching the game.' He smiled slightly.

'Why were you watching me empty the bins and not the game?' she said, holding his gaze.

Beni didn't know what to say; he just fidgeted nervously and tried not to look at her legs.

'I prefer football but my family all love rugby,' she said eventually, blushing.

'My dad got me into rugby. He was really tall, taller than I am now and I'm six foot three. He played for a local team when we lived in Yorkshire.'

'I didn't realise you'd lived in Yorkshire?'

'We moved to Middlesbrough too before we ended up in Manchester.'

'Why did you move around so much?'

'My dad was a university lecturer and he kept losing his job.' He shrugged.

'Your dad was a lecturer and yet he still abandoned his family? He should have known better.'

'Why? Smart people can be arseholes too, you know.'

'That's true. You've not seen him since you were a kid then? Not at all?'

'No, he's probably drunk himself to death by now but I wouldn't know. He just left. Rugby reminds me of him though. It reminds me that he wasn't a complete shit. And he taught me a few DIY skills before he left.'

'Like how to make shelves?'

'Yeah, that kind of thing.'

'Then why don't you have a bookshelf for all of your books?' she said, gesturing to the pile that she had stacked neatly against a wall during her cleaning frenzy.

'I should make one, I've just been lazy,' he said, rubbing the back of his neck.

'Too busy reading the books to build them a shelf?' She slid onto the floor and pulled out a copy of *Wuthering Heights* from the pile, flicking the classic book's pages fast, like a poker dealer shuffling cards. 'I was surprised to see this in your collection. I read it when I was younger.' She smiled.

'I wanted to know how it ends.'

'You're a bit of a Heathcliff.' She laughed, sitting back next to him. 'All wild hair and brooding intensity.'

Beni smiled slightly. 'So, this is what the place would look like if I had a wife,' he said as he looked around at his clean apartment.

'It could look like this if you just cleaned it. No wife required.'

'Sorry, you're right!'

'But if a woman lived here you would probably have a bookshelf already, and a coffee table.'

'What else?' he asked, leaning his head back against the sofa and closing his eyes.

'Photos all over the walls, some art, plants, maybe a painted feature wall,' she said, noticing that he was in pain.

'Photos of what?'

'Of you and your wife, of holidays and family.' She shrugged.

'Is that what your house in England looks like?'

Catherine nodded and looked at her nail polish, thinking of all the photos of Thomas that she couldn't bear to look at any more.

'When those guys pulled the knife on me, I thought, if I die here today, absolutely no one would miss me. No one would even notice I was gone,' he said, staring at his bottle of beer.

'You would be missed.' Catherine reached out and pushed her fingers through his hair without thinking.

'By who? I have no family.' His voice cracked.

'You have us, your friends,' she said.

'You wouldn't care. I'm in no one's photos, none that are on a wall.'

'I live in a hotel! As soon as I have a wall of my own again, I promise you will be up there.'

Beni looked at her sideways, the edges of his mouth pointing downwards.

'What can I do to cheer you up?' she asked, squeezing his hand.

'Let's argue about something. Distract me.'

'OK.' She smiled, turning her body to face him and folding her legs beneath her. 'What shall we argue about?'

'Do you think women are better at cleaning than men?'

'Rewind the clock and your apartment kind of answers that question for us.'

'That's not fair, I'm injured. I'm usually pretty tidy,' he said.

'Women are better at cleaning. I wish it wasn't true, I wish my ancestors had developed more kick-ass natural instincts in our bloodline, like precision shuriken-throwing, but alas, I am just really, really, good at hoovering instead.'

'Men just haven't been given the chance to polish their skills in this field. If you'll pardon the pun.' He smirked, pleased with himself.

'Oh, OK, you really do want an argument, don't you!' She laughed.

'I'm not speaking from experience, but from what I've heard and seen on TV, women just moan at men for doing things wrong when they try, and moan that they have to do it all themselves when they don't.'

'Women wouldn't moan if men did things correctly the first time. Are they pretending to be bad at that stuff to get out of doing it, or are they just genuinely terrible at it? That is the question.'

'No, the real question is, if men weren't pretending to be bad at it, would cleaning be yet another thing that they are better at than women?' He grinned.

'Watch it, you,' she said poking his bicep. 'Men used to go out and earn the money, right? So, the woman would stay home and keep the house clean, fair enough. But now women have to do both.'

'Not necessarily. Some men do both too, and some men even stay home with their kids now.'

'Some do.' Catherine nodded and stroked a hand along the cool leather back of the sofa. 'But that's still rare. We have just about evolved enough that women are free to do whatever they please; they can work, they can vote, blah-blah, but they still have to do all of that around their jobs at home. So effectively, women have two jobs: the one that pays and the one that doesn't. They get home from a long day and then have to do the cleaning, cooking and caring for kids if they have them.'

'And the man drinks a brandy and has a cigar? Come on, not all couples are like that.'

'My mum complained twenty years ago about the same things that my friends complain about now. Nothing changes. We're really not that evolved from 1950s housewives, but thanks to gadgets like microwaves and dishwashers we have time to fit in a quick eight-hour shift at work alongside our wifely duties, which cements an illusion of freedom, lucky us.'

'What do men do while the women hurry around doing everything?'

'You tell me! One of my friends said that when she and her husband fought, he would take her hands in his and say very sincerely to her, "you just have to remember that you're a mother", as though that was a good enough reason for him to sit and scroll through the internet while she did everything.'

'He said that to her? Are they still together?'

'Hell no!' said Catherine.

'She got unlucky, I'm sure most men aren't like that.'

'You think you'll be an evolved husband then one day?'

'Sure,' he said.

'You have to commit to one woman to be married, Beni, could you handle that?'

'I suppose that would depend on the woman.'

Catherine rolled her eyes. 'What about being creative? Women go to work for eight hours, cook and clean, take care of the kids and then sleep, while also being expected to keep themselves looking drop-dead gorgeous with exercise and beauty treatments and clothes shopping. Oh, and for one week a month they are gifted with unrelenting pain and discomfort that wipes them out too! What if they have a passion they want to pursue beyond all of that?'

'There are lots of creative, brilliant women out there. It's not stopped them.'

'Yes, but they're the exceptional ones who don't need much sleep. What about the rest of us average Janes who dream of doing something creative?'

'Lish, you're no average Jane.'

'I would wager that this is why men are always so much friskier than women too, because after working all day and doing all the house jobs, women are knackered.'

'Then women should relinquish some control and let men help more; they don't have to do it all themselves, or maybe they should stop trying to do both and choose between work or home.'

'Not everyone has the luxury of choice, and a man would never be made to choose between working or having a family.'

'Women have a biological need to be at home near their kids, to breastfeed and stuff.'

'They did before breast pumps and formula were invented. Now mums can throw their kid at a nanny or grandparent as soon as their C-section stitches heal, and carry on climbing the corporate ladder. Of course, those women are judged, just like the ones who stay home full-time are judged. You can't win as a woman unless you stretch yourself between the two worlds, and even then you end up with resentful kids, and colleagues who discredit your contribution.'

'Then ... men should share the housework; women should let them.'

'Maybe men could learn to share the housework more evenly, but won't that just tire them out? Soon everyone will be too knackered for sex!' She laughed, and re-folded her legs into a new position.

'No way, that won't stop people!'

'With all the entertainment out there, is there actually time for sex? Sex used to *be* the entertainment, but now, everyone's too busy with other stuff. I read that a lot of millennials are now celibate by choice.'

'I've seen you and Stef, it doesn't seem like you're struggling in that department.'

'We aren't living together. I don't work right now or have a house to take care of, I don't have to wash his pants.'

'Do you imagine washing his pants one day?'

Catherine shook her head.

'I've not been with anyone long enough to get bored of the sex and no one has ever washed my pants.'

'From what I've heard, you've never been with anyone longer than a night.'

'Don't believe everything you hear about me, Lishy. But yeah, that's true.' He smirked.

'Do you know there is now a pyjama top you can get that has a phone holder in the back, so that when you roll over, your partner can pop their phone in and use you as a TV stand?'

'What? No way, who would use that?'

'What better example is there than that, that we are literally turning our backs on intimacy and human interaction in favour of looking at a screen. It's insane isn't it?'

'Any couple that use that are just sad,' he said.

'Is it any different to having a TV in the bedroom?'

'You can both watch that though, no one is being used to prop it up.'

'Remember what I told you about my flight out here? How it descended into madness without any inflight entertainment? I wonder how many people joined the mile high club before the staff started strapping people into chairs?' She laughed.

'Are you a member?' he asked, looking at her sideways.

'No! But I bet you are. If I turned the TV off right now, if I took away our source of entertainment, what would we end up doing to entertain ourselves I wonder?'

'We have a lot of books to read, remember.'

'OK, then how long would it take if we were trapped in here with no books and no TV for us to turn to sex for entertainment?' she said, a slight smile curling her closed lips.

'I think the bleach fumes have gone to your head,' he whispered.

Catherine turned off the TV with a click of the remote, waving it theatrically in the air. She looked into his eyes, the room suddenly much darker without the blue light of the TV, and she leaned in towards him, her hand on his leg.

'Lish!' he said quickly, stopping her just before her lips touched his.

'I guess longer than ten seconds.' She laughed, turning the TV back on.

'Are you trying to give me a heart attack? I thought you were going to kiss me,' he said, touching a hand to his chest and feeling his heart beat like a drum.

'I was conducting an experiment for the purpose of our argument; do you feel distracted?'

'What would you have done if I'd kissed you back?'

'I knew you wouldn't.'

'Why wouldn't I?' he asked, frowning.

'So, you see, in conclusion, whether men or women are better at cleaning soon won't matter at all.'

'Why not?'

'We'll soon be extinct, because people have much better things to keep them busy now than having children.'

'You should save that chilling speech for Gloria's social worker,' he said with a small smile, then winced in pain and reached for his calf.

'Is there anything I can do?' she said, touching his leg lightly.

'Why did you think I wouldn't kiss you back?'

'You're Stef's friend.'

'Right, yeah.'

'His best friend,' she said.

'Val is his best friend. We are close I guess, not as close as we were though.'

'Why not?'

'I don't see him as much now he's with you.' He shrugged.

'Sorry.'

'It's not your fault. If I were him, I'd rather be with you too,' he said, instantly cringing inside at having said it out loud.

'You would?'

'Getting high and playing video games with a mate or being with a girl, I know what I'd rather be doing. I don't blame him.'

Catherine laughed nervously. 'You could get a girlfriend if you wanted one.'

'I don't want one.'

'Right,' she said, feeling oddly offended.

'I never thought Stef did either. I remember when he first told me about you, and told me how you met.'

'What did he say?'

'He said you were the most beautiful but saddest girl he had ever seen, and he followed you to the beach to make sure you were OK.'

'He came along and cheered me up. It was just after I took on Gloria and I was freaking out. He was amazing, actually. Really helped me through that time, I couldn't have done it without him.'

'That's how he met me too.'

'He followed you to the beach because you're so beautiful?' She laughed.

'No, he saw me looking sad and he came over to see if I was OK. He kept talking and talking at me, smiling that big stupid smile of his, telling me a story about a customer with a wooden hand or something, and we became friends.'

'He's so happy all the time.'

'Or he's good at hiding when he's sad?' Beni said.

'Have you ever actually seen him look sad?'

'Once.'

'What happened?'

'Oh, I don't think I should tell you.'

'What was it?' asked Catherine.

'It was when Val agreed to go out with me.'

'Right. Is that why you two didn't have more than the one date then?'

Beni nodded. 'He looked so upset, I couldn't do it to him.'

'So, you liked her then?'

'She wasn't worth ruining my friendship with him over.'

Catherine smiled. 'Bros before hoes?'

'Yeah,' he said, looking at her lips and taking a deep breath. 'Do you have to get going soon for Gloria?' he asked.

'No, but if you want me to go, I can do?' she said, getting ready to stand up.

'No, I don't want you to leave,' he said, his hand on her arm. 'Where is Gloria, anyway?'

'She's staying at her little friend's house tonight. She was so excited, bless her. You know Maria from the bar? It's her daughter, Leonora. She's a bit younger but they get on great.'

'You and Maria have become close then?'

'She's been a good friend; she cares for Leonora on her own too, so we have each other to chat to about things and I look after Leonora sometimes so Maria can have a break. She owns the bar, you know? It belonged to her mum and dad, and now it's hers.'

'I didn't know that. She is there a lot more than she used to be, come to think of it. When I first started going there, she would only work once in a blue moon. So, if you don't have to leave, do you want to watch a film?'

'Sure, why not, what's your favourite film? It's a tough one, but I think I would have to say *Die Hard* three,' she said.

'What? You can't tell me *Die Hard* is your favourite film and then ruin it by putting three at the end of it! *Die Hard* one is the best.'

'You are just so wrong.'

'Number one had Alan Rickman!'

'I agree it's amazing, but number three has Samuel L.

Jackson and it doesn't end with him hugging his flaky wife, Holly.'

'She wasn't flaky, she just valued her own career above his,' Beni said.

'Oh my God, I am the worst feminist ever!' Catherine said, smacking her palm against her nose and laughing. 'She is actually a badass, a woman on film in the twentieth century that wasn't in her kitchen or picking up the kids from school.'

'You know what we have to do, right?'

Catherine grinned. 'We have to watch them all.'

Beni nodded. 'So, after all your talk of film being art, *Die Hard* three ends up being your favourite film ever?' he said, shaking his head and tutting.

'That film is a masterpiece. I could watch it every day for a week and still love it. Not all art looks the same: it's a Warhol not a Rembrandt.' She smiled, getting up to get them some more drinks and some ice.

Beni watched her in the kitchen and sighed before turning his attention to the television to search for the trio of films for them to watch.

'Sorry to touch your leg, but the ice won't stay in place if I don't hold it. Please don't accuse me of sexual harassment,' said Catherine once she was sitting down again, holding her free hand in the air in a gesture of conciliation.

'If hairy man-calves are what get you going, then go right ahead.'

'It doesn't look swollen, does it,' she said, prodding his leg muscle gently.

Beni felt his hairs stand on end as her fingers touched his skin; he wasn't sure if it was because the ice was so cold or because it was her doing the touching.

'No, it's not swollen,' he said. 'And surely if it was broken it would be going a funny colour by now?'

'That's very sensible reasoning, doctor, why did they even bother inventing the X-ray machine?'

'You can't sit like that all night holding it against my leg.'

'It will melt soon and be a puddle on the floor, so don't worry about that.'

'OK. If you insist,' he said, moving her hair behind her ear without thinking, and looking at all the freckles on her arm.

'What about your ribs, do you want me to make some more ice for there?' asked Catherine, her cold fingers softly grazing his T-shirt where the bruises were.

'It doesn't really hurt there,' he said, instantly regretting it as she pulled her hand away.

'Let me know if you want more paracetamol or another drink or anything.' She smiled once the ice was melted, curling her bare legs against him on the sofa, getting comfortable.

'Here we go, are you ready to watch the best film ever made?' said Beni, hitting play.

'I will be after we've watched one and two.' She grinned. 'Can I draw on you while we watch?'

'Go on then,' he said.

'You're like a doodle bear.' She laughed, and pulled a pen from her handbag.

'A what?'

'Can you remember those teddy bears that you could draw all over and then wash?'

Beni shook his head, wondering if the bears had enjoyed being drawn on as much as he did. 'Do you do this with Stef?' he asked as he watched her draw the first few lines in black ink across his forearm, his hand resting on her leg.

'No, his arms are too hairy. You have the perfect amount,' she said, running her fingers briefly over the dark fuzz on his arms.

'So, when you have smudges of ink on you, he knows it's from me?' he asked quietly.

'I guess so,' she said, looking into his dark eyes. 'Kind of like Anck-Su-Namun in *The Mummy*, when the Pharaoh knew that someone had touched her because the make-up on her arm was smudged.'

'You and your random film references. Didn't they bury Imhotep alive for touching her?'

'Yep.'

'Maybe we should stop this then.'

'Are you worried Stef will bury you alive?'

'I'm worried we could break his heart,' he said seriously.

'It's just ink with us. Imhotep was banging her too; I think that was the main issue?' She laughed.

'Lish,' he said, pulling his arm away gently.

'Where do you think he is right now, if you had to put money on it?'

Beni sighed. 'Probably with Val?'

'Can't one friend draw on another friend's arm while watching *Die Hard* without it being reduced to something sordid?'

'Maybe it is sordid?' he said, trying not to look at her legs for the thousandth time.

'OK, I won't do it any more. I'm sorry, I didn't mean to make you feel uncomfortable,' she said quietly, feeling embarrassed and giving him the pen.

'I love hanging out with you, I'm glad Stef followed you to the beach, I'm glad we're friends. I just don't want to hurt him.'

'Neither do I,' she said, not looking at him.

Beni turned the pen over and over in his fingers, thinking about Stef being with Val at that moment, playing his usual memory montage of Catherine in his mind as though she wasn't sitting next to him, thinking about her smiling, about her tattoos, how blue her eyes were.

They sat in silence watching Bruce Willis ride in a limo, and after a minute or two Catherine said, '*The Mummy* might be my favourite film ever, actually.'

'We can watch that one another night?' said Beni, handing the pen back to her with a tiny smile and a sigh.

They watched all three *Die Hard* films, and at around two o'clock in the morning, Beni was standing at the door, his arm covered in ink, begging her not to get a taxi at that time of night. He offered her his bed, which she declined, knowing he would never be able to sleep on the sofa with his injured leg.

'I'll be fine, my taxi's just there. You can watch me get into it.'

'I'm glad you now agree that *Die Hard* one is the best.'

'Yes, but I might just think that because we were less tired when we started watching it.'

'Stay here and argue with me about it?' he said, holding the tips of her fingers loosely, caring less and less about upsetting his friend.

'I can't, I need to be back at the hotel when Maria drops off Gloria first thing.'

'Thanks for everything, for distracting me.'

'Any time.' She smiled, put her shopping bags on the floor and hugged him tight around the middle. 'There's more ice in the freezer. Put it on your leg and call me if you need help with anything.'

'I will, boss.'

'Beni ...' she began seriously, pulling away from him but keeping her hands on his waist, 'I know what loneliness is like. If you ever want to talk, I'm here ... I would miss you a lot if you weren't around, so please don't get into any more knife fights?'

Beni nodded, not quite meeting her eye.

'When your leg's better, do you want to go to the beach with me and Gloria?' she asked, smiling again as she stepped into the outdoor corridor with all of her bags.

'Yeah, I'd like that. But is there enough sun cream in Mexico for you to be able to spend a whole day at the beach?'

Catherine laughed. 'See you soon, hopalong.'

The Night Out

Catherine walked in to a busy bar in Playa Del Carmen. She hated arriving places first and having to wait for her friends, it was a great source of anxiety for her and she usually got to places a few minutes late to avoid such an ordeal. She wasn't really sure what she was so scared of: being seen alone, unplanned human interaction? In the past, she had variously hidden in the toilet, had three drinks within twenty-five minutes, and had once even done a few laps of the block rather than just sit and wait for her friends like a normal person.

The walls of the bar were covered in mirrors and black and white art, Edison-bulbed chandeliers hung above red velvet and diamanté-bordered high tables and a Justin Bieber song was playing loudly. Like most bars in the town, this one was loud and chaotic, waitresses moved around in short dresses serving tables and there was also a long queue at the bar.

Thankfully, just as she was beginning to spiral, she spotted that Beni was already there, but as Catherine got closer, she realised that he was talking to a girl. She didn't know what to do; she couldn't go and interrupt his conversation but she also didn't fancy doing a lap of the block in the heels she was wearing, so she decided to go and hide in the toilet for a while. As she went to walk up the stairs, however, a tall blonde man with excessive sideburns stepped in front of her and asked if he could buy her a drink.

'No, I'm fine thanks,' she said, feeling as sober as she ever had in her whole life and wishing she had the sloshy confidence of wine moving her limbs and lips for her like a more socially adept puppet master.

He persisted, putting his hand firmly on her upper arm. 'Come on, let me get you a drink?'

'I told you, no!' she said angrily, trying to peel his hand away. 'Get off me, you fucking arsehole!' she said even louder, starting to panic.

'Don't be so uptight!'

Her handbag fell on the floor, and she gritted her teeth as she tried to pull away from him with all her weight but he still didn't surrender, just laughed and swayed slightly on the spot.

Beni glanced around, wondering if any of his friends had arrived yet, and spotted Catherine near the stairs with a man he didn't recognise. Thinking she looked upset, he rushed over, abandoning mid-sentence the girl he had been speaking to.

'Hey, there you are, Lish,' he said once beside her, picking up her bag from the floor.

Relieved, Catherine tried to wriggle free of the man's grasp subtly, hoping her friend wouldn't need to get involved, that his presence would be enough to scare off the inebriate holding her hostage.

'Let go of her, man,' said Beni, pushing the guy hard as he realised what was happening, his face contorting quickly with anger.

'She wants me to buy her a drink,' slurred the man.

'No, I really don't,' Catherine said, attempting again to

break free of his grip, which was becoming more and more painful. 'He won't let go of me.'

Beni leaned in close to the man's face, put a hand calmly on his shoulder and began to squeeze. 'Let fucking go of her, or you won't be holding on to anything for a long time.'

The drunk man winced, released Catherine's arm and staggered off.

'Hey,' said Beni, touching her face. 'Are you OK?'

She nodded, but she just wanted to leave.

'Here's your bag. Where were you going? Didn't you see me?'

'I didn't want to interrupt; you were talking to that girl.'

'So, you were off up the stairs because ...?'

'I hate being on my own and sober in places like this, I was going to go and hide in the loo for a bit.'

He closed his eyes and smiled a tiny smile. 'You weirdo. You should have just come over to me, I'd already got her number.'

Catherine frowned and ran her trembling hand over her arm, red from where the drunk idiot's thumb and fingers had dug into her flesh. 'I think I might just go back to the hotel.'

'Wait, don't leave. Why are you so upset?'

'Have a good night,' she said and then walked off, squeezing through the crowd, leaving Beni and his larger frame to fall a few steps behind.

'Wait, wait, wait,' he said as he caught up to her outside, grabbing her hand.

'The others will be here soon,' she said, trying to pull away.

'Don't let him ruin your night. Come on, we'll just go to another bar?'

'I don't feel like it.'

'Come on, just one drink?'

'You sound like him! Let me go!' she shouted, snatching her hand from his and walking away. She only got halfway down the street before stopping, however, and as soon as she did, Beni's hand slipped into hers.

'I'm lucky you're wearing heels tonight, not-so-Speedy Gonzales.'

'I'm sorry, you're not like that guy at all.'

'Please don't go, I've been looking forward to seeing you,' he said, still holding her hand.

She sighed, then nodded. 'OK, let's go somewhere else.'

They walked a bit further down the busy street and sat down at a booth in a small, rustic bar that had hundreds of clocks on its walls and a bright yellow ceiling. A waitress came and took their drinks order and Beni looked at Catherine across the table. The bruises on her arm were becoming more obvious, no longer single marks, they were beginning to blend together to form one big red-and-purple discoloration and he felt bad that he had minimised what had just happened. She looked shaken up and wouldn't look him in the eye, so he moved to sit next to her in the snug booth, wanting more than anything to hold her, but he didn't: she wasn't his to hold.

'I had fun at the beach the other day,' he said softly.

'So did I. Gloria loved it too, it's a shame the others couldn't come with us.'

'Next time.' Beni shrugged as he rolled up the sleeves of his checked shirt, not caring in the least that they hadn't been there.

Their drinks soon arrived, and Catherine ordered another glass of wine before starting the one in her hand, which she gulped as soon as the waitress walked away. The burning liquid stung her insides just like the threat of tears was stinging her eyes, but she felt better for it. She looked closely at her arm, at the clusters of tiny red dots forming the bruises. 'Pickled prick,' she said.

They were sitting close; his arm was behind her, resting on

the back of the booth, and more than once the fabric of her floaty pink dress touched his denim-clad knees.

'Why didn't you tell him to fuck off like you did with those lads at the water park?'

'I did, but he wouldn't let go. I tried to pull away. Do you think I just let him do this?'

'No, sorry.'

'Muchas gracias,' she said to the waitress as she delivered her second wine. 'Thanks for getting him off me,' she said to Beni.

'Everywhere we go, men grab you.'

'It's tough being a woman.' She shrugged. 'Do I look like a slut? Is this dress slutty?'

'No, no. You look really nice. It's fine. Really.' He wanted to tell her she looked amazing but didn't.

'I thought maybe I was putting something out there. Isn't that what men give as a defence? "Well, the girl was dressed a certain way, officer, she gave me no choice."'

'Lish. He was a drunken idiot; you didn't do anything wrong.'

'I should have just gone for a walk around the block instead of heading to the loos.'

'You should have just come up to me. Do you think I care about that girl more than you?'

'She was pretty.'

'Always just come up to me,' he said, tucking her hair behind her ear, watching her lips.

She smiled. 'How hard did you squeeze his shoulder?'

'Hard. But believe me, if I'd seen what a mess he'd made of your arm that would have been the least of his worries. I'd better not bump into him again tonight,' he said, touching the bruises on her arm lightly.

'That's the second time you've offered to beat someone to a pulp to defend my honour.'

'I would go to prison to defend you,' he said with a smile in his eyes. 'Nothing like that will happen again, I won't let it.'

'You aren't always around.'

'You have a boyfriend who can defend your honour too, you know,' he said, his jaw tensing.

'Stef's a lover not a fighter. Literally. He kisses me and gropes me to make sure everyone knows I'm his; it works, no one ever tries it on with me when he's around.'

'I can't use that tactic, I'm afraid,' Beni said, wishing he could.

'I should have punched that guy or something. I shouldn't need anyone to rescue me.'

'I hate seeing you sad.'

'Let's forget about it. Sorry for being such a buzzkill, it's been a long and stressful day.'

'You're not a buzzkill; I understand why you're upset,' he said, putting his hand on hers.

'The police came to talk to Gloria today.'

'What happened?'

'I called Mr Hernandez, the lawyer that's been helping us, and he insisted that we not say anything until he got there. It was all very awkward waiting for him for forty minutes while a policewoman eyed us up across the table like we were criminals.'

'What did he say when he got there?' asked Beni.

'Not much really. I get the feeling he just wanted to be there so they couldn't twist anything that Gloria said?' Catherine shrugged and her forehead creased in an uneasy frown.

'And what did she say, what did they ask her?'

'They asked her about what she saw and how she got the bruises on her arm the night her parents died.'

'What did she say?'

'She didn't say anything.'

'Nothing at all?' Beni frowned.

'Absolutely nothing, she just clammed up,' said Catherine.

'Was she upset?'

'Not really. I thought maybe I should have cancelled tonight and stayed with her but she seemed fine and she wanted to see Leonora.'

'Why on earth are they asking her this now? It happened months ago.'

'I know,' said Catherine, running a hand through her hair, sighing loudly and sipping her wine quickly. 'That's essentially what the lawyer said to them and they eventually backed off. I'm glad he was there.'

'Tell me something about you that I don't know.'

Catherine smiled and thought about it. 'Sometimes I zone out in the shower and end up washing my hair three or four times. Now you.'

'I used to wear eyeliner back in the day, I went through a full-on Jack Sparrow phase.'

'Are you just saying that to cheer me up?'

'Nope, I thought girls would like it.'

'That's amazing.' Catherine laughed. 'Have you messaged Stef that we've changed bars?'

'Yep.'

'So, how's work been? It's spring break around this time, right?'

'That was weeks ago. The Opal is like your hotel really, more families and old people than crazy spring-breakers, so we don't really notice it either.'

'No eager Ericas from El Paso to fall for the Italian Stallion act then? That's why you're out here chasing the chicas?'

He shook his head and made the sound of a buzzer. 'Alliteration! Am I going to have to stage an intervention?'

'I'll stop, I'll stop! I'm sorry!' she said, holding up her hands in surrender.

'You can have one a day.'

'Can I save them up for the days that I drink?'

He smiled slightly and paused. 'Yes,' he said finally.

'Good.'

'Oh, Stef's messaged me back, he's running late anyway. Apparently Val has been to the dentist and had some work done, so she won't be drinking tonight and we're not to point that out in any way. I wonder what she's had done?'

'She's been nicer to me lately. Maybe we're turning the corner and will finally take the next step from acquaintances, to frenemies.'

'Fingers crossed.'

'You don't have any tattoos, do you?' asked Catherine, taking a pen out of her bag.

'You've seen me in swimming trunks,' he said with eyebrows raised.

'I don't know. You could have been hiding one somewhere. Would you ever get one?' she asked, taking his hand, which he offered with no protest for her to start drawing on. She twisted away from him, hiding her work; he enjoyed being so close to her, relished how warm her skin felt when it fleetingly touched his.

'I don't know. What would I get?' Beni said, distracted by long blonde strands of her hair brushing along his hand as she wrote, and fighting the urge to wrap his arms around her waist and kiss her neck.

'Well, what do you love?'

'Beer?'

'You can't get a beer bottle tattooed on you. What about something for your mum?'

'Like "mum" in capitals inside a love heart on my shoulder?'

'No!' Catherine laughed. 'What's your mum's name?'

'Rosie.'

'That's a nice name, you could get a rose?'

'Right here on my face, with mum written underneath it in Chinese!'

Catherine shook her head in mock despair. 'I'm nearly done. You can't wash it off, you have to leave it on all night, OK?' she said, finishing off with a few more pen marks here and there.

Catherine turned to face him when she was done, a big smile on her face as she watched him squint at what she had written.

'I love *Die Hard* three,' he read out loud, amused, rolling his eyes.

'Tattoo design free of charge, honey.' she said, doing an American accent.

He tapped his bottle against her glass. 'You have some ink on your dress, by the way.'

'Oh no, we really should retire this game,' she said, pulling out a bottle of hand sanitiser from her bag to erase some of the ink that had smudged onto her skin. 'I always end up with more ink on me than you.'

'How is it on your elbow?' he asked, wiping at it with a napkin, leaning even closer to her. 'You always smell of coconut.' He sighed as she turned to face him.

'Probably because I wash my hair three or four times a day.' She smiled, only then realising that his arm was running behind her, that they were sitting so close, and her insides suddenly filled with swimming fish as she watched the scar on his lip.

'Is your arm hurting?' he asked.

She shook her head; she had forgotten how to speak.

'Sorry,' he said with a jolt, moving away from her.

'Sorry for what?'

For being completely obsessed with my best friend's girlfriend, he thought, fighting the urge to kiss her again. Catherine shot a look past him and he turned to see Stef walking towards their table, holding drinks. As always, Val wasn't far behind, and Beni wondered how long they had been at the bar for, and what they had seen.

They both slid out of the booth to greet their friends; Stef kissed Catherine and ran his hands down her body.

'Wow, steady on, tiger,' she said, not smiling.

'Sorry, I've just missed you! I haven't seen you for over a week,' he whispered in her ear. 'Beni, do you mind if I sit next to Lish?'

'Of course not.' Beni grunted his approval, feeling jealousy wrap its fingers around his vocal cords as he moved to sit on the other side of the booth.

'What happened to your arm?' asked Stefano when they were all sitting down.

'Oh, nothing. Someone fell over and grabbed my arm to stop their fall,' she said, not looking at Beni.

'How was your trip to the beach with Gloria last week?' Valentina fired this question at Beni without even so much as a hello first.

'It was great, why do you ask?' he replied.

'Just taking an interest. Where's Gloria tonight, Catherine?'

'She's staying with her friend.'

'That's good that she has a friend, she must get tired of all the babysitters,' Val sniped, sipping some water from a bottle.

'How did your trip to the dentist go, Val?' asked Catherine, causing Beni to choke a little on his beer.

'Fine, why do you ask?' Val gave Stef a betrayed look.

'Just taking an interest,' said Catherine with a fake smile.

'So, you had fun at the beach?' said Stefano, kissing Catherine's neck, probably as a silent way of telling her to stop poking the pit bull.

'Gloria loved it; we spent the whole day there. She buried us both in the sand, which she found absolutely hilarious and can't wait to do again.' Catherine smiled at the memory of Gloria rolling around laughing as the grown-ups tried to wiggle themselves free.

'Yeah, we could take you next time, Val, and let her bury you,' said Beni, no hint of a smile at all.

'Maybe it's silly but I just can't get over how much pelicans look like pterodactyls when they swoop down,' said Catherine, trying to defuse the tension. 'Every single time I see them, I imagine Richard Attenborough's welcome greeting in *Jurassic Park*!' She laughed, and then proceeded to hum the theme tune, and mimic Sam Neill's timeless awed expression. Val brought this out of her, just like the bullies had done in school. She was desperate to crack her dispassionate façade, but while the Neill impression made the boys laugh at least, Valentina just rolled her eyes. They were firmly back in the acquaintance zone, it seemed.

'Puedo tomar una trago, por favor?' Catherine asked the passing waitress. 'Does anyone else want another drink?'

'I'll have another beer,' said Beni.

'Me too,' Stefano said to the waitress.

'Pelicans are actually related to prehistoric birds, so Lish hasn't completely lost her mind,' Beni said.

'Imagine living in a time where reptiles were flying through the sky?' said Lish.

'And we've lost her.' Stef laughed.

'Shut up, I'm just saying, imagine chilling on your sunlounger and a big lizard with wings comes along and snatches you up and no one is the least bit surprised, they just

133

put another line on the tally chart for hotel guests snatched that week and carry on folding towels!'

Stefano kissed her cheek. 'They would notice you'd been snatched; everyone knows you at the hotel.'

'I saw that they're building some big houses up past the rocks while we were at the beach; I think I might go and check them out.' Catherine shrugged.

'Those big ones?' asked Beni, frowning.

'Yeah, the big ones, why? What's wrong with that?'

'They were like, full-on mansions. I didn't realise we were friends with J.Lo.'

Catherine laughed. 'J.Lo? Why J.Lo?'

'She was the first rich person that popped into my head.'

'It can't hurt to look. They'll have amazing views being up on the rocks like that, and if I don't find any of Gloria's family soon it makes sense for us to put down some roots ready for the adoption. We can't live in that small room forever and it would be a good investment.'

'Some of us mere mortals have no choice but to live in small places,' said Val.

'Sorry,' said Catherine, reaching for Val's hand, the wine starting to work its social magic. 'I just don't want to move too far from the hotel, Gloria feels comfortable there. And think of the parties we could have in one of those big houses.'

Val nodded, and slithered her hand away just as the waitress delivered more drinks.

'I thought you were going to go back to England if you adopted Gloria officially?' Beni said.

'Well, my company is doing well over there thanks to my brother running things. My house has been rented out. I have more keeping me here right now, to be honest,' she said, glancing at Beni.

'Like me!' yelled Stefano putting his arm around her. 'Don't go back to England, I would miss you more than oxygen, my polpetta!'

'It takes about three minutes to die without oxygen, Stefano. You would really miss me for three whole minutes?'

To Catherine's shock, Val let out a small laugh, probably overjoyed at the thought of Catherine leaving the country, or maybe imagining her choked-out and oxygenless, but still, she would take it. The ice queen was melting!

'What do your family think to you staying here for so long? It's been seven months now hasn't it?' asked Valentina.

'I think they're just happy that I'm happy. My brother's been really supportive.'

'Doesn't he want to visit you?' asked Val.

'Rob's never really been interested in travelling, but if I get one of those big houses he'll have to visit! What about you and Stef, weren't your families a bit bemused when you came out here?'

'Well, mine think I live in LA,' said Stef.

Distracted by some glasses shattering loudly, Catherine looked over her shoulder to see the waitress being handed a dust pan and brush by a smiling barman, 'Wait, did you just say they think you live in LA?' asked Catherine, turning to face Stefano.

He nodded and looked at Val with a smile, 'We moved to LA first to become big movie stars, but all we did was get high and we ran out of money pretty fast.'

'Did you do some modelling there? Val, you're beautiful, surely you could have modelled?' said Catherine honestly.

Valentina gave her a quarter of a smile in thanks for her compliment, but then Stef kissed Catherine and told her that she could be a model too, and the smile was wiped from Val's lips in an instant.

'Stef actually did some modelling,' said Beni, smiling a little. 'Why don't you show Lish that poster you did?'

'Oh God, I don't want you to see that!' said Stef, trying to find it on his phone, and placing a hand over his eyes, apparently in embarrassment, once he did.

It was a poster for a Vegas casino; he was clean shaven and his hair was gelled flat, unrecognisable but for his beaming grin, and pictured throwing a dice while a leggy blonde clung to his arm.

'Oh, come on, that's not embarrassing, although I do think you look much better with a beard,' said Catherine, stroking his face.

'Stop talking about my beard, Beni will cry – he can't grow one!' said Stefano in a loud whisper.

'Leave him alone, he has stubble,' said Catherine, looking at the angles of Beni's square chin.

'This is as far is it goes, I can't go full Viking like Stef,' said Beni, pulling a sad face with smiling eyes.

'Beni, you don't need one. You're a Jean-Paul Belmondo type, a Marlon Brando. Neither of them had beards and they were sex symbols in their time.'

'So, I was sexy in the 1950s and Stef is sexy right now? Is that what you're saying?' asked Beni.

'Oh, no! I was trying to defend your lack of beard, and now I don't know what to say,' said Catherine with a grimace. 'You're both sexy now, and Stef would have been a pariah with this beard back in the 1950s. Let's just be glad that we live in a time when it's socially acceptable to be either a Marlon ... or a Manson!'

'Manson?' Stef raised his eyebrows. 'As in, Charles?'

'He had a beard, didn't he?' asked Catherine.

'She was just being alliterative with Marlon. See, this is why I'm rationing your alliterations,' said Beni.

'What's "alliterative"?' asked Stefano.

'Where you say things that begin with the same letter or sound, like white wine or brown bear,' said Catherine.

'Belmondo or Barry Gibb?' The suggestion came from Val.

This time Catherine laughed, shocking herself. Were they getting along again? What had that dentist done to Val? She was up and down like a yo-yo.

'Barry Gibb – good one!'

'Who is Jean-Paul?' asked Beni, sipping his beer.

'When I studied film, at every level they make you watch *Breathless* about five times because it was one of the first films to start using the shots and cuts and devices used in modern cinema; it's kind of a big deal. The lead actor was Belmondo. He was odd but very sexy, the intense bad boy type that steals cars and shoots at cops.'

'Yes! I see how you made the connection between Beni and that guy then.' Stefano laughed. 'Beni is always on the run from the law, a real bad guy.'

'It was really just the lack of facial hair that I was comparing. I like a beard, don't get me wrong, but not every face needs one.' Catherine blushed, not daring to look Beni in the eye. 'I love his name too, Bel-mondo – "beautiful world" in Italian?'

'Was he Italian?' asked Val.

'No, he's French, but no one's perfect.' Catherine shrugged, and smiled. 'So, when did you leave Italy?' she asked.

'We did some travelling first before going to LA,' said Stefano. 'We actually went to England during that time.'

'I hated it, so crowded, and everyone was so uptight,' said Val.

'Let me guess, you went to London? Well, that's like me saying, "Oh yeah, I've been to Italy and it was shit" after a few nights in Milan – equally, if not more shit than London, and in no way Italy at its best, right?'

'I really liked London,' said Stef.

Val snorted. 'British people are so stressed; they're always rushing around and saying sorry for no reason.'

'Is that a joke between you then? That we're like that?' said Catherine, looking at Val and Stefano.

'No, no! She's just joking,' said Stef.

'You are stressed and British, aren't you?' Val shrugged.

Catherine sighed. 'I'm British, but first and foremost I'm English.'

'Fine. English people are stressed-out, unfeeling robots. Is that better?'

'I'm proud to be English. We might be stressed out and emotionally constipated a lot of the time, but blast a nineties classic on a night out and even the most hardcore metalhead or uptight business mogul will sling an arm around the stranger next to them and sing their heart out! That's England – sentimental, always apologising, tries its best and openly, effervescently emotional only when drunk. England. And it's bloody brilliant. Right, Beni?'

'Yeah,' he said, almost actually smiling at her.

'I think I might be homesick.' Catherine gave her wine glass an embarrassed grin.

'British people are arrogant too, they always think they can barge in and fix things,' said Val, with one of her disinterested eyes rolls.

'Maybe so, but most of the time we're just trying to help.'

'So that's why your Empire spread all over the globe taking what wasn't theirs? To help people?'

'You're from Rome!' said Catherine, exasperated. 'How can you sling mud at us for being like that? The Romans even invaded England. Are you high right now?'

'All I know is what I saw in England, and you. You're very

uptight, Catherine, and look how you bulldozed in and took Gloria.'

'Stef, are you going to say something?' said Beni, giving Val an evil stare.

'I'm uptight and arrogant? That's funny coming from you,' said Catherine.

'OK, let's change the subject,' said Stef, clearly feeling awkward.

'You know what, you're about to be the most uptight person in this bar, Valentina.' Catherine nodded, and finished her drink. 'How many people do you think are English in here?' she asked, standing up and looking around the bar, which was much busier than when they had arrived.

Val shrugged. 'I don't know.'

'Let's find out, shall we?' said Catherine, with wild eyes.

'Lish, what are you doing?' asked Stefano.

'What are you going to do?' said Val, finally showing some emotion with a tiny frown, looking at Catherine like she imagined she was about to go berserk.

'Get ready to make a swift exit in case this goes south,' Catherine whispered to Beni across the table with a smirk, before walking over to the DJ in the corner of the heaving bar. She slipped him some ten-dollar bills to let her speak on the microphone and play a song and, after turning and pressing a few buttons, the DJ stepped to one side.

'Hello!' Catherine's voice boomed, and everyone in the bar stopped what they were doing to look at her wobbling on a chair with a microphone in her hand.

Beni raised his hand to his face, dreading what she was about to say, wondering how many men he was going to have to punch to get her out of there.

'I'm conducting an experiment. Out of interest, can you give me a cheer if you are from England or Britain?'

Over half of the room cheered, and Catherine smiled defiantly at her group of friends across the room.

'My friends are from the Continent, and they think we are all posh, stressed-out robots. I want them to see what happens when this next song comes on. Don't let me down, OK?'

An Oasis song began to play and, sure enough, everyone in the bar started to sing. Catherine looked around thinking it was miraculous, even the bar staff were arm in arm, singing away. She walked over to a laughing Stef and a sulking Val and gave them an "I told you so, bitches" look, realising that she probably was arrogant after all, after a few wines, at least.

'What's that on your arm?' asked Stefano, tilting his head and holding Catherine's wrist in the air once the song was over and normal chit-chat had resumed.

'Can you still see it?' Beni laughed. 'I can't believe it worked.'

Along Catherine's forearm in large letters was the word 'beautiful' in Italian, the skin on the letters was white as snow and all around it was vaguely tanned, making the word stand out once you noticed it.

'I cut out the letters and made a stencil, stuck it to her arm, and then the rest of her arm we covered in factor thirty for safety. She told me she never tans so I wanted to prove that she could.'

'You wrote bella on my girlfriend's arm? With a stencil you made?'

'Well, what would you have written?' said Beni, his jaw tensed.

∾

They moved on to another bar where they bumped into some more friends, including Anton, and then went on to a club, and after many, many, drinks, they were hitting the dance floor hard.

Catherine could feel Stefano's hands all over her body as they jumped around and danced all night, his kisses tasting sweet thanks to the shots that Anton kept bringing to them.

Beni was sitting down watching Catherine dance; she was swinging her hair around like Janis Joplin, bouncing on the balls of her feet in time to the music, mouthing all of the words to everything from Metallica to Muse, and all the while, Stefano was running his hands all over her. It made Beni feel sick.

At around three o'clock in the morning, Catherine noticed Beni sitting alone at a table and danced over to him.

'Are you excited for our trip to the Hammock Hideout?' she shouted to Beni over the booming music and the sound of her own tinnitus.

'YES!' he shouted back, making fun of her.

Catherine giggled and corrected her volume. 'Come and dance with us?' She took his hands in hers and attempted to pull him onto the dance floor.

Beni shook his head and stayed firmly anchored to his chair.

'Don't you like dancing with me?' she asked.

'I don't want to hurt my leg again.'

'Oh, of course, I'm so sorry for not asking sooner! How is it?'

'It's a lot better now.' He was obviously lying – if she was sober she might have noticed.

'I'm glad it's better!' she yelled, continuing to wiggle to the music on the spot, holding his hands.

'Come and sit down for a minute, you're going to be knackered tomorrow.' He yanked her hands like a magician pulling a tablecloth from under a load of dishes, and she landed on his lap in a heap.

Their faces were close together and Catherine found it more difficult than ever not to lean in and kiss the tiny scar on his lip.

Don't kiss her, he told himself half-heartedly, the remnants of his willpower dissipating rapidly as he enjoyed the weight of her body in his lap.

'I'm tired,' she announced, slumping onto the seat next to his and resting her head on his shoulder. 'Thanks for making me sit down, Bel-mon-do.'

'It's OK, light-weight-Lish. You've had a busy night. What you did in that bar earlier was crazy.'

'It was either that or physically attack Val for being such a cow.'

'Stef should have said something to her; so should I, I'm sorry.'

'I feel like I dealt with it.' She laughed. 'But I'll be cringing tomorrow. Why am I such an embarrassing drunk!'

'What would I do without you around causing chaos, eh? You make things much more interesting than they used to be.'

'Me?' she asked, pointing at herself, shocked.

'Yeah, you. Promise you'll never stop drawing on me?' he whispered into her hair.

'I promise,' she whispered back, dragging a finger lightly over the words scrawled on his hand.

'What's this! Lish, why have you stopped dancing?' shouted Anton, bopping over to them, flicking his legs and head in time to Fall Out Boy's version of 'Beat It'.

'I'm tired, Anton. You are the lord of dance, I concede the title.' She laughed, bowing down to him from her seat. 'I think that beautiful boy over there might appreciate your flicky heels more than us right now,' she shouted, and not-so-subtly pointed out the obviously interested party on the other side of the room.

Anton winked at them and shimmied away.

'I think I'm drunk,' slurred Catherine, laying her head back on Beni's shoulder.

They stayed like that for a while, watching the others dancing like loons. Eventually, he went to help her up, intending to put her in a taxi home, alone.

'Why didn't you tell them how your arm really got hurt?'

'I don't know. Habit?' She shrugged.

'Habit? What do you mean?' he asked, but Stefano came swooping over before she could answer.

She smiled as Stef whispered in her ear, and after pecking Beni on the cheek and saying goodbye, she was gone.

The Smoke

Catherine and Stefano stumbled out onto the pavement where a cluster of chatting smokers lined the kerb. The street was filled with bars and clubs, and people staggered, swayed, danced and skipped in groups from venue to venue, singing and laughing with their arms around each other, having the time of their lives. Music pumped loudly out of each club on the strip, and to compete with the hum of the base tones, many conversations were being held at a much higher volume than usual.

Catherine leant herself against a brick wall and observed the deafening night-time antics like a zoologist studying animals from the safety of a tree branch. She turned to watch Stefano, who was smoking, and standing a few feet away so as not to get the smoke on her hair and clothes. Smoking was smelly, unhealthy and disgusting, but for some reason seeing a man smoke was still sexy for Catherine, especially when he did it. At a distance, anyway.

Once he had flicked his cigarette butt onto the tarmac, Stef walked over to her, put his hands on her waist and kissed her. She put her arms around his neck and pulled him close; she could still taste the sweet alcohol, now mixed with the bitter caramel flavour of tobacco on his tongue. His hands held on to her tightly and she was glad to have him propping her up – with her eyes closed, gravity had become watery.

He sighed as they paused a moment. 'I love kissing you. You're like strawberry ice cream,' he said, smiling one of his big grins and running his fingers along her arms.

'You're like pistachio and coffee ice cream then.' She smiled, tiptoeing to peck him once more on the lips.

'What about Beni? What ice cream is he?' he asked, taking a step back from her, the smile sliding from his face.

'What? Why are you thinking about Beni?' she said, shocked, but thoughts of Beni as chocolate-chip ice cream filled her foggy brain and her insides tingled.

'Do you like him?' he asked.

'Where is this coming from?'

'You said he was sexy earlier. You spend a lot of time with him, more than with me, and I've seen the way you look at him. You even have a message from him on your arm right now telling you that you're beautiful, for God's sake.'

'Are you jealous?' she said, standing close to him again, sliding her hand down his chest.

'Kind of. I know me and you have our own thing, don't we. I'm not saying you're mine. I'm just asking how you feel?' He shrugged.

'Well, how do you feel about Val?' she asked, reaching her fingers beneath his T-shirt and holding his gaze, feeling his muscles tense.

Neither of them said anything for a long time. Catherine continued to caress the skin of his stomach and he stroked the small of her back.

'She doesn't want to be with me,' he said eventually, kissing Catherine's neck.

'You must be blind to actually think that. She never leaves your side!'

'Does that make you jealous?' he asked.

'Sometimes. It makes me wonder if I'm in the way.' She arched her neck as he continued to kiss it.

'That's how I feel about you and Beni.'

'There's nothing between me and Beni.'

'We both know that isn't true,' he said, running his fingers along the message on her arm, then across and around her upper body. 'You must think he's good-looking, other women certainly do. I've lost count of the number of women I've seen him with over the years.'

'He's your best friend. He's a player. I don't want to lose what we have just to be a notch on his bedpost, and anyway, nothing will ever happen because he loves you,' Catherine said. 'He doesn't want me, I promise.'

'He would be mad not to want you,' said Stef, breathing more heavily as they pawed at each other. 'I want you every time I see you.'

'Sex is sex and love is love, and not everyone is lucky enough to have both,' she said, pulling away from him. 'You should talk to Val. If you want to be with her then you should be.'

'Did he hurt your arm?' he asked, holding her shoulders lightly and looking at the bruises.

'What? No, of course he didn't. Some guy grabbed me and wouldn't let me go. Stef, Beni loves you, he wouldn't do anything to upset you.'

'He was always so down about things but he seems different now, since he met you. I want him to be happy. If you like him, you should see how he feels about you?'

'He doesn't feel anything about me.'

'*You* must be blind if you think that.'

'You would be OK with it, would you? Give us your bless-ing?' said Catherine, not looking him in the eye.

'Well, we wouldn't hang out any more, we wouldn't be friends. But I wouldn't kill him or anything.'

'I don't want to lose you and neither does he. He told me he doesn't want a girlfriend, that he will never have feelings for anyone longer than a night. So, nothing will happen. End of. But if you want to make things work with Val, then you should. Don't let me get in the way.'

He sighed loudly and turned away from her. 'It's compli-cated, you wouldn't understand.'

'Try to explain it to me?' she said, wrapping her arms around him and leaning her face into his back, feeling like she could fall asleep on him, tranquilised by the alcohol.

'Me and Val were together once. I thought we were in love, it was all going great. Then suddenly she decided we had to break up. I was heartbroken and I left, but she followed me.' He turned around. 'Ever since then it's like she wants to be near me but not with me, like she just doesn't find me attractive any more or something. She wants me around, but not the sex.'

'That's not possible,' said Catherine, wishing that he was still kissing her.

'I don't understand what changed, so I don't expect you to,' he said, shaking his head.

'Maybe one day she'll change her mind again. The way she looks at you, the hateful way she looks at me ... it's obvious she wants you for herself.'

'It was her idea for me to date someone else.'

'It was?' said Catherine, frowning.

'She suggested it years ago. But I didn't even consider it until I saw you.'

'You haven't dated anyone else? Just me and her?' Catherine shook her head slowly in disbelief and took a few small steps back towards the wall, pulling him with her by the hand. 'Kiss me,' she said, looking up at him and biting her lip.

He didn't move. The lights from the club danced across his face and his blue eyes sparkled beneath a tiny frown.

'Kiss me,' she repeated, reaching her hand beneath his T-shirt again and pulling at the waistband of his trousers.

He just looked at her, defiantly.

'What do you want me to say?'

'Tell me to stop seeing her. Tell me to choose between you and her, that's what most girls would do.'

'What?' Catherine laughed in surprise.

'Tell me to choose you,' he said, his heart beating fast beneath her hand.

'What would that achieve? She's your best friend. You would miss her, wouldn't you? You love her, don't you?'

'I want to love you.'

'Why, because it's easier? Because I let you touch me, kiss me, fuck me and she won't?'

'I'm sorry,' he said.

She shrugged. 'We can't choose who we love.'

'Why does it have to be so difficult?'

'Talk to her, maybe it's not as difficult as it seems.'

'I've been in love with her since I was sixteen. Believe me, I've tried everything, we've talked and talked, she just won't even consider me any more, she doesn't want me. And I'm done trying. You know I have feelings for you, don't you?'

'You can't have sex like we do and not feel anything. I know you like me, and I like you.'

'Maybe it could be more if we would just let it?'

'Maybe, but if you open the door to me, you close the door to her.'

'I need to close the door,' he said, running a hand nervously across his blonde beard as tears filled his eyes.

149

'Stef, don't be upset,' said Catherine, sobering up slightly and wrapping her arms around him.

'I'm so drunk.' He laughed into her hair. 'I'm not making any sense, am I?'

'This is all hard to make sense of,' said Catherine, placing her hands on either side of his face and looking up into his weary wet eyes. 'If it hurts you to have her around then you need to talk to her, ask her to move on?'

'She will be all alone without me.'

'She would meet someone new eventually.'

'I guess.'

'But that's too hard for you to deal with, isn't it? That's an idea you can't stand either?'

'Maybe I need to get away from here. I should leave and go somewhere she can't find me.'

'That's one option.' Catherine smiled, but her nod was hesitant.

'Would you miss me?' he asked, his smile starting to return.

'Like oxygen. For three whole minutes.'

'So, we're sticking with passionately not in love, then are we?' asked Stefano, putting his hand on her cheek.

'I think that's for the best, don't you?'

'For now, I think so, but don't be jealous of Val. There's nothing there any more.'

'Don't be jealous of Beni.'

'I'll do my best,' he said, smiling, holding her waist again. 'Even when I see the ink smudges on your clothes.'

'Will you please just kiss me?' she said, looking into his eyes, and this time he obeyed.

'Let's go to your place,' said Catherine, taking him by the hand.

The Brother

'Ayup,' said Catherine's brother as his image appeared on her computer screen. He was at work and was wearing his shirt and tie. His red hair and beard looked neat and the office appeared to be quite tidy in the background, which was all a relief as she had been imagining him and the office in squalor.

'Hello,' said Catherine. 'Gloria, Robert is here, come and say hello,' she shouted in Spanish. 'She's just out on the balcony with her new binoculars.' Catherine smiled.

'Letting her play alone on the balcony? You are the best mum ever,' said Robert.

'Shut it, I never let anything happen to you, did I? Mum was far more neglectful of us. Gloria! Come on!'

'Talking of mum, she asked after you the other day.'

'I hope you didn't tell her anything,' said Catherine, her smile disappearing.

'Of course not, she still doesn't even know that you're in Mexico. She just assumes you've become even better at avoiding her.'

'I've been here nearly eight months, Robbie. It's laughable

that I can be living in another country and my mum hasn't even noticed.'

'Don't you miss her even a little bit?' he asked.

'I've missed my sadistic dentist more than I've missed the woman who accused me of killing my husband!'

'That was a long time ago,' Robert said, folding his hands on the desk in front of him, looking awkward.

'Robbie, I love you. I don't want to argue, please let's just forget about her. How are you doing?'

'I'm really good.'

'You look good, have you lost weight?'

'Yes, I have. You look thinner too, are you doing OK?' he asked, frowning.

'Oh, I'm fine. It's all fruit and booze out here, that's all.'

'You haven't been taking your medication for a while now though? Do you want me to try and post it to you?'

'No, customs for meds are really strict here, it would be a waste of time. If I need to, I'll go and see a doctor. I'm OK, don't worry.'

'How's your romance going with the Italian?'

'Stef's good.'

'I meant the other one,' he said, raising his eyebrows.

'Shut up.'

'You always have much more to say about Beni than you do Stefano.'

'Hola, Robert!' shouted Gloria, running into the room and putting her mouth right next to the computer screen.

'Come here, sit on my knee for a second. You see that man there? That's my brother, Rob. You usually speak to him on the phone, but now I have this computer we can see him too. Isn't that cool?' said Catherine in Spanish, hugging Gloria around the waist as she sat on her knee.

'That's him?' asked Gloria, prodding the screen with a small finger, then looking at Catherine for reassurance.

'Yeah, that's him. Wave at him,' Catherine said, waving too.

'Hi, Gloria!' Robert said, waving back. 'Where are your binoculars?'

Catherine translated his question and Gloria grinned, holding them in the air for Robert to see.

'They look great!' he said, curling his hands to form binoculars of his own.

'His hair is orange,' whispered Gloria to Catherine.

'It is.'

'I like it,' she said, touching the screen again where his head was bobbing around.

Catherine smiled. 'She's saying she likes your hair.'

'Gracias, Gloria! You've just erased many haunting memories from my school days by saying that.'

'He says he likes your hair too,' said Catherine in Spanish.

'That's not what he said!'

'Oh, didn't he? What did he say then?'

'Nope, he said the word "school".'

'You are getting too clever for me to lie to.' Catherine smiled. 'Can you say something in English to Robbie?'

'Hello, Robbie, I am Gloria. I am six years old.'

'Hello, Gloria, how are you?'

'I'm very well thank you, how are you?'

'I'm very well too.'

'You are so clever!' said Catherine, squeezing the child close. 'Go and look for birds, and don't climb on the balcony or the furniture out there, OK? You could fall.'

'OK, I'll be careful,' said Gloria, waving at Robert again as she slid from Catherine's knee.

'She's learning so fast. I still translate most things; I don't want her to feel excluded from conversations. She got the binoculars today, she thinks she's a spy.'

'She's great, Catherine,' said Robert.

'So, how're things with work?' she asked as she watched Gloria on the balcony for a couple of seconds.

'Everything's going great; I'm loving being the boss,' he said, stretching his arms behind his head in a macho way, puffing out his chest, and smiling.

'I knew you would be,' she said, rolling her eyes.

'Did you get the email I sent over last night?'

'Yeah, and I think they all look great. If they've had their surveys done and Mick's happy that there are no red flags, then put an offer in as soon as possible.'

'I suppose I'll have to go and see Ronnie Ross for a signature,' he said, scowling.

'Yes, he has to sign any documents for me by proxy, there's no getting round that.'

'You put me in charge but gave all the power to your lawyer.'

'Don't be moody. I had visions of me coming home and finding you'd signed everything over to mum.'

'I would never do that.'

'It's not because I don't trust you. It's just that you sit on the fence, you always have. I love you but you don't stand up to either of us.'

'OK. Well, Ronnie isn't so bad I guess, and it means I can't be completely blamed for things if they go tits-up.'

'That's the spirit! I'll call Ron tomorrow and get him to meet you. If there's anything else that I can be doing from here, just let me know. I can sort emails and things if you're struggling?'

'I'm not struggling.'

'OK, OK, I know you can handle it. I just feel bad leaving it all to you. Now I've got this laptop I can attend some meetings virtually; I'd like to do that.'

'You could have done all this on your phone you know, you technophobe. And don't feel bad; you worked your arse off to get us this far, you hired me and taught me everything, and you made me rich. I'm happy to do this for as long as you want to be out there, and I would never ever let mum take this from you. You earned it.'

'You know how bitter she is about the success we've had; I just worry what she might be capable of.'

'I get it, believe me. Just ... please don't stress. I'm looking after everything, I swear.'

'I know. I'm proud of you, you've really stepped up. You're only twenty years old and you've handled the responsibility so well. I'm grateful, Robbie. So, things are great then, you don't miss me at all?'

'Do I miss you bossing me around? No! Do I miss our office film trivia and accent competitions? Of course.' He smiled.

'I miss you too. Do you know if Sarah's had her baby yet?'

'She's your friend, why are you asking me?'

'She isn't talking to me; I think she's still pissed that I'm missing her wedding. Find out when she has it, won't you, and send a big, fat, expensive gift?'

'She'll get over it. You couldn't abandon Gloria to go to what will definitely be one of many weddings that Sarah has.'

'You're so mean. Please send a gift.'

'I'll do it, don't worry. You're so good with Gloria, I couldn't imagine it before I just saw you together.'

'You couldn't imagine me being nice to a child? Thanks, baby brother.'

'You know what I mean, it's hard to imagine your new life over there. Yeah, I've seen photos and we talk on the phone, but it's different actually seeing you with her.'

'I'm getting better at this parenting thing as I go along, and thank God I've had friends here to help me. I'd have been lost without them, especially Maria.'

'She owns the bar, right?'

'That's right.'

'And the private detective is still out looking for Gloria's family?'

'Yep, still looking. Are you dating anyone?'

'Why do you ask that?'

'Why so defensive?' she said, and smirked.

'I'm not defensive. I am seeing someone actually, but it's early days,' he said, blushing slightly.

'Oh, how exciting! What's she like?'

'She's nice. My age, an estate agent.'

'Why don't you come out here to visit and bring her?'

'Nothing says "I'm a psycho" like dragging the girl I've been dating for a couple of weeks off to Mexico to meet my sister!'

'Well, in a month or so then?'

'Who would run things while I'm gone?'

'Mick could handle things for a couple of weeks?' said Catherine.

'Mick? The plumber?'

'He's also our handyman and surveyor! And anyway, plumbers are very clever – they can fix submarines if those army adverts are anything to go by.'

'He is clever, but I don't think he knows what an Excel spreadsheet even is. He types text messages with one finger, and a few weeks ago he told me that everything on his phone had been translating into Portuguese for months and he didn't know how to fix it. He'd just accepted that his phone was now Portuguese,' Robert said, shaking his head and smiling.

'Oh, dear.' Catherine laughed nervously, hoping that would never happen to her.

'How's the singing going? I can't believe you convinced them to let you sing Eurovision songs. You're living the dream.'

'You should come and visit so you can see it for yourself!'

'No, I'm all right just imagining it, thanks.' He laughed.

'So, there was something I wanted to talk to you about,' said Catherine.

'Go on ...'

'How do you feel about us adding a holiday home to our portfolio?'

The Hammock

'Buenas tardes, beautiful,' Stefano said, getting out of the driver's seat and kissing her beside the car in front of the hotel lobby.

'You're going in the middle, Lish,' said Anton, who had also got out of the car to let her climb in.

Catherine settled in, between Anton and Beni with her legs parted slightly around her bag on the floor. She was wearing a red shirt dress, tied in the middle, and the boys were wearing shorts and T-shirts. Valentina was in the front passenger seat, looking annoyingly glamourous in a thin white dress with an orange bikini visible beneath it, and with freshly shortened hair that showed off her bejewelled ears and slender neck.

Maria was staying at the hotel for the night, having a minibreak from the bar and leaving her sister in charge so that she could relax by the pool with the girls and enjoy the hotel buffet. With Gloria safe and happy, Catherine started to relax as they began their journey.

'Gloria has painted something for each of you,' said Catherine, suddenly remembering and handing out the wrinkled pieces of paper.

'I look like a surfing yeti,' said Stef as Catherine held his in front of him while he drove slowly through the hotel grounds. 'Is it time I shaved this beard?' He laughed.

'Aww that is so sweet,' said Anton as he looked at the painting of himself and Gloria, blue water swirling around them.

'I think that's you in the wave pool with her,' said Catherine, smiling at him. 'Val, she was most eager to impress you because she knows you paint too.'

'I love it,' said Val quietly, running her fingers over the painting of herself in a black dress. 'She's really good, Catherine, I wouldn't have thought a six-year-old painted this.'

Catherine glanced at Beni's painting and smiled awkwardly when her eyes met his. His was a drawing of him and Catherine holding hands on the beach, with Gloria building a sandcastle nearby.

It was an hour's drive to where they were going – to an overnight experience with unlimited drinks, a campfire, and hammocks as beds – and Stef's old car was proving to be too small for all five of them and their bags.

'Am I squishing you?' asked Catherine.

'No, it's fine,' Beni said.

'You're squashing me!' said Anton, pushing her even closer to Beni.

Catherine laughed and pushed him back.

'Road trip!' shouted Stefano from the front, turning up the radio.

Valentina was just staring out of the window, silently mouthing the words to the Sum 41 song that was playing, and seemed even more distant than usual.

'Just sit forward a second?' Catherine said to Beni, then she linked her arm with his and put her shoulder behind him slightly so that they could all fit more comfortably, at the cost of her and Beni being more intimately positioned. 'Is this OK?' she asked, her hand on his arm.

'It's fine,' he said, looking at her parted knees for a second.

'Anton, do you have more room now?' Catherine asked, no longer able to look at him as she was curved towards Beni.

'Much better,' he said loudly over the blasting music.

'You're warm,' Catherine said to Beni.

'Sorry,' he said, his heart beating quickly, watching Stefano's eyes in the rear-view mirror.

'No, it's good. It's cold in here with the air con on,' she said, absentmindedly running her fingers up and down his arm, trying to steal his heat.

They sat like that for twenty minutes and he thought she might have fallen asleep until she abruptly wriggled free.

Being careful to not wake Anton who was asleep against the window, she leaned forward to whisper into Stef's ear, and then turned to smile mischievously at Beni.

'What's going on?' he said.

'The air con is freezing my ...' she indicated her lap with her eyes and started laughing. She took his hand and placed it at the top of her thigh. 'I've just asked him to turn it down. Feel how cold I am. I'm like a frozen chicken.'

'You're cold,' he managed to say, feeling her smooth, ice-cold skin, his blood rushing from his brain to another part of his body.

'Leave your hand there a second? Warm me up?' she whispered, hooking his arm again and sinking back into position.

The heat from his hand soon warmed her but she didn't ask him to take it away, instead she closed her eyes and wondered what it would be like if his hand were to reach underneath her dress. They each remained quiet for a long time, both imagining the same scenario and neither of them realising it.

'I watched the rugby last night so I could talk to you about it,' she said eventually.

'But you hate rugby.'

'I liked all the dramatic Madonna-microphone referee bits; I didn't realise they were so strict. But to be honest, I didn't understand a minute of it, so I don't exactly have much to say.'

'What don't you understand?'

'Who does what, who goes where, what the point of any of it is ... I got bored and started organising my earring collection into colour order. That was fun.'

Beni smiled and turned over her forearm to face the roof, drawing lines and dots on her soft skin as he tried to explain it all.

'That tickles,' she said as he explained what a try, scrum and fly half all were, but she wasn't really listening, too busy focusing on his touch.

'Do you understand it now?' he asked after their lesson.

'Umm, not really. You explained it well but I just switch off with that kind of thing. I speak three extra languages but try and teach me even to play Monopoly and my brain flatlines.' She laughed.

'Like me with Eurovision! So ... your bikini is red today then?'

'How did you guess? Can you see it?'

'Your toes are painted red; it's one of your golden rules, isn't it?'

She smiled. 'You remembered that?'

'I hoped one day I might see you in a red bikini with blue toe polish so I could call you out on it, but you haven't broken the rule yet,' he said.

'Sorry to disappoint.'

You never disappoint, he thought with a sigh.

She wanted to pull his hand a fraction closer to her, part her legs just a millimetre more, she was flushed.

Beni kept his eyes on the rear-view mirror, wondering if Stef could see how close he and Catherine were, but he didn't glance back at them once, he didn't seem to care. He was too busy driving the car and giving side glances to Valentina, who sat sulking next to him with her legs on the dashboard.

When they got out of the car, they were greeted by an enthusiastic American called Mark who walked them from the dusty car park along a path through some trees. As they got closer to the beach, the sound of lapping waves grew louder and numbers painted in swirling white lettering began to appear on every tree in sight. Lockers were bolted to the bases of the trunks and hammocks swung from the branches, rippling in the faint breeze. As they stood beside the last row of trees, Catherine and her friends could see the beautiful beach in its entirety, with its powdery white sand and crystal-clear water beneath miles and miles of cloudless blue sky.

'These hammocks are strong; two people can share if you can't bear to be away from your partner for the night. Remember your hammock number though, or you could end up sharing with a stranger!' said Mark, causing Anton to wiggle his big eyebrows at them all.

'There are no rules here,' Mark continued, showing them the toilet and shower blocks, the bar and the firepit. 'You can smoke, drink, do what you please, but obviously be sensible, and don't wander out of this area. We have guards at each end of the beach and in the trees for your safety; there are wild animals here in Mexico and I don't want you wandering off and getting attacked by a jaguar, so please be mindful! Be kind to each other. Don't go swimming stoned off your faces in the dark, and be careful around the campfire ... it's hot!'

'How many guests have you got booked tonight?' asked Anton.

'We are expecting about thirty tonight, there should be a good atmosphere. For now, go swimming, get some lunch or drinks at the bar. Enjoy yourselves. The campfire will be lit at around 10.00 pm.'

'Thanks,' they all chorused.

'I am hammock number one,' said Catherine, walking off to find it, wanting to get away from the group for a second, away from thoughts of Beni, to let her cheeks stop burning and her heartbeat slow.

Her hammock was a few trees back from the beach and far away from the bar and toilets.

'This is nice and private,' said Stef, smiling as she shoved him for startling her.

'Until more people show up, I suppose it is. I'll be the first one to get eaten by the big cats though.' She laughed nervously. 'What number is your hammock?'

'Does it matter? Aren't we going to end up sharing?'

She looked at the piece of material hanging from the tree. 'You think we can both get in that? I don't even think I can get in on my own.'

Not entirely gracefully, they managed to sit in it together and then, as if he were reading her mind, he reached under her dress and slipped his fingers into her bikini bottoms.

'What are you doing?' she said, taking a deep breath, a shiver running through her.

He looked around as if to check no one else was coming, then kissed her neck and continued to play with her. 'You think I don't know when you're horny by now?' He laughed.

She closed her eyes and gave in to it.

The day passed quickly, more young travellers arrived and after hours of swimming and sunbathing and drinking, the sun began to set and the campfire was lit. Everyone remained in their swimwear into the night, their bikinis and shorts having dried against their bodies beneath the blazing sun. Some girls wore just their bikini and nothing else, some wore crochet coveralls and some wore shorts with their bikini tops on show. Catherine, however, wore tight denim shorts and her dress open like it was a kimono over her bikini top, the vodka and soft firelight just about giving her the confidence to do so. It was a hot night and as well as the smell of smoke, the sour stink of the mosquito spray clinging to everyone's skin clawed at the back of her throat.

In the firelight, Beni thought Catherine looked as close to perfect as any woman he had ever seen in his life. The dancing flames blushed her pale skin, making her appear as though she were glimmering, her hair was wavier than ever thanks to the salt water, and her eyes were like diamonds encircled by smudged mascara. He looked at the tiny creases in her tummy as she sat chatting to Anton, at her curves, her smile, the sand on her ankles. She had been dancing all night, the life and soul of the party. He stared at her, not caring who saw. He got up from the fireside and walked towards the trees, running his hand across his face, telling himself to snap out of it.

'She's beautiful,' said a brunette who was suddenly standing beside him.

'What?' said Beni defensively.

'The girl in the red bikini. You can't keep your eyes off her.' She smiled, swaying a little, clearly quite drunk.

Beni turned around to look at Catherine. She and Stefano

had started dancing again and his hands were running all over her bare skin.

'That's got to hurt,' said the woman.

'What do you want?' snapped Beni, starting to walk off.

'I think you're hot, I want you to kiss me,' said the girl.

'You're drunk,' he said, pushing her away gently.

'Look, I just want a drunken, meaningless kiss. Kiss me, you can imagine I'm her.'

'What's the catch?' he said, giving her a shy smile.

'No catch, but maybe you'll like it.'

He reached out for the girl's waist, pulled her towards him and their mouths collided, not unpleasantly yet there was a coldness in his chest that slithered down his arms and his spine. He felt anchored to the floor as the woman's tongue massaged his and the taste of beer and sticky lip gloss coated his lips. Her hair was still damp as he held it off her face. He pressed his eyes shut but couldn't imagine that kissing Catherine would be like that at all and he soon stopped and walked off, his eyes burning with emotion and campfire smoke, leaving the girl alone in the trees.

Catherine danced with Stefano and Anton, laughing as they each spun her around and as she stumbled, dizzy, from one to the other she saw Beni, somewhat hidden by the trees, kissing a girl, and she stopped still. It was like a gunshot had gone off right next to her ear. Everything around her seemed to go silent except for a high-pitched screaming and she wondered if it was the sound of jealousy's battle cry as it polluted her bloodstream. She gathered herself before, she hoped, anyone had noticed, and carried on dancing, laughing in appearance only as her mind spiralled.

From then on she danced and drank until she felt exhausted, eventually resting on the sand to drowsily watch the rest of the guests having fun.

'Spin-the-bottle!' someone shouted, and everyone gathered in a circle.

Catherine looked between Beni and his latest conquest, she was beautiful with brown hair running down her back, olive skin and a svelte figure. Catherine couldn't stand the idea of watching them kiss again so she staggered over to her hammock.

Catherine sat in her hammock like it was a chair and her feet dragged along the floor as it swung back and forth. She was drunk, to the point where you feel everything and nothing at the same time, so while her heart ached for a man that didn't want her, she didn't notice her bare feet and ankles being scratched by debris on the jungle floor.

'Not enjoying spin-the-bottle?' she asked as Stefano walked towards her, unsteady on his feet.

'The girl I wanted to kiss wasn't in the circle.' He smiled.

'I'm not the only girl in that circle you would have enjoyed kissing,' she said quietly.

'I'm going to try and sit next to you,' he said, looking at the hammock like a gymnast looks at a padded floor.

'OK,' she said, half-heartedly trying to shuffle up to make room for him.

After some manoeuvring, he was beside her. He lit a cigarette and she lay on his chest as they swayed back and forth in their out-of-the-way hammock.

'Do you believe in ghosts?' he said.

'Why? You haven't seen one, have you?' She looked around them, imagining faces in the trees.

'No, don't worry, but that kind of answers the question.' He laughed, exhaling smoke into the darkness.

'I always think I don't believe in them, but then sometimes I'll be scared to open my eyes in the dark for fear of seeing something, so deep down, I must believe? Do you?'

'I think so.'

'Have you ever seen one?' she asked.

'Not that I know of, but maybe we see them and they erase our memories?'

'That makes sense.'

'What's your favourite colour?'

'Stef, are you interviewing me?'

'I want to get to know you better. I know your favourite sex positions and the face you make when you orgasm like the back of my hand, but I don't know much more.'

'What face do I make?' She laughed, looking at him and poking his ribs as he impersonated her.

'It's quite similar to your impression of Sam Neill in Jurassic Park.' He grinned.

'I'm as surprised that a boy knows how to make me feel like that, as he was that dinosaurs were alive and kicking.' She giggled.

'Haven't boys made you feel like that before?'

'Sometimes. Not as consistently as you.'

'We're good together, aren't we. Let's just get married and be done with it.'

'Don't joke about that. I'm very drunk and emotional, I might just say yes.'

'It's good to know you would have to be drunk to say yes to me. I saw Beni kissing that girl. That's just what he's like.' He shrugged.

'I'm not sad because of him.'

'Then what's wrong?'

She sat up and looked him in the eye. 'Why was Val so sulky in the car?'

'I told her I wanted to spend today with you and that I would sleep in your hammock.'

'You're trying to push her away then?'

'Trying to,' he said, holding Catherine more tightly.

'You're very serious during sex. Like this,' she said frowning. 'I know you're done because you suddenly start smiling again.' She laughed.

'My favourite colour is blue,' he said, laughing too.

'Mine is turquoise.'

'What's your favourite word?'

'Hmm ... I like albóndigas.'

'Meatballs?' He smiled.

'Al–bond–eee–gas,' she said, exaggerating each syllable and looking at him with a pout. 'It's a sexy word, don't you think? What's yours?'

'I don't know, actually. Lish?'

'That's not a word!'

'I like saying it though. Lish,' he said, exaggerating the shh in his gravelly voice.

'Do you miss Italy?'

'I miss my mum a lot. Does that make me sound like a mamma's boy?'

'What do you miss about her?'

'Mainly knowing that when I'd walk into the house she would be there to listen to me, make me some food, look after me.'

'She sounds like my grandma, a proper old-fashioned mum.'

'Yeah, she is old-fashioned. She never had a job, she just looked after us all. She was always there.'

'You have sisters, don't you?' asked Catherine.

'I grew up with my mamma, three sisters, my dad and my cousin, all of us in quite a small house near Rome. It was manic but I loved it.'

'Always someone to talk to?'

'Yeah.' He smiled. 'My sisters are all so happy and friendly, but they never stop talking. And my mamma's cooking is amazing, she makes the best cheesecake for our birthdays. One year she made one for my sister Magda, who was about nine. I was eleven, and I ate a huge chunk of her cake the night before her birthday and was awake all night worrying about the fallout. But when we got up, there was no slice missing. My mamma had made a brand new cake at, like, five o'clock in the morning to cover my crime.' He laughed.

'You got away with murder then? My mum's like that with my brother.'

'Well, on my birthday that year, which is just a few weeks after Magda's, she made my cake smaller to punish me. She didn't say anything, she said it all with her eyes. I should call her soon, see how she is. What was your home like as a kid?'

'My mum was never there. She was in sales and she worked hard, so hard that sometimes I wondered if it was an excuse to be away from us. Of course, now I know she did it to keep a roof over our heads. My stepdad really did try his best but he wasn't always that nice. My mum divorced him when I was a teenager. A lot of the time it was just me and my brother in the house, which was fine, only a handful of traumatic incidents.' She laughed.

'Like what?'

'I almost always burnt his dinner; he never lets me forget that. One time, a bird got trapped in the house; we were having some work done in the bathroom and it must have flown in through the hole in the wall. I was about sixteen, so naturally woke up at about one o'clock in the afternoon in the school holidays, and as I stood on the landing stretching, trying to wake up, a crow flew past me. I started screaming and Robbie came running out of his room and then he started screaming, and we were both running around the house screaming until we spotted that the neighbour over the road was looking out of his window. We started to gesture to him like there was a serial killer keeping us hostage and to get help, and he called the police!' Catherine was laughing as she told the story, like she always did when she remembered it. 'The police showed up and helped get rid of the bird, and then they searched the house to check nothing else was going on and found Robbie in the downstairs cupboard hugging the hoover, traumatised. My mum was so mad at me.'

Stefano laughed. 'That's funny.'

'When did you last see your mum?' she said.

'About five years ago?'

'That's a long time. What's your dad like?'

'He's the opposite to my mum and sisters. He's very quiet and doesn't really know how to show his emotions, but he's a nice person. Beni reminds me of him sometimes.'

Catherine sat up and looked into his blue eyes for a long time before he put his hand at the back of her head, and kissed her softly.

'I'm glad you're mine ... even if it's just for tonight,' he whispered.

They carried on talking for hours about everything from their favourite actors, to bones they'd broken, to drugs they'd tried – which for Catherine was none. Eventually they pulled up their feet into the hammock and fell asleep in their secluded corner as the rest of the group partied.

The Hangover

‘Buenos días, Lish,’ said Beni, looking stern as he sat down next to her on the beach, his T-shirt balled up in his hand, his hair as messy as ever.

‘Hola.’

‘I checked on you this morning, there were no lizards.’

‘Why are you speaking Spanish?’ she asked, running her hands over her face a few times.

‘Because you struggle to speak it when you’re hungover and I thought it might be fun to see you try.’

‘Fun to see me struggle, more like.’

‘This place is amazing; I could stay here forever,’ he said, rolling his r’s like a pro.

Meanwhile, she hacked through her brain fog like a jungle explorer with a spoon for a machete. ‘Why did you check on me?’

‘I didn’t want you getting trapped in your hammock all day because there was a lizard nearby, but I saw Stefano was there already,’ he said, hoping his bitterness wasn’t obvious.

‘I feel like I’m dying,’ she said, lying back on the sand, not caring that it was getting in her hair.

'You had a lot to drink last night,' he said. 'I watched you dancing for a while and it was like I'd hit fast forward, you were moving so fast.'

'Oh God, was I a nightmare?'

'No, you were funny.' He lay down next to her, propping himself up on his elbows.

Catherine tried not to stare at his abs and the sand clinging to his strong arms. 'I stink of smoke,' she said, sniffing her dress, feeling disgusting.

Beni just carried on looking at the sky, which was turning a deeper shade of blue by the minute, eventually closing his eyes against the glare of the climbing sun.

'Why didn't you want to play spin-the-bottle? I saw you get up and walk off in a huff.'

'In a huff?' She laughed, cringing inwardly as she imagined herself drunkenly stomping off. 'I didn't want to play because I'm not American or fourteen!'

'Because you didn't want to see Stef kiss Val?' he said, turning to face her.

Catherine rolled onto her side, her head resting on her hand as a pillow, her elbow digging into the sand, propping her up. She thought *No, because I didn't want to see you kiss that girl again,* but she swallowed those words along with some bile.

'That game just causes trouble when couples are involved. It's the same with Never Have I Ever. You leave the game thinking great, now I know all the places you had sex before you met me!' She smiled.

'Well, spin-the-bottle actually ended pretty quickly and we started playing Never Have I Ever.'

'Oh, I am so glad I left!'

'Sometimes it's a good way to find things out about people.'

'What happened after I left? What did you find out?' she asked eagerly.

'Anton's kissed a celebrity, a lot of people have had sex on a beach – probably this one, a guy admitted to having sex in front of his dog – he said he'd never and then he drank.'

'Eww, like he forced the dog to watch or the dog just happened to be chilling in the same room?'

'I don't know,' he said, distracted by her cleavage. 'Wake him up and ask him.' He flicked his eyes towards a nearby hammock and smiled.

'Oh god, that's him?' she whispered.

'Another said, "Never have I ever had recurring sex dreams about my mum's best friend." One girl kept saying nice things like, "Never have I ever tried cherry ice cream," but then she was drinking when other people said "I've never punched anyone, I've never stolen money, I've never wanted to kill someone."'

'What about you?' asked Catherine.

'I've never had cherry ice cream,' he said, a smile in his eyes.

'No, I mean what did you say on your turn?'

'I said, "Never have I ever liked *Die Hard* three more than number one because I'm not insane."' He raised his eyebrows.

She laughed. 'You didn't say that.'

'I would have if you'd been there. No, I drank to never having been loved instead.'

'You are loved! That's so depressing, you mood hoover.'

'I meant romantically. A few people drank, it made everyone sad for a few seconds actually. Maybe that's why that guy admitted to doing it in front of his dog, to lighten the mood.'

'You could be loved in a second if you stopped whoring around and focused on just one woman.'

Beni lay his head back on the sand and covered his face with his arm; he felt like screaming. All he did was focus on one woman and she had no idea how he felt.

'What about Val and Stef?' asked Catherine.

'Val was even more moody than usual last night; she barely spoke to anyone. She drank to having kissed her best friend and to wanting to kill someone.'

'Surprise, surprise,' said Catherine under her breath, wondering exactly how Val planned to kill her. 'What about Stef?'

Beni shrugged. 'He walked off not long after you went. What would you have said?'

Catherine thought about it, but her head kept filling with things that she couldn't admit to Beni. 'Hmm, does it have to be something you've not done?'

'Depends if you want to drink or not, I guess?'

'You know, I've never kissed anyone from the south of England, they're like a different species down there.' She laughed.

'The guy with the dog would have been more than happy to help remedy that, I'm sure.'

'Ugh, he was a southerner too?' She smiled. 'Did Stef kiss anyone during spin-the-bottle?'

'I don't think so,' he said, shaking his head.

'Did you?' she asked, her heart beginning to pound.

He didn't answer, he just shrugged again.

'You're making a shrug angel in the sand,' she said, pointing to where the sand had moved. 'Here, I'm going to make a sand angel of you. Are you ready?' she asked as she lay flat on her back again and started shrugging and looking moody. 'I'm Beni, whatever,' she said, deadpan, then started to giggle.

He watched her and smiled, a real smile that she was too busy laughing to see. 'Well, this is your sand angel from last night,' he said, lying flat and kicking and thrusting in all directions imitating her dancing, sand flying everywhere.

Catherine put her hand over her mouth to stop herself from laughing too loud, she didn't want to wake everyone up.

'Let's look at them,' Beni said, standing up and offering her his hand.

They looked at their creations, a high-shouldered otherwise normal-looking human imprint and an erratic mess.

'That is us in a nutshell right there,' she said, stretching and pulling her hair up into a ponytail. 'Try not to shrug for one whole hour.' She put her hands on his shoulders lightly and looked up at him.

'OK,' he said, wondering how she still looked so perfect, even when she was hungover and tired. He brushed a speck of sand off her cheek in one sweeping Mr-Miyagi-type hand movement and looked at the ground. 'You have so many cuts on your feet,' he said, suddenly noticing them.

'Twigs and stones, no shoes and a lot of vodka.' She grimaced.

'Does it hurt?' he asked, still speaking in Spanish.

'It's my own fault that I'm hurt,' she said, looking into his eyes, thinking about how selfish she had been the previous night. She'd been happy to let Stef kiss her but felt jealous of Beni kissing someone else. He wasn't hers; she had to stop thinking about him.

'I'm going to swim, clean the wounds,' she announced.

He nodded, and looked out to sea as she unbuttoned the dress she was wearing over her bikini and tossed it to the ground.

'Is it cold?' he whispered as she stepped slowly into the water.

'Come and see,' she said over her shoulder.

They walked out until the water was at their waists and then sank their shoulders under quickly. They looked at the beach, at all the sleeping people in their hammocks and at the guards in their huts. And then they looked at each other, their heads bobbing just above the water.

'Why were you awake so early?' she asked.

'I just couldn't sleep in that hammock, you?'

'I have a lot on my mind at the minute, I haven't been sleeping much. I love being in water,' she said, leaning her head back and floating, her aching muscles starting to relax. 'We're always touching something. When we sleep our backs are on the bed, when we stand our feet are on the floor. Being in water is like cutting all the ties we have, we're not touching anything and nothing touches us.'

He reached out and clasped her hand, stopping her from drifting away with the lazy current. She held on, entwining her fingers with his, not wanting to let go but she did. She put her feet on the seabed and crouched in front of him, swishing her arms gently to fight the soft waves and stay in one place.

'Lishy, I think you're still drunk.'

'Floating is like being in space, I bet. Isn't it sad that we'll never get to go to space?'

'Maybe we will, who knows?'

'When the world is ending and they recruit a property developer and a bartender to save the day?'

'You think they won't want perfect pina coladas on Mars?'

'Alliteration!' she shouted, then grimaced and quickly checked to see if anyone had woken up. They hadn't.

'I read a while ago that there's a film that's been made that won't be released for 100 years. That made me feel so shit; we will never get to see it.'

'I read about that too, but there are lots of things we won't live to see,' she said.

'I suppose.'

'Maybe you could be frozen, and wake up just in time to watch it, like in *Demolition Man*. Me and Gloria watched that the other night.' She laughed.

'Maybe I'll just live to 130,' he said.

'You'll have to stop smoking and eat less pizza.'

'My body is a temple.'

'Will you remember this day when you're 130, floating in the sea with your old friend Catherine?'

He smiled. *How could I forget you?* he thought. 'How did you get out of that hammock this morning without waking Stef up by the way?' he said.

'I have cat-like reflexes, like a ninja,' she said, splashing him with the flick of a finger.

'I know, I saw them last night. You dance like Jackie Chan fighting ten men.'

Catherine laughed. 'I don't even know how we both got *in* the hammock last night. I remember we talked a lot; it was nice actually getting to know him a bit more.'

'What did you talk about?'

'Pillow talk stays on the pillow, Benedetto, unless you want to tell me what you and that beautiful brunette talked about?'

He shook his head. 'We didn't talk.'

Catherine felt sick, and not just because the vodka was swishing around in her stomach each time a wave hit them. He really was a lady's man, all the rumours were true, she thought.

She lay her head back in the water again and let herself be swayed by the tide, imagining him with that girl. Beni, meanwhile, thought about all the private things that she and Stef had discussed, their relationship no longer just sex, and a silence fell over them as the movement of the water pulled them apart.

The Glow

'Hola, chicas!' said Anton as Gloria and Catherine joined him at a table in a bustling Playa del Carmen restaurant.

Tourists swaggered along the main street dodging overzealous vendors, and music played from every bar on the strip creating a buzzing, busy atmosphere only slightly tamer than it was at night.

Anton was wearing a loud, short-sleeved shirt with perfectly ironed shorts and his sunglasses were parked atop his dark quiff of hair.

'Hola!' shouted Gloria, climbing onto the chair next to his and letting Catherine push her closer to the table, the chair legs screeching along the floor with each push.

'She wanted to sit next to you, she talked about it all the way here.' Catherine smiled, feeling a bit flustered. Gloria had been in her life for nearly nine months, yet she was still not used to the chaos that just leaving home could cause. 'I'm sorry we're late,' she said, giving him a one-armed hug and sitting down. 'You look very tanned today.'

'You don't see me in natural light very often.' He grinned.

'Hola, Gloria, I love your outfit and Kitty has even plaited your hair! You look adorable. Have you been having fun with Kitty?' he said in Spanish, his sunglasses wilting off his head as he bowed forward, until they were practically over his eyes.

'Yes, we have been swimming lots and me and Kitty are reading a book,' said the little girl.

'What book are you reading?'

'I don't know,' said Gloria, looking around the restaurant, at the water feature, at the singers walking around with guitars, at the waitresses rushing around. There was a lot going on and she was clearly having a hard time focusing on the conversation.

'You don't know? Well, if you remember, will you tell me?' said Anton, smiling at Catherine and placing his sunglasses on the table.

Gloria nodded. 'Do you like swimming, Anton?' she asked, wriggling in her seat. 'I love swimming.'

'We will have to go to the wave pool again soon, wont we?'

'I like swimming because we play games and it's fun,' she said, finally looking at him, seemingly content that she had seen all there was to see in the restaurant.

'Oh, Gloria, tell Anton about the James Bond game that Beni taught you. That's your favourite at the minute, isn't it?' said Catherine.

'Kitty throws things into the pool and I am a spy and I swim to the floor of the pool and get them back for her.'

'What makes that James Bond? Are you throwing women's underwear into the pool?' Anton whispered to Catherine out of the side of his mouth.

Catherine laughed. 'It's James Bond because spies often have to swim into secret lairs, don't they, Gloria?'

'So, what *do* you throw in?' asked Anton.

'Mainly some toothbrushes and one of my old mascaras.' Catherine laughed.

'Ahh, typical spy things to have to scuba-dive for. Do you wear goggles, Gloria, or can you open your eyes under water?'

'I can open them under water now but I have some big goggles too with a thing that goes over my nose,' she said poking her little nose with her finger.

'Just like a proper spy!'

Gloria agreed, smiling widely, and continued to talk about swimming and spies for another ten minutes in a mix of Spanish and English, the latter of which was improving every day thanks to cartoons, Catherine reading with her, and the play time she was enjoying with the American and English tourists in the kids' club.

They finally ordered some drinks and food from the clearly worn-out waitress and then Gloria entertained herself with a colouring book.

'Look at the yummy mummy carrying all the essentials in her Gucci handbag!' Anton wailed, as Catherine pulled out some crayons.

'You know it's a fake, right? This bag? I got it down one of these side streets,' she said with a wink.

'I don't believe you for one second.'

'Your birthday party was so much fun, and your new man seems lovely.'

Anton grinned. 'It was great wasn't it, and he is gorgeous!'

'Tell me more about him? I spoke to him a little at your party but he was too busy following you around adoringly to chat for long.'

'He works at the airport, he's twenty-seven years old – which so am I, by the way, if it should come up,' said Anton, eyes wide as he pursed his lips. 'And I'm really happy!'

'Well, that last bit is all I'm interested in,' she said, squeezing his hairy hand. 'And bravo for keeping your age on the down-low by the way, even though he attended your fortieth birthday party.' She laughed, secretly thinking that Mateo didn't seem that bright.

'Thank you for my gift, I can't believe you did that! Lunch is on me today.'

'Don't be silly!' said Catherine, batting away his offer with her hand.

'What about you and Stefano? Still passionately pretending not to love each other?'

'We don't love each other.'

'So, if he broke up with you tomorrow, you would be fine with it, would you?'

'I'd miss him, of course I would, but I'd be fine.' She shrugged.

'I know exactly what you would miss about him, young lady!' he said, sipping his drink and pulling a face at its sour taste.

'If we broke up, I wouldn't just miss him, I would miss you too. I would even miss Val, she's been a tiny bit nicer to me lately. I think she's starting to like me.'

'Don't get too excited.'

'Why? What have you heard?' asked Catherine.

'Nothing, but this is Val – she likes Stef and that's it. And if you and Stef ever break up, you will get custody of me, let that be a comfort to you,' he said, tapping her on the hand.

'Oh, I will.' She laughed. 'What do you know about Stef and Val?'

'Why, are you jealous? Because if you were, that would be a classic sign of love.'

'No, I'm just curious what you know about them. Maybe we should set Val up with someone?'

'I tried that once, with Beni. It didn't work out. I think he prefers blondes, to be honest,' he whispered, giving her a knowing look.

'I love Beni!' said Gloria.

'I think she has a bit of a crush on her swimming coach,' whispered Catherine in Italian.

'We've all been there,' said Anton, offering Gloria's little hand a high five. 'Doesn't it make Stef jealous how much time Beni spends with you both?'

'A little. But he can't exactly complain, he spends a lot of time with Val. And what is there to be jealous of Beni for?'

'I am just going to put this out there – Beni is gorgeous. He is, don't deny it, it's just a fact of life. I saw you snuggling up to him in the back of the car when we went to that hammock place. I saw how many shots you did after he went off with that tacky girl, and I saw how upset he looked at my party.'

'What are you saying?'

'That if I was Stefano, I would watch my back. Beni wants you.'

'Me and Beni are just friends. And really, me and Stef are just friends too,' she said, folding her paper napkin into a fan anxiously.

'Friends who have a lot of S–E–X!'

Gloria's head popped up.

'She knows letters now, you know.' Catherine cringed, trying not to laugh. 'Speak Italian if you are going to talk sesso e peccato!' she whispered.

'Sesso e peccato!' He laughed, taking a long drink and banging a hand on the table. 'Gloria do you want to listen to some music?' he asked, giving the little girl his phone and headphones and finding a child-friendly playlist.

'Now we can talk sex and sin.' Anton laughed.

'Beni wouldn't touch me with a ten-foot barge pole. He loves Stef.'

'Touch you with a ten-foot what? Is that an English sex thing?'

Catherine laughed. 'I just mean that nothing will ever

happen with him, because he doesn't want to upset Stef, and neither do I. Besides, I'd heard that Beni was a lady magnet, and I saw it with my own eyes at the Hammock Hideout. I've never been into men like that,' whispered Catherine, conscious of Gloria still being able to hear them.

She needn't have worried though, as Gloria was busy bopping her head to Abba while happily colouring in.

Anton nodded. 'We've all seen him in action with girls over the years.'

'I haven't heard from him or seen him at all since your party. He didn't seem himself, I'm worried.'

'It was only last week, maybe he's just been busy? He did seem even more brooding than usual, but I just thought he'd had too many drinks. I'll try and meet up with him soon and find out what's going on.'

'I've texted him a few times but he's not got back to me, it's not like him. I was really worried, but Val said she'd seen him at work and that he was OK. Maybe he just has a girlfriend?'

'Maybe. Would that make you jealous?' asked Anton, narrowing his eyes slightly.

'What? What is everyone's fascination with jealousy?' said Catherine, not looking at him.

'It's a sin, bella! All of the best conversation topics centre around sesso e peccato!' He laughed. 'Don't avoid the question. Would you be sad if our Benedetto found a Juliet?'

'Of course not!' said Catherine, at an unusual volume. She couldn't help but disagree with herself though, and her face suddenly felt warm.

'I'm just teasing you. Now that I'm in love I just want to spread the good vibes around. I want you to fall in love too.'

'Well, I don't think that will happen any time soon.'

'Do you want to know what I think?'

'You're going to tell me anyway, so go on.' She smirked.

'I think you love them both. I think you and Stef started off casual and now you're having feelings for him, and I think you've always loved Beni, from the minute you met. There were sparks between you, I remember it.'

'You're crazy.'

'You guessed he was English before he had even spoken a single word, it's like you recognised him from a past life,' said Anton putting his hands up like a mime against a non-existent windowpane. 'Fate!'

'Oh no, please, don't start talking to me about past lives and fate again, I can't handle it.' She laughed.

'The universe gives us gifts, if something is right in front of you then you should reach out and take it.'

'The universe has bigger fish to fry than my love life.'

'I think you're in love,' he said in a sing-song voice.

'I am in love,' said Catherine, giving Gloria a motherly glance.

'I remember the day you walked up to my desk and demanded I get you the police and a lawyer.' Anton laughed. 'I thought, wow, who is this bossy B–I–T–C–H, but then when I found out what you were doing I thought you were amazing. And look at her, she's doing so well, Lish.'

'She's great, so much better than half the kids I see at the hotel. Some of them are absolute nightmares.'

'Maybe you're biased because she's yours.'

'She's not mine,' said Catherine, staring at the mushy paper straw in her Diet Coke.

'She could be, you could just fire the private detective and go through with the adoption now?'

'I'm sure being a mum while living in a five-star hotel is very different to being an actual mum in the real world. I don't know if I could cope with it. If in a few more months he still hasn't found anyone, then the universe will have spoken and I will keep her.'

'It's the universe that gave her to you in the first place,' said Anton.

'Why are you here, Anton? Why did the universe make you come to Mexico?'

'I had nowhere else to go.'

'The world is big and wild and there are plenty of other places you could have ended up. Why here?' She held up her hands to indicate their surroundings, the bustling bar a perfect example of the beauty and chaos of touristic Mexico.

'The short story is that I met a boy.'

'And the longer version? Who's back in Italy, do you still have family there?'

'Just my mother.'

'What's she like?'

'She's ... a character!'

'Like mother, like son.' Catherine smiled.

'She was a dancer and would be out all hours but she was always there for me when I needed her, with a full face of makeup, and smelling of perfume and cigarettes.' He smiled at the memory. 'But, when I was around eighteen years old, she met a man and he moved in with us. He was OK at first but soon he was ruling the roost and my mamma let him. One day, he gave me some money and told me to leave.'

'What an arsehole.'

'He could have thrown me out with nothing, at least he gave me some money. And he has always treated my mum well. I was an adult too, not a kid any more; he did me a favour, made me stand on my own two feet.'

'That's good then, I guess?'

'My mamma did lose her sparkle when she met him, but we all

do, don't we? When we meet someone that loves us, we stop trying so hard to shine. I haven't seen them in years, I can't imagine what she's even like now. I can't envision her at five in the morning in a tasselled dress and perfect lipstick any more; I imagine her in slippers and night cream. I just hope she's happy.' He shrugged.

'You don't think she stopped dressing up because he told her to?'

'No way. She was tired, she wanted to chuck out the heels. He's not a bad guy really.'

'They never seem bad, Anton. Maybe you should give your mum a call? See how she's doing?'

'I will. It's been a while.'

'So, you came here after he kicked you out, then?'

'No, I didn't go far at first. I used the money he gave me to rent a small place in my hometown. I already had a job so I was fine for a long time on my own. Then I met a gorgeous man from Spain and we went travelling. While with him I worked as a kitchen gardener at a hotel in Scotland for a year, hiked the Inca Trail, went swimming with sharks in Fiji – we did everything and worked every kind of job. Eventually, we ended up in Cuba.'

'Così romantico.' Catherine smiled.

'It was, until the bastard cheated on me, so I left him and ended up here. That was about eight years ago. The cost of living is so cheap here, the people are nice, the weather is beautiful. I'm happy.'

'What about your dad? When they kicked you out, couldn't you go to him?'

'I don't know who my dad is.'

'Have you thought about doing one of those DNA test things to find out your heritage?'

'Are you suggesting this because of my tan today? I spent

three hours at the beach with Mateo, that's why I'm extra glowing today, not because of who my daddy is.' He laughed.

'No, not because of your tan! I've been thinking of getting a test done for Gloria, to help her understand her heritage. Shall I order you one too?'

'It can't hurt I suppose, it might help to narrow it down a bit in my mamma's memory. Then, once a handful of daddy options are on the table, I can re-enact *Mamma Mia*.'

'Please don't sing, the mariachi band will come over here,' said Catherine in a panicked whisper, leaning towards him.

'Let them come over, it's fun! Mamma Mia!' He started to sing loudly.

Catherine slumped in her chair, hiding from the fast-approaching guitarist in a sombrero who was offering his musical services along the kerbside restaurants. Thankfully, before he got to them the waitress brought over their food and Anton stopped singing.

'Wow, your food looks so yummy!' Catherine said as she took away the headphones and cut up Gloria's chicken.

'It does!' said the little girl. She jammed her fork into the pieces of chicken with one hand and continued to colour in with the other.

'I'll get you a DNA test, and you haven't become any less fabulous since being in love you know,' Catherine said to Anton as she moved her food around her plate.

'Give it time, my mother didn't throw out her heels straight away,' he said, chewing a piece of bread.

'Don't some bugs light up to find a mate, and when they find one they switch off their glow? Maybe humans are just like that – when we've found the right person there's no need to be so bright and shiny any more?'

'Can't we be bright and shiny even when we've found someone who loves us?'

'Maybe we just start to sparkle in different ways? Or glow just for them?'

'I don't know, bella, this whole glowing-ass metaphor is dying a death!' He laughed. 'But it is kind of exhausting being so brilliant 24/7. It would be nice to switch off my light for a while.'

'Anyone worth loving will love you when your light is off and still love you when your light is on, without feeling threatened that you're trying to attract someone else with your glowing arse.'

'Love you when you're in the tasselled dress, and still love you in your slippers?' he said thoughtfully.

'Exactly. Why don't we just use the dimmer switch?' Catherine shrugged.

'Good idea!' he said, raising his glass. 'To dimming our lights, not switching them off.' He clinked his glass against Catherine's, and Gloria's bottle of juice too, which made the little girl smile.

'So, what is your light doing right now?' he asked, eyebrows high.

'You tell me.'

'You're like a disco ball when Stefano is around, a strobe light in a club.'

'Shut up.' She smiled, tapping his arm.

'But you shine even brighter when Beni is around,' he said seriously.

'I love Beni!' shouted Gloria again.

Catherine laughed and put her hand to her face, thinking, *Me too.*

'Oh God,' she said before continuing in Italian. 'I'm trying to be a good role model. I googled inspirational quotes for women the other day and the top twenty were all about appearance. Can we not be inspired by something else, people?'

'You are a good role model.'

'She watches me do my make-up before I see Stefano and she's just listened to us talking about glowing for the sake of men, and not glowing for the sake of men. She's going to be putting illuminator powder on her Christmas list at this rate.'

'Just be honest with her about your womanly ... experience,' he said, grimacing and waving his hand around in the direction of her lady parts.

'Kitty is reading *Matilda* to me,' Gloria said suddenly in Spanish.

'Is she? Do you like it?' asked Anton, looking between Catherine and Gloria.

'Yes, Matilda likes reading and so do I.'

'What do you like about reading?' asked Anton.

'Kitty says it gives you superpowers because you end up knowing so much more when you read and being smart is very important.'

'That's right,' said Catherine, beaming, glad that out of all the inane things she said every day, Gloria had remembered something positive.

After their meal with Anton, some shopping and a risky paddle in the sea with all of their bags, Catherine and Gloria arrived back at the hotel and walked over to one of the hotel excursion organisers. Today there was a young man on the desk; he was probably no older than nineteen, he had black hair and a streak of acne across his forehead. Catherine was glad he was there because it was him specifically that she wanted to talk to.

'Buenas tardes,' she said as they approached his desk.

'Hola, do you want to book an excursion?' he asked eagerly.

'Oh, well, maybe actually, but not right now.'

'Then what can I help you with?' he asked, his shoulders sagging slightly.

'Well,' – she paused briefly as she read his name tag – 'Ricky, this is for you,' she said, untangling her many bags and handing over the one intended for him.

'Why is it for me?' he asked, giving a confused glance to Gloria who was standing at Catherine's side, bobbing up and down in excitement.

'I sing here, in the corner. I've seen you talk to guests about these so many times, and I've heard you say that you want one, that you're saving up. It just broke my heart a little. When I was a kid, I wanted a hamster so much, it took me like a year to save up for its cage and its food and everything, and when I finally got it the poor thing died after five hours, scared to death by my cat! Now I'm lucky enough that if I want something, I can just buy it.'

Ricky carried on looking at them both, clearly confused.

'I'm friends with Anton,' Catherine said, pointing at the concierge desk, which at that point was being manned by someone else. 'Don't be mad, but he said you've been having a tough time at home. Anyway, we were in a store today and I saw it, so I got you one.' She shrugged.

He peered into the bag and his eyes seemed to grow to twice their normal size. 'I can't accept this, it's too much.'

'Just take it!' said Gloria. 'Kitty bought it for you, to make you happy!'

Catherine stroked the plaited black hair on Gloria's small head. 'I don't want to offend you, I just wanted to do something nice. Please accept it?' said Catherine softly.

'I'm not offended, I'm in shock,' he said, and a smile spread across his face. 'Thank you so much.'

'The receipt is in the bag. There's a travel charger and a few games too, I paid in cash so if there are any problems you can take it back. Don't tell anyone I got it for you, OK?'

'Why would you do this for me? You don't even know me?' asked Ricky, looking into the bag again.

Catherine smiled. 'You work so hard, you are here all the time and you're a good person. You deserve it. I will think about that excursion, Ricky, thanks,' she said taking a leaflet from his desk and walking away.

The Surprise

I t was getting dark; the sun was already halfway down the sky as Catherine and Gloria walked through the busy lobby, looking for Stefano who had asked them to meet him there. When they couldn't find him inside, they wandered out onto the lobby steps and spotted him standing with the bellboys, chatting and smiling.

'Happy birthday, beautiful,' he said, running over and kissing Catherine softly on the lips.

'Thanks.' She smiled.

'Hi, Gloria! I know you both like driving around on these things, so I borrowed one,' he said, darting over to stand in front of one of the hotel's long golf buggies that were used to ferry guests around the resort.

'Have you got something to do with this, Javier?' Catherine asked in Spanish, smiling at one of the bellboys, who was laughing and leaning against a wall.

'Maybe, Lish, but don't thank me yet – he might crash the thing within minutes, he's not an expert driver like me.'

'Oh, thanks,' she said with a smile, pretending to look worried. 'We love riding on these, don't we, Gloria? Are we

195

going on safari through the jungle?' asked Catherine, crouching down, sensing that Gloria was feeling shy.

Gloria nodded and then smiled as Javier put his bellboy hat on her head, making her look like a tiny Victorian explorer.

'You can look after this for me while I enjoy my break,' he said.

'How's your wife doing, Javier? It was so kind of you both to give us those toys, she loves them.'

'Oh, no, we were glad to help – what you're doing is great. My wife is fine, thanks for asking. How is everything?'

'Everything's great.' Catherine smiled, stood up straight and then held on to Gloria by the shoulders. 'I'd be lost without my little buddy now.'

'Are you ready?' asked Stefano. 'I'm taking you both on a tour. Madame ...' he said, offering his hand to help Catherine into the passenger seat before lifting Gloria onto her lap.

'We will be back in time for my gig, won't we? I'm on at eight o'clock,' Catherine said as he climbed in beside them.

'We will definitely be back in time, don't worry,' he said, kissing her.

'Wave goodbye to Javier, Gloria!' said Catherine.

Stefano drove them around the winding paths of the resort, passing lazy iguanas and dozens of coati – racoon-type creatures – that were tiptoeing to look in bins and digging their paws and noses into the grass in search of snacks. Amusingly, their curved tails sticking in the air gave them the silhouette of a herd of miniature long-necked dinosaurs, so much so, that Catherine always did a double take whenever she encountered them.

As they pootled along, their golf cart narrowly dodged hotel guests sporting wet hair and flip-flops, and Stef made up funny facts about things that they drove past as though he were a real tour guide.

'This water fountain doesn't actually have any water in it, it's all special effects and glitter,' he said matter-of-factly.

'It looks like there is water in it to me,' Gloria said, craning her neck to get a better look.

'The hotel has spared no expense on the special effects. If you touch it, it even feels like water,' Stef said, smiling at Catherine who was trying not to laugh.

'Oh, Villa 42, that's where the Queen of England stays when she visits Mexico. It has a gold toilet and the bed is made of marshmallows so that it's extra comfy,' he said seriously, looking around as if searching for something else to tell them about. 'And be careful to never touch that umbrella over there. Legend has it that in 1987 a woman touched it and was struck by lightning, so it's very unlucky, and also, very made of metal.'

'Well, I'm glad we know that now,' said Catherine, giggling.

'That bench has been sat on 900,784 times, and those steps up there are very slippy. I have fallen down them about six times!'

'Finally, a fact I believe,' whispered Catherine, grinning at him.

'Gloria, that lizard there, his name is Carlos and he is the boss, the lizard king. His tongue is three metres long and he has to roll it up to make it fit in his mouth.'

'Eww!' said the little girl as she crawled all over them both to get a better look at Carlos who sat stock-still on the grass, minding his own business, probably feeling a bit self-conscious about being stared at.

'That's the sea over there. Unlike in the hotel's fountains, the water there is real, and is very salty.'

Catherine laughed. 'You should become a real tour guide, you have all of the inside info.'

He smiled. 'That towel hut was completed in 1999; it took fourteen years to build.'

'What is it made out of then, Mr Tour-Guide-for-the-Insane?'

'Jelly beans and chocolate wafers originally. That's why it took so long – no one took the Mexican heat into account and it melted, so now it's made of broken table legs and sticky tape.'

Catherine smiled, looking at him for a second as they drove along, feeling lucky.

After covering the whole resort, they made their approach back to the lobby and Catherine could see that there was a group of people standing on the front steps, probably waiting for a coach to the airport, she thought. As they got closer, however, the group started to sing 'Happy Birthday' and she could see Anton holding a cake covered in candles.

As well as it being Catherine's birthday, in a few days she and Gloria were moving out of their hotel room and into a new house; this might be the last time she would see some people for a long while and she started to feel emotional.

'Surprise!' said Stefano, beaming at her from the driver's seat.

'You're so sweet,' she said kissing him on the cheek.

They hopped out of the buggy and Catherine blew out the candles on her cake with help from Gloria. She hugged everyone in sight and thanked them, telling each person that she was going to miss them, smiling and crying the whole time.

'You're only moving ten minutes away,' cried Anton. 'And you will still be working here twice a week!'

'I know, I'll still miss it though! Will you visit me at the new house all the time?'

'Yes, I'll be there all the time,' said Anton, looking around before pulling her to one side and pressing a small bag into her hand. 'Beni couldn't make it, he had to work but he wanted me to give you this.'

'You saw him then? How is he?' asked Catherine.

'He's not doing great, but I'm keeping an eye on him.'

'I should go to his flat and talk to him.'

'Honestly, I think it's best if you leave him alone for a while.'

'Is he mad at me or something? I don't know why he doesn't want to see me any more.'

'He just needs space from us all at the minute. Don't waste your time worrying about him, he's a grown-up. When he's ready, he will come back to us. Anyway, did you like the present I got you?'

'It was amazing, a two-hour massage next to the sea. I was so relaxed afterwards that I almost forgot that Gloria existed, poor kid.'

'I'm glad you liked it; I got the results back from that DNA test, by the way.'

'Ooh, what did it say?' asked Catherine.

'I'm 63% Italian–Greek, 18% North African, 10% Western European and I'm even a bit Russian.'

'That's a mixed bag. Mine was so boring, your ancestors were much more adventurous!'

'I do feel much more interesting than I did before I spat in that tube.' He laughed.

'Did you speak to your mum, then? Does she have any idea about who your dad might be?'

'She said she would think about it.' He shrugged. 'Thanks for getting it for me. What were your results?'

'I'm about 90% English and a tiny bit Scandi. Boring! Gloria is 55% Native American, so I think that means she has Mayan ancestry? I'm looking further into it. So, North African is Egypt, Algeria, that kind of area, isn't it? Could that be from your mum's side, or is it definitely from your dad?'

'I suppose it could be from mum. I'll let you know if she gets back to me with anything. Anyway, enough about me, go and open your present from Beni and enjoy your birthday cake.

I love you.' He kissed her on the cheek and went to chat to Stefano.

Catherine looked at the gift tag on the bag; it was addressed to both Catherine and Gloria so she took Gloria by the hand and led her over to a quiet corner, leaving everyone else to chat and eat cake around one of the big tables next to the bar.

There were two boxes inside, labelled with their names. They opened Gloria's first. Inside was a beautiful shell necklace on a silver chain, the shell was painted turquoise with pink shapes all over it like leopard print.

'That is so cool!' said Catherine as she put the necklace around Gloria's neck. 'Beni sent this for you.'

'It's beautiful,' said Gloria, squeezing the shell as it rested on her chest.

Catherine opened hers next, a slightly bigger box containing earrings that matched Gloria's necklace, beautifully garish, dangling earrings which she loved. Nestled next to them in the box was matching turquoise gel nail polish and a note which read:

To Lish,

Happy Birthday. I'm sorry I couldn't be there to surprise you, but I had to work. I saw these earrings and knew you would like them and I knew you wouldn't wear them unless you had the correct shade of turquoise nail varnish so I found that too. I hope Gloria likes her necklace, I thought you might like to match. Best of luck with the house move and everything.

Beni.

'Let's take a photo and send it to Beni, shall we?' said Catherine, popping the earrings into her ears.

They pulled their best pose for the camera and Catherine sent the image to Beni with a simple "We miss you" message.

Gloria wasted no time running up to Anton and Stefano to

show them her new necklace, and then she sat down with Anton to eat some cake.

'Are you OK?' asked Stefano, having wandered over to Catherine in the corner.

'Is Val at work?' she asked, wondering why she wasn't there, glued to his side as usual.

Stef nodded as he sat next to her and ran his fingers down her cheek, getting a good look at the gift he must have guessed was from Beni, now dangling from his girlfriend's ears.

'Do you ever miss those first couple of months when it was just me and you?' he asked.

'Before you met Gloria, do you mean?'

'No, not Gloria. I mean my friends. Sometimes I wish I could rewind time and not show them to you. Maybe you would see me differently if you didn't know about the Val skeleton hanging in my closet?'

'Whether I knew about it or not, it would still be there wouldn't it?'

'Yeah.' He sighed, staring at the marble floor.

'Did you ever talk to her about how you feel?'

He shook his head. 'No point. I see her much less now.'

'How do you feel about that?'

'I'm OK,' he said, smiling. 'It's time. I want to see you more. When you move into your house, I'll be able to stay over, right?'

'Thanks for my safari around the resort, it was funny,' she said, kissing him, putting her hand at the back of his neck and feeling his tighten on her waist, pulling her close to him. 'I should go and set up. Can you stay and watch me with Gloria?'

'Of course I will,' he said.

'First night with the pianist and drummer. Exciting!' she said as she walked off to get Miguel.

Their performance went well and afterwards, Jose the entertainment manager informed them that they would be moving to the outdoor stage from the following week because they had become so popular.

Stefano walked back with Catherine to her room, holding Gloria in his arms as the little girl dozed on his shoulder, her legs dangling. She was fast asleep and didn't even wake up when he lay her on the bed, took off her shoes and covered her with a blanket.

Catherine smiled as she watched him, and her heart beat fast as she thought about how sweet and gentle he was with Gloria.

Stefano took a bottle of Prosecco and two glasses from the desk, a birthday gift from the hotel, and handed them to Catherine as they stepped out onto the balcony. He lit a cigarette and leaned over the railing, blowing the smoke into the darkness like a dragon while Catherine leaned against the wall furthest away from him, holding the bottle and glasses limply, her mind wandering.

'You were amazing tonight,' he said, smiling at her.

'Did you see how happy Miguel was when Jose said we were moving stages? It's more money, the nights will be different though; we'll be doing Tuesdays and Fridays from now on.'

'Aren't you going to pour some drinks?' he asked.

She took a deep breath, there was no avoiding it any more. She put the bottle and glasses down on the balcony table and leaned back against the wall. 'Stef, I'm late. I haven't had a period in a long time.'

'How late are you?' he said, stubbing out his cigarette instantly and moving over to her.

'I've missed one completely and now it looks like I'm missing another.'

'What does that mean?'

'It might not mean anything; some women miss periods all the time, I thought it was just stress.'

'Do you miss them often?'

She shook her head. 'What if I'm pregnant?'

'We're so careful, you can't be.'

'Nothing is 100%, is it?'

'Would we keep it?' he said, placing his hands on hers, on her stomach.

'I'm all for having the choice, but what if I have an abortion and this was my last chance to have a baby? Plus, I would probably have to fly north to have it done, to America. Do they approve of abortion here? I doubt it. And I can't leave Gloria.'

'Do you want a baby, though? Do you want my baby?' he whispered, his face close to hers.

No, she thought, but then she imagined a cheeky, blonde little boy running around looking like Stef and being as laid back as him, trying to pet stray dogs like he did and cartwheeling on the beach and the idea didn't seem so bad.

'I'll get a test soon. The lobby shop didn't have any, and when I went into Playa I was with Gloria the whole time, I didn't want her earwigging and having a hundred questions. Nothing is certain right now. Don't worry about it yet, not until I've done a test. I've not been eating very well and I've been stressed out about the house, it might just be all that wreaking havoc?'

Stefano just blinked at her for a minute, he seemed to be thinking things over. Then suddenly, he kissed her. 'You're so beautiful, you're an amazing woman. If you're pregnant, it will be a new adventure,' he said, his frown dissolving into a huge smile. 'Anyway, I could do with a mini-me to pass on my wisdom to.' He laughed.

'All that wisdom would go to waste otherwise.' She smiled.

'You're all I've thought about lately. I'll stop seeing Val and we will be together properly. We can be a family, if that's what you want?'

'I don't know what I want.' She stumbled over the words, feeling overwhelmed.

'It's OK. Sorry, I didn't mean to pile a load of pressure on you.'

'Thanks for being so nice, I thought you were going to freak out.'

'Are you freaking out? You still look worried,' he said, pushing her hair off her face.

'I'm worried about Beni too. Anton says he's not doing well right now and I don't know why he's stopped talking to me?'

'Maybe he has a girlfriend?' Stefano shrugged, then walked over to the chair and sat down.

Catherine nodded. 'Val's seen him recently ... maybe they're dating?'

'I don't think so. No, they can't be. But maybe if he does have a girlfriend, she's the jealous type and won't let him see you?'

'I hope that's what it is, I just want to make sure he's OK,' said Catherine, feeling sick.

'Lish, this would be my baby, right?' Stef asked, not looking at her.

'What? Do you think I've cheated on you?'

'No, I'm sorry. I just needed to check because of you thinking about Beni right now.'

I'm always thinking about him, she thought. 'Of course, it would be yours,' she said, walking over and sitting on his lap, running her hand through his hair and kissing him, biting his lip, and then smiling as he dragged her quietly into the bathroom.

The Smile

When Stefano had gone home, Catherine tried to sleep but for hours she just tossed and turned. She felt like she was halfway between being awake and trapped in a dream and each time she rolled over in bed some new form of anxiety pulled the covers from her. In the end, conscious that her tossing and turning would soon wake up Gloria, Catherine got up as quietly as she could and tiptoed down the dark hallway. Once in the bright, quiet cocoon of the bathroom, she sat on the tiled floor and leaned against the bath which was still damp from the shower she had taken with Stefano.

Why at night do places so familiar to you start to feel alien? she wondered, as she looked around the room noticing things she had never bothered to really see before, like tiny cracks in tiles and a transparent sticker on the mirror. She turned and put her hand against the shower tiles and her stomach flipped as she thought about Stefano's wet body pressing her against them hours earlier.

She sighed loudly and lay down on the cold floor, a hand over her eyes to block out the harsh light. She tried to think about other things but her thoughts kept drifting back to why Beni might not want to see her any more and about possibly being pregnant. She pondered reasons that might make her stop seeing someone; could she make things right by going to see him? Could he really be dating Valentina? Why could she not just forget about him and get on with her life?

Then there was the gift he had sent and in the blacks of her closed eyes she saw painted seashells twirling like space stations. Catherine snapped her eyes open again and stared at the light bulb on the ceiling, imagining that it was the flash of a neuralyzer that would erase her memory, *Men-in-Black*-style. She felt manic, her insides fizzed and her eyes burned with exhaustion; she felt sick and dizzy, and didn't know what to do with the energy that was jumping around beneath the surface of her skin. She thought about what her life would be like if she had Stefano's baby. She imagined it wriggling around inside of her, its curly blonde hair grazing like hessian against her organs. Eventually, she crawled back into bed, and at some point must have fallen asleep because the next thing she knew, Gloria was fidgeting around beside her looking for the television remote.

'Kitty, can I go to kids' club today?' she asked the instant that Catherine's eyes fluttered open.

'What time is it?' said Catherine.

'I don't know.'

'Pass me my phone please?'

'Here you go,' Gloria said, handing over the phone, full of energy, Catherine's long gone.

'It's only eight o'clock. You can go to kids' club this morning if you like?' said Catherine, sitting up.

∼

Later that morning, Catherine took a shuttle bus over to the hotel next door, hoping that Beni would be working. She didn't intend to speak to him, she just wanted to see with her own eyes that he was all right.

She walked through the hotel grounds, which looked similar to hers but this one had flamingos in a pond next to the lobby and a far grander reception area with chandeliers and mirrors everywhere. As it was further inland there were also far more lizards, and she kept having to dodge them as she walked the narrow paths to the pool bar.

She was so busy looking at the ground for surprise iguanas that as she turned a corner and finally looked up, she saw Beni and he saw her, throwing her plan of spying on him from behind a tree firmly out of the window. He was wearing a white shirt, he looked tired, his hair was messy and yet as she walked towards him, her heart started pumping faster than her body could handle and she felt like she might pass out, she was so happy to see him. All the sunloungers were taken, music played loudly and people splashed around in the pool, but Catherine didn't notice any of that, she only had eyes for Beni.

'Hi,' she said, taking a seat at the bar.

'Hi,' he said back, barely looking at her. 'How was your birthday? Do you want a drink?'

'Do you think that's why I'm here?' she said, annoyed that he wouldn't look at her.

'Why *are* you here?'

'Beni, what did I do? Why don't you want to see me any more?'

'You haven't done anything, Lish. Not everything is about you, you know,' he said, picking up a glass and pretending to clean it, determined not to look at her.

'I'm sorry, you're right,' she said quietly, feeling like an idiot.

'I just need space from everyone at the minute.'

207

'Just tell me you're OK and I'll leave. I've been worried about you.'

'I'm OK, I promise,' he said, finally looking into her eyes. He thought she looked exhausted.

'OK. Well, thanks for my gift, and Gloria's. We love them,' she said, her eyes shining with tears. She swallowed hard and turned to leave.

Beni watched her walk away and sighed, relieved that she was going, but then just before she turned the corner, he saw her jump at what he assumed must have been a lizard and he smiled. He put down the glass he was cleaning and ran after her.

'Lish, wait,' he said as he got close to her.

She turned to look at him just as he fell to the floor, clutching his chest.

'Beni?' said Catherine, falling to her knees to help him. 'Are you OK? Did you trip on that damn lizard?'

'I can't breathe,' he said, gasping for air.

'Oh my god. Por favor ayuda! Help! Call an ambulance!' she shouted at passing staff and guests who all scrambled to help. 'It's OK, it's OK,' she soothed as she undid his white shirt to reveal his chest, which was rising and falling in sharp movements.

A first aider arrived within minutes, looking flustered, holding a medical kit and wearing a worried expression.

'Why are you here? He doesn't need a bandage! Call an ambulance!' shouted Catherine.

'That won't be cheap, madam, and he works here,' said the nervous man.

'It doesn't matter what it costs. He's my friend, call them now, to the best hospital! Please!'

A crowd had gathered nearby and people propped themselves up lazily on their loungers to rubberneck. Another member of staff brought over a damp cloth that Catherine held to Beni's head, triggering a flashback to when she had done the same for someone else a long time ago; the cold compress hadn't saved them.

'It's going to be OK. I've watched enough *Grey's Anatomy* to know that this is probably something to do with you being punched in the ribs a few months ago. Have your ribs been hurting?'

He nodded and reached out to hold her hand.

'They will probably just need to stab you in the side with a biro to let your lung inflate properly,' she whispered.

'What?'

'Sorry, I don't know why that was meant to comfort you. I just mean it's going be OK, they can fix this, just keep breathing for me?'

Beni smiled, an actual smile, and held her hand tight as his breaths became even more laboured.

'Calm down, it's going to be OK. Now isn't the time for smiling at me,' she said, kissing his hand, tears splashing onto his fingers.

'You're like my guardian angel,' he gasped. 'You always show up when I'm at my lowest.'

'Stop talking, just focus on breathing. I'm starting to think I'm a jinx. I should have stayed away from you like you wanted, I'm sorry.'

'No, that first night you came to the bar with Stef,' – he paused, trying to catch his breath, his eyes closing – 'I was going to end it. I had a box of pills and a bottle of vodka ready to do it, but instead I went to the bar and I met you.'

'Shh, just breathe in and out. Your hair's getting long on top,' she said, pushing some wavy dark strands off his forehead. 'If it were blonde and less wavy, you'd look a bit like Jack from *Titanic*.' She smiled. 'I learnt a new word the other day: deuter-agonist. It's used to describe the second most important character in a book or film, so in *Die Hard*, Hans would be the deuteragonist, and in Harry Potter, it would be Ron. Jack is the deuteragonist in *Titanic*, apparently. That really surprised me because you see things from his point of view just as much as Rose's. But I guess, actually, she's telling the story isn't she, when she's old, so that does make sense.'

'You're trying to distract me,' he wheezed, and smiled again, gripping her hand weakly. 'So now you think I look like I'm from 1910 instead of 1950?'

'Part your hair in the middle and you could look like you're from the 1990s too.' She smiled.

'I need to get it cut!'

'I like it.'

'I've missed you,' he gasped, coughing a little. 'Tell me more about films and words. Teach me.'

'OK, umm ... did you know that pleonastic sound is when a sound is exaggerated in a film, like the squelch of a knife going into someone, and that contrapuntal sound is when the sound doesn't really match what's happening, like a happy song playing at a funeral?'

'What else?' he gasped. 'Keep going.'

'I really like the theory that film is a way for us to dream while we're awake. Some films literally emulate the way that we dream by playing with angles and the way things move to make it feel strange, like jumping from one scene to another with no explanation, playing with timelines, using creatures and colours that seem odd or don't actually exist in reality. But even a standard, linear Hollywood film like *Die Hard* is like a dream in the way it allows us to escape for two hours and live vicariously through the main character. It's even been suggested that films, like dreams, allow our subconscious to act out its desires and stop us from actually doing the things that subconsciously we would love to do, like murder or sleeping with inappropriate people. Everyone is less violent now than they were, aren't they? I'm pretty sure that's a fact. Maybe we have cinema to thank for that?'

'All seems plausible to me,' said Beni.

'Stop talking. My questions are rhetorical and purely for effect.' She smiled. 'So, with video and DVD, and now streaming, we get to pick which dream we have at the click of a button, any time we want. How long until our actual dreams can be recorded for us to see, and what will they look like, I wonder?'

'Keep going.' He smiled, his eyes closed.

'Try to stay awake for me. It's not that boring, is it?' She laughed nervously, watching his chest rising and falling much less rapidly. 'The ambulance will be here any minute. You'll be OK, I promise,' said Catherine. She racked her brain for more film theory to talk to him about for another fifteen minutes, until the ambulance arrived and he was rushed to the hospital.

Catherine stayed with him the whole way, watching from the corner of the vehicle as they placed an oxygen mask on him and examined his chest. Once in the hospital, they hurried him off on a bed leaving her to sit in the waiting area, where time seemed to stand still. Catherine people-watched as staff and patients moved around the busy space, which was filled with chairs and magazines and frustrated, poorly people either desperate to be seen or, like Catherine, desperate for news.

'Mrs Lish?' a female doctor finally called out after a few hours.

Catherine practically ran towards her.

'Benedetto is stable. He's just woken up and he's not really with it, but he keeps asking for you. Do you want to come and see him now?' she asked kindly, and led Catherine down the corridor to his room.

Catherine walked into his private room and sat down next

to the bed. It was a small room, sterile and whitewashed, with a few beeping machines in the corner, no natural light, just a big hospital bed, a chair and a sink. Beni was wearing pyjama-like bottoms and no top; he had a dressing over the left side of his chest and a mask over his face. She slid her hand into his and held on to it as though they were about to arm wrestle. She lifted it gently to her face and started to sob.

'Lishy,' said Beni, raising the mask as he spoke, his voice croaky.

'What happened? Have they told you?' she asked, leaning in and kissing him on the forehead.

'Pneumothorax,' he said. 'You were right, they had to stick a tube in my lung. Turns out some of my ribs had broken and there was a tiny bit of bone sticking out. It was just a matter of time before it stuck into my lung.'

'The air seeps out and instead of being in your lung pushing out, it starts to deflate it from the outside,' she said, running her fingers along the length of his arm nervously.

He raised a weak smile. 'God, how much *Grey's Anatomy* do you watch?' He let go of her hand and touched her wet face.

'I used to work in a hospital, just as admin but it's surprising how much you pick up from reading letters and talking to nurses.'

'They've given me some painkillers; they said they'll knock me out any minute.'

'So, what are they going to do about the sticky-out bone?'

'I don't know. They probably told me but all I could think about was you.'

'I should have forced you to go to the hospital ages ago. This must have been painful for a long time.'

'Other things hurt more.' He attempted to shrug but winced.

'Do you want me to stay? I'll stay here all night, Anton has Gloria.'

'No, you've done enough. This seems like a fancy hospital, I'm guessing I have you to thank for that?'

'It's all paid for, they just need your last name for the paper-work but I told them you would give them your details.'

'Don't you want to know it?'

'You're saving it for a rainy day, aren't you? Don't waste it on today,' she said, smiling.

'How are things with you and Stefano?' he asked and watched as her hand went instinctively straight to her stomach and he felt like his lung was collapsing all over again as he connected the dots.

'Good,' she said, feeling guilty that she was the type of girl who was in love with one man and possibly having another's baby, like a soap opera character.

'Lish, I think you should go,' he said quietly.

'You're right, you need to rest. I'll visit you tomorrow?'

'No, please don't visit me,' he said, his eyes snapping open. 'I don't want to see you, and I don't want anyone to know that I'm in here.'

'Why don't you want me to visit? I don't understand?'

'You annoy me,' he said angrily, closing his eyes so she wouldn't see how difficult it was for him to lie.

'What do I do that's so annoying?' asked Catherine, a defensive edge growing in her own voice.

'Well, for a start, you're moving in to a big mansion after telling me you don't want to take Gloria away from everything she knows. That isn't what she knows, Catherine, that gated complex may as well be in Malibu or Beverly Hills. You're full of shit.'

'I'm moving there because it's close to the hotel and, trust me, if the house was in either of those locations, I couldn't afford it.'

'You're just not who I thought you were.'

Catherine sat stunned for a few seconds. 'I'm not who you thought I was? Then I don't know who I am either.'

'Lish,' he said, touching her face as fresh tears rolled down her cheeks.

'I can't stay away from you, Beni.' she said softly, looking into his eyes.

'You need to stay away.'

'Why?'

'You know why,' he said drowsily.

'Tell me why,' she said, squeezing his hand, but it was too late, he was asleep.

Catherine fixed his mask back in place and then sat back in her chair. Her stomach growled. She hadn't eaten anything for at least two days, not even a piece of birthday cake. In the midst of all the chaos, the pangs of hunger reminded her that she was in control of one thing at least. She felt dizzy and nauseous, however, and was struggling to process what had happened in the last few hours.

She watched Beni for a while, noticing for the first time how long and dark his eye lashes were, and ran her eyes over his body. She felt like a voyeur but she couldn't stop herself. Tears were running down her cheeks but she couldn't feel them, she just felt numb.

After what felt like hours, she lightly penned *Get well soon Belmondo* on his hand so he wouldn't forget that she had been there, kissed him on the forehead, wiped her face and left.

~

Catherine got a taxi back to the hotel and found Gloria and Anton by the pool eating ice creams. Gloria was lying on a sunlounger in her pink bathing costume and sunglasses looking like a total diva and Catherine couldn't help but smile.

'Has she got sun cream on?'

'Yes, plenty of sun cream, don't worry. Are you OK? What happened that was so urgent?' asked Anton, sticking his ice lolly stick in a glass and standing up to greet her.

'I'm sorry I had to ask you for help out of the blue like that. The private detective called, he thought he had some news about Gloria's family, but it was a dead end,' she whispered.

'You look traumatised, come here,' he said, pulling her into a hug as she began to cry.

'Anton, I'm lying.'

'What really happened?' he asked into her hair, steering her out of Gloria's eyeline so she wouldn't see that Catherine was upset.

'I need you to keep this a secret. I'm only telling you because you may have to pull some strings for him at work,' she said, looking him in the eye.

'What? Tell me,' he said, frowning.

'Don't tell him that I told you. Plenty of people saw him collapse, just say one of them told you.'

'Who collapsed?'

'Beni. I went to see him. I know you said not to, but I just needed to see him to make sure that he was OK. He collapsed and was rushed to hospital.'

'Is he OK?'

'He's stable, he's resting. He told me to stay away from him.'

'Which hospital is he at? I'll go now.'

'The one not far from here. Here's a card from the ward he's on,' she said, handing him a glossy white rectangle with the address and telephone numbers embossed on it.

'How is he affording that? His insurance is better than mine,' he said, looking at the card in his hands, his eyebrows high.

'I've paid for his treatment and whatever he needs, I'll cover. Can you please be there for him and tell me if he needs anything else?'

'Lish,' he said softly, wiping her face, 'why don't you just admit you're in love with him?'

'There's no point, it may be too late,' she said.

'Why is it?'

Catherine slipped a pregnancy test, still in its box, out of her handbag.

'Oh God,' said Anton, frowning at the box. 'Shall we go to your room so you can do it while I'm here?'

Catherine nodded, beginning to cry again, and Anton hugged her tight.

They went back to Catherine's room and ordered room service, got Gloria ready for bed and told her a bedtime story. She took a while to settle down with the added excitement of Anton being there and it being quite early, but finally, when she was asleep, they went into the bathroom and Catherine did the pregnancy test.

'If it's negative, I will drive to the hospital right now and tell him how I feel,' said Catherine, sitting on the floor, clutching her legs, waiting for the two minutes to be up and for her fate to be revealed.

'And if it's positive? Will you tell Stef straight away?' asked Anton, perching on the side of the bath, looking anxious.

'No, I'll need to think about it. What will I do?'

'Can you imagine being with him properly? Can you imagine him being a dad?'

'I don't know. He knows I might be pregnant, I told him I was late. He was kind of excited.'

'Stef is always excited, he's like a puppy.' Anton smiled.

'I already have Gloria, what's one more child to take care of? I could do it on my own?'

'Gloria will be happy, someone for her to boss around.'

Catherine smiled. 'And you. You would be an uncle to a mini Stefano.'

'I don't think I have the energy for that.' He laughed. 'So, positive Stef, negative Beni? Like flipping a coin, with more urine involved than normal.'

Catherine nodded and watched the little window on the test like it was a bomb that would explode if she looked away, and finally, when its verdict was reached, she looked at Anton. He didn't need her to tell him what it said, he just skittered instinctively onto the floor and wrapped his arms around her as she began to cry.

The Wave

'You're still avoiding Stefano, then?' said Anton from the driver's seat as they cruised along the highway.

'If I see him, I'll have to tell him that I'm pregnant and then I'll have to deal with it. This way, I get to pretend none of it's happening for a bit longer,' said Catherine, looking out of the window.

'There's a time limit on this, Lish. In a few more months you'll have a kicking, screaming baby and you won't be able to pretend any more.'

'I'm not quite three months along yet, I have ages to be in denial,' she said, waving her hand in the air.

'You can't avoid him forever. Isn't he wondering why you won't see him?'

'It's only been a few weeks. I've just moved into the house, so I keep telling him that I'm busy sorting everything out there.'

'And he just accepts that? Doesn't he want to help you, be with you?'

'You know what he's like. He really is like a puppy, bounding around doing what he wants to do, living in his own world,' she said.

'Doesn't it bother you?'

'No. I don't want to see him yet and why kill his mood with this news until I have to?'

'And you're putting it off because you've finally, finally realised what I knew all along – that you love Beni!'

'Shush,' said Catherine, looking at Gloria on the back seat, bopping her head, wearing Anton's headphones and smiling.

'You need to tell Stef about the baby. God, your life stresses me out!'

'You love all the drama I bring to the table, don't lie!' She laughed.

'You're right.'

'Stef said if I was pregnant, then we would be together, that he would stop seeing Val completely. But to be honest, I don't want him to stop seeing her, I was happy the way things were. I don't want a faithful husband and a baby; I'd rather have a friend and a baby.'

'So, when you tell him, you'll break up?'

'Yes, I think so.'

'Oh,' he said, looking surprised. 'And then will you tell Beni how you feel?'

'Nope, that ship has sailed too.'

'So, you won't be with either of them?'

'It's what's best for everyone, that's what I've decided. Stef can be involved with the kid if he wants, and if not, that's fine too. And I'm not seeing Beni any more, I'm just going to have to get over him. This is all my fault; I will deal with the consequences.'

'But the consequences are you being on your own with two young kids and not being with the man you love.'

'Life is mad, isn't it. I only came out here for a holiday.' She laughed loudly, wondering if this was the mental breakdown she had been anticipating.

'It's not your fault and it's not Stef's fault. Accidents happen.'

'I know it's no one's "fault", and we should probably stop talking about this like it's a tumour. It's a baby, it's a good thing.'

'It is a good thing.' Anton smiled.

'My problems are pretty pathetic in the grand scheme of things. Gloria nearly starved to death on a beach and I'm sad because I'm pregnant with the wrong gorgeous, kind, funny man's baby.'

'It's going to be a beautiful baby; I just hope it gets your brains.' Anton turned to her briefly and flashed a grin.

Catherine laughed and pushed Anton's arm. 'You are so mean.'

'You love that I'm mean.'

'I hope it's more like him than me.'

'If it's like him you'll spend the next eighteen years worrying about it sticking a fork in the plug sockets or being bitten by a wild animal it's chased or it cartwheeling off a cliff or eating poisonous flowers because they were pretty or ...'

'OK, I get it!' She laughed.

'It would be better for it to take after you.'

'I would rather have it be like Stef, happy and accident-prone, than sad and safe like me.'

'You know Stef once tried fitting as many sweets in his mouth as possible and he nearly choked to death? Beni had to do the Heimlich on him.'

'Oh God.' She smiled. 'It's going to be a handful, isn't it.'

'Do you want a boy or a girl?'

'I don't mind really, but I keep picturing a boy.'

'You look happy,' said Anton, glancing at her.

'I am happy. Now I've said my plan out loud it feels like the right thing to do. I'm going to break up with Stef, I'll ask him to come over tomorrow.'

'Still want me to stay at yours tonight?'

'Of course. Is Mateo at work this evening? How are things with you two?'

Anton nodded. 'Things are going really well, we're thinking of going on holiday soon.'

'Oh, where to? I'm so jealous!'

'Maybe Boston or New Orleans? I fancy a city break. That's one thing I miss about Europe, all the cities that are close together and each one so different.'

'I love that too. A quick two-hour flight from London and you can be in Berlin, or Copenhagen or Bucharest. When did you last leave Mexico?'

'I haven't since I got here, it's paradise. I never even thought about it until recently.'

'I miss the cold weather and old towns of Europe.'

'Me too, minus the cold weather. New Orleans looks different and interesting, I'm hoping we go there.'

'So, why the sudden desire to go somewhere?' asked Catherine.

'Mateo hasn't seen the world like I have.' He shrugged.

'Yes, you've managed to cram much more travel into your twenty-seven years than he has,' she said, smirking at him.

'What can I say? I'm a jet-setter.' Anton laughed as they approached the exit for the water park.

'Oh, Gloria, we're here!' said Catherine, turning to smile at her and gesturing for her to take off the headphones.

'I can't wait to go in the wave pool again,' said Anton, looking in the rear-view mirror at Gloria, who was dancing in her seat, refusing to stop listening to the music.

～

Catherine had moved into one of the residential properties owned by the hotel. They were all big, modern and rendered a bright white, and were just a stone's throw from the hotel itself. She had chosen one with a gated path to the beach at the end of its garden and a guard stationed just a few feet away in a cabin. She had convinced herself and her team back home that having a holiday home in their property portfolio was a good investment, and while by no means cheap, the house prices in that part of the world were not the most expensive, so the large four-bedroom home that overlooked the sea seemed like a steal.

'Are you as exhausted as I am?' asked Catherine, flopping onto the sofa in the sitting room of her house.

It was a small room, just big enough for a large cream corner sofa and three big boxes of Gloria's toys. A huge TV was fixed to the wall opposite the sofa and, despite the air con that was blasting, a fluffy rug made the space feel cosy, earning the room the nickname of 'the snug'.

'I am tired,' said Anton with a yawn. 'It didn't take you long to put Gloria to bed, did she just pass out?'

'She was asleep within seconds of her head hitting the pillow.' Catherine smiled. 'Sun exposure and lots of chlorine are parenting musts.'

'There's a bestselling book idea: "How to sedate children".' He laughed.

'She loves you. She might even like you more than me, you know.'

'Do you still want to watch a film or are you too tired?'

'Yeah, I'll watch one if you want to,' she said as the exhaustion her like a wave again. 'I'll go and get some snacks; do you want a drink?' she asked, standing up.

'Have you got any wine in? Or is that just cruel of me because you can't have any?'

'No, that's not cruel, that's pure evil,' she said, smiling. 'Is red OK?'

'That would be great.'

'OK, you decide on the film,' she said, but as she clutched the door handle, the exhaustion hit her again and the room started to spin.

'Oh God, you're bleeding,' said Anton suddenly, catching her as she fell. He lay her gently on the rug and watched as blood pooled around the crotch of her pyjamas. 'What do I do?' he said, his face stricken with panic.

The Wolf

Catherine wanted Gloria to see more of her homeland's culture, so for her seventh birthday, just six weeks after Catherine had turned twenty-seven and with the help of Ricky the excursion rep, she had arranged a private tour of the Coba ruins. They were going there in the morning, and in the afternoon, she was having a girls-only tea party at their new house.

The private tour included pick up and drop-off, so at eight o'clock in the morning a large black car pulled up at the house to collect Catherine and the birthday girl, and Maria and her daughter, Leonora, the latter having agreed to come along as guests.

To start with they thought that the driver/tour guide was quite odd. He insisted they call him The Wolf, had a shadow of D'Artagnan-esque facial hair and mainly talked to the grown-ups about his opinions on Donald Trump, which were surprisingly positive for someone on that side of the wall. Despite his strangeness though, Maria seemed to be having a ball with him sitting up front, which left Catherine to enjoy the passing scenery in peace next to the two sleepy little girls.

Once at the site, The Wolf gave them two options to get to the temple: they could either walk from the car park, or ride there in two-seater tuk-tuks. They opted for the faster option and were soon whipping through the trees, with their driver, Brian, peddling faster and faster to amuse Gloria. Catherine clung on to her giggling companion for dear life, but eventually relaxed enough to watch the light splinter through the passing trees and glance at some small Mayan buildings along the way.

Brian chatted to them while he peddled. *No mean feat,* thought Catherine, *talking and peddling on a hot day.* Sometimes she got out of breath just climbing the stairs, so she made a mental note to do more exercise.

Once at their destination, they stood waiting for The Wolf to catch them up and Catherine looked up at the huge temple, at its dark grey steps, crumbling in places, looking like a giant's staircase leading out of the trees into the sky.

'This is the Ixmoja pyramid, it's why most people visit us here. As you can see, you can climb to the top if you want to,' said The Wolf as he appeared next to them.

Like Brian, he had biked all the way there but was barely out of breath. He had even ditched his bicycle in a heap next to the tuk-tuks and jogged the rest of the way, seemingly eager to not keep them waiting.

Catherine gave Maria an impressed look and they both tried not to smile.

'How many steps are there?' asked Leonora, her big brown eyes looking up at The Wolf, waiting for an answer.

'120 steps, and from the top you can see views all over of the trees and the lagoons.'

'Kitty, I don't want to climb that thing,' said Gloria, holding on to Catherine's leg.

'I'm glad you said that, because neither do I.' Catherine laughed. 'Shall we just watch other people do it?'

'Well, I'm going up!' said Maria, walking off, the bangles and bracelets up her arms making their familiar rattle as she moved. 'Len, stay there with Lish, OK?'

'I'll come with you,' said The Wolf, after Catherine gave him an encouraging eye flick and smirk to indicate that he should follow Maria.

A large group of tourists arrived not long after them and stood around their guide for a few minutes before starting the climb. Catherine and the girls had a lot of fun watching them all. There was a mixture of brave souls, some charging hands and feet up the steep slope to the top with no fear, and others clearly not so happy with heights who got an impressive halfway up before they froze in fear.

Maria and the guide got to the top quickly, using the thin rope down the centre of the steps to stop themselves from falling, and Catherine tried to take a photo of them, zooming in as they waved from the top.

'It's more rugged than Chichen Itza, isn't it?' said Catherine when The Wolf was back on solid ground. 'Do you think they will stop people climbing it soon to preserve it?'

'It's 138 feet high, so much taller. You know why chicken pizza is more popular? American investment!' he said, rolling his eyes. 'It's just a sun dial! Here we have an actual temple, miles of archaeological site.' He sighed and put his hands on his hips. 'But no one has heard of this place. Had you, before you came here?'

'No, I hadn't,' said Catherine.

Despite his bitterness towards the rival tourist attraction, The Wolf turned out to be a great guide and made things interesting for the children. Next, he showed them the Mesoamerican ballgame arena, a long rectangular space with a sideways stone basketball-like hoop on each wall. He explained how players would have to try and get the ball through the hoop using just their hips, and produced a fist-sized rubber ball from his bag to show them. After some instruction, he threw the ball at Gloria and Leonora, who had fun trying to bounce it back to him, largely without success.

'So, before we finish the tour, I just want to tell you about the ceiba tree,' he said, gesturing to the many trees surrounding them once that they were back at the pyramid, near the tuk-tuks.

'In some of our neighbouring countries, this type of hollow tree is thought of negatively because, sadly, the trees were used to hang slaves. People in countries such as Cuba believed that the soul of the poor man or woman hanged would get trapped in the tree, and so the trees became bad omens. The Maya here, however, worshipped the ceiba tree, still do. It's considered a link between the underworld and heaven. Put simply, they believe your soul ascends the trees on the way up to heaven, or slides down the roots to hell. They celebrate the trees, there-fore, much like we do in Christianity where the tree is a symbol of life.'

'I always loved that idea of climbing the branches up to heaven. My grandmother used to tell me stories of the Mayan culture, her ancestors were Maya,' said Maria, nodding proudly and looking at the tops of the trees.

'Gloria has Maya ancestry too, 55% to be precise. I really want us to learn all about her heritage,' said Catherine to The Wolf.

'Race is a very interesting issue in Mexico,' said The Wolf, turning to Catherine. 'Most Mexican people are a mix of different races, mainly Spanish and Maya, but also African, and other European races like German. The majority of us are classed as mestizo, mixed.'

'I suppose England is the same, though. We have a really diverse population now,' said Catherine, handing Gloria a bottle of water and combing the girl's hair with her fingers to untangle the knots.

'But the difference here is, you could take two people whose families have lived in Mexico for hundreds of years, both equally "Mexican", and yet they could look totally different. In England, immigration wasn't too common until the mid twentieth century.'

'You're right. I suppose our little island stayed as it was, while our men went off around the world getting indigenous people pregnant. Sorry about that.'

'Exactly. But perhaps in England's case, it's similar to light-skinned people like yourself being a mix of locals and Vikings, and those with more olive skin being descended from the Normans? We are just a bit more diverse than the fifty-shades-of-white in Europe, and the Spanish invaded Mexico a few centuries later than the Normans invaded England, so it is more recent in our history.'

'That makes sense. You are very wise, Wolf, this has been really interesting,' Catherine said, looking at Maria with a slight smile.

'Like with Coba, unless you visit Mexico, most of this information never seems to make it to the rest of the world. A good example is Mexican television. You will notice that they mainly favour the more European-looking actors and actresses, which doesn't reflect the population accurately at all.' He shrugged.

'When I was living at the hotel it seemed most of the staff were Maya, or Maya descent, is that quite common?'

'Yes, especially in this region of Mexico. Unfortunately, they are probably paid less because of their background.'

'That's awful,' said Catherine, stroking Gloria's dark hair and worrying that her little girl could face similar prejudice one day.

'So, Maria, you have Maya ancestry? What about Leonora,

her dad must be more European?' asked The Wolf, glancing at the little girl, whose skin was much fairer than her mother's.

'Oh, you should let me get you one of those DNA test things that tells you your heritage!' said Catherine, starting to feel like she should get commission from the company that sold them.

'No, thanks,' said Maria.

'It's so much fun, please let me get you both one?'

'Lish, I said no,' said Maria seriously. 'Thanks though. I just don't want our DNA on file somewhere, it's creepy.'

'I don't blame you. The government could frame you for murder,' said The Wolf without any hint that he was joking.

Following another joyous ride back to the car park with Brian, whom Catherine tipped a $50 note for doing such a great job, they headed back to the house. On the return leg of the journey, The Wolf and Maria talked non-stop about Iron Maiden, his young son and, most importantly, his divorce.

Maria was smiling from ear-to-ear when they got into the house, and she admitted in a whisper that the guide had given her his number.

'That's great! He was nice,' whispered Catherine.

'He was, wasn't he. And just the right side of strange.' Maria laughed.

'I'm glad you said that and not me! Right then, girls, do you want to go and play while we wait for the other ladies to get here?' said Catherine.

Leonora and Gloria quickly ran off down the hallway.

The downstairs of the house consisted of an entrance hall with a large, slightly curved staircase to one side, and leading from that space were two doors. To the left was a downstairs bathroom, utility room and the 'snug'. If you turned right, you walked into a large kitchen/dining/living space that was bright and sparse, as the kitchen cabinets, walls, and even the sofa were all white. It was characterless, Catherine not yet having had the time to put her eclectic stamp on it. The only colourful feature of the room was the row of bifold doors at its end that framed views of the sea and its breaking waves as if it were a giant Monet canvas.

'Wow!' said Maria as they walked into the kitchen and she saw the view at the end of the room. 'This is such a beautiful house! I am dying of jealousy. Actually dying!'

'Well, you can visit whenever you like. I mean it. Day or night, just show up, mi casa es tu casa. Gloria would absolutely love more people to go swimming with.' Catherine smiled as she poured some iced water for them both.

'Who else is coming today?' asked Maria.

'Valentina, I think. And you know Miguel who performs with me at the hotel? His wife is coming with their two daughters who are twelve and thirteen; they're such a lovely family.'

'That's nice.'

Catherine began preparing the food for their tea party while Maria sat down at the breakfast bar and stared out at the ocean, seeming to be in a trance.

'When do you think you'll see The Wolf again?' asked Catherine, emphasising his name with an accent and a wiggle of her eyebrows.

'Well, when can you babysit?' asked Maria, her trance ending abruptly at the mention of her new tour-guide friend.

'Any time. I owe you about a hundred!'

'You don't owe me shit, you're my friend.'

'Thanks so much for today, Maria.'

'No, thank you! It's not every day I get a free day trip with

the added bonus of meeting a sexy, non-threatening weirdo.'
She laughed.

'Thank you for being such a good friend to me, and for
helping me with Gloria so much.'

'Don't be going all nice on me, Lish, I can't handle it.
Anyway, Leonora loves spending time with you. You've spoilt
her with all that hotel buffet food, she turns up her nose to my
cooking now!'

'Well, I can't cook, so now that we're living here she'll be
back to appreciating your food, I promise you that.' Catherine
laughed. 'I love that Gloria and Len are such good friends.'

'They play so nicely together. I was never like them, I was a
monster child,' Maria said.

'I can believe that!'

'My poor mama, what I put her through at times.'

'Leonora is only six, there's still time for her to go rogue.'

'God, I hope not.'

'You're a brilliant mum,' said Catherine.

'So are you. Sorry, I know you don't like being called a mum
but you basically are, and you're great.' Maria patted Catherine's
hand.

Catherine couldn't help it, the tears shot from her eyes like
a sprinkler.

'Oh God, what's wrong?' said Maria rushing to hug her
friend.

'Sorry, I'm fine,' Catherine said and then quickly wiped her
face.

'What's going on? Tell me.'

Catherine took a deep breath, 'I lost a baby.'

'Oh no.'

'I don't know how I'm supposed to feel.'

'You're not supposed to feel any specific way, Lish, you just
feel how you feel,' said Maria, squeezing Catherine tight.

'I just keep thinking about what could have been, what it would have looked like, how Gloria would have acted like a bossy little mum and I feel so guilty. I've let everyone down.'

'These things happen, they're more common than we realise. How far along were you?'

'Almost three months.'

'Oh honey, I'm so sorry. Is that why you didn't drink at Anton's party? I thought that was weird.'

Catherine nodded. 'I wasn't sure then, I was just being careful.'

'So, you did everything right, it just wasn't meant to be. I didn't know I was pregnant with Len until I was nearly four months, and I did all sorts in that time.'

'I didn't drink, but I wasn't eating properly.' Catherine sighed, staring at her more pronounced wrist bone, her stomach feeling comfortingly empty. 'I didn't really want a baby to start with, but I was coming around to the idea. I feel so numb about it all.'

'Does Stef know?'

'No.'

'How are you physically? Did you go to the hospital?'

'Yes, I'm OK,' said Catherine.

'You should have called me; you should have talked to me about it sooner,' said Maria, squeezing her one more time before letting Catherine go.

'Who would have thought when I walked into that bar with Stefano, that the barmaid would end up being one of my best friends?'

'Bar owner!' Maria reminded her, wagging a finger in fake chastisement.

'Sorry, I am so terrible for assuming you just worked there and didn't own the place. You are a girl boss.' Catherine smiled. 'How's business?'

'Not as good as it was when you and your friends were there all the time.'

'We haven't been getting together as a group as much lately.'

'How are things with you and Stefano, apart from all this?'

'To be honest, I haven't seen him much, I've been avoiding him. But things are OK,' said Catherine, thinking about Beni.

'You lucky girl, he's gorgeous. So, you've invited Valentina? Does she go anywhere without Stefano?'

'Sometimes I get on OK with her and other times it's like she hates me.'

'Well, you know exactly what I think – I think she loves your man.'

'He's not *my* man. I hope she comes today; Gloria really likes her, they're both arty souls,' said Catherine, pulling herself together and popping some mini enchiladas in the oven.

She stacked shop-bought cupcakes on a cake stand, blew up some balloons and just as she was laying the table with multi-coloured paper plates and napkins, Valentina walked in, not bothering to knock. She was holding a big wrapped present and Maria and Catherine exchanged a quick look of surprise.

'Hi, Val, thanks for coming.'

'Thanks for asking me,' she said.

'Gloria!' shouted Catherine into the hallway. 'Val is here with a present for you!'

In pounced the birthday girl at lightning speed to see her new gift. She tore off the brightly coloured wrapping paper and handed the rubbish to Catherine sporadically until a beautiful painting set complete with brushes, paints, a canvas and sketching paper was revealed.

'Oh Gloria, that's so nice, isn't it!' said Catherine.

'I love it!' said the birthday girl, hugging Valentina tightly around her middle.

'We could paint together soon if you like? We could have a play date,' said Val.

'Kitty, can we? Can Val visit soon so we can paint?'

'Of course she can. Thank you, Val, that's a really lovely gift.'

Val gave them all an awkward look and then she joined Maria who was sitting back at the breakfast bar.

'This house is a bit much, isn't it?' said Valentina, looking around like she had smelled something funny.

'It is big for just the two of us.'

'So, when's the housewarming?' she asked, plucking a cupcake from its stand and taking a big bite.

The Note

After a few hours of playing games and eating junk food, everyone had gone home but Valentina, who sat waiting on the sofa for Stefano to give her a lift home. Gloria was lying next to her, cake covered and sound asleep after a long, busy day.

Catherine was cleaning the kitchen when there was a knock at the door and Val jumped up to answer it, thinking it was Stef. But it wasn't, it was the private detective that Catherine had hired.

Catherine asked Val to sit with Gloria while she spoke to him in the back garden and it wasn't long before she walked back through the kitchen to show him out.

'That didn't take long, has he found someone?' asked Valentina quietly.

'Come outside?' asked Catherine.

Val followed her onto the veranda, which overlooked a square infinity pool and miles of glittering ocean beyond it. There was a large outdoor sofa and hot tub in one corner of the paved outdoor space, and a large mosaic-topped table in the shade, where they sat down.

'He brought me this letter; it's from the neighbour that lived next door to Gloria's family,' said Catherine, her throat feeling dry.

'What does it say?' asked Val.

'You can read it if you like?' Catherine said, handing over the folded piece of beige paper.

'I ... I have dyslexia. Reading something written in another language is especially difficult for me. Please will you read it out? Only if you want to, of course.'

Catherine nodded and began to read. 'To Mrs Lish, your private detective came to speak to me many months ago and I have been thinking of writing to you ever since, but I couldn't find the words. I want to say sorry for not speaking to the police about this, but I worried about getting into trouble. I want little Gloria to know the truth about what happened to her family. Ana was a sweet girl and Jorge seemed like a nice man when they first moved in next door. He was polite and always smiled at me. They seemed happy enough whenever I ran into them, and soon they had a baby, little Gloria.

'After a couple of years of them living there I started to hear them arguing. At first, I thought it was nothing unusual, me and my husband used to have our fair share of arguments, so I ignored it. But Jorge lost his job, and he started to drink heavily and soon strange men began to visit the apartment. Rumours started that they were taking drugs, and little Gloria was often left wandering the corridors at night. I tried to intervene, but Jorge threatened me – he said if I got involved, he would push fire through my letterbox while I slept. The once nice, polite boy had changed, not only in personality but in looks too; he had aged twenty years overnight, his teeth were rotting, it was plain to see that he was on drugs. Ana, however, looked as angelic as ever. When I saw her around, which became less and less often, she was so shy, she wouldn't look up from the ground to meet my eye. She always wore long dresses with long sleeves, even in the scorching heat, and I suspected he was hurting her, but I was a coward and did nothing. Everyone assumed she was as bad as her husband and turned their backs on her. She was all alone. Eventually, they had another baby and it cried all the time ... Are you OK, Val, shall I keep reading?' asked Catherine, seeing how upset Val looked.

'It's OK, carry on.'

'One night, I heard Jorge shouting louder than ever, I heard plates smashing and screams and the baby's cries were wailing like a siren, and then suddenly they stopped, like a switch had been flicked. I was certain Jorge had put his hand over the baby's mouth, or maybe Ana had, to stop Jorge from hurting him? But either way I didn't hear the baby cry again. A couple of hours later I watched little Gloria run from the apartment, too quick for me to catch up to her. I left the next day to go and stay with my sister for a few weeks, my nerves were shot to pieces. When I got back, I found out that they had died and that Gloria had been found by a kind stranger on a beach and was being looked after.

'Gloria needs to know that her mum was not on drugs. She was a sweet, kind girl who was mistreated and let down by her friends, family and neighbours, including me. I'm so sorry.

'Your detective tells me that you do not know how they died. Well, I have heard around the neighbourhood that Jorge had a stab wound in his stomach, which I am sure he deserved! I don't know what happened to the baby or Ana, but I think it is safe to assume Jorge was to blame in one way or another.'

Catherine looked at Val when she finished reading the letter. Neither of them said anything for a while, they just sat and absorbed the note's contents.

'I can't believe I didn't consider this as an option. I just assumed they were both bad people. This didn't cross my mind,' said Catherine.

'Why would you? When we live sheltered lives, we tend to see things as black and white.'

'You think I'm sheltered?' Catherine laughed, shaking her head.

'You are the whitest, most privileged person I know. You have a lot of money, which you throw around, a nice family, you're always smiling ... you seem kind of sheltered to me.' Val shrugged, raising her eyebrows at the table.

'I didn't grow up with money, and I may "throw it around" now and then, but I try to do good with it. I'm close to my brother but I haven't spoken to my mum in years, and my husband wasn't always the nicest to me, you know,' she said, looking at the letter in her hands. 'He was depressed and jealous; he was controlling and violent,' she said, putting her fingers to her neck, remembering how it felt when he would put all of his weight on her, squeezing, watching her eyes bulge before letting go just in time.

'I didn't know.'

'You shouldn't assume things about people. I shouldn't have assumed the worst of poor Ana, I should have known better.'

'What happened with your husband, did you leave him?'

'No, he died.'

'Oh god, Stefano didn't tell me.'

'Stef doesn't know,' said Catherine, thinking, *He doesn't know me at all*.

'How did he die?'

'He killed himself by driving his car off a bridge. I've never told anyone that. Beni kind of knows, but not the full story.'

'Do you want to talk to me about it?'

'Do you care?' asked Catherine.

'It would be nice to understand you better.'

Catherine nodded and looked at the sea. 'I fell pregnant, but I had an abortion straight away. I just couldn't face bringing a baby into that situation. I waited until he was rough with me again and then told him I'd lost it because of that. He blamed himself, that's why he did what he did, or so the suicide note said. I didn't mean for my lie to do that, I just thought it might shock him into getting help. I was going to end it all too, despite everything I really did care about him and I couldn't deal with the guilt. I didn't think I could cope without him either; mainly because he had told me every day for so long that I couldn't do this, and I couldn't do that. But after a while, I realised I was free, that I wasn't as worthless as he'd had me believing. I never told anyone about the way he treated me, no one else needed to know.'

'What a bastard, how could he do that to you?' said Val, frowning.

'I gave up so many things for him, but it wasn't enough.' Catherine shrugged. 'I loved him so much but he just couldn't see that. He didn't believe that I loved him, because he couldn't love himself. And of course, as his jealousy got worse, and he started to treat me badly, to beat me, I did stop loving him, he *was* losing me. He changed so much from the boy I met in uni.' Catherine took a deep breath. 'He wasn't well, I pity him.'

'He hurt you, he controlled you, don't you hate him?'

'He's dead, what good would hating him do now? I hid the note he left for me that said he was sorry, and when the police came my bruises were hidden, so they didn't ask questions. It had been raining and his death was ruled an accident; it was better that the family didn't know the truth.'

'Why are you still wearing your wedding ring?'

'Well, the widow that takes off her ring is a bitch, right?' Catherine said, looking at the white gold band and realising that her hand was trembling.

'Take it off right now and throw it into the sea,' said Val.

Catherine smiled slightly, then looked at the ring again, wriggled it off her finger and put it on the table.

'Why are you telling me this, if you've never told anyone else?'

'Because I feel terrible for misjudging poor Ana. And ... I see the jealousy in your eyes when you look at Stef. I don't know what's happened between you, but I do know you need to address it before it turns toxic. Why did you break up? You obviously still love him.'

'We didn't work. You know Stef, he only sees the positive side of things,' said Val, staring at and running her fingers along the mosaic tiles on the table's surface. 'We weren't a good fit.'

'Then why don't you just find someone else and move on?'

'It's not so easy to stop loving someone, is it? Logically, I know we aren't right together but try telling my heart that.'

'Do you want to talk to me about it, about anything?'

'I really don't want to. Not because it's you, I just don't like talking about this stuff, but thanks for asking.'

'I want us to get along,' Catherine put her hand on top of Val's.

Valentina smiled. 'I can be 10% nicer to you?'

'I'll take it! You really are so beautiful, you know; you could have anyone you wanted. It's hard not to be envious of you at times.'

'Do you think I wouldn't swap my bony ass for your va-va-voom in a heartbeat? We all want what we don't have,' said Val, her eyes flicking up and down Catherine's slender frame.

'You're right.'

'You make Stef happy and it's good to see him happy. I'm sorry for being a bitch.'

'I want to see you be happy too,' said Catherine.

'I'm sorry I haven't taken the time to get to know you.'

'There's still time. Gloria loves you; will you visit and paint with her?'

'Of course. Maybe she could be the next Frida! So, why don't you talk to your mum any more?'

'She accused me of killing Thomas. What she thought I did to him, I don't know. We lived in a tiny village, if I'd cut his brakes, he would have rolled into a lamp post long before he went flying off that bridge.'

'Why did she think that?'

'I don't know. I was acting a bit funny, I guess. I probably did seem guilty because that's how I felt, but it's not like I'm some character out of *Dynasty*, forever hatching schemes. Why would she do that to her own daughter?'

'What did she do exactly?' asked Valentina.

'She went to the police,' said Catherine, letting out an annoyed scoff, anger seething through her.

'Mio Dio, what a cow,' said Valentina, screwing up her face.

'Seriously, the biggest cow on earth.'

'Why did she care so much about him?'

'Me and Thomas had been together for a few years when my mum started dating his dad,' said Catherine with disgust.

'What?'

'I know, I was mortified. Thankfully, it was after our wedding. That would have been one crazy confusing head table otherwise, wouldn't it?'

Valentina nodded, and picked at the jagged edges of the tabletop.

'In the end, she cared more about her partner's son than her own daughter. She didn't know what he was like, I know that, but she was still accusing me of something that I couldn't and wouldn't ever have done. I was twenty-three and all alone but for my teenage brother and a handful of old friends who forgave me for ignoring them for years. Even if I had killed him, shouldn't she have been on my side anyway? If Gloria killed someone, I would be on hers.'

'She's your mother, she was wrong to do what she did and I don't blame you for not speaking to her any more. You are definitely not sheltered.' Val smiled.

Catherine laughed. 'Thanks.'

'Are you going to have a housewarming party, then?'

'Will you help me to plan it?'

'Yes! Let's do a fancy-dress theme?' said Valentina, the most enthusiastic Catherine had ever seen her look about anything.

'What theme?'

'It would have to be movie stars, you love films!'

'What would you go as?'

'Let's both go as badass Tarantino bitches.'

Catherine smiled. 'OK. But we will have to coordinate; Stef's head would explode if we both turned up as The Bride.'

'I am seeing less of him. I'm stepping back, you know, I really am,' said Val seriously.

'You don't have to do that.' Catherine shrugged. 'If you want to be with him, then you should be.'

'I want him to get on with his life. I need to leave him alone, I know I do.'

'Maybe it's me who should step back and let you be together?'

'No,' said Val, frowning.

'You know me and him aren't serious, we never will be. He loves you, Val, you do know that, right? If you want him, you should take him, he would be so happy.'

'I'm never going to take him, Catherine.'

'Can I be honest with you? You won't tell him this?'

'I won't tell him.'

'I don't know how much longer me and him will be together for. He is the kindest, purest and most fun person I have ever met, but I don't love him and he doesn't love me. I thought love didn't matter, but it does. I don't want to hurt him, I care about him, I love being around him ... he's hard to walk away from,' she said, putting her hand on Val's and giving her a knowing look.

'Are you missing Beni?'

Catherine nodded, instantly feeling sad, emotion stinging her eyes, her heart aching.

'Are you going to talk to Gloria about her mum, then?' asked Val quickly.

'We already talk about her when Gloria wants to, she misses her. I wish I had some photos of her mum to put around the—'

Loud thuds began to echo inside the house and Catherine stood up quickly to go and answer the door. Her mind raced as she walked through the kitchen, pondering why Val had asked about Beni and then changed the subject so rapidly. Was she right? Were they dating? She didn't dare to ask, and although it was breaking her heart, it was none of her business who he dated anyway. She had to forget him.

The Discovery

I
t had been eleven months and twenty-two days since she had found Gloria on the beach, and Catherine was sitting in her kitchen looking out at the sea and enjoying some peace and quiet. She had hired a tutor to visit three times a week to get Gloria up to speed ready for starting school, and during the two-hour sessions, Catherine did what many mums and women in general do during their downtime, she cleaned the house, washed clothes and prepared food. She also checked her emails and talked to her brother, happy to be more involved with the business again.

With all her jobs done, Catherine was enjoying a rare moment of calm; for her, these were dangerous though, as they allowed her mind to wander. She couldn't quite believe what a crazy life she was leading, especially compared to how things had been a few years before, when she would spend her time between her home and the office with little in between. She could never have guessed what was around the corner for her.

Suddenly, there was a knock at the door, shattering her calm. It was the private detective again and before Catherine had even had chance to invite him inside, he proudly announced that he had found Gloria's great-aunt living nearby.

He was a tall man and extremely thin, which made the suit he was wearing appear sharp and angular. His hair was very neat, like a Lego man, and his face was expressionless; it was like a mannequin had come to life. Catherine had never enjoyed their interactions.

'If she's been living nearby all this time, how is it that you haven't found her before now? I've been paying you for nearly eleven months and now, with just over a week to the deadline, you suddenly find someone?' said Catherine, allowing the annoyance to show on her face and be heard in her voice.

'I have worked on your case tirelessly, Mrs Lish. I got you that letter from the neighbour a couple of weeks ago, and this aunt has moved around a lot, going from rental to rental, not leaving a forwarding address. I thought it was a dead end until one of her old neighbours called me last night.'

Catherine sighed. 'What do we know about her?'

'Not a lot at the moment.'

Catherine gave him a disapproving look that she hoped implied he wasn't worth the money he charged.

'This is her address. She is Gloria's great-aunt on her father's side, and she is sixty-eight years old.'

Catherine took the piece of paper from him, and for a split second as she held it in her hand, she thought about how easy it would be to rip it in half and pretend she knew nothing about this relative that might take Gloria away from her.

That afternoon, Gloria and Catherine got into a taxi. They drove thirty minutes down the highway, before turning onto a slightly smaller road and pulling up outside Maria's bar.

'Thank you so much, Maria,' said Catherine, hurriedly pressing Gloria into her care, saying goodbye and getting back into the taxi.

They drove for no more than ten more minutes before the taxi stopped in front of a run-down duplex with clothes hanging on the balconies and litter on the street. Before Catherine got out of the car, feeling uneasy, she asked the taxi driver to wait for her. The manicured lawns and bright white interiors of her make-believe life felt foolish all of a sudden as she stepped into the real Mexico. The sounds of waves lapping were gone, replaced by shouting and music and cars revving.

Catherine walked up to the front door, double-checking the address on the now crumpled piece of paper in her hand before knocking loudly. She waited for a full two minutes before a thin lady with silver-streaked hair, who looked far older than sixty-eight, answered the door breathlessly, hunched over a walking frame.

'Are you Izelda Garcia?' asked Catherine, speaking as clearly and loudly as possible in her best Spanish.

'Yes, dear, that's me. How can I help you?' asked the older woman, still struggling for breath.

'I'm here about your great-niece, her name is Gloria. She is your nephew, Jorge's daughter. Do you want to go and sit down and we can talk inside?'

Izelda looked up at her, probably to see if Catherine looked threatening. Just like Gloria had done that day on the beach before agreeing to go with her.

'Well, all right,' said Izelda, turning in slow motion with her walker like a bus doing a U-turn on a narrow country lane.

They walked down the corridor at a snail's pace and into a small sitting room with a terracotta floor and bare stone walls, which was packed with knick-knacks and photographs.

While Izelda collapsed into her chair and tried to catch her breath, Catherine sat down on the sofa opposite, looking around the room, waiting. Once the infirmed lady seemed more comfortable, Catherine pulled a photograph from her handbag.

'This is your great-niece, Gloria,' she said, presenting it to Izelda.

The older lady pulled the photo out of Catherine's hands and held it close to her spectacled face. 'Jorge's daughter, you said. My sister's Jorge? He has a child?'

'That's right.'

'She's a pretty thing, isn't she.' Izelda smiled.

'Do you know what happened to Jorge, Mrs Garcia?'

'No, but I imagine that I could guess,' she said, handing the photograph back to Catherine.

'He died and so did Gloria's mother,' Catherine said softly.

'That's awful. He always loved a drink, Jorge did. Was it that? Was Ana a drinker too? I didn't know they had a child.'

'Jorge was a drug user, but Ana wasn't. She tried her best for the children, I think. Jorge was ...' Catherine struggled with how to say it; she didn't want to upset the lady but was determined for Ana's memory to no longer be soiled. 'It's thought that Jorge was abusive. I'm sorry to tell you that, but I am led to believe that it was largely because of the drink and drugs.'

The news seemed to hit Izelda hard, the corners of her mouth turned down and her eyes clouded over.

'They had a little boy too, but unfortunately he died. I found Gloria on a beach, very badly malnourished and quite neglected in every sense.' Catherine watched as all the colour drained from the older woman's face. 'But it's OK,' said Catherine, leaning towards her and taking her wrinkled hand in her own. 'I've been looking after Gloria for almost a year now and she couldn't be any more transformed from that scared little girl I found on the sand. She is independent and bright and really funny; she loves art and swimming.'

'Where are you from, dear?'

'I'm from England. Sorry, is my accent terrible?'

'No, your Spanish is excellent, just a slight accent. Do you live here, then?'

'Kind of. I was here on holiday when I found Gloria.'

'You stayed here all this time just to look after the girl?'

Catherine nodded. 'The police couldn't find any family. I didn't want her to go into an orphanage so I stayed and I hired a private detective to find a family member who could take her in, but it's taken him a long time. He said you moved around a lot?'

'Yes, I'm not at all well, you see. Each time I moved it was because a piece of my body was failing me. At first it was just my hands. I couldn't work any more so I had to move to a smaller apartment; then my lungs failed me and I needed somewhere cleaner, closer to the sea air; then my legs gave up on me and I needed a ground-floor apartment. But I won't be moving again, dear. This is small, not far from the sea and on the ground floor. My next move will be up to heaven.'

'I see,' said Catherine, unsure how to continue after such a declaration.

'I'm in no fit state to look after a child,' said the older lady, gripping Catherine's hand again and looking at the photograph of Gloria on Catherine's lap. 'She is so like her father, almost identical. She looks happy enough with you, can't you keep her?'

Catherine let out an audible sigh of relief. She couldn't help it, it just burst out of her before she knew it was coming. It was as though she had been holding her breath since the detective had told her about his discovery.

'I'm sorry, I was trying to do the right thing by coming here today. I thought Gloria should be with family, but if I'm honest, the thought of letting her go was breaking my heart.'

'She deserves a family, a chance at life. You should adopt her, make it official.'

'I will,' said Catherine. 'Do you have any other family? Do you have children?'

'I have a son that lives in America. He sends me money when he can, God bless him, he's a good boy.' She smiled, nodding to a photo of a young family on the wall.

'Are they your grandchildren?' asked Catherine.

'Yes. I've never met them but we talk on the phone. I can't go there with my health and if he comes here, he may not be able to go back.'

Catherine nodded in understanding. 'You could do a video call with them?'

'I don't have the gadgets for that, dear, and I wouldn't know how.'

'I have a laptop; I'll help you. I'm rubbish with technology too, but I think I know how to do it now.'

'That would be great.'

'I would really like Gloria to know more about her family, do you want to meet her? I can go and fetch her now if you like, she isn't far away?'

'I would love to meet her,' said the lady, smiling.

Catherine dashed out to the waiting taxi and went to pick up Gloria from Maria's. She hugged her friend at the side of the road again and told Maria that she would call her and fill her in on everything as soon as possible. Once again back in the taxi, Catherine explained to Gloria that they were going to see her great-aunt Izelda and that she was to behave herself as the old lady was quite poorly.

When they arrived at Izelda's, Catherine let them both in to the apartment, as per the older woman's instructions so she wouldn't have to sprint to the door again. Gloria walked shyly into the sitting room and sat so close to Catherine that she was practically on her knee. It wasn't long before the little girl came out of her shell, however, as aunt and great-niece caught up on everything from favourite types of cake to how high Gloria could jump, the latter of which she demonstrated several times.

Izelda showed Gloria photos of her dad when he was a child, her grandparents, and her mum and dad at their wedding. Gloria took it all in silently and Catherine wondered what the small girl was thinking, if she understood or not.

'My mum and dad are dead,' she said suddenly to her aunt.

'I'm so sorry, sweetheart,' said Izelda.

'But they loved me very much and asked Kitty to look after me,' she said, and then continued to flick happily through the photo album that was perched on her knees.

'That's right, and didn't they choose well?' said Izelda, giving Catherine a kind smile. The two women then chatted for a shockingly long time about English tea and the perfect consistency for guacamole.

'He is a bad man,' said Gloria abruptly, having opened a new book of photos.

'Who is?' asked Catherine, looking at Izelda in surprise and sliding the album from Gloria's grip. 'Who's a bad man?' she asked, looking at the page of photos, wondering who Gloria could mean.

'Him, he's the man that hurt my arm,' said Gloria, pointing at a young man standing near to Ana on her wedding day.

'That man is the one that bruised your arm? He gave you the bruises you had when I found you?' asked Catherine.

'Yes.'

'Sweetheart, are you sure? I thought your dad hurt your arm?'

'No, papá didn't do that. He hurt mama, but that man hurt my arm, he grabbed me.'

'Izelda, who is this?' said Catherine, reeling from all the new information that Gloria was unexpectedly sharing. She held the photo album under the older lady's nose and pointed to the man.

'That's Ana's brother, Luis.'

'She has a brother? God, that private detective is useless.'

'He's been in and out of prison. I only met him a few times at family events, you wouldn't want him caring for her, dear,' said Izelda quietly.

'Gloria, do you remember anything else that happened that night?'

'Papá kept asking my mama for something, but she wouldn't give it to him. He got mad and she told me to hide.'

'You are such a brave girl, thank you for telling me that. If you remember anything else you know you can tell me, don't you?' said Catherine, hugging Gloria tightly. 'Izelda, could you please tell me more about Luis? Anything at all might be useful.'

'I think he worked with Jorge, at a wholesale company or a factory, something like that? That's how he met Ana, through Luis, I remember them saying that at the wedding. Sorry, I don't know anything else. I wouldn't go looking for him, he's no good.'

Sometime later, Catherine and Gloria hugged Izelda goodbye and promised to visit again very soon with the laptop. They got back into the taxi for a final time that day clutching a handful of family photos, including the one of Ana's brother, and they drove back to their home.

That evening, Catherine called Maria and told her every-thing and thanked her for helping yet again. She called Anton, Stefano and even Val, and told them all about it. She wished she could call Beni, and in that moment, she missed him more than ever. Then, she called Mr Hernandez and asked him to start the adoption process. He suggested that changing Gloria's surname would make getting English citizenship more straightforward when the time came, and so Gloria Castillo would soon become Gloria Castillo-Lish.

Finally, she called the private detective and gave him one more task: to find Gloria's uncle.

The Invitation

Catherine stood in her hallway, looking at herself in the floor-length mirror, twisting this way and that to take in what she was wearing from every angle. It was the night of her fancy-dress housewarming party and her costume consisted of a pink leopard print skirt that hugged her figure, and a sheer, cobalt Bardot top, with an even brighter blue bralette underneath.

As she turned to go back into the kitchen to continue setting up, there was a loud knock at the door, and after one more self-conscious tug on her skirt she felt marginally ready to greet the first of her guests.

'Beni?' she said in surprise, as he stepped into her home. 'I wasn't expecting you.'

He was wearing a white T-shirt, red jacket and black trousers, with his hair shaped into a messy quiff, but Catherine didn't notice his outfit, she could only see how uncomfortable and tired he looked.

'I thought we weren't seeing each other any more? Oh, but if you're here to see Val and the others then they aren't here yet, but feel free to come through and wait?'

'Why would I want to see Val? I'm here to see you,' he said, putting his hand lightly on her waist to stop her walking off. She looked so thin, he thought, and then with a jolt, he took a big step back and handed her a gift bag at arm's length. 'This house is insane,' he said, spinning in a slow circle to take it all in.

'It's a bit much, isn't it. I feel a bit gaudy, like a Real House-wife of Riviera Maya or something. And I mean, look at me, I'm dressed for it too.' She smiled nervously. 'Thanks for this, it's lovely,' she said, taking a purple photo frame with a photo of her and Gloria in it out of the gift bag. 'Did you take this photo? I don't think I've seen it before.'

He nodded. 'At the beach. God, it's like a hotel,' he said, looking up at the high ceiling, avoiding making eye contact with her blue-sheathed cleavage.

'Gloria loves playing hide and seek here, I lose her at least ten times a day,' she said in a whisper, leading him from the hallway into the large kitchen. 'But don't tell the social worker that!'

She placed the photo frame on a shelf and it suited the space perfectly, as after some decorating, the huge room was much more colourful. Bright cushions littered the white sofa, and photos and framed paintings by Gloria covered one wall. Colourful accessories gave the previously clinical kitchen life, and a turquoise rug, mirrors and table runner made the dining part of the room look at one with the ocean just beyond the glass doors.

'Where is Gloria?' asked Beni, looking at the photos of himself and his friends on her wall.

'She's been with Maria today so I could clean and tidy. She'll be here soon.'

'I heard you're going ahead with the adoption. You never found any of her family, then? I can't believe you've had her for over a year already,' said Beni.

'So much has happened since I last saw you, so many times I wanted to call you and tell you stuff,' she said, looking at the floor.

'Like what?'

'That useless private detective finally found a great-aunt from her dad's side. Come and sit down outside with me for a minute?'

Catherine had hired young helpers from the local area to come and act as waiting staff. They were almost all younger siblings or children of her friends from the hotel and were inexperienced and very shy. More than once since they had arrived, she had found them in a panicked huddle in the middle of the kitchen, watching the burritos cook in the wall oven while nervously chatting.

'Come on, guys!' she cheered at them in Spanish as she passed through the kitchen with Beni following her. She issued some words of encouragement and handed them some trays to take outside, giving the bubbling burritos a concerned glance herself.

Out on the sunny veranda, Catherine and Beni sat down on the plush white sofa as the young hired help bustled around and finished setting up for the party.

'Wow,' said Beni, taking in the view.

'So, there's a great-aunt, but she's not very well ...' continued Catherine, filling him in on everything from the neighbour's letter about Jorge and Ana, to aunt Izelda and trying to find bad egg, uncle Luis.

'Be careful, Lish, that guy sounds dangerous,' said Beni, who had been watching Catherine's blue eyes sparkle as she spoke. He had missed her so much.

'Can I get you some drinks, Miss Catherine?' asked a young girl in a white dress.

'Oh, yes please, Isabella, can we have a beer and a white

wine? You don't need to call me Miss Catherine, OK? You look beautiful. Beni, this is Maria's sister, Isabella.'

Beni nodded and smiled in greeting and Isabella scurried off to the kitchen to fetch the drinks, looking like she had seen a ghost.

'So ... I've met with the social worker a few times and I've talked to Gloria about it all and she's happy, the adoption should be finished soon, it's exciting.'

'I'm glad it all worked out,' he said with a tiny smile.

Catherine watched Beni. He was jigging his leg up and down and kept looking around, he seemed agitated. He accepted his beer from a blushing Isabella and began to drink it quickly.

'You're James Dean, then?' said Catherine, smoothing down the collar of his jacket.

'Straight from the 1950s,' he said with a hint of a smile. 'And you're Alabama from *True Romance?*'

'Oh good, I was worried no one would know who I am.'

'You look great.'

'I'll leave you to chill out here then, the others will be here soon,' she said as she stood up.

'I want to talk to you, please don't go,' he said, grabbing for her hand.

'Beni.' She sighed, not looking at him. 'I don't know how to be around you any more. Do you remember what you said to me in the hospital?'

'Kind of.'

'How is your rib and everything?' She frowned at him, watching his shaking knee.

'I'm fine, thanks to you.' He looked up at her, the gaze from his brown eyes had an unfamiliar edge to it.

'Lish!' Anton came running out onto the veranda and swept her into a hug.

'Hi, you look great!' She laughed, running her hands through his pigtails and prodding his beard. 'Thanks so much for coming,' she said, hugging him tightly again, for a long time, needing it after the exchange with Beni.

'Hi, Beni,' said Anton, looking at Catherine in surprise. 'Mateo is just parking the car. Oh, Lish, this place is a mansion! I can never quite believe that you live here, I love the new decor,' he gushed, clicking his sparkling red shoes together.

He handed Catherine a big candle with a pink bow wrapped around it and she was still giggling as she accepted it.

She cringed. 'It's too big.'

'The candle?'

'No, no, the candle is lovely, thank you!' she said, putting it gently onto the glass table. 'No, the house is too big. I'm still not used to it; it feels a bit over the top.' She sat back down next to Beni, close to him.

'Well, why don't you offer a room to Beni?' said Anton, sitting down opposite them and sipping the champagne that Isabella had just delivered.

'Why would Beni want to live here?' asked Catherine.

'Beni is searching for somewhere new to live at the minute,' said Anton, looking between the two of them, his pigtails swinging slightly.

'Shut it, Anton, that's private!'

'No, screw your pride, Beni, it makes perfect sense to me. She has all this space and you're about to be evicted! He will be homeless in a few days, Lish.'

'Oh my God, Anton!' said Beni, his leg bouncing frantically again.

'You're about to be evicted? What happened?' asked Catherine slowly, concern coursing through her.

'Umm, my landlord expects me to pay rent. He's very unreasonable like that.' Beni rubbed his neck awkwardly and faked a tiny smile. 'I'm sorting it, I was hoping to keep this quiet, it's embarrassing,' he said, shooting Anton a scathing look.

'Anton, could you give us a minute please?' asked Catherine seriously.

Anton threw up his hands theatrically and rolled his eyes before stomping into the kitchen.

Catherine turned her knees towards Beni. She was close enough to see the murmurings of stubble along his square jaw and strong neck, and just the familiar smell of his aftershave was enough to make her feel flushed.

'If you want to move in, you can,' she said.

'I can't do that.'

'I wish you'd told me about being evicted sooner.'

'Why, so you could pay my rent? I'm not a charity case, it's enough that you paid for my medical bills, I saw how much it cost. I'll never be able to pay you back.'

'You look knackered, what's going on with you?'

'I've got it under control ... kind of.'

'Got what under control?' She twisted in her seat to face him head on, then placed her hands on his shoulders like she was afraid he might float away if she didn't stay tethered to him.

'I've been drinking, a lot. I was in pain for so many different reasons and I fixed it all by reaching for the bottle,' he said, staring at the ground. 'I lost a week's wages when I hurt my leg and even more when I had the surgery and I struggled to catch up. I fell behind with the rent, I felt bad, so I went out drinking again, then I had even less money. It was a cycle. I'm just like my dad.'

'You're not your dad, Beni ... but should you be drinking that?' she asked, eyeing the bottle in his hand.

'Probably not.'

'It's OK to not be OK sometimes, but if you struggle again you need to talk to someone about it, not just walk away from everyone.' Her eyes misted as her grip on his shoulders wavered and slid down his strong arms.

'I'll be fine. One of the reasons I pushed you away was because I didn't want you and Gloria to see me like that. I was a mess.'

'I've been so worried about you, I've missed you.'

'I promise I'll talk more and I'll stop drinking,' he said, taking her hands in his. He couldn't take his eyes off her trembling lip, plump and bright red from a slick of lipstick.

'I think I need to stop drinking too,' she said, looking at her glass on the coffee table.

'You? Why?' asked Beni, realising he must have been wrong about her being pregnant and feeling like an idiot.

'I've drunk more this year than I ever have in my life. I drink to calm my nerves, and to deal with social anxiety especially. You must have noticed how different I am when I drink? I need to stop using booze as a mask. So, when you move in, we'll stop drinking together, OK?'

'I can't move in, Lish.'

'OK, well, think about it, the offer is there. I'm just glad you're here now,' she said, remembering for the hundredth time what he had told her about having vodka and pills at home.

'Won't Stef think it's a bit weird that you're living with me?'

'You're his best friend, surely he'd rather you live here than on the street?'

'Won't he get jealous?'

'You know it's not like that with me and him, we do our own thing.'

'I heard he's seeing less of Val now, maybe he cares more about you than you think?'

Catherine looked at him, hunched, looking sad. She just wanted to tell him how she felt, wrap her arms around him and protect him from whatever was hurting him.

'I honestly hate it here,' she admitted, looking at the sea. 'I'm not sleeping, it's too big and I'm scared. I'm scared all the time.'

'Isn't Stef here with you every night?'

She shook her head. 'We have no neighbours yet; they're still selling the houses, one by one, so it could be months until I live within ten houses of anyone. It's thirty-four steps from my bed to Gloria's room. If someone broke in and tried to snatch her, I'm thirty-two more steps away than when we were sharing our little hotel room. I've started sleeping with a night light on and have a carving knife in my bedside drawer.' She stopped to take a few calming breaths. 'I know we're not far from the hotel, that the hotel is really just beyond those trees over there, but it all feels so different here. It's been really lonely,' she admitted, clutching his arm.

'Why isn't Stef here more?'

Catherine shrugged. 'You said in the hospital that I'm full of shit, and you're right, I am. I could have moved me and Gloria into a small apartment somewhere nearby, I didn't need to buy this big house. You know why I did?'

'Why?'

'I thought there would be fewer lizards up here on the rocks next to the sea.'

He felt horrible as he absorbed this confession. She looked so crestfallen, so wounded. He pushed the hair back from her face. 'And are there less lizards?'

'I saw two already today,' she said, smiling slightly.

'I'm not surprised, there are marine lizards, you know. I don't know if they have them here but they like rocks next to the sea and normal iguanas won't mind it here either.'

'What? Why would you tell me that!' she said, looking horrified.

Beni smiled, an actual smile. 'I'll move in. You've made me

worried about you. I don't want you to be scared out here and it's a great offer. I'll protect you from the sea lizards and potential kidnappers.'

'Thanks.'

'Gloria is lucky to have you and this gigantic mansion. Please forget what I said in the hospital, I was just trying push you away ... and it worked.'

'A lot has happened, Beni. I didn't want to stay away, but it was for the best.'

'But now you don't mind living with me?' he asked, looking confused.

'Things are different than they were,' she said, touching his face, looking into his eyes.

'Friends again?' he asked, his heart beating fast.

'Yes,' she said, hugging him tight. 'Everything is going to be OK. You look after me, and I'll look after you.'

'I've missed you so much,' he whispered, smelling the coconut scent of her hair and closing his eyes.

'I had better finish sorting the food.' Catherine stood up and smoothed down her skirt. 'Gloria is going to be so happy to see you, she's missed you.'

Beni watched her dart back into the kitchen and start frantically taking trays out of the oven before greeting a yellow-suited, green-faced Mateo, and hugging Anton again. The house was filling with people quickly. Next to arrive were Miguel and his wife, dressed as wizards, then a fairy-winged Maria with Gloria and Leonora in princess dresses; a man that Beni didn't recognise stood beside them in an Iron Maiden T-shirt and a blonde wig and glasses.

Beni continued to sit out on the veranda by himself, watching as the kitchen filled with superheroes, vampires, and long-dead movie stars, as the waitresses, bartenders, maids and holiday reps from the hotel all bustled in to the space. Finally,

Stefano walked in with Val, dressed respectively as Indiana Jones, and Mia from *Pulp Fiction*, the latter wearing a cropped black wig, and a big white shirt as a dress. Beni watched Stefano pull Catherine into a hug, kissing her all over her face while her oven-mitted hands groped at his back and knocked off his hat. Val stood watching them, but then she too hugged Catherine and stood talking to her for a while as though they were friends. Beni finished his drink and went in search of another.

~

'Hi, Mateo,' said Catherine, hugging him carefully so as to not get any green face paint on her. 'How's work?'

'It's been busy, but I'm getting plenty of overtime, which is good.'

'That's great. Anton ...' she said, hugging her friend close, one of his pigtails sticking into her closed eye.

'I knew Beni would come back eventually,' he said.

'Did you tell him about tonight? I didn't invite him.'

'No, I didn't. He must have heard about it from some of the others and thought it was a good time to see you?'

'I'm so glad he's here,' said Catherine.

'He looks much better than he has in a long time,' said Anton.

'Hey, Catherine,' Miguel said, tapping her on the shoulder and handing her some flowers.

'Hi, Miguel! Hi, Sophia! Thank you for these, they're beautiful. You both look great!' she said, turning to one of her helpers and asking him to put the flowers in a vase and to get them some drinks. 'Where are your girls?'

'My mum is watching them, it's nice to have a night off, as horrible as that sounds.'

'Oh, don't worry, I know all about needing a night off from a little girl. And you have two. Double trouble!' She smiled.

'Hola, Lish!' said Maria, walking in with Gloria and Leonora.

'Hola, chicas! Oh, girls you look amazing, look at your dresses,' said Catherine, bending down to hug them.

'I'm Cinderella and Len is Belle,' said Gloria, moving from side to side, letting her dress swish at her feet.

'I know, I can tell. You look just like real princesses! I've put some snacks and games and presents in the snug for you both, why don't you go and play in there away from all the boring grown-ups?'

'OK!' they both shouted excitedly.

'Hi, Wolf,' said Catherine, standing up. 'I'm glad you could make it. Are you Garth from *Wayne's World?*'

'See, people can tell who I'm meant to be,' he said to Maria.

She smiled and rolled her eyes. 'Lish doesn't count, she's like an encyclopaedia of movies. If someone else guesses it, then I will admit I'm wrong!'

'Thanks for inviting me,' Wolf said to Catherine, who smiled and dashed off to take more things out of the oven and put more in.

She waved as other guests started to arrive, and sent her helpers off one by one to get them drinks, like launching fighter jets from a warship.

'Lish!' said Stefano, squeezing in to the busy room.

'Hello, Mr Jones,' she said, still wearing the oven gloves when he began kissing her all over her face. 'Val, I love your outfit!' she said, pulling away from him and throwing her arms around Valentina. 'You even have the bloody nose, it's perfect!'

'You look amazing too. How do you make a prostitute outfit look classy?'

'I don't know how to answer that,' she said, and they both laughed.

'Is everything going to plan so far? Is the food done? Do you need help with anything?' asked Val.

'I just need to mix some big bowls of punch,' said Catherine.

'I can do that,' said Stefano, looking at Val and Catherine warily. 'You two OK?'

'Of course! Be sure to make it lethal, I don't want anyone leaving here sober,' said Val.

'All the stuff is on the table over there, Stef,' said Catherine, pointing, then threw a concerned look at Beni sitting outside alone.

'I thought you said you hadn't invited him?' said Stefano, following her gaze.

'I didn't invite him; I don't know who did.' She shrugged.

Catherine kicked off her sandals at the bottom of the sweeping staircase. The party was in full swing out on the veranda as her friends ate and drank and danced beneath a canopy of fairy lights that had been twinkling away since the sun had set. It was quiet next to the staircase, she could only just about hear the distant music and muffled laughter.

Upstairs, she walked into Gloria's room quietly to check that the girls were sleeping, but was surprised to find them with Beni, sitting cross-legged on the floor playing a game.

'What are you three doing? I thought you were asleep, little ladies?' Catherine asked while sinking to the floor awkwardly in her tight skirt.

'Gloria wanted me to see her room, I didn't get much choice in the matter,' said Beni. 'And that was three games of Buckaroo ago.' He gave Catherine a 'help me' look that she recognised from before she'd had a kid in her life.

People without kids generally don't know how to say no to

other people's children, they just go along with almost everything they request out of politeness, only really arguing on safety grounds.

Catherine smiled. 'Girls, this game will be the last one, OK? It's your bedtime and Beni has to go and see his grown-up friends.'

'All right,' said Gloria grumpily, sticking her tongue out as she concentrated on attaching a cowboy hat to the donkey's saddle.

'Are you OK, Leonora? Remember, your mummy is just downstairs if you need her at all,' said Catherine, showing her again how to use the walkie-talkie that Gloria often summoned *her* with, like an Edwardian lady of the manor ringing a bell.

Half an hour later, when Gloria and her friend were finally tucked up in bed, Catherine showed Beni the room that would be his – a large double with its own bathroom. Tour over, they walked through her master bedroom and out onto the upstairs balcony, which wrapped around the back of the house. You couldn't see the downstairs patio from up there because of the retractable wooden canopy covering it; likewise, if her guests wanted to see the balcony, they would have to swim to the edge of the infinity pool or walk halfway down the path to the beach. No one could see Beni and Catherine, therefore, as they sat side by side on a small bench looking out at the black ocean and star-speckled sky.

'I got lucky with the weather. There was meant to be a storm tonight, but it never showed up. Touch wood,' she said, knocking her knuckles against her head.

'There's plenty of space inside if it does.' Beni shrugged.

'Thanks for being so lovely to the girls.'

'It's OK. To be honest, it was perfect timing; they stopped me from getting hammered. I was just about to drink my third whisky when Gloria came running over wanting to show me her new room.'

'You were drinking again? Tonight?' asked Catherine, spinning in her seat to face him. She could smell the alcohol on him now, and though it was dark on the balcony, with the light coming from the bedroom providing only slight illumination, she could see the burden in his eyes. 'Talk to me, what's going on?'

'You had Isabella bring me a beer, you knew I was drinking.'

'There's a difference between beer and whisky.'

'Not to an alcoholic.'

She put a hand on his and neither of them said anything for a long time, they just sat with each other, not knowing what to say.

'This place is amazing,' he said eventually, closing his eyes and imagining the expanse of sea that would be visible from that spot in daylight. It made him feel so small.

'It's great having the house buzzing with people,' she said, listening to her guests enjoying themselves.

'You're so funny. You want them all here, but you don't want to talk to any of them.'

'Of course I want to talk to them.'

'You didn't know I was up here, so what were you coming up here for?' He tipped his chin in the air, waiting to be proven right.

'Just to check on Gloria ... and maybe to have a sit down somewhere quiet for a minute,' she admitted, smiling.

'See, you were coming up here to hide.'

'Maybe you're right. I like it all going on around me, but sometimes I don't want to be involved. I like living on the private side of one-way glass.'

'Do you want me to leave you on your own?' he asked.

'The first night we met I'd run away and was hiding, remember, outside the bar? You can always hide with me.'

'What did you mean downstairs when you said that things are different now?'

'Why have you never had a girlfriend, Beni? Tell me the truth.'

'That's a random question.'

'Can you please just answer it?'

He sighed, and slouched in his seat, looking defeated. 'Everyone that I've ever loved has either left or died. After a while you just accept that you shouldn't love anyone, it's less painful that way. You said that to me, remember? Isn't it the same reason why you didn't want to love Stef?'

'I don't love him because I don't love him. Love isn't a choice, is it?'

'Well, I know that now.'

'Are you in love with someone? Who?' she asked, feeling her heart stop.

He sat up and reached to push a strand of hair from her face. 'Haven't you realised that I'm too busy looking around the room for you, to notice anyone else? Don't you know that I would do anything for you? Isn't it obvious that I'm completely fucking in love with you?'

Catherine's stomach instantly filled with butterflies and her cheeks burned. 'You are?'

'Don't look so shocked, of course I am. You're the kindest person I've ever met, and you're beautiful and smart. You're funny and weird and when I'm with you I feel happier than I've ever felt. That is, until you start getting off with Stef right in front of me. Then I feel like punching something, mostly him. Anton's party was the last straw.'

'Because you saw us together?'

He nodded. 'I watched you all night, he didn't leave you alone for a second. I wanted to kill him.'

'He's your best friend,' said Catherine.

'Not any more.'

They sat in silence in the half-light, each lost in their memories.

The Piñata

Anton had thrown himself the birthday party, he was turning forty. However, he had given everyone strict instructions to not actually mention his age at his party, and this included no cards with the number on, no balloons, and certainly no candles on the cake. He promised that should anyone make the error of mentioning such F-word – or C-word in Spanish – they would be banished from his life forever.

The party was held at Maria's bar, and in the taxi, Catherine made sure to repeatedly tell Gloria that uncle Anton was turning twenty-five, in the hope that she would forget about Catherine previously talking about it being a higher number, a number the little girl had recently learnt in English.

When they arrived, Catherine was amazed at how different the bar looked covered in banners and gold balloons. The tables and chairs were pushed together more tightly to make way for a small dance floor, and the usual rock music had been replaced by hits from the eighties, indie and pop.

'Hola, Maria!' said Catherine, hugging her friend and

watching as their two girls ran over to the pool table to play. 'It looks great! Is Anton here already?'

'He's gone in a taxi to pick up his boyfriend and his cake,' said Maria.

'Good, I have a surprise for him,' said Catherine, pulling a piñata from within a huge plastic bag.

'I was wondering what was in there!' Maria laughed. 'What did you fill it with? Candy?'

Catherine grinned. 'That's the surprise!'

Soon Stefano arrived with Val and some of the other staff from the hotel that Catherine didn't know.

'Lishy, Lishy, Lishy, I've missed you,' he said, running his hands through her hair and kissing her as he picked her up and spun in a circle.

'I saw you a few days ago!'

'It's a long time to be away from you.'

'Hola, Beni,' said Maria.

'Hi,' said Catherine, breaking free from Stefano's embrace and walking up to Beni. 'What did you get Anton?' she asked, peering nosily into the gift bag he was holding.

'Italian wine,' he said, breathing in her perfume while she was standing so close to him, watching her earrings waggle and the ruffles on her playsuit dance in the breeze.

'Where is Anton?' asked Val, who had sat herself down at a nearby table without greeting anyone.

'He's gone to pick up a cake and his boyfriend,' answered Catherine, excitedly.

'You seem extra hyper today, Lish,' said Beni.

'I just can't wait to give Anton his present! How are you doing? How is your leg?' she asked quietly.

'I'm fine,' he said, looking outside at the rain that had just begun to fall.

'Lish, shall we hang up your piñata before Anton gets back?' shouted Maria from behind the bar.

'Oh yes!' said Catherine, dashing over to help Maria and Stefano to lift it. She climbed onto a chair and stretched to attach it to a beam on the ceiling. Stefano held the chair still for her and ran his hands up her long legs as he did so. Once the piñata was in place, she let it dangle above the centre of the dance floor, holding her hands close by in the air to test if it would stay put without their help. As she began to climb down from the chair Stefano swept her off her feet and held her in his arms.

'What are you doing, King Kong?' she asked, kicking her legs like Ann Darrow.

He didn't answer, just kissed her and carried her off to the bar.

Anton arrived fashionably late, holding an age-neutral chocolate sponge, with his boyfriend at his side, and was clearly emotional as his many friends flooded him with hugs and birthday wishes.

'I'm not drinking tonight, I have Gloria with me, so that means you get double shots,' said Catherine, placing a shot glass from a tray that Stef was holding into each of Anton's hands.

'Oh, well if you insist ...' Anton laughed.

'Happy birthday!' Catherine giggled, watching his face grimace at the taste of the tequila.

'Thanks, beautiful. Hi, Stefano!' he said, pulling his friend in for a hug.

'Buon compleanno!'

'This is Mateo,' said Anton as he put an arm around the tall, handsome man next to him.

'Hola! Mucho gusto,' said Catherine, handing him a shot and flashing a big grin.

'You already met, you know,' Anton said to Catherine.

'We did?'

'Well, you pointed him out to me on the dance floor. I consider you our matchmaker,' said Anton, and then wandered off to greet more of his guests.

Catherine and Stefano played endless games of pool with Gloria and Leonora, finally taking a break when Maria's sister, Isabella, mercifully took over babysitting duties.

Anton seemed to be having fun, music was playing, everyone was chatting and dancing and having a good time, and in the midst of all the chaos Catherine walked up to Anton in the centre of the dance floor and handed him a bright blue stick.

'Piñata time,' she said, smiling widely, unable to contain her excitement any longer.

Maria turned down the music and helped Stefano to move everyone into a circle around the dance floor, while Catherine put a blindfold on the very inebriated birthday boy and kissed his cheek before taking a big step back.

He swung the stick lots of times, missing on many attempts. Finally though, the stick connected with the tissue paper hard enough for it to spill open, at which point he lifted the blindfold, elated at hearing the contents spilling onto the floor. He looked at the ground, which was littered with glow sticks, miniature perfume bottles and lollipops, and in the middle of it all was his gift from Catherine: car keys.

He snatched them up immediately and hugged her, before shouting to everyone watching that he finally had a new car.

~

Valentina walked outside and sat beside Beni with a thud. 'Catherine's bought Anton a new car,' she said, pulling a face. 'Per l'amor di Dio! Who does that? Who buys their friend a car?'

'You know what she got me for my birthday?' he said, necking a glass of whisky in one gulp.

'What?'

'A bookshelf and a photo of us all in a big frame to put on the wall.'

'Do you feel jealous that Anton got a car, then?' asked Val, rolling her eyes.

'No. My point is, she buys you what you need. Anton's needed a car for a long time. She doesn't do it to be a show-off, she just finds something you need and gets it for you.'

'I wonder what she'll give me, then,' said Val, looking at her feet.

'Maybe she could wrap Stefano in a bow and hand him over to you,' said Beni, slurring his words slightly and topping up his glass with more whisky from the bottle at his feet.

'What?'

'Val?'

'What?' she said angrily, like a teenager bored of her parents asking her questions.

'Why aren't the two of you together?'

Val looked stunned.

'I'm sorry to ask, Val. Actually, I'm not sorry at all, it's like a giant bloody elephant in the room.'

There was a long pause, tension sparking in the air like a live wire flailing in a storm.

'Why do you suddenly care?' asked Valentina.

'I'm sick and tired of your attitude. You drag everyone down, and you're horrible to Lish. Just come out with it. Why do you hang around him like a dog following its master? It clearly upsets you that he's all over her, so why aren't you together?'

'You're drunk.'

'I'm very drunk, so if you don't tell me right now, I'm going to stagger into the centre of that room and ask you this question again at the top of my lungs, and then everyone else will be just as eager to hear the answer as me.'

He glared at her and Val shrank back from him a little, her brow furrowed in concern.

'I can't say it out loud, Beni. Please, I can't talk about this,' she mumbled.

'Does he love you?' he asked.

'Yes,' she said.

'Then why can't you be with him?'

'I can't tell you.'

'For fuck's sake! Then just let the poor guy go!' he said, shifting forward, ready to stand up.

'I can't let him go!' she hissed.

'Why not?'

'Because I love him.'

'Then if you love him, and he loves you, why are you not with him?' asked Beni loudly, throwing his hands in the air.

'I can't be with him ... because he's my brother,' she whispered.

'You're in love with your brother? That's sick,' said Beni slowly, his face screwing up in disgust, feeling like she had just slapped him across the face, sobering him up.

'It's not as straightforward as it sounds,' said Val, putting her head in her hands. 'I lived with my mum until I was twelve years old, and then she became ill and had to give me up. She went into a mental health facility and I went to live with my mum's stepsister and her husband – my aunt and uncle – who up to that point I had never even met before. From then on, they raised me, and Stefano is their son.'

'So, he's your stepcousin?'

'Yes.'

'Fucking your cousin is weird, but if you're stepcousins that's OK, isn't it? You don't share blood?'

'We couldn't help it. It didn't happen straight away, not until I was seventeen and he was sixteen.'

'So, he isn't really your brother, he just kind of is, because you were raised together?'

'My uncle found out about us when I was about twenty. He caught us together and he went crazy! He was so angry, so we took off and we went travelling. Eventually, and I don't know how he found us, but my uncle showed up at our hostel one day in France when Stefano had gone out, and he finally told me the truth.'

'And what was the truth?'

'That he, that my uncle, was really my dad. That means that me and Stef are actually half-brother and sister. I was sick, right then and there, when he told me. I screamed and hit him and he just sat there and took it. He begged me not to tell anyone, and I didn't want Stef to know either, so I promised to keep the secret.'

'He had an affair with his wife's stepsister? What a dog,' said Beni, in total shock.

'My mother would talk about the mysterious figure that was my dad and how much she loved him. She told me that he had died, but the truth was, he was living just a few miles away with her stepsister. She loved him and he just tossed her to one side, is it any wonder she went mad?'

'Maybe she should have thought about that before she slept with her stepsister's husband?'

'And what about my uncle? He was the married man, but it wasn't him that suffered, was it!'

'Is your mum OK now?'

'She died while she was in the facility.'

'I'm sorry.'

'I didn't visit her much while she was in there, I was so mad at her for being weak, for abandoning me.'

'You were just a kid when she left, it's not surprising that you resented her.'

'I don't any more,' said Val, looking up at the sky.

'What happened when Stef got back, what did you tell him?' asked Beni, speaking more softly.

'I broke up with him and he went to America.'

'If he left then how are you here with him now?'

'I missed him. It was like my arm had been chopped off, I couldn't breathe without him being around. He's my best friend, the love of my life.'

'Oh my God, this is so sick.'

'I found out where he was, in Los Angeles. I thought we could make a go of it, no one knew that we were related there and as long as we agreed not to have children, I thought, what's the harm?'

'The harm is that it's illegal, it's incest,' he said, pulling an even more disgusted face. 'Have you done anything since finding out?' whispered Beni.

'We've kissed,' she said quietly, not looking at him.

'Has he kissed you since he's been with Lish?'

Valentina nodded faintly.

'Fucking arsehole,' said Beni smashing his arm against the bench. 'He's cheated on her with you?'

'He must be so confused. It's not his fault, he doesn't know any of this,' said Val quickly, and placed a gently restraining hand on his leg.

'Does your uncle know that you're out here with him?'

She shook her head. 'My aunt doesn't know any of this, and if they knew we were together then my uncle would have to come clean, it would destroy the family. That's the real reason we can't be together. Yes, we could live happily ever after, but it would mean cutting out the family and he wouldn't understand why we had to do that unless I told him the truth. And he loves his mother, he would never be able to cut her out.'

'Where do they think you are?'

'They think I'm in Spain.'

'Val, why don't you just tell him the truth so he can understand what's going on? Maybe he would be happy to go and live in some southern state in America with you and just accept that he's in love with his sister?'

'Because it drives me crazy and I don't want him to ever feel this way. Can you imagine how it feels to love someone and it make you feel physically sick at the same time? It's horrible, Beni.'

'You need to leave, then. If you love him, you need to back off and let him live his life.'

'I know I do. Do you think he and Catherine could be happy if I left?'

'He could be happy with anyone else, he just can't be happy with you,' said Beni looking at the floor, thinking about Catherine being Stef's happily-ever-after and feeling the whisky creep from his stomach into the back of his throat.

'Do you think he could be happy with Catherine, though?'

'Why are you asking me?'

'I can see that you love her, everyone can. Even Stef knows,' said Valentina quietly.

'If he knows, then why does he do that? Why does he kiss her and grope her right in front of me?' he said, knocking back more whisky before he had chance to be sick.

'Maybe he's marking his territory? It's kind of obvious that she has feelings for you too.'

'She doesn't have feelings for me, why would she? He's such a hypocrite, "marking his territory" while harbouring an all-consuming love for his fucking sister and pouncing on her every chance he gets!'

'He doesn't know that I'm his sister! And you can't tell him,' she pleaded, suddenly grabbing Beni's arm.

'Val, I won't tell anyone, it's not for me to tell.'

'Thank you.'

'You'll really never tell him? He will never know the truth, never know why you refuse to be with him?'

'He can never find out.'

Beni nodded.

'It's strange that Catherine's not drinking, isn't it?'

'Not really, she has Gloria with her.'

'Since when does that stop her?'

'What are you getting at?'

'Maybe she's pregnant?' said Val, swirling the lemonade in her own glass before taking a sip.

Feeling sucker-punched, Beni thought about how easy it would be for Stef to wrap his arms around Catherine and never let go if she had his child, especially if Val left. But then he looked at Val, sitting beside him looking deflated, and he heaved a sigh.

'You need to leave. I won't say anything, but as much as I don't want Stef to fall in love with Lish, as fucking shit as it makes me feel thinking she might have his baby, better that they get to properly love each other than to carry on living in this twisted, fucked-up four-way we're all in at the minute. I'll leave them alone too.'

'You won't be able to stay away, you're as bad as me,' she said.

Tears burned his eyes. 'I love her so much,' he said, his voice cracking, 'that I'm willing to let her go if that's what will make her happy. Can you say the same about Stef? Or are you just too selfish to let him go?'

'I'm too selfish.'

Beni stood up and went to walk inside, unsteady on his feet.

Val jumped up and grabbed his arm, pleading with him not to say anything.

'I'm just going to the loo. I won't say anything, but if I find out you're still hanging around them, if I find out you're still causing them any grief, then I will tell Stefano. Do you understand?'

Val nodded.

He walked into the bathroom and stared at himself in the mirror. Having drunk almost half a bottle of whisky already, he was starting to feel sick; the room swayed around him. As he looked into his own hollow eyes, images of Catherine flashed in his mind and he knew that he had to walk away from her. This jealousy was killing him, loving her was killing him. He thought about Stef kissing Val and him touching Catherine's legs and was once again filled with rage; he pulled back his fist and smashed it into the wall. Blood and bruising exploded instantly across his knuckles. He couldn't even feel it.

As Beni stumbled out of the bathroom, bouncing against the walls and almost tripping over his own feet, he walked straight into a smiling Catherine.

'There you are, have you been hiding? Isn't it me that hides at parties?' Her smile disappeared quickly as she watched him sway in front of her, saw how red his eyes were and then noticed the blood dripping from his hand.

'Here I am,' he slurred.

'What's happened?' she asked, snatching some napkins from

the bar and folding them around his hand to stop the bleeding. She put one hand on his cheek and watched his lips as he spoke.

'I fell over, and accidently punched the floor.'

'You fell over. Really?' she said, raising her eyebrows at him.

'Tell me something about you that I don't know?' he asked, putting his uninjured hand on her waist.

'Umm, OK ... I love the smell of petrol and hate the smell of papaya. Now you.'

'I'm scared of flying.'

'That's rational,' said Catherine, looking up at him, still holding his injured hand tightly in hers.

'And I hate getting my hair cut,' he said.

'Because of all the needless chatter? Me too.'

'I hate raspberries, they're all bumpy and mushy and gross,' he said, looking disgusted.

'But do you like raspberry flavoured things?'

'Yes,' he said, pushing her hair back from her face.

'I feel like I am seeing into your soul with this new information.' She laughed.

'You smell nice,' he said, leaning towards her and kissing her cheek roughly.

'You're hammered, did you drive here?' she asked, stepping back from him and letting go of his hand. Fortunately, the napkin clung to the drying blood on his knuckles without her help, and the bleeding had seemingly stopped.

'Your eyes are so blue in the middle, and then they get darker at the edges.'

'Let me drive you home,' she said.

'I thought you were too scared to drive here?' he said loudly, swaying without her propping him up.

'I'd brave it for you.'

'If you drove me home, I'd have to insist you stay with me

all night so I could drive you home in the morning?' he said, putting his hands lightly on her waist again.

'I can't do that, Beni.'

'Why haven't you been drinking tonight?' he asked, watching her eyelashes blink as if in slow motion, like a butterfly's wing in a nature documentary. His thoughts corkscrewed and curled until they were a mass of jagged razor wire that was impossible to untangle, and he held his breath waiting for her to answer.

'I have Gloria with me. Why, am I boring sober?'

'You're never boring.'

'I'm not letting you leave my sight until you're safely in a taxi,' she said.

'Here.' He sighed, placing his car keys into her hand. 'Give them to Maria, I'll come and get my car tomorrow.'

'Shall I call you a taxi, then?' she whispered as she wrapped her arms around him like a forcefield, protecting him.

He let her hold onto him for a full minute; he counted down the seconds as he stroked her hair and craned his neck to rest his chin on her shoulder. 'I've got to go,' he said when the minute was up, pushing her away.

The Confession

Beni and Catherine sat next to each other on her balcony, listening to the music and laughter below them as their friends continued to celebrate Catherine's house-warming.

'Beni, I should have stopped Stef from being so touchy-feely in front of you, I'm sorry.'

'I know you didn't do it to hurt me, but it did. I had to stop seeing you, I couldn't deal with it any more. Seeing you with him was killing me, that's why I started drinking. But being away from you was so much worse.'

'I'm so sorry that I hurt you.'

'Wasn't it obvious that I liked you?' he asked, running his hand across his face.

'Sometimes I thought you might. You're not exactly easy to read,' she said quietly. 'Why didn't you just come out and say how you felt?'

'Why would I tell you? You're with Stef, I didn't want to hurt him and you're happy with him, aren't you? I have no money, I work in a bar. What do I have to offer someone like you?'

'Do you think Stef is the heir to an oil fortune he hasn't told anyone about? Do you really think I'm so shallow that I care how much money you have?'

'I care. And besides all that, feeling that way was terrifying. I couldn't stop thinking about you. I didn't want to love you, but I couldn't stop it.' He stood up and paced back and forth in front of her.

Catherine caught his hand as he walked by and ran her fingers across his knuckles, looking up at him. 'What did you punch that night at Anton's party? You told me you fell over. Did you hit Stef?'

'No. Don't you think you might have noticed if I'd hit him? Your face is never more than two inches from his! I punched a wall,' he said, snatching his hand away angrily.

'I'm so sorry. All of your problems are because of me, you have to let me fix it.'

'My problems are not your fault, me loving you is not your fault and me drinking to numb how I feel is definitely not your fault,' he said, pacing again. 'At first, I told myself to stop being a dick and I tried to turn off my feelings. But every time you would bite your lip or laugh or touch my arm I just fell deeper and deeper under your spell. I thought it was a crush and that it would pass. I've never felt like this, I had nothing to compare it to.'

'But it wouldn't go away?'

'Every time I saw you it got worse. I just wanted to grab you and kiss you. Eventually, I thought I should just stop being selfish and walk away and let you be happy with him,' he said, standing still and bowing his head to the ground. 'You have no idea how hard it was ignoring your messages, telling you to leave at the hospital.'

'So why did you come here tonight?' she asked. 'What changed all of a sudden?'

'I'm selfish. I missed you. I couldn't stay away any longer, and no matter how much time passed without seeing you, I still felt the same. So many times, I ...'

Catherine looked up at him. 'What?' she said.

'Stop it!'

'Stop what?'

'Biting your lip, it kills me when you do that,' he said, with his hand on his face.

She drew her thumb across her lips slowly. 'You should have told me how you felt.'

'I wanted to in the hospital, but I thought you were pregnant. I thought you were going to open the door to me today looking pregnant. I'm so pathetic. I was willing to watch you have his baby and live happily ever after because not being near you was worse than having my heart ripped out every time I saw him touch you.'

Catherine swallowed hard and stared at the floor. 'I was pregnant.'

'You were? What happened?' He frowned.

'I lost the baby.' She shrugged, trying not to look upset.

'I'm sorry. When did it happen?'

'About a month ago.'

'I would never have wished for that,' he said, getting on his knees in front of her.

'I did.'

'You didn't want it?'

'Not at first, but then just as I got used to the idea, I lost it. That's what I get for wanting one man and having another's baby. I'm a bad person.'

'What?' he said, shock etched on his face.

'I wanted to tell you how I felt,' she said, putting her hand at the back of his neck and looking him in the eye.

'How did you feel?'

'Isn't it obvious?'

'But you were having his baby?'

Catherine nodded. 'I wanted to tell you the day you collapsed. I did a pregnancy test that night. If it was negative, I was going to run back to the hospital and tell you everything, but it was positive.'

'So, you had to choose him?'

'I didn't choose him, Beni. I didn't even tell him I was pregnant. I avoided him, and before I could tell him, I'd lost it. I was going to break up with him and stay away from you too; it seemed fairer to just be on my own, to have neither of you.'

'Do you still like me?'

'Stop tensing your jaw like that.' She smiled, touching his face.

'Why, do you like it?' he asked, a smile twitching the corners of his mouth.

'You tense your jaw when you're thinking hard about something. At first I thought it just happened when you were angry or sad, but then one day I asked you to work out the exchange rate for me and you did it then too.' She laughed.

'You bite your lip when you're nervous. So many times I've wanted to bite it for you and tell you not to worry.' He grinned.

'I can't pretend any more,' said Catherine, letting out a sigh. 'I can't pretend that we're friends. We never were, I don't feel this way about my friends. You're the only person I open up to, and I think about you all the time.'

'What exactly do you think about?'

'Use your imagination,' she said to the floor, smiling.

'I want you to say it,' he whispered, using a finger to raise her chin so he could look into her eyes.

'I think about what it would be like to kiss that scar on your lip, a lot.'

'Then you should do it.'

'Remember that night at your flat, when I leaned in to kiss you? I turned off the TV and I joked that without it to enter-tain us, we could do something else?' she whispered, pushing a hand through his thick brown hair, watching his jaw tense again. 'I wanted to kiss you. I wanted you more than I've ever wanted anything.' Catherine took a big breath of evening air. She was grateful for the loud music masking their conversation from the revellers below, thankful for the darkness that concealed her blushing cheeks.

'Why didn't you just kiss me, then?' he asked, his heart hammering.

'You stopped me. You're a good guy, it would have been wrong to do that behind Stef's back. I'm glad we didn't. You said you didn't want us to break Stef's heart, remember? So, after that I thought you must not like me, at least not enough.'

'I wish you could have read my mind that night. It was like fireworks were going off in my brain. I didn't watch a single bit of *Die Hard*, I was too busy listening to you breathing, and thinking about your hand on my leg.'

'Stef guessed that I liked you, he asked me about it. But he reminded me of what a player you are, and I saw you with that girl at the hammock place. I felt stupid for even thinking you would want me. I can't compete with those girls; they don't have the baggage that I have. I didn't want to ruin what I had with Stef to just be another notch on your bedpost.'

'I don't care about any other woman but you,' he said, letting her push her fingers through his hair again, his own running along the exposed area of skin on her thigh just above her knee. 'That girl ... we just kissed. And Stef said all that so you wouldn't think about me any more.'

'Well, it didn't work.' She shrugged, looking into his eyes.

'How do you feel about me now?' asked Beni.

She bit her lip as she ran her fingers along the dark stubble on his jaw and sighed.

'If you want me, I'm yours,' he said, moving his thumb across her red lips and cupping her face in his hand.

'Even though I'm a nervous film nerd, and a widow with a kid?' she said, looking at him incredulously.

'I love that you're a nerd, I love Gloria, I love you. I met you about ten months ago, didn't I?'

Catherine nodded.

'I haven't slept with anyone for nine of them. All I think about is you.'

'What?'

'I mean it.'

'No one, in all that time?'

'I just couldn't do it. I tried to move on, but I'm yours, Lish. You've turned me into a pathetic, snivelling, lovelorn moron.' He laughed, shaking his head. 'I would honestly do anything for you, and before I met you I wouldn't do anything for anyone. So, now you know how I feel, what do we do?'

'Beni,' said Catherine as she realised his fingers were working their way further and further up her leg. Not knowing what to do with herself, she stood up and walked towards the bedroom door, towards the light and the exit. But, she stopped before she got there, choosing instead to lean against the wall, look up at the black sky and take a few deep breaths as her head spun.

'Why didn't you break up with him when you lost the baby?' he asked, moving from the floor to sit on the bench, not looking at her. 'I saw him kissing you earlier, you're still together.'

'I felt so guilty, and then everything with Gloria and the adoption happened. I've barely seen him, I've been avoiding him for months.'

'So, who do you choose?'

'I don't want to hurt anyone,' she said, rubbing her eyes.

'I shouldn't move in,' he said, walking towards her. 'I can't live here with you; I don't know what I was thinking. It's hard enough as it is, without you being within reach, and knowing you're down the hall kissing, touching, fucking Stefano. I would rather live in my car.'

'You can't live in your car,' she said, holding his hands, pulling him close to her. 'And I don't need to choose.'

'What do you mean?'

'It's you, it always has been,' she said, not daring to look him in the eye.

'You would really choose me?' he asked, putting his forehead against hers.

'My heart stops beating properly when you're around.'

'But what about Stefano?'

'He's in love with Val, he told me.'

Beni froze, thinking about Val's confession. 'Then why were you even with him if you knew that?' he asked.

'It kept him at arm's length, but when I told him I was late, he said if I had his baby he would stop seeing her.'

'You could have had him to yourself, but you still didn't tell him?'

'I wanted you,' she whispered. 'And he wanted her. Us being together for the sake of a baby would have been pointless. I was avoiding him until I had the guts to break up with him, but the baby had other ideas.'

'Lish, that's not your fault.'

'I wished it away.'

'If wishes worked, you would have been mine a long time ago.'

'This is all my fault, I've been so selfish. I should have broken up with him when I started to have feelings for you.

But I was all alone here, I didn't want to lose the only friends I had.'

'Do you love me?' he asked, his arms around her.

Catherine stared up at him for a long time. 'How do you know if you love someone?'

'You were married, don't you know?'

'It's easy to forget. How do you know that you love me? Maybe you only want me because you couldn't have me?'

'You know when I realised that I loved you?'

'When?'

'I have no idea. It's not like in films when one thing makes you fall in love. It's a thousand different things.'

'Like the way your arm muscles tense when you change gears while driving?' She smiled.

'Or how delicate your skin is,' he said, kissing her wrist while looking into her eyes.

'Those big brown eyes.'

'The way your earrings waggle around when you're chattering away about random films.'

'The way you make fun of me,' she said, arching her eyebrows at him.

'The way you coordinate your nail varnish to things, you weirdo.'

'The way you make me feel safe.'

'Is that all I make you feel? Safe ...' he asked as he leaned towards her slowly.

She felt his breath on her neck before his lips touched her skin for the first time and electric shocks shot through them both. She ran her fingers through his hair, closing her eyes as he kissed her neck over and over again, his hands sliding down her body.

He stopped to look at her, putting a hand at the back of her head, preparing to finally kiss her red lips.

'Our first kiss shouldn't be behind his back,' she blurted out, pushing him away.

Beni stroked her hair and then put his forehead against hers again for a long time, just enjoying being close to her, their lips just centimetres apart.

'We're bad people,' she said to the sky.

He shook his head. 'If we were bad people, we would have kissed the first night we met, when I drove you home. I would have told you I thought you were perfect, and you would have told me you liked my twitchy arms and face. Instead, I spent all this time thinking I had no chance with you and being scared to death of being in love, and you just thought I was a man-whore with no feelings.'

'I do love your face,' she said, smiling up at him with sadness and worry in her eyes.

'If we weren't so bloody English, we could have saved ourselves so much heartache. We should have just said how we felt.'

'So, you think I'm perfect?'

'You are to me. Just one kiss?' He sighed, pressing himself against her gently, moving his hands down her body again and imagining the taste of her lower lip.

'We can't.'

'No loopholes? Can I kiss your neck again?' He smiled.

'We shouldn't. I need to talk to Stef. I'm going to break up with him and then you can kiss me as much as you want to,' she said, playing with the buttons on his jacket before tiptoeing to kiss the stubble on his jaw.

'We should go back to the party.'

'Can't we just stay here forever? I can't face it,' she said as they walked into the bedroom. 'What if Stefano kisses me?'

'Then I'll look away.'

'I can't believe this is happening.'

'Just do what you think is right,' he said.

'I won't kiss him obviously, but I don't want to push him away in front of everyone. It would be weird, he would know something was wrong and there's no point us all having a brawl tonight. I don't want to hurt anyone.'

Beni looked at the floor, feeling angry, sad and above all, frustrated.

Catherine watched Beni frown at the floor and didn't know what to do. They stood there for a few minutes in silence until she walked over to the table and grabbed a pen. She pulled off her sheer top, stood close to him in just her blue bralette and watched his frown disappear.

'Have you changed your mind?' he asked, looking at the perfect skin along the curve of her breasts.

'Write me a message here,' she said, lowering the cup of the lacy bra slightly and handing him the pen. 'That way, even if he does kiss me, you know I'll be thinking about whatever you've written here; I'll be thinking about you touching me, not him.'

He felt like he was a starving man standing in front of an all-you-can-eat buffet and being told he could only clean the cutlery. But if this was what it took for him to be with her without a fight, without embarrassing her, without losing their friends, then he would do it. He was dying to blurt out that Stefano had kissed Valentina so that Catherine wouldn't feel so guilty, but it was just one more night and then she would finally be his.

He accepted the pen and wrote her a message in small letters across her chest; he wrote slowly, and she ran her nails along his back as he did it. Her obvious arousal stimulated him even more and it took all of his willpower not to throw her onto the bed.

When he was done, she repositioned her top, pulled the sheer blouse back on and spun in a circle.

'Can you see it? Can you see any ink?' she asked.

'It's hidden. Only I know it's there,' he said, scooping her towards him by the waist.

'This is torture, isn't it?' said Catherine, seeing his frown deepen once more.

'I'll look away if he kisses you.'

'OK, but don't punch any of my walls, they're new,' she said, kissing his fist.

'When will you talk to him?' he whispered as they walked down the stairs, fingers entwined.

'Tomorrow,' she whispered back.

'I'll come and see you before my shift.'

'There you are!' said Stefano, his voice echoing in the vast hallway.

They quickly snatched their hands apart.

'What have you been doing?' Stefano was smiling from ear-to-ear as always, like an innocent kid.

'Well, three games of Buckaroo with Gloria for starters, and I was just showing Beni the spare room. He's going to be staying here for a while until he can find somewhere else, he's lost his flat,' she said. Technically no lies told in that sentence, she thought, but her conscience was still screaming at her like the brakes on a rusty mountain bike.

'That's great! Lish hates it out here, all these big rooms and no carpets; she misses her tiny English cottage. She needs a housemate to keep her company.' Stefano slapped Beni hard on the back, painfully hard, and then put his arms around the two of them as they walked back outside to rejoin the party.

As they got outside, Catherine could see Miguel strumming his guitar with his wife dancing at his side in the traditional Spanish style, arms above her head, stamping her feet; when the song ended, everyone clapped.

'Come on then, Lish, sing for us!' slurred Anton from

Mateo's lap, his beard covered in green face paint, his wig crooked.

'No way! I'm off duty,' she said, waving her hands around in protest. She felt flustered enough, she could do without singing in front of everyone too.

'Come on, Catherine,' said Miguel. 'It's good practise and I want my wife to see us, she hasn't seen me perform with you. Please?'

'OK, anything for you, Miguel.'

'Thanks.'

'Any requests from the crowd?' Catherine joked at volume as she positioned herself on a stool.

'Italy! Eurovision!' shouted Beni.

'Remember that one, Miguel?'

'Yes, ready when you are.'

Beni watched her as she began to sing. She looked nervous and vulnerable with her long wavy hair tucked behind her ears and her feet bare; he just wanted to hold her.

As she sang the Italian song, the guests started to recognise it, and by the time she hit the chorus everyone was singing 'Vol–ar–ay' at the top of their lungs, arms around each other, swaying as they helped her sing the Oh oh oh ohs. Beni watched her self-consciousness melt away, she was soon smiling, her arms were flung wide, and her voice became louder and even more beautiful.

Catherine and Miguel sang a few more songs after that and then they were replaced by a punk rock playlist. Stefano wrapped his arms around her and kissed her when she finished singing, but she wriggled away and said she needed to get a drink, glancing at Beni's stern face as she skipped into the kitchen.

The Dilemma

atherine woke up the morning after her party to see
Gloria standing next to her bed.

'You look green,' she said with her little head
tipped to one side.

Catherine felt green. 'I'm just a bit hungover, honey,' she
said, sitting up slowly to give the room enough time to stop
spinning. 'Come on, hop up here,' she eventually said, smiling as
best she could.

'Where is Leonora?'

'Her mummy took her home last night, sweetheart. Did you
have fun?' asked Catherine, trying her hardest to speak Spanish
with the remaining half of her brain cells.

'Yes, I did.'

'Did you have fun playing Buckaroo with Beni and
Leonora?'

'Yes. Beni said he liked my new room. He is so cute.'

'Gloria, you are so cute!' Catherine laughed, giving the little
girl a squeeze. 'Are you hungry?'

'That depends,' said Gloria.

'On what?'

'Will you make me pancakes? It's Sunday.'

'OK, but let's go and brush our teeth first?'

Teeth brushed – wondrously, for Catherine, without vomiting – they headed down to the kitchen, which looked like a bomb had hit it.

As Catherine looked around and assessed the carnage, the spilled drinks, the rubbish, the half-eaten plates of food, she startled as she spotted Stefano asleep on the sofa.

'Oh shit,' she said under her breath, gesturing for Gloria to be quiet.

Everything that had happened the night before came rushing back to her like a train hitting her hard between the eyes, and she blushed crimson as she thought about running her hands through Beni's hair and how much she had wanted to kiss him. But then a smile spread across her lips as she remembered him telling her that he loved her.

She made pancakes and cleaned the kitchen, barefoot and wearing her pyjamas, tiptoeing around so as not to wake up Stefano, wanting to put off the awkward break-up chat for as many minutes as possible.

'Morning,' he said eventually.

'Morning. How are you feeling? asked Catherine, concentrating hard on scrubbing a sticky stain on the kitchen counter instead of looking at him.

'I'm fine, I must have crashed out down here, sorry. Hey, trouble,' he said, giving a big smile to Gloria, who was sitting at his feet, kicking her little legs against the sofa and eating her pancakes.

'Gloria, remember when I told you not to wake Stef up?'

'Yes.'

'Well, you've woken him up.'

'Oh, sorry, but I was hoping when he woke up, maybe we could go swimming?'

'I can do that. I'm half fish, you know,' he told Gloria earnestly, smacking his lips together, imitating a fish.

'Where are your gills?' she asked, narrowing her eyes.

Stefano looked at Catherine and raised his eyebrows before standing and ruffling Gloria's mass of dark hair. 'You have to wait an hour after eating before you go swimming, it's the law,' he said, stretching and yawning in his crumpled, caramel-brown Indiana Jones shirt.

'Kitty, can you tell me when it's been one hour, please?'

'Yes ma'am,' said Catherine with a salute as Gloria sat down on the floor and started playing with one of her toys.

'Stef, I actually need to talk to you before you leave?' said Catherine quietly as he approached her.

'I'm leaving?' he said, checking that Gloria wasn't looking and pulling Catherine close to him for a kiss before she could stop him. 'I was hoping we could spend some time together; I haven't seen you at all lately.'

As his arms wrapped around her, Catherine's hand flew to her chest and she rushed to the bathroom, pretending to feel sick. She looked in the mirror and lowered her pyjama top; Beni's words were still there, inked on her chest, and her stomach flipped as she thought about him writing every single letter.

She composed herself and hurried back into the kitchen. Stefano was making them some coffee and Gloria was still lying flat on the floor, playing. Catherine stood on the spot feeling like she was sinking into the tiles. She needed to do it there and then, she needed to break up with Stefano.

'Stef, let's take our coffee outside, shall we? We need to talk.'

'OK,' he said, giving her a huge oblivious grin.

She tried to smile back as the coffee maker made its rattling swooshing noises, but Catherine felt like her insides were doing something very similar.

'Is everything all right? Do you still feel sick?'

'No, I'm fine, thanks.' This was a lie.

Just as the coffee started to spill into the cup, Stefano's phone started to ring. He frowned at the screen and as he answered it and walked towards the veranda, Catherine took over making the coffee. Soon, rushed and agitated Italian filled the kitchen, and when Stefano hung up the call he looked upset and began to shout.

'Gloria, sweetheart, I think Stefano has had some bad news and he's upset, could you go play in the snug for me?' said Catherine, leading Gloria out of the room by the hand.

When Catherine returned, Stef was preparing to leave, looking around frantically for his car keys.

'What's happened?' she asked.

At that moment Beni let himself in the front door, and Catherine, not wanting Beni to jump to conclusions about what had upset Stef, explained the situation at the speed of light. 'Stef has just had a call and is really upset. Can you do me a favour and go check on Gloria, she might be a bit freaked out, she's in the snug, down the hallway.'

'Sorry, sorry!' cried Stef, 'I didn't mean to scare her.'

'It's OK, she'll be fine. What's happened?'

'It's my sister Magda, she's in a coma.'

'Oh my God, I'm so sorry, what happened to her?' Catherine asked, pulling him into a hug that he collapsed into, sobbing.

'She was hit by a car. She's so young, she can't die.'

'She'll be OK. People wake up from comas all the time, they're our body's way of taking some time to repair itself,' she said reassuringly, uncertain if she was right or not.

'I should go and see her; my mamma will be devastated.'

'You know I would come with you, but I can't leave Gloria. Why don't you take Valentina?'

'No, no, I will go on my own.'

'I can lend you some money for her flight if that's the issue?'

'Valentina won't come with me to Italy, she won't go back there, not yet. I'll go on my own. Thanks, though.'

'If there is anything else I can do, just tell me.'

'Well, can you keep an eye on her while I'm gone?'

'I'm sure Val will be fine without you for a couple of weeks, Stef, she's a big girl. I didn't think you saw her that much any more?' said Catherine, frowning slightly, annoyed at being asked to babysit the woman who, in his mind, was still her love rival.

'Please just have dinner with her once or twice, or coffee or something? She doesn't have anyone else.'

'OK, of course. She's been coming over to paint with Gloria anyway. Don't worry about anything here, just go and be with your family.'

'Thanks,' he said. 'She's been coming here?'

'Yes, Gloria loves her. It's like having a private art teacher who I pay with food.' Catherine smiled. 'We've become friends.'

'Oh, right, I didn't know.'

'Magda will be OK. And the first thing she'll see when she wakes up is that dumb face of yours.'

Stef smiled, wiped his eyes with his shirt sleeve and moved his face close to hers for a second before kissing her softly on the lips.

'I'll miss you like oxygen,' he said, then ran to his car.

A few minutes after the front door had slammed shut, Beni wandered into the kitchen and found Catherine with her head in her hands at the table.

'His sister's in a coma, he's flying to Italy to be with her,' she said.

'Oh no.'

'She was hit by a car. Is Gloria OK?'

'Yes, she's fine. She was worried about him so I told her that his cat had escaped. Sorry, I panicked.'

'His cat?' Catherine smiled.

'She asked why he was upset, and I thought, a cat escaping is a child-friendly reason to be sad, isn't it?'

Catherine laughed and held his hand as he sat down beside her on the long bench. He was in his work uniform, his white shirt open at the collar.

'Did he sleep here last night?' asked Beni, his jaw tensing faintly.

'He was asleep on the sofa when I came downstairs,' she said, running her nails through his chest hair, up his neck and along his taut jawline.

'Oh, right,' he said, enjoying her attentions.

'I'm not dressed yet, I'm a total mess,' said Catherine, suddenly realising what she was doing and that he had never seen her without make-up before.

'You look amazing,' he said, holding her at arm's length as she squirmed and blushed.

'Gloria wanted to go swimming,' said Catherine, covering his eyes and smiling.

'Then we can go swimming,' he said, grinning beneath her hand, kissing her palm. 'I'll go to work a bit late; someone will cover for me.'

'What are we going to do now?' she asked with a sigh, lowering her hand and looking into his eyes. 'I know it's awful, but all I could think was, *I can't break up with you now,* and I can't, can I?'

'No, I guess not.'

'But while I'm with him, I can't be with you. I meant what I said last night; I don't want to cheat on him.'

'Then we'll wait. I've waited all this time for you, I can wait some more.'

'I read what you wrote here,' she said, touching her chest: 'Soon I'll be kissing you, I've never wanted anything more in my life, I love you,' she recited, her cheeks turning even more pink, goosebumps springing to life on her arms.

'I can wait,' he said. 'How long will he be gone? A week? Surely he can't take too much time off work.'

'He wants us to check on Val, invite her over for dinner and stuff. I suggested he take her with him, but he said she won't go back to Italy. I wonder why?'

Beni got up and pretended to look for a glass in the cupboard, not wanting Catherine to see how angry he was that Stefano had asked her to do that.

The Wait

It had been six days since they had almost kissed on the balcony and five since Stefano had left for Italy.

Beni had moved his things into the spare room down the hall from the woman he loved, and had to pretend like nothing had changed. He couldn't sleep beside her, they couldn't talk about the fact that they had loved one another for almost a year already in secret, he couldn't kiss her, or touch her or make love to her. It was hell. For this reason, they were awkward around each other, like magnets that were once drawn together now pushing each other away.

They put on a show for Gloria, and when Anton and Val visited it was almost normal, but the Stefano-sized hole in the group was immense and Beni began to feel hopeless. He felt angry at himself for being so selfish, that at a time when his friend was grieving for his sister – who was still hooked up to machines in a hospital bed on the other side of the world – he was pining for the touch of his girlfriend.

Then one night, Beni woke to the sound of crying. Still drowsy, he climbed out of bed and hurried down the corridor to check on Gloria. She was fine, sound asleep swathed in pink blankets and surrounded by dolls and spy gadgets. Relieved that she was OK and that she wasn't being kidnapped, he walked back along the hall and pressed his ear to Catherine's bedroom door. From there, he could clearly hear her sobbing, moving around, gasping. He put his hand on the door handle but hesitated, not wanting to embarrass her by admitting he had heard her cry, but he couldn't stand to hear her upset and do nothing either.

When he walked into the room it was clear that she was still asleep and having a nightmare. She was writhing around and the tears on her cheeks kept catching the light from the hallway as she moved. He walked over to the bed and lay down, pulling her body to him so that her head rested on his bare chest; he wrapped his arms around her, making shushing sounds, rocking her until she slowly woke up.

'What happened?' she asked hazily, wondering why he was in her bed.

'You were having a nightmare,' he said, not letting her go.

With just his underwear on and Catherine wearing a vest and shorts, their hot skin was touching in multiple places. He could feel her breathing start to slow and her eyelashes blinking against his chest. She was fully awake but hadn't told him to leave so he didn't. It seemed like neither of them dared to move, like they thought if they stayed still enough, the universe might let them be together without the consequences, without it hurting anyone. Just once. In that bubble. Beni stroked the soft skin of her back and buried his face into her hair, and after a few minutes she kissed his chest and raised her head to look at him.

'You heard me crying and you came to look after me?' said Catherine.

'I'll always look after you. What were you dreaming about? Was it the vengeance-seeking sea turtles again?'

She smiled slightly and rested her head back on his chest, running her fingers across the hair on his stomach as she spoke.

'There was a car crash. It happened over and over. On a loop. A car crashes and I'm trying to get there to stop it but I'm too late every time. And then I'm in a house and there is a door and someone different leaves through the door on each loop. They know I did something, something bad, and they're mad at me.'

He could feel fresh tears pooling on his skin and he held her even tighter.

'You won't lose anyone else. You won't lose anyone else,' he repeated, over and over until she calmed down again. 'Everything is fine, it was just a nightmare.'

'I don't want to lose you.'

'You won't.'

'I don't want to hurt anyone.' She looked up at him, her blue eyes glimmering with tears. 'I just want to be with you, I want us to be happy.'

'I'm yours, I always will be and we're going to be so happy.'

'And you'll never hurt me?'

'Never.'

'No, I mean it. You wouldn't ever hurt me or Gloria, would you?' she said.

'I would never hurt you; do you mean physically?'

'You'll never tell me to lose weight, or tell me to change my outfit, and you won't call me a slut for wearing lipstick or ... hit me or anything?'

'Who did that to you?'

'Thomas.'

'I will love you no matter what you wear or what you weigh. I will never call you names and I would never, ever, lay a hand on you or Gloria, I swear.' He held on to her even more tightly.

'OK, I believe you, but you're squeezing all the air out of me,' she said. 'You're hugging me to death, Lenny.'

'Sorry.' He laughed, loosening his hold.

'Do you ever have nightmares?'

'Sometimes, and as a kid I used to get them bad, but my mum would tell me that we have nightmares so that when we wake up, we remember not to take real life for granted.'

'That's a nice way of looking at it. What do you have night-mares about?'

'I have one repeatedly where I'm in a burning building, and I need to jump out the window but I'm too scared of heights. So, for what feels like hours I'm just trapped between the flames and the drop.'

'That sounds horrible,' she said, still running her fingers across the skin of his stomach. 'I hate dreams where you have everything and then you wake up and you actually don't, like when you dream you've won the lottery.'

'The worst thing would be for this to be a dream. For me to wake up in my flat all alone.'

'It's not a dream,' she said, looking him in the eye and smiling.

'Gloria was playing with her dolls earlier, in the snug. I walked in and she was bashing them together so I asked her what they were doing, and thankfully she said the doll was performing "mouth-to-mouth resusigigation".' He laughed. 'She couldn't pronounce it, bless her. It made me smile and she ran at me and hugged me. She said, "You should smile more so that Kitty knows you love her."'

'She is so smart, that girl. She's seen straight through us all along.'

'She said her doll had been electrocuted.'

'We watched *Jurassic Park* not long before you moved in, and she was performing CPR on me every five minutes.' Catherine laughed. 'She's freakishly strong. I thought she might crack my ribs, so I told her to practise with the dolls instead.'

Beni smiled. 'It did feel like she had me in a headlock when she hugged me.'

'She's a tough cookie, no one will ever mess with her.'

'I'm going to sleep in here from now on, just sleep. I'll sneak in so Gloria doesn't see; is that OK?'

Catherine nodded and held him tight, falling asleep in his arms.

A few nights later, when Gloria had gone to bed, Beni walked out onto the veranda. It was dark except for the fairy lights and the moon and it was silent but for the sound of the hot tub bubbling away, which is where he found Catherine.

'There you are,' he said, taking off his shorts and T-shirt.

'Hi,' said Catherine. Her eyes were closed, and her voice cracked slightly.

'Are you OK?' asked Beni as he climbed into the bubbling water.

'I'm sitting on a jet of water that is hitting me in exactly the right place.' She giggled.

'Oh wow,' he said, feeling instantly aroused. 'Should I leave?'

'No,' she said, opening her eyes. She moved over to him and placed his hand beneath the water.

'What if Gloria wakes up?' he said, anxiously looking at the patio door.

'She knows not to come downstairs without us. She will walkie-talkie me first if she needs anything.'

'OK,' he said, relaxing.

'Watch me. You can look, can't you? It's not cheating if we don't touch?'

He nodded, transfixed by her as she slowly removed her bikini top. But he couldn't stop himself, he disobediently reached out and caressed the wet, tattooed skin of her waist and tried to pull her towards him.

'No touching me, just yourself.' She smirked as she sat back in position.

Beni watched her breasts rise and fall in the water as she took heavy breaths; he watched her lips as she moaned quietly. His own breathing quickened, he wanted to touch her more than anything, and it was like she'd read his mind because her eyes soon snapped open.

'You can't touch me. But I can. What shall I touch, here?' she asked, placing a hand on her breast and massaging, looking him in the eye, watching him enjoy her performance.

Beni nodded. 'I want you.' He exhaled noisily, closing his eyes.

She moved her fingers across her chest, through her hair and bit her lip, all the while imagining that it was him touching her. 'I want you too,' she whispered as her face eventually contorted and her body shivered.

Catherine giggled and put her bikini top back on, moved to sit beside him, and rested her head on his shoulder. With the bubbles turned off, it was silent out on the veranda but for the crickets and the swishing of the gently swaying trees in the distance; even the ocean was more muted than normal.

'Why are we doing this?' asked Beni.

'Doing what?'

'Why can't we just be together?'

'You know why. I don't want to cheat on Stef, he doesn't deserve it,' she said, knowing that what they were doing was already cheating and feeling sick with guilt.

'Lish, I have to tell you something ... Stef's kissed Valentina while he's been with you. If she had let him, he would have gladly done more. He's cheated on you.'

'I'm not exactly surprised,' she said, shaking her head.

'You're not?'

'He loves her. I find it hard to be around you and not kiss you, and it's the same for them.'

'We've gone almost two weeks not touching each other to protect his delicate little heart. Why are we bothering if he's in love with someone else?' said Beni, looking annoyed.

'I'm not doing this purely for his sake. It's also because I can't be with someone who doesn't trust me again. If I give in to you now, sooner or later you will throw it in my face. You'll say: "Look how we got together. You cheated on Stef, are you cheating on me?" And nothing I say will be able to remove that doubt from your mind.'

'I'm not Thomas.'

'I know you're not, but I can't risk ruining this.'

'I will never treat you like he did.'

'I don't think he ever thought he'd be like that until he was.'

'When did he start to act that way with you? Why did you marry him?'

'I was young, and at first I liked how protective he was. He wasn't violent at all, we were just a normal couple, travelling, studying ... The first time it got really bad, we were on a night out and some guy came over and started chatting me up. After about a minute and a half I told him I was married and he walked away, and I didn't think about it again, but when we got back to our flat, Thomas lost it. He blamed me, said I was sending out signals, and that was the first time he hurt me. Before then, he'd just been controlling and moody with me when he got jealous; he only turned violent after we were married.'

'He was very insecure, that wasn't your fault.'

'I just don't want to plant any seeds of doubt in your mind.'

'What we're doing right now could be classed as cheating, Lish,' he said, kissing her hand. 'But you and Stef aren't in love, and he has the weird thing with Val. It's not black and white.'

'I know,' she said, feeling anxious. 'I still feel like I've ruined this.' She closed her eyes and cringed at what they had just done together in the hot tub, wishing they hadn't.

'It's not ruined. I can see how much you're struggling with this; I know you wouldn't cheat on me.'

'Have you ever cheated on anyone?' she asked.

'No. My dad accused my mum of cheating once and all hell broke loose, so I would never cheat and I would definitely never cheat on you. Even before we lived together, being with you felt like being home and I haven't had that for so long. I will never do anything to risk losing you,' he said, kissing her cheek and putting his arm around her.

'Oh wow, you make it even harder to resist you when you say things like that.' She sighed.

'Good, I don't want you to resist me.'

'Do you believe in God?'

'Random. No. Do you?'

'No, but surely there must be something going on, even if it's that we're all plugged into *The Matrix*?'

Beni nodded, but wasn't exactly convinced.

'Anton once said we should listen to the universe, that if something is right in front you then it means that the universe has gifted it to you.' Catherine smiled. 'Wonder how many shoplifters would get off if they claimed that as part of their religion.'

'Anton says a lot of very wise things,' said Beni, running his hand along her thigh.

'I, on the other hand, think the universe watches us and

gives us things based on the choices we make ourselves. Karma,' she said, pushing his hand away with a smile.

'Kiss me. Just once?' he whispered; his mouth close to hers.

'Maybe you're here to test me, like Eve and the apple, and if I kiss you then a load of bad karma will head my way.'

'Maybe I'm your karmic reward for being so perfect.'

She scoffed. 'No chance of that.'

'Kiss me, please?'

'No,' she said unconvincingly, running her hand along his torso and up his neck, leaving a line of water in his chest hair. 'But maybe we could talk about some loopholes.'

'Like, we can kiss each other but not on the lips?'

'Or any other intimate area.' Catherine giggled. 'Same for touching.'

'So, I can touch you here?' he said, placing his hand beneath her bikini top.

Catherine nodded.

'But not here?' he asked as he ran his other hand up her leg until she stopped him just in time.

She nodded again, biting her lip. 'Let's go to bed?'

The Phone Call

‘It sounds like someone's being murdered out here!’ Catherine said, stepping into the pool, her eyes darting around everywhere, doing a quick lizard check.

Beni laughed. ‘It's OK, there are no lizards. Gloria is a shark though and she's trying to kill me,’ he said, running through the water towards Catherine and scooping her into his arms, kissing her cheek.

‘Oh no! Poor Beni, Gloria!’

‘He isn't Beni, he's a seal!’

‘Oh, well that's OK then.’ Catherine smiled, her arms around his neck.

‘Don't come any closer, Mrs Shark, I have a hostage and if you eat me, you eat Kitty too!’ he said, and gave an evil laugh.

‘Oh, and I thought you were hugging me because you love me, *Belmondo*,’ whispered Catherine into his ear.

‘A shark would just eat you both.’ Gloria shrugged, and swam towards them.

‘Oh no!’ said Catherine, humming the *Jaws* theme tune as Gloria got closer and closer and then ‘killed them’ by splashing them.

'Well, now I've been disembowelled by a shark, I suppose I should go and make some dinner,' said Beni.

'You're cooking tonight? Are you sure? You seem to always cook.'

'I told you I'd make an evolved husband one day; I want to take care of you.' He kissed her on the cheek again before getting out of the water.

'When will it be ready, should we get out now too? Will it be after six o'clock?' asked Catherine, clinging to the side of the pool, watching the water run down his arms, wishing he was still holding her.

'It will be after six. It's OK, you can carry on swimming for a while.'

'Gloria do you like living here?' asked Catherine after they had done some floating.

'I like this pool.'

'Do you know much about England? We might move there one day.'

Gloria shook her head from side to side exaggeratedly, looking horrified.

'Well, it's very different to Mexico.'

'They speak English there.'

'That's right, they do, and it's not hot like here. It's sometimes hot, but mostly it's cold.'

'I will have to get new clothes if it's cold.'

'You will need a big coat and some boots in the winter.'

'Is there a sea there?'

'There is, but not where I live. Instead we have lots of green grass and trees and big hills.'

'Is there swimming pools?'

'Kind of, but not like here. They are usually indoors.'

'Inside?' said Gloria, looking shocked.

'They have to be inside because it's so cold outside, and it rains a lot.'

'I don't think I like England.'

'I think you'll like it. It'll just be different until you get used to it, and we will come back here a lot,' said Catherine softly.

'Do we have to go?'

'Not for a while. But Robert is there, and my house, so I need to go home at some point.'

'Kitty, can I ask you something?'

'You can always ask me anything.'

'Are you my mum now?'

'Umm, well you don't have to think of me as your mum, but you can if you want to. It's completely up to you, sweetheart,' said Catherine with a shrug and a smile, not wanting Gloria to feel any pressure.

'Maybe, then?'

'If that's what you want, then great. Or you can just call me Kitty forever, I like the idea of being called that when I'm old.' She laughed.

'You are old,' said Gloria with an evil grin, splashing water at Catherine.

'I am going to remind you that you said that when you're my age and you're clinging on to the illusion of youth!' Catherine laughed, splashing Gloria back, and chasing the giggling eel around the pool.

'If you will be my new mum, will Beni be my new dad?' asked Gloria, holding on to the side of the pool, catching her breath from laughing so much.

'Well, it's me that's adopting you, it's me that has promised to take care of you no matter what. Beni hasn't made that promise, so, if he leaves one day, we can't hold it against him really. Is that OK?'

'Yes. As long as I have you, I know I will be OK.'

'Same for me; as long as I have you, I'm OK too. You're my deuteragonist, the Ron to my Harry, the Hans to my John.' Catherine smiled, knowing Gloria wouldn't know what the hell she was talking about. 'I love you. I don't say that enough. You're a really good kid, Gloria, and you make me proud at least once every single day.'

'What made you proud of me today?' asked the little girl, swimming towards Catherine.

'There is a lot to choose from, but probably when you cleaned your room without me having to nag you to death, that was a proud moment.'

'You made really nice pancakes for me this morning, you should be proud of that,' said Gloria, putting her arms around Catherine's neck and pulling her in to a slippery hug.

'Thanks a lot for your feedback, madam. Come on, time we got you bathed and fed and ready for bed, you're turning into a prune!'

'A bath won't help with that,' said Gloria, trying to escape Catherine's clutches as she moved them both towards the pool steps.

'OK, smarty-pants, we'll make it a quick shower. Then food, a bedtime story and sleep!'

'All right,' said Gloria moodily.

After putting Gloria to bed that night and talking to Stefano on the phone, Catherine walked into the snug, closing the door behind her. She was wearing a navy satin camisole and shorts with lace trim, her hair was all over the place, extra voluminous after a speedy blow-dry, and after a day in the sun, freckles were emerging across her cheeks and shoulders like stars appearing in the night sky.

Beni was sitting on the big beige sofa in his usual night-time T-shirt-and-shorts combo watching TV. His leg was perched on one of Gloria's toy boxes and he didn't look at Catherine, he just stared at the screen with a deep-set frown.

'You don't look very happy, are you OK?' she asked, as she curled up next to him and kissed his jaw.

'My leg hurts. I pulled it in the pool earlier, I think,' he said, absentmindedly stroking her long legs, still not looking at her.

'Have you had some painkillers?'

'Yes, but I only took them about twenty minutes ago.'

'They'll kick in soon then, won't they?'

'Yeah,' said Beni, and sighed loudly.

'You really need to rest. You went back to work too soon, and since then you've been on your feet non-stop,' said Catherine, running her fingers up and down his arm.

'I had no choice but to go back to work.' He shrugged.

'I bet the only rest you had was in hospital. Why not take some time off work now?'

'I'd have no money coming in if I did that.'

'Well, so what? We don't need it.' She shrugged.

'I want to have my own money, Lish; I want to be able to buy you things and get Gloria the stuff she asks for without having to run to you with my hand out.'

'Sorry, I understand that. Maybe just take a week off then, or a few days?'

'I'll see how I go,' said Beni, still frowning.

'Is it just your leg that's bothering you?'

'I'll be fine.'

'Talk to me. What's wrong?'

'I really want a drink,' he admitted quietly, looking at the floor.

'I thought you were past the worst of that?'

'I'm past the shakes and headaches, but the anxiety is worse than ever, and usually when I feel this shit or I'm in pain, I have a drink. I'm not really sure how to handle this without one.'

'All we have is wine, and you hate wine so you can't have a drink. It's Pavlovian. When the pain goes away, you won't need it as bad, I bet?'

'Maybe.'

'Is it general anxiety, or is it about anything in particular? Can I help?'

'I heard you on the phone with Stef.'

'So? You don't usually mind me talking to him.'

'You were on the phone for a long time and you sounded so happy to talk to him today.'

'That's because Magda's woken up, and she's OK. He's going to stay a few more days with her and then he'll be flying back.' She smiled.

'It took an hour to tell you that? What else did you talk about?'

'All sorts. Gloria painting with Val, his birthday ... why are you asking? What do you think we talked about?'

Beni just looked at the TV and sighed again. 'I imagine he's missing all the sex you were having. I bet he'd like to talk to you about it on the phone.'

'Thankfully, with everything that's going on with him, that kind of thing hasn't come up, and if it had, I would obviously have ended the call.'

'When did you last have sex with him?'

'Why are you asking me that?' she said, pulling at his arm to get him to look at her.

'It's been weeks. Weeks since you told me that it's me you've chosen, but you still haven't, not really. I'm starting to wonder if you ever will. You chat to him on the phone, you won't let me kiss you. Nothing's changed. You're still stringing us both along and not committing to either of us, but at least he got to have sex,' said Beni, instantly feeling sick that he had said that to her, knowing how much it would hurt.

'Wow. You think I'm stringing you along? Really?' asked Catherine, letting go of his arm.

'I'm sorry. I'm being such an idiot, I know I am. You should leave me on my own tonight, I'm not myself, and ... you should probably hide the wine.'

'What am I supposed to do, break up with him via video call to Italy in between his visits to the ICU?'

'But Magda's awake now; you could have done it today?' he said softly.

'She's awake but she's not about to run a marathon! She's still poorly.'

'It's just hard. I want all of you. I don't want to think that there's a part of you that still wants him.'

'Beni, I don't want him.'

'You were going to have his baby.'

'Don't you think it kills me that I'm glad I'm not?' said Catherine, tears stinging her eyes.

'So, he knew you might be pregnant, but you never told him that you definitely were?'

'Yes,' she said, wondering what he was getting at.

'And he didn't ask you about it?'

'I avoided him.'

'If a girl told me she might be having my baby, I wouldn't let her avoid me, I would want to know for sure. Why did he never follow up?'

'I don't know, maybe he just assumed I wasn't?'

'Do you still have feelings for him?'

'What is going on with you? You know I don't! I want you; I choose you. If you don't believe me, you should ask Anton, he's the one that held on to me while I cried on the bathroom floor, crying about you.'

'Crying about me?' he said, looking at her with a confused expression.

'As soon as I saw that the test was positive, I knew I could never be with you. I cried for like an hour solid.'

'So, Anton knew you were pregnant, but Stef didn't?'

'Anton was there when I lost the baby too. He drove me to the hospital. I talked to him about everything – about breaking up with Stef, about loving you. So if you don't believe me, go and talk to him and he will tell you how I feel.' Catherine stood up and went to walk out of the room.

'I'm struggling with this,' Beni said quietly.

'Are you trying to make me feel shit? I know there are things I should have done differently; I can't change them now. I'm sorry that you feel bad, I'll leave you in peace.'

'Wait, please, I'm sorry. You asked me to tell you how I'm feeling, but now you're mad at me for telling you.'

'You're right.' She nodded, covering her eyes with her hand. 'I'm sorry. I just don't know what to say to make you feel better.'

Beni shook his head. 'You told Anton that you love me? You haven't even told me that.'

'You know I do.'

'I want you to say it.'

'I'm not going to say it because you demand me to,' she said, opening the door.

'Please don't run off. I can't chase you, it's not fair,' he said quickly. 'I heard you laughing on the phone with Stef, it made me jealous.'

'Because I laughed?' she said, stepping back into the room.

'I don't love him but I don't hate him, and neither do you. We just talked.'

'I know. You haven't done anything wrong,' he said, dragging his hand down his face. 'I've never been in love before; I've never had any reason to be jealous before loving you. My leg hurts and I'm desperate for a drink. I'm just feeling pathetic.'

'I don't know what to say.' She shrugged, looking at the ceiling.

'You just sounded so happy to hear that he was coming back.'

'Because it means I can break up with him, you idiot!'

'No phone sex?'

'At what point did you think I was doing that? When we talked about his sister's physiotherapy or when I asked him if there was a congestion charge in Rome?' She smiled, sitting down next to him again.

'I didn't,' said Beni, smiling slightly. 'I'm so sorry. I just feel kind of insecure about competing with him.'

'You shouldn't compare yourself to him, you're like night and day.'

'I suppose I'm night, am I?'

Catherine smiled and began running her fingers through his hair. 'I thought you were hot the minute I saw you. I couldn't stop thinking about you.' She smiled, blushing slightly. 'I never thought you would be insecure, not with your reputation.'

'My reputation,' he said, rolling his eyes. 'You know it's different with you. You can't feel insecure if you don't care. But I care about you. For the first time, I actually care about something.'

'In a few days, we will be together.'

'If I ever have to travel, will you phone sex me up?' he asked, lifting his chin, his eyes smiling.

'What do you even say during phone sex?' she asked.

'I don't know, let's practise?' he said with a tiny smile. 'Let's pretend we're miles apart on the phone?'

'OK,' she said with a laugh, feeling embarrassed already. 'If it will cheer you up.'

'I'm missing you,' said Beni, holding an imaginary phone to his ear.

'Me too. What do you miss the most?' she said, her thumb and little finger creating a fake phone that she pressed to the side of her burning cheek.

'Those beautiful lips, your long legs. I can't wait to see you. What do you miss about me?'

'I miss your twitchy face.' She smiled, then bit her lip and pulled his T-shirt over his head. 'I miss you touching me, and touching you,' she said more seriously, dragging her fingers down his chest and stomach with a sigh.

'What are you wearing?' he asked.

'Oh, you know, I'm just lounging about in some black lace knickers, matching bra, suspenders, red stilettos and bright red lipstick.' She grinned, her finger-phone back against her ear.

'Just a casual Sunday night kind of outfit, then?'

'Yep. What would you be doing to me if you were here right now?' she asked, looking into his brown eyes.

Beni looked at her, blonde hair tumbling all over the place, lips pink, her pyjama top straps falling off her shoulders.

'I'd kiss you,' he said, lowering his hand from his ear and leaning towards her. He started kissing her collar bone, then her neck and slipped her top further from her shoulders until her breasts were on show and began to run his hands over them, kissing them.

'What next?' she whispered, sweeping her nails along his back.

'You know what I want to do next,' he said, looking into her eyes.

'Take me roughly on the kitchen island?' She smiled.

'Oh, well yeah.' He laughed slightly, then winced in pain.

'What can I do?' she asked, sitting up and pulling her top back on.

'I'm sorry about everything I said. I don't want to make you feel shit, I'm as bad as Thomas.'

'You are not! It's not surprising that you're jealous of Stef right now, this is a fucking weird situation.'

'I just worry that you might have second thoughts. And that now happy, fun, smiley Stef isn't around, you're not finding my melancholy quite so sexy? Me and him balance each other out, maybe you do need us both.'

'I find the gaps in your clouds sexy, not the clouds. He's coming back soon. I'll break up with him and I'll be yours. If that's what you still want?'

'Of course, it is,' said Beni, putting his hand on her face, trying to remember how it felt before she was in his life, how it felt to not have the ache in his heart, to feel absolutely nothing.

'Listen, I'll go back to England if this doesn't work out. I'm pretty much done with living here now. I really miss the drizzle and cold. The only thing keeping me here when Gloria has her passport will be you, so if you want me out of your life, that will be easy.'

'Don't say that,' he said sitting up, trying to hide another grimace as a twinge of pain shot through his calf once more.

'Can you please just forget Stef and let me take care of you?' said Catherine.

'Sorry.'

'We all get jealous, you're nothing like Thomas.'

Beni nodded with a frown and held her hand. 'Tell me something I don't know about you?'

'OK. I'm ready for you this time with one of my most embarrassing moments.' Catherine smiled, kissing his cheek. 'I pocket-dialled my office once while driving and when I got into work the next day my boss played me the message I'd left, which was basically me shouting "get off my arse, you wanker" over and over and, obviously, out of context it seemed quite threatening.' She laughed with a hand over her eyes. 'I get serious road rage.'

'Stef used to prank call himself when he was high and leave himself messages in different accents. He would wake up the next day thinking someone was after him; that went on for a long time.' Beni smiled. 'It was so funny.'

'Do you miss him?'

'Yeah.' He shrugged.

'I'm so sorry that I came between you.'

'It's not your fault. I guess it's just weighing on me that in a few days' time, I'll lose my friend for good.'

Catherine nodded. 'Maybe he'll be OK with us and you can still be friends?'

'I think me being a jealous knob with you tonight has proven that that can't happen.'

Catherine moved her fingers up and down his chest for a while. 'So, no embarrassing voicemails for you, then?'

Beni cringed. 'Well, no … but I pocket-dialled my mate's home number when I was about seventeen and his mum heard me having sex.'

'That's traumatising.' She laughed. 'Did she know it was you?'

'Well, the girl kept saying my name.'

'Of course she did,' said Catherine, rolling her eyes.

'So, you want to move back to England, then?'

'Not right this second, but yes, eventually.'

'Can I come with you?' he asked.

'Will you?' she smiled.

'I definitely can't take time off work if I need to save up for a plane ticket. What will you do with this place?'

'It's a holiday home, we'll holiday here?'

'No camping in Dorset for our family, then?'

'We can do that too. I quite like the idea of watching you put up a tent in the rain while me and Gloria sit in the car eating chocolate.' She laughed.

'We can go on family holidays to where the dinosaurs walked.'

Catherine smiled. 'You imagine a lot of walking boots and anoraks in our future, it seems?'

'Can't be bikinis and sun cream all year round, we'd get bored.'

'I wouldn't get bored if I was with you,' she said, climbing on top of him gently. 'Does this hurt your leg?'

He shook his head, looking up at her. 'I love it when you sit on me like this, I can feel your bum and legs more easily.'

He moved his hands from her waist down to her thighs, along the silk of her pyjama shorts and Catherine could feel him getting excited between her legs.

'You're a leg and bum man then, are you?' she asked, her heart beating fast.

'For you, I'm an everything man,' he whispered.

She kissed his neck and face, getting dangerously close to kissing his lips as passion took hold of them, and then she ran her hand down his body and slipped it into his shorts.

'I thought that was against the rules,' he said, breathing deeply as he pulled down her vest.

'This is a medical emergency,' she said, biting his earlobe, moving her hand, stroking him.

The Painting

It had been over three weeks since Stefano had left, and part of Catherine's new routine included Valentina coming over mid-afternoon once Gloria was finished with her tutor. They would paint at the kitchen table while Catherine or Beni cooked, and then they would all sit and eat together before Val went to work.

That day was not an average day, however, and while Gloria was in the study upstairs learning, Catherine had gone down to the beach for a walk to clear her head. Beni was preparing lunch earlier than usual and for some reason Val arrived an hour earlier than planned; the routine they had developed was shot to pieces.

'Sorry I'm early, Anton gave me a lift here on his way in to work, it saved me getting a taxi.'

'It's OK.' Beni shrugged.

'Where's Catherine?'

'At the beach. She's had a pretty full-on morning.'

'Beni, we haven't really talked properly since—'

'Since you told me you're in love with your brother?'

Valentina winced, like he had run a knife straight through her. 'You haven't told anyone, have you?'

'No, I told you I wouldn't. But what I don't understand is why you're still here. And what I understand even less, is why on earth you come here most days and let me and Lish cook you lunch!'

'Me and Catherine are friends now, and I love Gloria.'

'And that's fine while Stef's away, but what will happen when he comes back?'

'Well, actually ... Stef is flying back. He told me he would land tonight.'

'He's coming back tonight?' said Beni.

'I did what you said, I see him much less now,' said Valentina.

'And yet it's you he calls to say he's coming home, not Lish?'

'I don't know what to say, I hardly see him now. Him and Catherine have hardly spoken while he's been away, maybe that's why he didn't tell her?'

'You need to be seeing him zero! I bet he's called you every day while he's been there, hasn't he?'

'I know you and Lish are together so climb down off your tall horse.'

'High horse. And you don't know anything, we're not together.'

'Gloria told me you sleep in Catherine's room,' said Val, raising her eyebrows at him.

'She's confused, I sleep in my room.'

'Come on, Beni.'

'Fine, so what? Stef loves you and Lish is going to break up with him and he will go running back to you. Isn't that what you want?'

'No, it's not, because we can't be together. You know that!'

'Then you need to move on.'

'Threaten me,' she said.

'What?'

'Tell me that if I don't leave, you will tell everyone. It's the only way I will ever go, and I seriously need to.'

'Can't you just have the balls to leave without me threatening you?'

'Obviously not!'

'I'm not going to threaten you, Val.'

'How many times have you fucked Catherine so far?'

'Honestly, none,' said Beni, stirring the sauce he was making on the hob.

'I actually believe you.'

'Good, you should. She won't do anything behind Stef's back. She doesn't want to cheat on him, even though she knows he's kissed you.'

'You told her that?'

'Yes.'

'She really is nice, isn't she? She could have clawed my eyes out, but instead she invites me over to paint and eat pasta.'

'I do sleep in her bed. But we haven't "slept together" or even kissed.'

'That must kill you.'

'We're making it work,' he said, trying not to smile. 'You must know what it's like, lying in bed wanting to touch someone that you can't.'

'Is she definitely going to break up with Stefano?'

'Yes. Does he suspect anything?'

'Maybe. He asks about you a lot. Does she love you?'

'I think so, but she won't say it,' said Beni, sitting at the breakfast bar, letting the food bubble away behind him in various saucepans.

'That must kill you too,' she said, standing next to him.

'She'll say it when she's ready.'

'You love a woman who won't say it back, or let you fuck her.'

'A bit like Stef and you isn't it, only we're not blood relatives.'

'How long would you love her for if she gave you absolutely nothing, though?' asked Val, a haunted look in her eyes.

'I love Catherine more than anything. It might drive me mad over time, but I would go forever without touching her if I had to.'

'You love Catherine?'

Val and Beni spun their heads to see Stefano standing in the kitchen doorway.

'Stef, you're back!' said Val, speaking Italian. She had turned ghostly white, clearly panicking about how much he had heard. 'I thought you weren't landing until tonight?'

'I got the time difference mixed up,' he said, placing his rucksack down on the tiled floor.

'How is Magda?' asked Val.

'She's doing good, the physiotherapist thinks she should have full movement back in her arm soon,' he said, still staring at Beni.

Val sighed. 'Good.'

'You finally came out and admitted that you love Lish then, Beni? You beat me to it.'

'I'm sorry you found out like this.'

'When did you tell her, the minute my ass was on the plane?'

'I told her the night of her party.'

'You told her that night?'

'He beat you to it? You love her too?' asked Val quietly.

Stefano nodded at Valentina's question and stared angrily at the ground.

'With you going back to Italy and everything, we decided not to tell you until you got back. Stef, we haven't done anything together. We haven't, you know. She didn't want to cheat. There is just something between us. I tried to pretend there wasn't. I'm sorry,' said Beni.

'Sorry, he says. *Sorry?*'

'I'm not that sorry. You haven't exactly been the model boyfriend, have you?'

Stefano looked at Valentina and she looked at the floor, her cheeks turning crimson.

'You told him what we did?'

'I know you've kissed Val while you've been with Lish, and I told her. She knows you cheated on her.'

Stefano didn't say anything, he just looked at Val.

'It was just a kiss, right?' asked Beni, sensing the tension between them.

Valentina's whole body seemed to sag, as if utterly depleted of energy. 'It was just once ... we slept together,' she said eventually.

'You bastard,' said Beni, charging towards Stef like a freight train and punching him hard on the mouth.

'Please, don't!' said Valentina, hanging off Beni's arm, dragging him away.

'*You,*' – Beni shook her off – 'you said you were Catherine's friend. Get out both of you. Now.'

'I am her friend! That's why I invited you to her party. I wanted you to have a chance to be together.'

'You helped them get together?' said Stef, glaring at Val and touching his fingers to his bleeding lip. 'I'm not going until I talk to Lish, where is she?'

'She went for a walk on the beach, she's had a rough morning. It's a long story but we know what happened to Gloria's mum and dad now, kind of. I'll go and get her if you like, and she can hear all about you two,' said Beni, walking towards the veranda.

'No, I'm going to go and talk to her first,' said Stefano, pushing past Beni. 'She's still my girlfriend, I think I have the right to talk to her about this, don't you?'

'You have zero-fucking-right to anything, but as we used to be friends, I'll give you five minutes to say goodbye. Don't upset her.'

∼

Beni watched Stefano walk down the path to the beach before spinning around and walking back towards Val. 'I know you must be hurting right now, but you need to leave. Go somewhere and don't contact him again.'

'What? I'm not leaving him now. When Catherine breaks up with him, he'll need me.'

'Fucking hell. Exactly!' said Beni, slamming his hand hard against the kitchen table. 'He will want you. And you're his sister! If you love him, you need to leave, and now is the time.'

'Now is the time to abandon him? At his lowest point?'

'It will be a fresh start all round, he needs to move on.' Beni put his hands on her shoulders. 'If you don't leave, I'll tell him and he will know that he's been fucking his own sister for years and when he thinks about you from then on, he will hate himself. Leave now, and you remain in his memory as his first love, and your family won't be destroyed by this secret.'

'Would you really tell him?' she asked, looking sceptical.

'I'm threatening you. You need to leave right now. I'll stall him for as long as I can to give you time to pack up. You need to be gone before he can get to you or you will spend your whole lives in this fucked-up incestuous infinity spiral.'

'Why are you doing this? After what we did you could just kick us to the kerb.'

'You invited me to her party, you helped me and Lish get

together; I kind of owe you. Plus, do you think I want her to know about all this? She's hard enough on herself as it is without finding out the man she was with for a year preferred his own sister to her all along!'

'I'm scared,' said Valentina.

'You can live without him, Val. He's your first love. All first loves are like this but not everyone gets a happily-ever-after with the first person they fall for. It's shit and it's unfair, but if you love him, you need to leave him.'

'Where should I go?'

'I don't know. Put your finger on a map and go there. I'll call you a taxi. Go straight to your flat, pack up and just leave. Here ...' he said, handing her an envelope of money that Catherine kept in a drawer for emergencies.

As Valentina's taxi pulled away, Beni stuck a barbecue skewer into one of the tires on Stef's car and placed a sharp-looking rock on the driveway behind it. Then he took Stef's phone from the kitchen counter and dropped it into a jug of water, leaving it submerged until it turned off. He then dried it on a kitchen towel to erase any evidence and continued cooking lunch, his hustling heart beating fast.

Catherine was sitting on the beach with her legs pulled up beneath her, her chin resting on her knees. The sky was becoming cloudy, the wind was picking up and though the sand was still warm from the recently departed sunshine, the air felt cool. Sensing movement behind her, she glanced over her shoulder to see Stef approaching.

'What are you looking at?' he asked.

'You're back,' she said, smiling as he plonked himself next to her. 'And that's the sea.'

He kissed her on the lips without warning, their last kiss.

She tasted a metallic tang and realised that he was bleeding. 'What happened to your lip?' she asked, rubbing her own to remove the blood.

'It's fine,' he said, waving his hand.

'How's Magda?'

'Much better.'

'Good,' she said as she put an arm around him.

'So ... I just overheard Beni telling Val that he's in love with you.'

'Oh God, Stef, I'm sorry. That's not how I wanted you to find out. Did you fight?'

'What exactly is going on with you two? Because, he can love you as much as he wants, but if you don't love him back then we don't have a problem, do we?'

'I do love him.'

'I'm such an idiot,' he said, covering his frowning face with his hand. 'I was coming back here to tell you that I love you. I've had time to think while I've been away. I've missed you. I wanted to be with you properly, none of that passionately-not-in-love bullshit. Actually with you.'

'We haven't been seeing each other properly for months now, don't you think it's taken you a long time to realise that you miss me?' she said softly, stroking his back.

'I didn't just realise, Lishy. You stopped wanting to see me, do you think I didn't notice? I thought you'd found out about me and Val but I was too much of a coward to ask you,' he said, looking at the sand.

'I only just found out that you kissed, it wasn't that.'

'What was it then? Why wouldn't you see me? Because I'm not Beni?'

'Stef, I should have told you this sooner. I didn't want to upset you, but now that other people know, it feels wrong that

338

you don't. I was pregnant, but I lost the baby. That's why I was avoiding you.'

'Why did you avoid me?'

'Because, at first I didn't want to tell you about the baby. I was scared and I buried my head in the sand, and then I lost it and I didn't want to upset you.'

'You should have told me; I could have supported you. I'm not a kid, everyone always treats me like an idiot that can't handle things.'

'I'm sorry that I didn't tell you.'

'I'll tell Val to leave me alone for good. We could make this work?'

'You love her, you wouldn't be able to stay away.'

He took a deep breath. 'You're right ... I slept with her a few months ago. I'm so sorry.'

'You did?' said Catherine, taking her hand away from his back.

'It was just once. I was drunk and I regretted it instantly.'

'It's OK.' She shrugged.

'After it happened, I realised my feelings for her were just swirling around the drain. They were there but they were going, and I decided to focus on you.'

'Very poetic, Keats,' she said, a smile inexplicably hitting her lips. 'I wish you'd just told me.'

'Could you have forgiven me? Loved me after that?' he asked, smiling bashfully back at her.

'Probably not.'

'Exactly. I didn't tell you because I didn't want to lose you. I'm so sorry for what I did.'

'I knew you loved her, it's OK. It doesn't really matter now. Given the opportunity back then, I might have cheated too.'

'I really thought me and you could make something out of all this mess.'

'We loved other people; it would never have worked.'

'I knew Beni liked you, I knew it. He was always watching you. It got to the point where I would kiss you even more in front of him to make him look away.'

'We drove him crazy, you know; he could have taken me but he didn't because he didn't want to hurt you.'

'I'm sorry. I kissed you because I couldn't not kiss you too. God, I'm going to miss kissing you.'

After a few minutes of quiet between them, of just listening to the waves hitting the beach, Catherine stood up. 'I read recently that Picasso once said that lots of his paintings were the "sum of destructions".'

'What does that have to do with this?' he asked, standing too and dusting sand off his clothes.

'Well, he would paint something and destroy it with another painting. And he would do it again and again until he was happy. He didn't just paint something and think: Yeah, good enough.'

'You could be my finished painting?' he said, holding her hand.

'I'm not. Val isn't either, I don't think. She's all over the canvas. I've made my mark but there is still a long way to go before it's finished. You need to paint over us and start again.'

Stef put his arms around her and she leaned into his chest.

'I'm really sorry,' he said.

'So am I. One day we will look back on this and it will be inconsequential, just another layer of paint, but right now I hope that bleeding lip hurts you, you son of a bitch.' She smirked up at him.

He smiled back. 'You still have a little blood here,' he said, wiping her lip with his thumb. 'Don't want Beni getting the wrong idea, do we?'

'I hope you and him can be friends again. I hope we can all

be friends again someday. I'll never forget how you helped me. If it wasn't for you ...' Tears brimmed in her eyes, but she held them back as a look of mild panic flicked across Stefano's face when he saw them.

He scratched his head. 'Oh, umm, Beni said you know what happened to Gloria's mum and dad?' he said.

Catherine was glad of the change of subject. 'The private detective came to see us this morning. He found Gloria's uncle. He's been in prison for the last few months for a host of things, and he's never getting out,' she said as they made their way back up to the house.

'Did he visit him in prison then? Did he actually talk to him?'

Catherine nodded. 'When Gloria's dad, Jorge, lost his job, her mum turned to her brother for help and they started selling drugs.'

'Her mum did?' he asked, looking surprised.

'It just goes to show you should never underestimate an oppressed woman. She was good at it too. At one point they were doing quite well, apparently, but Jorge got a taste for the product and messed up a few times, and annoyed the wrong people.'

'So did her brother say how they died?'

'His account is that he got to the flat and found Jorge passed out, but alive. Ana was dead. He said it looked like she had been strangled, and he wasn't sure what was wrong with the baby, but he wasn't breathing. He had no marks on him. Gloria was hiding, and when she went to run off, he grabbed her, which I suppose explains the bruises on her arm? He smashed Ana's phone, took what little money was hidden in the apartment and left. The police caught up with him a few months later during a robbery. He shot a woman.'

'But what about Jorge? Did he kill him?'

'He claims that he doesn't know what happened to him and the private detective believed him.'

'He must have done it ... unless he's protecting someone else?'

'Could be.'

'So, Jorge killed Ana, maybe? And then someone found Jorge passed out on the floor and stabbed him?' said Stef, screwing his face up as if trying to make sense of it.

'I suppose we'll never know the full story,' said Catherine, remembering the colour of the water in the sink the night she found Gloria. She had assumed that the dirt on her tiny clothes was mud and sand; now she wondered if it had been blood.

She stopped walking and stared at the sea for a moment, thinking about that night and what Gloria might have seen. Had she watched her father kill her mother and her uncle kill her father? Did the neighbour stop pressing her ear against the wall long enough to actually act and kill the man she believed was abusive? Did some of Ana's clients, looking for a fix or money owed to them, hurt the whole family? Or did Gloria go back to her home that night and make sure her scary father could never frighten her again?

All Catherine could do was hope that one day, Gloria might tell her more, and that the truth wouldn't be too hard to bear.

The Beginning

C atherine and Stefano walked back up to the house
and were greeted by an anxious-looking Beni who
reluctantly accepted Stef's offer of an unfriendly
handshake. Beni explained that Valentina had been called in to
do an earlier shift at work last minute, which Stefano accepted,
and with his phone dead – he assumed from lack of battery, not
because Beni had given it a bath – he couldn't call her.

Stefano hurried out to his car but soon returned,
announcing that one of his tyres was flat and so was the spare, a
happy coincidence as Beni hadn't remembered to stab that one.
Stefano said he would get a taxi, but Beni refused to call him
one, saying he didn't want him to have an excuse to come back,
even to collect his car, which Catherine thought seemed harsh.
Breakdown service was arranged instead.

Gloria finished with her tutor and was happy to see Stef
again. They sat together and he listened to all her stories from
the previous few weeks, and he told her about Italy and the
aeroplane which, having never been on one, she was fascinated
by. He told her that it was a time machine that flew him back in
time to Mexico, and Gloria sat there with her mouth open in

shock. They all ate dinner together, silent apart from when Gloria had something to say, and a couple of hours later, Stef, with a new tyre, pulled off the drive.

'Gloria can you please go and play in the snug while me and Beni clean up in here?'

'Can I watch cartoons?'

'Of course you can,' said Catherine, crouching down and kissing her on the cheek.

Catherine dragged Beni out onto the veranda by the hand and as they sat on the sofa, relief coursing through them, rain began to rattle on the canopy above and splash into the pool.

'I gave Val the money from your drawer for a taxi,' said Beni suddenly, looking guilty.

'There was $300 in that drawer. Where's she going, Guatemala?' Catherine laughed.

'She's leaving, and if Stef knew, he would stop her. So, I drowned his phone and stabbed his tyre. Are you mad?'

'I'm not mad, Danny Ocean! It's exactly what they both need, to get away from each other. I just hope she goes through with it. I could see from his split lip that you know they slept together?'

'Are you OK?'

'I'm fine. It's not like I was so innocent either, and anyway, aren't I the other woman in their love story?' She shrugged.

'I'm so mad at him for wasting our time together on their fucked-up bullshit.'

'They are part of our love story, Beni. Their bullshit helped us to fall in love. If you'd had me straight away, you wouldn't be interested now.'

'You don't really believe that, do you?'

'I think you needed time.'

'If we'd just been honest with each other about how we felt we could have avoided all of this. From now on, let's be brutally honest, OK. Is there anything you want to tell me?'

'Like what?' she asked.

'Anything. Now is a good time to say it, at the beginning.'

'No,' she said, but thought, *I had an abortion and now I don't think I can have kids; I have an eating disorder, and I don't speak to my mum because she thinks I murdered my husband.*

'Nothing at all?'

'Well, actually ...' She sighed, not wanting to start things dishonestly. 'I'm worried I can't have kids, I'm not on speaking terms with my mum and I have a bit of an issue with food. Oh, and Thomas's death wasn't an accident; he killed himself and I hid the suicide note.' She pulled a face, bracing for his reaction.

'I don't care about having our own kids, we can always just adopt a load. As for your mum, I know what it's like to be estranged from a parent; you don't have to explain why. And knowing you, you hid his note to protect his memory, not because it would have voided the life insurance, and I know about the food thing.'

'You know already?'

'Not to sound creepy, but I've spent the last eleven months watching your every move. I know you have an issue with it and it worries me, you've lost a lot of weight. What's causing it?'

'I was diagnosed with obsessive compulsive disorder as a teenager and that eventually evolved into controlling my food too. It's been in my peripheral ever since, but most of the time it's OK, I can handle it. It gets worse when I start to lose control though, so for a while now it's been getting bad again, things have been so crazy. I hope Gloria hasn't noticed.'

'Gloria is fine. I've seen the lengths you go to to hide it from her, to hide it from everyone. So, it's not that you want to lose weight really, you just need control?'

Catherine shrugged. 'It's both. I've always been tall and just naturally bigger and heavier than all of my petite friends. Feeling so different, especially as a teenager, was horrible, so I started dieting obsessively. It didn't make me feel any better, of course, just made me really poorly. It was a horrible time of my life that just got worse when I was with Thomas because he used it all against me. On the one hand I know full well that losing weight has never done me any good, and yet the thought of relinquishing control, terrifies me; eating ten minutes earlier than I have scheduled in my head, terrifies me.'

'So, what are we going to do about it?'

'I'll go and see a doctor. I need some anxiety medication, I ran out ages ago. I know I can get over this because I've done it before. I just need a routine and no drama for a while. I'll be OK, don't worry.' She smiled.

'I'll always worry about you.'

'And I'll worry about you.'

'I'm going to tell you every single day that you're perfect exactly as you are,' he said, putting his arm around her.

Catherine leaned into him and kissed his neck before resting her head on his shoulder. They listened to the rain and watched, amazed, as bolts of lightning struck the sea multiple times in the distance.

'So, who invited you to my housewarming? Was it Anton?' she asked when the light show eventually moved so far away that they couldn't see the lightning itself any more, just the flash of illuminated clouds.

'No, actually, Val told me about it.'

'Val?'

'She knew I was in love with you. We made a deal that if she stayed away then I would too. But she wasn't staying away. I guess that's why she invited me? To give us a chance?'

'Ohh ... for a while I thought you and her were ... She kept asking me about you and changing the subject, and she always seemed to be the only one that had ever seen you. It makes sense now; you were in cahoots. Why did you tell her to stay away?'

'I wanted you to be happy. She's the one that suggested you might be pregnant at Anton's party.'

'She suggested that?' Catherine frowned at the rain. 'Have you seen her drink lately? I don't think I have in months, even at my party. Have you seen her wear anything fitted?'

'No, but I wouldn't really notice that kind of thing.' He shrugged.

'That dentist appointment she had, remember that?'

'Vaguely.'

'Maybe that was really a doctor's appointment?'

'You think she's pregnant?' said Beni, trying not to look too horrified at the possible brother-sister, mum-dad, aunt-uncle situation.

'I don't know. Maybe? It adds up. If so, I hope he catches up with her, I feel bad now. So, Val knew you loved me, and Anton knew, even Stef knew but I didn't.'

'The one time it would have helped for Anton to gossip about something.' Beni smiled.

'I begged him not to tell you how I felt.'

'So did I.'

'Is there anything you want to tell me?' asked Catherine.

'No, I think you've already extracted all my secrets, talk show host. Is there anything you want to ask me?'

'When did you get this scar?' she said, running her finger across his lip, along the tiny scar that she had spent so long looking at, wanting to kiss.

'My dad hit me, the day he left.'

'He hit you?'

'Is this your idea of pillow talk?' he said, running his hand along the back of his neck awkwardly.

'No, but we have our whole lives for that now, don't we?' She smiled and began to run her fingers through his hair, watching his jaw tense and the scar on his lip move as he spoke.

'You can't delay kissing me forever, you know,' he said, touching her bottom lip with his thumb and sighing. 'I won't stop wanting you.'

'Tell me what happened?' she said.

'OK ... My dad was always drunk. Most of the time he was just merry with it, he would pass out before getting aggressive or anything, so as drunks go, he wasn't all that bad. We were visiting my nonna in Italy and my mum had gone to the market—'

'I thought your grandma lived in England?'

'No, in Italy, but we went there all the time and she visited us. Anyway, my mum came back with some vegetables and cheese and stuff, and her and my nonna started to put the food away in the cupboards. The next thing I know, my dad bursts in through the door, I had never seen him that drunk and upright.

He started yelling at my mum that she was a tramp and that he'd seen her with another man. He pushed my nonna aside and I remember a load of potatoes bouncing along the floor as she dropped them. I got in his face and he hit me, his watch smashed against my mouth, there was blood everywhere.'

'Where was this? Where was your grandma's home?' asked Catherine, a chill shooting down her spine.

'Tuscany, not far from Florence. Why?'

'Your grandma died that day, didn't she?'

'How do you know that?' asked Beni, looking at her in astonishment.

Catherine couldn't believe it. When she was a young girl her mum had developed a love of all things Italian. She started singing opera songs around the house, badly, she made godawful fishy pasta meals that even the cat was too fussy to eat and she loved drinking Italian wine on a Friday after her shift at work. For her mum's fortieth birthday, therefore, her stepdad had taken the family to Tuscany and they had stayed in a beautiful village encircled by yellow fields.

They rented an apartment in a building which was old but charming, a mix of holiday rentals and permanent residences set over three floors. Across the hallway from Catherine's family was an old lady, and she had guests staying with her. There was a boy. Catherine guessed that he was about a year older than her at twelve or thirteen and she quickly developed her first ever crush.

For the rest of the holiday, she was intent on making him notice her. She would sit out on the stairs and read her book hoping he would walk by. She would sing at the top of her voice in the shower hoping he would hear her through the vents. She even started to learn Italian to impress him and she carried on learning it for years afterwards.

'I was sitting on the stairs reading my book when I heard what sounded like thunder coming from the apartment across from ours; it made me jump. The next thing I knew, a man came out of the flat and went hurtling down the stairs, bouncing between the wall and banister as he went,' said Catherine.

'Oh my God,' mumbled Beni.

'I could hear crying in the apartment, so I walked slowly in. The boy and his mum were crouched over an old lady who was lying on the floor. I wasn't sure what was wrong with her, she just looked pale and she was struggling to breathe. The boy's mum was in shock, she was frozen on the spot, so I walked over, carefully stepping around the potatoes on the floor and I took the boys hand—'

'And you said we should call an ambulance,' said Beni, looking shocked.

Catherine nodded. 'We called an ambulance and I got the old lady a cold flannel and I put it on her head. She smiled and said she loved her Nicolas, which I assumed was the young boy's name; I remember, because I blushed as I thought: I love him too.' Catherine smiled.

'Me and the boy sat on the stairs and I read to him from my book to distract him while the paramedics came. She died. The old lady died. She'd had a heart attack, hadn't she?'

'You read *Wuthering Heights* to me and we didn't move until the paramedics carried my nonna down the stairs on a stretcher. I can't believe I didn't recognise you.'

'I can't believe it either, you were the first boy I ever had a crush on.' She smiled. 'I can't believe I forgot your face,' she said, stroking his cheek. 'You've changed so much. You didn't speak. I thought you were Italian–Italian, not English–Italian.'

'You've changed too. So, you guessing I was English in the bar that night ...'

'Just a lucky guess. Your poor grandma. So, who's Nicolas?'

'My dad. I guess she didn't want us to blame him. My dad's name is Nicolas Beneventi.' He smirked, watching her face light up.

'Your name is Benedetto Beneventi? Beni Beni?' She laughed.

'Shut it!' he said poking her in the ribs. 'Are you sure you weren't just sitting on the stairs to hide from some social event?'

'No! I wanted to get your attention.' Catherine laughed, covering her face. 'I wanted you to fall in love with me. I thought blocking your exit might help, but you didn't even notice me.'

Beni smiled. 'I did notice you; your hair was more red back then, wasn't it?'

'It still kind of is, but the sun's bleached it while I've been here.'

They looked at each other for a long time.

'This is insane.' Catherine laughed. 'We absolutely can't tell Anton, or he will never shut up about fate!'

'Maybe it is fate?' said Beni, shaking his head in disbelief.

'I didn't know he'd split your lip. There was so much blood I thought your nose was broken.'

'It was.'

'I'm sorry he did that to you.'

'It was a long time ago. He was sick and he just sank deeper and deeper into the mire. I can relate. He left us out of shame, I guess.'

'I'm sure he regrets it all now?' she said softly.

'Maybe.'

Catherine touched her fingers to the scar on his lip and watched him frown in the fading light.

'Can we be together now? Can I kiss you?' he asked.

'I told you once that I would never love anyone again ... but as it turns out, it's not something you actually get to decide,' she said, taking a deep breath and climbing onto his lap, her bare knees sinking into the squashy sofa cushion, her face centimetres from his.

'Is that a yes?' he whispered, his stomach doing somersaults.

She nodded. 'Ti Amo Benedetto.'

Beni sat up straight and kissed her bottom lip as softly as blowing the tiny white parachutes from a dandelion and everything around them seemed to disappear. He reached his hands beneath her dress and ran them along her thighs and the lace of her underwear before grabbing hold of her and pulling her even closer to him.

She ran her nails through his hair and down his back, letting out microscopic moans as his tongue moved in a rhythm with her own and his hands stirred beneath her dress.

After wanting to for so long, he finally bit the supple skin of her lip and the taste of cinnamon sugar hit him like a drug, causing him to stop and look into her eyes, at her parted lips, at her wavy hair and her freckled shoulders. He wanted to take it all in.

'Will you marry me?' he asked quietly.

'What?'

'Remember the old man you stole the walking stick from?'

'Borrowed ...'

'Well, when I returned it, we got talking and he seemed lonely, so I started to visit him every now and again. His wife died a long time ago, he doesn't have any family; I told him everything and he gave me a ring and told me to propose to you.'

'Francis from number four gave you a ring?' She smiled.

He nodded. 'So will you?'

'Why don't you ask me to be your girlfriend first? We haven't even had sex yet, what if we're terrible together?' She laughed.

'I would walk over hot coals just to hold your hand.'

'If you still want to marry me in a few months, then ask me again.'

Beni smiled and kissed her, the second of a thousand kisses. 'OK, girl-on-the-stairs. Will you be my girlfriend?'

The Couple

'Have you boiled the pasta?' asked Beni as he walked into the kitchen barefoot in dark jeans and a white T-shirt, smelling of aftershave and soap, his hair slightly damp from the shower.

'Yes, chef,' said Catherine, letting him wrap his arms around her and kiss her like he had been away at war, not just upstairs getting ready for half an hour.

'Shall we call them to cancel and just have dinner for two instead?' he suggested in between kisses, pressing her against the kitchen counter.

'No!' Catherine smiled, slipping away from him.

She walked over to the big dining table, which was decorated with duck-egg-blue place mats, and napkins that Gloria had folded into melted-looking origami shapes.

'We never get the place to ourselves,' he said, walking after her slowly.

'We're a couple now and it feels grown-up to have a dinner party. I really want you to get on with Maria and The Wolf.'

'The Wolf.' He scoffed, rolling his eyes.

'You'll like him. He's strange but very clever, and Maria is amazing. She's helped me so much with Gloria.'

'OK, OK, I'm looking forward to it, but as always, I would just rather spend my time alone with you,' he said, hugging her from behind as she lit the many candles on the table.

'Go and finish cooking. I need to call Miguel and check that Gloria is OK.' She smiled.

'She'll be fine with his girls. Who will look after Leonora tonight, do you think?'

'I'm not sure. It was Maria's idea to have a kid-free evening. Maybe The Wolf's mum has her?' Catherine shrugged.

'Can we at least just call him Wolf? Does it need to be "The" Wolf every time?'

'Tonight, is going to be so much fun,' said Catherine, smiling and raising her eyebrows at him as he started aggressively stirring the pasta into the sauce.

Beni looked up at her and smiled. They had been together for nearly three months, and for the first time since he was a kid, Beni was finding it easy to smile. Catherine still wasn't used to it; she half-flinched every time he did it, like when fireworks made loud bangs, and the surprise made her smile too.

'I love you,' she said, grinning.

'I love you more.'

She glanced at his feet. 'You should probably wear shoes to a dinner party, I think? Isn't the idea that we're meant to feel like we're in a restaurant but in our house?'

'Oh my God, so we have to cook the food, decorate the table, you've spent the last three days cleaning and now you're telling me I have to wear shoes? We might as well go out!'

'This is what sophisticated, grown-up couples do.' She laughed. 'I'll make it up to you later, I promise.'

'Oh really?' He smiled. 'Fine, I'll put shoes on. Go and call Gloria quickly, they'll be here any minute.'

Just as Catherine had hung up the phone following a very animated chat with Gloria – who had been making up dance routines with Miguel's daughters and, by the sounds of it, snorting sugar – there was a knock at the door.

'You don't need to knock.' Catherine smiled, pulling her friend into an instant hug. 'Hi, Wolf,' she said over Maria's shoulder.

'Hi,' he said, hovering awkwardly in the doorway.

'You guys haven't been here since the house party.'

'I know,' said Maria, pulling away, not quite seeming herself.

'Come through?' Catherine smiled, leading them into the kitchen. 'Beni's made dinner. He's a much better cook than me, you will both be very glad to hear! Beni, you know Maria, obviously, and this is her partner, The Wolf.' She smiled, trying not to laugh and hoping that he wouldn't either.

'Hi, I'm Beni,' he said, wiping his hands on a towel quickly before shaking The Wolf's hand.

'The table looks beautiful, Lish.' Maria smiled as they sat down.

'Do you want some wine?' asked Catherine.

'Yes, please, we both like red.'

Catherine flicked on some music and went to the wine rack, selecting a bottle at random. She had never known much about wine; she only knew how it made her feel, which is why she would be drinking iced water, and Beni, lemonade.

'Thanks, and thanks for having us over,' said The Wolf, swirling and sniffing the wine in his glass.

'Any time, I'm so glad to see you both. How's Leonora?' Catherine asked, sitting down opposite them.

'She's fine. She's at a school friend's house tonight,' said Maria.

'Oh, I see. We wondered where she might be, and guessed maybe at your mum's, Wolf,' said Catherine, smiling at him.

'No, no. My mum wasn't available.'

'You were wondering where she was? Why?' asked Maria with a frown.

'Gloria is at Miguel's, so it just made us think about where Len would be.' Catherine shrugged, puzzled as to why her friend was acting so strangely.

'Here you go,' said Beni, placing big bowls of seafood pasta in tomato sauce in front of their guests and then Catherine before sitting down to join them.

'This looks so nice, thank you,' said Catherine, kissing him on the cheek.

'Thanks, this looks great. So how is it living here? Have you got used to being outnumbered by the girls yet?' asked The Wolf.

'The last few months have honestly been the best of my life.' Beni smiled, glancing at Catherine and then at his bowl of food. 'I'm so lucky.'

'You've certainly landed on your feet,' said Maria, looking at the pasta in her bowl too.

'What does that mean?' asked Beni.

'I just mean that you've got it all now, haven't you. Have you seen Stefano lately?'

'I see him around the hotel sometimes, there's no bad blood any more. He's not exactly how he used to be, he's quieter, but I think in time he'll be OK.' Beni shrugged.

'Poor guy. Have you heard from Valentina?' asked Maria.

'No, we don't know where she is,' said Catherine.

After a few moments of quiet, and of listening to chewing, forks scraping across ceramic and the hum of music, Catherine sighed. 'Is everything OK, Maria? You don't really seem yourself.'

'I'm sorry, you're right. I'm just not feeling great today.'

'Are you OK?' asked The Wolf, stroking a hand across his girlfriend's back.

'You don't have to eat the pasta if you don't like it, I can make you something else?' said Beni, giving Catherine a worried look.

'No, it's really nice, thanks,' said Maria.

'Do you want some water?' asked Catherine.

'I'm fine. You're happy then? That's the main thing,' said Maria, looking directly into Catherine's eyes, as if searching for something.

'Really happy. And you two too?' asked Catherine, looking between her guests.

'We're moving in together,' said Maria, a smile spreading across her lips.

'That's great! Are you moving into the flat above the bar?'

'Yes,' said The Wolf, with his mouth full.

'If you have a lot of stuff to move, I can help if you like?' said Beni.

The Wolf nodded and smiled, chewing frantically so that he could speak. 'That would be great actually, if you don't mind? I'm bringing my couch and I don't think I'll get it up the stairs on my own.'

'Just let me know when,' Beni said.

'Me and Anton are taking Gloria to the water park next Saturday, do you want me to take Leonora with us?'

'Just you and Anton?' Maria said.

'I'm at work,' said Beni.

'Anton loves that water park, we go all the time now. I think Gloria will get bored of it soon and break his heart.' Catherine laughed. 'We could take your son too, if you like, Wolf? If you have him that weekend. He and Leonora must be close now.'

'That would be really nice,' he said, looking at Maria. 'We could have a day to ourselves for once, I'm not at work?'

'Yes, that would be nice, thanks, Lish.'

'What's his name, your son?' asked Catherine, trying not to laugh as she knew Beni would be dying to ask if it was "The Pup".

'Cristian.'

'Nice.' Catherine smiled, looking at Beni and seeing the glint in his eyes that she'd guessed would be there.

'I suppose you'll need bunk beds then, for when Cristian comes to stay?' Beni asked, to stop himself from laughing.

'Yeah.' The Wolf nodded.

'I can help with that too, if you like?' said Beni.

'You're so helpful nowadays aren't you, you're like a different person,' said Maria, gulping her wine.

The Garden

Tall, curvaceous and long-limbed, Catherine Lish walked along the cobbled streets of Florence, Italy. It was early morning and the sun was only just starting to appear over the orange rooftops of the romantic city's skyline. She thought everything in the Tuscan metropolis was beautiful, from the church spires and statues to the artists' work propped on easels and the city's many bridges; even the ground she was walking on with its uneven cobbles was a sight to behold.

Feeling euphoric, she smiled at a sour-faced woman walking an overweight dog and considered visiting a café that had just appeared in her eyeline across the square. She could already taste the coffee.

'Catherine?' said a male voice, stopping her in her tracks.

She turned and saw a man walking towards her, but a blinding beam of sunlight meant that she could only make out broad shoulders in a white shirt with the sleeves rolled up, and a satchel hanging at his side.

'Hi, do I know you?' she asked in Italian, shielding her eyes with her hand, the draped sleeve of her pink dress blowing in the breeze.

'It's me, Beni,' he said, as he stood in front of her, blocking the light.

He looked exactly the same, he smelled the same, the scar on his lip was still there, his hair was just as wild. Catherine's heart stopped beating for a second at the sight of the man who had so often walked through her dreams. Was she dreaming now? she wondered, looking over her shoulder to check that the chubby dog was still waddling across the square and hadn't transformed into a T-Rex.

'What are you doing here?' she asked, stunned.

'I live here now,' he said as he watched her check her watch, look around and give him a nervous smile. She was just as he remembered her.

'What about your daughter, Beni?' She frowned, feeling all the hurt from eight years earlier like it had happened just hours ago.

'Her and Maria never really needed me around. I left Mexico years ago. What are you doing here?'

'Gloria. You remember Gloria, right? She's here studying art; I've come to visit her.'

'Of course I remember her. Do you really think I would forget?'

'I don't know, I don't know you at all, do I?'

'You know me better than anyone. Even after all this time that's still true. How have you been?' he asked, stepping closer to her.

'I should get going,' she said, turning to leave.

'Catherine, please?'

'I can't do this, Beni, I'm sorry.'

'We never even talked about it, you just left me. Please, there's a rose garden up here. Can we just walk together for a while and talk?'

'Fine, but what is there to talk about? You told me you were the father of my friend's child, so I left. End of story?'

'It wouldn't have changed anything between me and you, why did you just leave?'

Catherine glared angrily at the sky for a second as memories of the pain she had felt continued to assault her like a heavyweight boxer. Tears started to sting her eyes, and as they walked along the quiet street her legs became jelly beneath her.

'I was completely in love with you, Beni. We were talking about our future. We were so happy and then in an instant it was all smashed to smithereens. Do you think I wanted to share you with Maria, my friend, after everything with Stefano? It was like fucking *Groundhog Day*! And especially when I thought I couldn't have kids of my own.'

'I wish I'd never told you about it. I wish Maria had never even told me.'

'When did you find out that Leonora was yours? That's what I've always wondered. Were you sneaking off to see them while we were living together? Did you and Maria plan the whole thing so you could take my money or something?'

'No, of course not, how can you even think that?'

'These are the things that have been going round and round in my head for eight years.'

'I didn't know at all; I had no idea, I swear,' he said, turning and holding on to her arms. 'Maria told me, and I told you just a few days later, once I'd processed it. I kept it quiet for just a few days, that's all.'

'Why should I believe you?' she said, wriggling free of his grip and walking ahead.

'Me and her, it was just a one-night mistake years before, it meant absolutely nothing. Until you came along, I didn't even know she had a kid, she just worked at the bar I went to with my friends. Even when I met Leonora, I still didn't realise.'

'How can you say it meant nothing? You have a child with her!'

'She's not mine, not really. She thinks of Pedro as her dad.'

'Pedro?' said Catherine, frowning.

'Oh, that's The Wolf's real name,' he said, putting air quotes around "The Wolf" and rolling his eyes.

'Why did you leave Mexico? Why aren't you with them?'

'They mean nothing to me.'

'She's your daughter, how can you say that?' said Catherine, shaking her head.

'Sharing DNA with someone doesn't instantly make you love them, you know; you have to work at it and Maria didn't want me being involved with Len at all. I send money and gifts on her birthday and stuff, and she knows I'm here if she needs me. But she doesn't need me.'

'Then why did Maria bother to tell you in the first place?'

'I've wondered the same thing a thousand times. I think she was worried that I would eventually work it out for myself, or that you might.'

'Look, it's all in the past now,' said Catherine as they walked through the gates of the small park, which was dotted with rose bushes and iron benches. 'So how come you ended up here?'

'My dad tracked me down online and asked me to come and see him. He sent me money for the flight and everything. I had nothing to lose, so I accepted the offer.'

'That's great that you've sorted things out with him. You've forgiven him?'

'Yeah, he's turned himself around. He's sober, he got married again and I have a little sister, which is weird.' He laughed.

'That's great,' she said as they sat down on a bench.

'He works at the university and he helped me to get on to the geology course. I'm almost done now.'

'So, you've been here a while then?'

'About five years.'

'Do you live with your dad?'

'I'm thirty-seven years old, I don't live with my dad.' He smiled. 'I have a flat, a few streets that way,' he said, pointing. 'I work in a restaurant to pay the bills. And I still don't drink – at all.'

'I'm happy for you, I really am. Are you going to train to be a teacher, then?'

'I think so, or maybe I'll carry on studying. You once told me it wasn't too late, and you were right. So, Gloria goes to school here? Isn't she too young for university?'

'She's nearly sixteen and she's doing a year at an all-girls boarding school. It specialises in fine art education. She's beautiful and smart and so sassy.' Catherine smiled. 'She's so talented, I'm really proud of her.'

'That's great,' he said, his heart aching as he watched her smile.

'So, are you married?' she asked.

'No, there's been no one serious since you.'

'But our grand romance lasted just six months?'

'No one's ever come close to you. I've never loved anyone but you. Why did you leave me like that?' He sighed, bowing his head.

'I just had a horrible vision of the future and it's not what I wanted at all. I had to get out of there.'

'Our future could have been anything we wanted it to be.'

'I didn't want to live in Mexico forever, you knew that, and I didn't think you would ever leave your daughter there. I felt betrayed by Maria, hurt that you hadn't told me about you and her sooner, and I had absolutely no desire to play the part of the wicked stepmother.'

'Leonora loved you, you wouldn't have been wicked.'

'Step-parents are wicked for a reason, you know. Having a stepchild is like playing an infinite game of Never Have I Ever; you have to talk to and spend money on them, and all the time they remind you that the person you love, once loved someone else. I never wanted to be a step-parent, it was shit enough being a stepchild, being the spanner in the works that no one wanted around. It was best that I left.'

'Don't you think in the end, though, that stepkids become an extension of the person you love? I know Gloria wasn't your blood, but I loved her because she would say and do things and I would think: That is pure Lish.' He smiled. 'Do people still call you Lish?'

Catherine nodded. 'Maybe if you hadn't kept Leonora a secret, it would've been different.'

'I didn't keep her a secret. You should have just talked to me about it. I don't understand how you stopped loving me so quickly. I will never ever forget the look on your face when I told you. One minute you were looking at me like I was everything, and then it was like you didn't care about me at all. The next thing I knew, you'd packed yours and Gloria's bags, and you'd left.'

'I didn't stop loving you, Beni. Do you think it was easy leaving you? I just didn't want any more toxic shit in my life. I just wanted things to be happy and simple and I knew it wouldn't be if I'd stayed there with you. I had to think about Gloria, she had been through so much. The last thing she needed was me, the person she relied on, to start spiralling and becoming ill again.'

'So, are you happy now?'

'I'm really happy,' said Catherine, a smile pulling at her lips.

'You're married then?' he asked, taking a deep breath, bracing himself.

'No.'

'Did you have more kids?'

'I have twin boys.' She smiled.

'Are you and the dad not together, then? Or you are but you're just not married?'

Catherine laughed. 'The dad is actually someone you know.'

'It is? Who?'

'It's Anton.'

'What? So, you and Anton?' he asked, frowning.

'No, I didn't turn him, if that's what you're thinking.'

'So, where do you live now? Does he live in England with you?'

Catherine nodded. 'We kept in touch after I left Mexico, and a couple of years later he had a run of bad luck. He broke up with Mateo, and then his mum unfortunately passed away, and he was in Bologna with her when it happened, during the pandemic. Did you know?'

'Yeah, that was a tough time. I was still in Mexico when he left,' said Beni, trying to wrap his head around the fact that she and Anton had children together.

'He didn't know his dad, and from her deathbed his mum finally told him who it was and that he had lived in London. So, when he was able to, Anton came to stay with me and Gloria and I helped to track him down, but it was too late, his dad had died a few months earlier too.'

'Poor Anton,' said Beni.

'But it turns out that his dad had known about him all along and was racked with guilt for not being a part of his life. He had never had any other children and had left everything to Anton in his will. All the money was being held in trust while lawyers tried to locate Anton.'

'Was it a lot of money?'

'Yes, a lot of money. A *lot*, a lot. Anton carried on staying with me and Gloria for a while as he got his head around everything, until one day he realised he didn't want to leave and so he moved in properly. Then, we were driving along a country lane one afternoon, and we saw this huge old house. It was stunning, but it was crumbling to pieces. We bought it together, we renovated it and it's doing really well as a hotel and spa.'

'Putting all those months that you lived in a hotel to good use, then?'

'Yeah.' She smiled. 'And we both wanted kids. We were already business partners and best friends, so we did the whole turkey-baster thing and we had the boys. They're nearly four now.'

'Wow. So, all that time me and Stef were fighting over you, Anton played the long game and swooped in at the very end.' He laughed.

'He's my best friend, nothing more, and we don't live together now; he lives down the road with his boyfriend, Fraser. Anton will die when I tell him I've run into you. He missed you.'

'Do you still have the other company with your brother? You managed to survive the pandemic and everything?'

'Yes, we were lucky. And I'm an auntie now, Robert got married and had a daughter.'

'So much has happened.'

'With you too. Is there anything else?'

'I saw Stef last year; he came to Italy when his dad was sick, and he got in touch with me. We met up. It was good to see him, like old times.'

'That's great. How is he? Is he still here or did he go back to Mexico?'

Beni looked at her with a frown. 'Don't you know what happened?'

'What happened with what?'

'He died,' said Beni slowly, looking at her with sad eyes.

'No ... what? How did it happen? When?'

'His mum called me not long after we'd met up. It was a head injury; he fell while hiking in Slovenia.'

'Oh my God,' said Catherine, starting to cry, breathing quickly, hyperventilating.

'It's OK, it's OK,' Beni said, putting his arms around her. 'I'm sorry, I don't know why I assumed you would already know.'

'I need to go,' she said, trying to escape from the hug.

'You really loved him, didn't you?'

'No, Beni, you don't understand. Valentina doesn't know, I have to tell her.'

'You found her?'

Catherine nodded, feeling dizzy as she continued to panic. 'When I left you, me and Gloria didn't leave Mexico straight away. We stayed at a hotel in Cancun for a couple of months while I dealt with renting out the house and sorting visas and stuff for Gloria to live in England. While I was there, I hired that useless private detective to help find Val.'

'Why did you do that?'

'I was worried about her. I was convinced that she was pregnant when she left, and the more I thought about it, the more it made sense.'

'So, where was she?'

'She was in France and she'd had Stef's baby.' Catherine smiled slightly before a few more tears fell down her cheek. 'She's going to be devastated, how do I even tell her?'

'Was it all right? Were there any problems with the baby?'

'That's a weird thing to ask,' said Catherine, raising her eyebrows.

'Sorry. I mean, how was the baby?'

'He looks just like Stefano. Bright as a button, though.'

Beni shook his head in disbelief. 'Did he know that he had a son?'

'No. I kept begging her to tell him, but she wouldn't. Eventually, she told me everything. I know why they couldn't be together now. And you know too, don't you?'

Beni nodded.

'Another secret you managed to keep from me.'

'That's not fair, it wasn't my secret to tell.'

Catherine stared at the moss-covered gravel at their feet as tears ran readily down her cheeks and dripped from her chin.

'This is all my fault,' said Beni. 'I'm the one that told Val to leave him. I stole you away. His mum said it was an accident, but what if it wasn't?'

'Val said she was always going to leave before Angelo was born, she was just holding on until the very last minute, it's not your fault at all,' said Catherine, putting her hand on his. 'And of course it was an accident, he was the most accident-prone person on the planet, the big-hearted buffoon. Don't think like that, he wouldn't have—'

'Why? Because he was always smiling and seemed so happy?'

'He wouldn't have done that, there is no way. He wouldn't do that to his mum or to Val.'

'Maybe he wasn't thinking about them.'

'He wouldn't do that. It was an accident.'

Beni nodded, not meeting her eye. 'Don't tell me Val lives with you too?'

'Not with me, but nearby, and she works at our hotel,' said Catherine with a tiny smile, sniffing, and wiping with her sleeve at the never-ending emotion spilling from her eyes.

'Stef never got to meet his son,' said Beni.

'I know,' she said, looking at his frowning face. 'I can't believe he's gone.'

'Are you going to call Val and tell her?'

'What will I even say?'

'I think I still have Stef's mum's phone number, in case she wants to call her aunt?'

'Every now and again, usually when I'm with Angelo, I think about Stef smiling at me the day we met. Maybe that's where he is now, cartwheeling on the beach looking for sad people like us to cheer up?'

Beni smiled, his own eyes watery as he touched her face. All the words in the world had left his brain and he had no idea what to say.

'I'll call Anton later and see what he thinks we should do,' she said, pulling away from Beni and wiping the fresh tears from her cheeks.

'How did Gloria cope with moving to England?' Beni asked, desperate to stop her crying.

'She hated it at first. She missed swimming every day mainly, but she soon replaced that with climbing trees and getting muddy, and finding frogs to freak me out with instead of lizards.'

'And what are your boys called?'

'Nat and Nico.'

'Alliterative.'

'You remember all that?'

'Every time I hear or read something alliterative, I think of you.' He smiled.

'With a name like yours that must have been a lot.'

'Every single day, pretty much,' he admitted, looking at the ground. 'Do they have your last name, or Anton's?'

'Both, of course: Bianchi-Lish. They look just like Anton. They're going to be so hairy, the poor things,' she said, smiling.

'Did you ever go back to Mexico?'

'We visit Gloria's aunt Izelda at least once a year. She's still going strong.'

'God, I can't believe it's been eight years,' said Beni, putting his head in his hands. 'Have you been in love with anyone ... since me?'

'Why are you asking me that?' she said, looking away from him and frowning at a nearby rose bush.

'Can you just answer the question?'

'I tried to. Before I had the boys, I dated a few guys, but it didn't work. And I haven't had time to even think about it since they were born,' she said.

'That's the only reason, is it? You've been too busy?'

'How could I fall in love with anyone else when I was still in love with you?' she said, still looking away from him.

'It's not too late for us, you know,' said Beni.

'What?'

'I still love you and you love me.'

'There's too much water under the bridge, don't you think?' Catherine said, standing up and beginning to pace around.

'Life is so short, look at what happened to Stef.'

'We tried this once before and we both ended up getting hurt!'

'Look at how much has changed since then, though. You were so much stronger than me and it rubbed off. You turned me into a better person, a stronger person. I'm not as lost, I've nearly got my degree, I feel like I might actually deserve you now,' he said, standing in front of her.

'Beni, I didn't leave you because you didn't have a degree!'

'But you have kids with someone else now too and I can handle it, we're on an even footing.'

'Even footing? I didn't shag Anton and keep it a secret from you! I didn't keep my kids a secret from you!'

'I didn't think my stupid, drunken one-night stand with Maria mattered. It happened years earlier. But you're right, she was your friend, and when we got together we promised to be honest with each other and I kept that quiet. But I swear I didn't lie; I didn't know about Leonora, I promise I didn't know. I didn't know, Lish.'

'OK, OK,' said Catherine, touching his chest lightly, not wanting to see him upset. She was having difficulty breathing, the emotion was strangling her. She had thought about him so often that seeing him in the flesh was like seeing a film star step out of the screen, and once again she looked around to check that she wasn't dreaming. 'You're right, things are different now.'

'Let's just finally be together,' he pleaded.

'I was just walking along minding my own business an hour ago, and now you're here looking like that, telling me that you love me. This is a lot to process!'

'Lish, we met when we were kids. We fell in love on the other side of the world and now we've run into each other by chance yet again. The universe is telling us to be together. Please, can't we try? I'm going to carry on loving you anyway, you might as well be around for it?' He smiled.

'How would it even work? You live here.'

'I graduate in June, I'll move back to England. I'll train to be a teacher there.'

'Gloria finishes school then too.'

'Is that a yes?'

'It's a maybe. I'm here until Sunday. I see Gloria on her breaks from school and for a couple of hours each evening. If you're not busy, I can spend the rest of the time with you, and on Sunday, we can decide if this is a good idea or not?'

'OK,' he said, smiling at her.

'Has something bad happened to you recently?'

'No.' He laughed. 'Why?'

'Then we should probably be careful. Don't I always show up when you're having, or are about to have, some bad luck?'

'I don't care. A piano could fall on me and it would be worth it.'

'Be careful what you wish for!' She laughed, looking up at the sky, checking it for falling anvils and musical instruments.

'You haven't changed at all,' he said, touching a hand to her cheek and watching her nervously chew her lip.

'Oh, I have. I've had babies. I'm older. I have definitely changed.'

He shook his head. 'Still as perfect as ever.'

'You have tattoos now,' she said, holding his hand in the air and running her fingers along his arm, over images of a compass, a rose ... and then she stopped and looked up at him. 'Belmondo?' She smiled, pointing at the word etched on his forearm.

'For you. "Beautiful world."'

'You soppy idiot.'

'Always, but only for you.' He grinned.

'You're really here, aren't you?' asked Catherine seriously as she closed her tear-soaked eyes and leaned into him.

'I'm here,' he said, enveloping her in a gentle, yet inescapable bear hug.

After a couple of minutes of getting used to being so close again, their lips connected, like hands reaching out in the dark and finding each other, knowing each other just by touch.

In that moment, Beni felt sure that everything he had done, every drink he poured but left untouched, every night he spent studying, every decision, good and bad, had led him back to her, to that garden and to the kiss that would finally unbreak their hearts.

Catherine grabbed the collar of his shirt, pulling him closer, determined to never let him go so easily again, and as he bit her bottom lip softly, in his familiar, velvety way, their eight years of distance evaporated. The scent of the roses around them and the quiet of the barely awake city made them feel like they we were in Eden, all alone, and for that splinter of time, nothing else mattered.

Acknowledgments

I started writing Bella Novela during the first UK coronavirus lockdown while still working full time as an administrator for the NHS. The extra time/ lack of social life that we were 'gifted' by that and the many subsequent lockdowns meant that finally, after years of having stories pop in and out of my head, I was able to tether one down and see it through to the end.

Writing this got me through the isolation of the pandemic, it gave me something to focus on when everything else felt so out of control.

It has been a dystopian couple of years for us all and I am aware there will be many people that will have had a far, far worse time than me. Whatever your experience, whatever your loss, however the situation has impacted your life, I hope you have had some glimmers of joy along the way too. This was mine. Bella Novela is definitely my pandemic lemons-into-lemonade story, and the people below are the sugar!

First and foremost, thank you to my incredibly supportive husband Stewart King. You listened to my constant worry for months, was woken up endlessly by me making frantic bedside notes at three AM and dealt with me ditching date nights when I was too wrapped up in it all to stop writing. You never once complained, you have given me countless pep talks and have been just generally amazing – you always are. I love you and I feel so lucky to have you in my life.

Before I took the plunge and contacted a professional editor, I reached out to an old college acquaintance Fabienne Mann, as I knew she was an avid reader. I asked if she would be willing to read a novel I had written and I honestly expected her to either reluctantly agree to read it out of politeness, or to just say no. Instead, she was boundlessly enthusiastic and read it not once, but twice. She gave me wonderful feedback, thoroughly proofread it and best of all we are no longer acquaintances but friends. I cannot thank you enough, Fab!

Thank you so much to my oldest friend, Natalie Knutton for spurring me on to finish writing the novel, as without your promise and eagerness to read the finished article, I may well have given up. All those years we spent as kids making up whacky plays with outrageous characters and storylines definitely helped too, so thanks for sticking with me all these years as my partner in crime. I hope we have many more years spent almost laughing off Icelandic waterfalls together.

Lucy-Anne Hastings, just like with everything else, I knew I could count on you. You are a great friend to everyone lucky enough to know you, I am just so glad to be one of them! Thank you for being patient with me when I was constantly asking for reassurance, your messages of support truly helped me to persevere.

Abbey Sisson, you were the first person to notice all of the *theres* instead of *theirs* that I had become blind to! I don't know how you found the time to read this while renovating a house but I am so grateful that you did. If you ever fancy ditching Audiology, a life in editing awaits! Thank you for being such a great friend, you're the best!

Claire Snape, when I doubted myself, you were a constant source of positivity, thanks for dreaming big for me! I'm hoping that with all of your Long Eaton connections we can make this a best seller – so thanks in advance for that too! More than anything, thank you for reinvigorating my love of reading in recent years, as that undoubtedly helped me to write this.

Aileen Walsh, thank you for reading my novel so super speedily and for the encouraging and in-depth feedback that made me happy-cry. It really meant a lot to me that you liked it.

Thank you to my mum, Karren Gourley for providing great single-mother inspiration for the book. I hope you know how proud I am of you.

Jack Gourley, my brother and best friend, thanks so much for your encouragement. I would be lost without you.

Thanks to Natasha Kalia, Carl Davies, Katie Macafee, Daniel Diskin, Lissa Connelly, Jean Davies, Sally Farmer, Becki Atkins and James Tuck, for the moral support, for not laughing in my face for trying to do this and for keeping Bella Novela a secret for so long!

Thank you to my talented, kind and supportive editor Cally Worden.

Thanks to beautiful Mexico for being so inspiring!

Finally, thank you to my A Level English teacher Mike Benford from Burton College. Your words have often echoed in my head whenever I have dreamt of writing something – 'She's a funny writer' – well I really hope this brings a smile to people's faces. Thanks for being so encouraging.

About the Author

Charlotte Harrison-King is from Derby, England.

Anyone that knows Charlotte will testify that there are unmistakable traces of her personality throughout Bella Novela, and so an 'About the Author' page feels fairly unnecessary if you have already read the story.

From her film and media degree to the *Jurassic Park* posters she had on her walls as a child, her stratospheric anxiety levels, fondness for rock music and fear of iguanas – this is a love letter to everything she loves and some things she loathes.

Whether you care to or not therefore, you will know this author intimately after reading her debut novel.

Share your thoughts with Charlotte
on Instagram @fourparrotspublishing
or email fourparrotspublishing@outlook.com